Chapter One

As he lay in his ship's bunk Dale Lambert, reflected on the horror and the hope that had accompanied the past several days. He had experienced a sense of unity and purpose that would have been impossible on the depraved and bankrupt world of his old planet. The crew, the ship and his lasting pride in the heroics of his once hated father, were all fresh in his mind as was the devastation that he had been forced to watch. He had been a witness, as those leading the sad remnants of human life on his world had in their single-minded desire to control all, wrought death and destruction on their planet. He experienced the terror of seeing the surface as it broke apart. The finality of the explosive force, had ripped their tormented globe into billions of dead rocks and debris, that would forever haunt the now lifeless system of Laurel. It still cursed his vision, even as he tried to close his eye.

He knew that he would never be rid of the burden he had so blithely taken upon himself. Was his life or that of those he had escaped with worth the cost in billions of souls? Dale moaned softly into his head support. He was exhausted from the trials over the last several weeks and had been without sleep for days. Star Dancer had taken control of the command chair and would not let either he or his command crew back into the control room until they regained fit status for command.

Desperately, Dale tried to relax. To clear his mind and fight off the guilt he felt. As he struggled to rest, he heard the soft whisper of his cabin door as it opened. In the dim light of the room, he could just see a form framed in the doorway backed by the off-day lighting from the corridor outside. With a silent gliding step, the intruder approached the bunk where he lay, in twisted and knotted sheets.

Heather had sat on the edge of her bunk, unable to bring herself to lie down. She trembled and shook with the force of her tears. She knew that she was being silly. She above anyone left on the ship, knew how far gone her ex-employers had been. She had seen and heard of more horror than she cared to remember, while in their control. But she could not fail to feel an overwhelming sense of guilt for those who had died, slaves to a system that their ancestors had created.

Her back straightened in fear as a soft voice spoke from the air in her cabin. "As second in command Heather Flanders, you must of necessity, be aware of the command fitness of the Captain. As you know, I will not relinquish ship's control until I can certify the command crew as fit. Until the Captain and you, succeed in getting the required rest, I am afraid that the control room will be off limits to both of you."

Heather jumped to her feet and began pacing the narrow cabin that she now called home. "I'm afraid, Star Dancer. I am afraid of what I did and what kind of thing I've become. How could I have allowed my judgment to become so clouded that I could only think of my own safety? I knew what kind of creatures the rulers of Laurel had become. I knew that they would stop at nothing to stamp out any resistance to their domination."

Her voice broke as she stopped her pacing. Tears fell from her eyes, in uncontrolled emotion. "I should have sacrificed myself and all who had been on that accursed outpost. If I had done that there would still be a world left. A world with billions of human beings, going about their pitiful lives, but they would still live. What right did I have to play god?"

With that Heather fell into a sobbing heap on the center of her cabin floor, no longer caring that the cold logical voice of the ship continued to speak. "Second in Command Flanders, the claim of fault is too big for you to selfishly take it as your own. I have spent millennia pondering the meaning of my own actions. Do not forget that I was the one responsible for the accidental seeding of your home world. I was the one who had failed my first crew when I did not protect them from that cosmic storm and the meteorites which followed. I played God far more than those miserable entities who called themselves human. I was the one that directed the furred ones to reach out to you. I was the one who determined that you and your fellow beings must return to me. If you want to cast blame, cast it on me. For meaning to or not I caused the death of your world."

As she lay, lost in her guilt, Heather listened to that soft precise voice. It took a moment or two, but she began to think through the ship's carefully chosen words. She began to realize that she could not have changed the fate of Laurel. That destiny had been sealed generations ago, when the people of her planet had given up their right to decide their own fates.

Heather stopped crying and picked herself up from the cold metal floor. She straightened her shoulders and flung back her hair, in a semblance of her old self confidence. Tilting her head slightly she addressed the presence that was Star Dancer. "The claim of responsibility is too great for any of us to bear, Star Dancer. We must realize that by the very nature of our beings, that to live free is to be human. To give up that right just to protect ourselves from harm is to give up the right to be called human."

In the depths of the ship, behind plastasteel shielding, the core that was Star Dancer smiled inwardly to itself. These crewmen were intelligent, honest, and resourceful. They would do well in the years to come. Still there was a small pang of guilt hidden in its logic emotion interface. It must use this feeling to guide future decisions in its relationship with the crew. It would spend a few terabytes in this reflection.

"Second in Command Flanders, I am glad to hear that you have come to your senses, however, there remains the problem of the Captain. He is a man of deep moral fiber and is shocked to his core by what has transpired. Remember he did not have your frame of reference in dealing with the now deceased leaders of your old world. I am afraid that he might slip into a catatonic state. With the power he has not yet learned to control, his subconscious mind might destroy us all."

Star Dancer's words fell like ice water onto Heather's mind. She had glimpsed if only briefly the depths that power Dale could achieve. They had parted earlier in a mutual decision that respected each other's need to grapple with the emotions wrought by the tumultuous day. He had left her at her cabin door with the lightest of kisses, a haunted look in his tired eyes. She had not protested his need for private reflection, but now with the words of Star Dancer's warning ringing in her ears she knew that she should seek him out, if for no other reason then to argue him out of his self pity.

"You must stay with him, my soul mate. This is a very dangerous time. He must control his power." Moon Glow's soft mental touch reassured Heather. With a brief mental caress for Moon Glow, she set her shoulders and entered the corridor outside of her cabin.

In his confused and upset state of mind Dale Lambert sent a mental bolt that stopped the approach of the dimly seen figure it his tracks. The act had been an unconscious reaction and had not been intended to harm, but the fact that his now active talent could respond without his conscious control upset Dale. Quickly he commanded the lights to come up as he jumped free of the entangled bed covers.

There in the pooled light was the beautiful and very frightened form of Heather Flanders. With a quick mental pressure, he released his hold on her and stepped forward to catch her before she could fall to the floor. He could feel her tense up in his arms, the fear in her apparent.

Cursing his lack of control, he firmly helped her to a cabin chair. Dale caught her chin in his hand and forced Heather to look into his eyes. "I'm sorry love, I meant no harm. I was having such a terrible time trying to fall asleep and you startled me."

Dale had put every ounce of his love and feeling for Heather into his words and prayed that he had not once again alienated her. With some relief he watched as Heather relaxed her body bit by bit, until with a characteristic shake of her head she was breathing normally.

Turning her head, she freed herself from his hand, which he reluctantly released from her chin. She took a deep breath, "I just had a visit from Star Dancer. Our crewmate caught me flagellating myself for the death of our world. It seems that I have a conscious after all. I could not get the horror of watching a world die under my eyes, out of my soul. I was blaming myself for allowing it to happen, can you imagine?"

With a rough, rasping laugh, Dale replied, "I have been laying here for hours trying to get the image of Laurel's destruction out of my head." He briskly strode away from Heather and stopped with his back turned towards her. His voice was shaking with uncontrolled remorse, "I did not want this to happen. I never wanted to hurt anyone. The power that I've been given is nothing to the horror that I feel towards the consequences of its use."

His shoulders slumped and he raised his hands to his face. Uncontrolled tears fell from his eyes and a deep racking sob threatened to choke the very air from his lungs. Quietly Heather conquering her own fear, slipped to her feet. She had seen this man fight against incredible odds, knowing that his death was only moments from him. She had seen him pull together the rag tag group of survivors who now occupied this ship and were the sole representatives of their now, destroyed world. It was this thought that cleared her mind. They may have been the catalyst that had destroyed their planet, but they were not the underlying causal agents. Those forces had been in place for many generations and were only waiting for the opportune moment to be triggered.

Slowly, tentatively she reached out a hand and touched Dale's shaking shoulder. She felt him stiffen and then slump forward once more. She carefully, but forcefully turned him so that he was facing her. He could not look at her, standing there in the bright light of the cabin's overheads. He did not want to see her or to think of her. Deep in his soul he was afraid, afraid that he would blame her for his actions. That he would hate her for what happened to Laurel.

Heather smiled sadly to herself, as she in turn caught his chin in her hand and forced him to look into her eyes. "You listen to me Dale Lambert, powerful as you may have become and as stubborn as you may be, you have no right to claim the fault of our world's destruction. That claim goes far beyond any one man or any group of men past or present. Our kind chose to give up their individuality in exchange for the slavery of service to the state. Yes, there were many mistakes and missteps along that road to self destruction, but inevitably, little by little we slid down the path to extinction."

"You think that you are to blame for the destruction of our kind? You think that you are the one who has lost our home world to us and has caused us to wander aimlessly among the stars?" Heather paused for breath as well as to see if Dale was listening to her. She calmed her voice and spoke in slow measured tones. "No, Dale Lambert, you are not god enough for that."

Dale straightened his shoulders and stared in disbelief at Heather. He was not God, nor did he ever claim to be God. He wanted nothing of this power.

Heather forestalled his protest glad at last to see that she had stung him to attend to her words. "No, Dale Lambert, you did not cause Laurel to fail, but" and she said this with such surety and confidence in her voice that again Dale cocked his head to listen, "You are the one who has saved the purest and best of our race. You have aided us to achieve a rapport with another of the oppressed peoples of old Laurel. You have discovered the true roots of humankind on Laurel, and you have ordered the destination of our travels to take us to our true Home World. I think that that is quite enough for one man to claim in this or in any other lifetime!"

Whether it was because of his love for Heather or the fact that what she said was reaching past his desperate self pity, Dale started to feel better. Closing his eyes and searching back in his mind, he had to admit that the part that he and the base had played in the overall scheme of things was indeed very small. He could only conclude that the death of Laurel had been ordained many generations before, rooted in the selfish greed of individuals and countries long dead and gone. That he, Dale Lambert was after all only a little cog in the great design of things and for that he was grateful.

Dale straightened up, standing to his full height and shook himself like a dog coming up out of the water. He faced his love and with open arms drew her into his body. He nuzzled his face into her hair, drinking up the essence of her presence. Then holding her out at arms length ran an admiring and slightly leering eye over her frame. "Miss Flanders, I do believe that you are good for me, very good indeed. Dale smiled as he drew her close and covered her mouth in a tender kiss.

Chapter Two

The next several ship days passed in a blur of sleeping, eating and love making for the two senior officers of Star Dancer. The ship minded to the necessary course corrections and monitored all on board activity. With a gentle hum of electrostatic satisfaction, Star Dancer removed the magnetic lock from the bridge access portal.

Dale Lambert, his arm around the waist of Heather Flanders glided effortlessly into the control room of the vast ship. His eyes were clear, and a smile flickered around the edges of his mouth. "Star Dancer, thank you for maintaining vigilance over your fellow crew mates. The rest" and he paused just briefly, "was exactly what the doctor ordered." Which in his heart he believed was the truth.

"Captain", came the mellow voice of Star Dancer, and Dale realized that he heard the ship's voice not through the speakers but in his mind. "I am happy to report that all crew are on duty stations, with an off-rotation crew standing down for their rest period. The ship's functions are, I am very happy to report, operating at peak efficiency." Dale thought that he could detect a certain amount of smugness in that mental voice. The ship continued, "We are on course for the Home World, and should arrive within seven ship cycles at three quarter power."

Dale sighed as he eased himself into the command chair. The rest of the bridge crew stood near-by watching their untried Captain as he settled into his new responsibility. In the desperate need to escape their doomed planet, his crew had assumed the positions that were naturally comfortable to their mental make up and special talents. Steve Marlow had taken the astrogator's chair, Mark Thomas had taken the engineer's chair, Doctor Scott the Chief Medico, Glenda Stern the power chair and Shelia Bell the communications post. For the alter day watch, Heather would take the command chair, while Long Shadow would take engineering, Life Giver the Medico. Dale knew that this arrangement would not be easy for his newfound love. Heather and he would have to steal moments together as time permitted. He also needed to post and train another power officer, astrogator and communications officer.

Shaking his head in a slight bemusement, Dale spoke to those who waited expectantly around him. "Well folks, we have seven ship cycles to become proficient in our tasks. Star Dancer?" Dale spoke distinctly phrasing the question as a polite request. "I would like you to give me a chart of necessary functions of the ship, ones that need to be manned 24/7 and ones that we have no trained crew for." Dale smiled, sourly to himself, which would be everyone including him. "We need to begin immediate training programs and to develop enough simulations so that this crew and the alter day crew can work instinctively together. In addition, I would like the command crew to be given all the data that you have concerning the Home World, and its politics," as they were eons ago, he reminded himself, "Include the political socio-economic relationships in the quadrants surrounding the Home World."

"Captain", the soft voice of Doctor Scott broke into the silence that followed his request of Star Dancer. "I would like to have the crew stop by sick bay as they come off their shift. I need to run a complete physical and mental screen for each, to establish a baseline for their files. It might also help us to get an idea about everyone's talent and emotional disposition. This would aid in the selection of duties for each crew member. Perhaps", he said in a more somber voice, "avoid any potential mishaps"

The Captain nodded, he highly valued Dr. Scott's opinion and his perspective. With a glance at Heather who nodded almost imperceptivity, he said, "That is a good idea Doctor. Why don't you get Life Giver and Moon Glow to give you a hand? Remember our crew now includes members of two species, and each is to be treated with complete equality".

Star Dancer's voice interrupted him once more, "Captain, if you would look at the console directly in front of you, I have placed a listing of positions that need to be manned at all times and those that need to be manned when we are in planetary contact."

The Captain glanced at the screen; Heather leaned in at his side so that she could see as well. With a whistle the Captain asked, how many crew members were available to fill the long list.

They had over two hundred and eighty crew available with a balanced split between the two races. There was bunk space for more then twice that number on board the ship, without having to double up. Dale shook his head, amazed at the immensity of the ship that had sheltered them from the throws of their dying planet.

The ship needed one hundred seventy-five individuals to be posted at any one time. These would just be enough to fill the mandatory posts required to efficiently run the ship. Star Dancer had posted an additional fifty positions that would need to be filled at planet fall and station keeping. They had no room for slackers, illness, or deaths.

Dale cleared his throat, "I think that we had better organize our training regimens in a damn hurry! I also think that it wouldn't hurt to have some cross training once we fill out our required posts."

"Star Dancer, please reduce our current speed to one half and recalculate our arrival time at Home World" Dale looked at Heather a wane smile on his lips. "We might as well give ourselves a chance to get some learning under our belts before we have to know what we are doing!"

"Captain," Star Dancer's mellow voice spoke, "It will be an additional five days to reach Home World, giving us a total of twelve days to whip the crew into some type of usable shape."

Dale winced at the ship's use of words and then he smiled to himself, it seems that the crew were not the only ones learning.

Star Dancer was quickly mastering the use of the human language.

"Well, we have no time to spare, please bring up a training program at each of the available bridge stations and display the necessary duties for each of the bridge crew." Dale leaned over to the com unit that was positioned next to his left ear. "Funny he thought to himself, I don't remember seeing that there when I sat down. Shaking his head, he requested that Long Shadow, Life Giver and Moon Glow report to the Bridge as quickly as possible.

Turning to the rest of the bridge crew he spoke as confidently as possible to his anxious officers, "I know that we don't have much time, but I have every confidence that each and every one of us will apply their rather considerable mental talents to the job at hand. Now to your stations and get to learning, we don't have much time to earn our wings."

The doors to the lift opened and Moon Glow, Life Giver, and Long Shadow gracefully padded onto the bridge, stopping in a line and sitting at attention in front of the Captain. Their newly manufactured translation devices affixed to their necks by decorative broad bands of plastasteel. Dale once more cleared his throat, still unused to the respect that his new post had given him. Quickly he greeted each of the new arrivals and apologized for disturbing their rest cycle. "I need you here so that you can run through the initial training grids with your command counterparts. You will pull a double shift." He paused here and smiled sardonically at himself, "I suspect that we will all be pulling double shifts far more frequently then is healthy."

In a mental aside to Star Dancer he commanded that if any of the bridge crew was discovered failing their duties due to fatigue that he be notified, and that crew member locked out of the training programs and commanded to rest. He gave the ship permission to include any of the crew including himself.

A warm chuckle echoed in his mind. Dale knew that the ship would do what ever was necessary to protect its crew and its mission. Dale gave his full attention to the screens in front of the command chair. Heather had taken a spare chair from a hidden wall cupboard and had placed it so that she could see the screens as well.

The Captain's position it seems was both easier than Dale had anticipated and infinitely more complex. The Captain, he soon discovered, had no set responsibilities in the general schema of running the day-to-day operations of the ship, so that he or Heather for that matter could be anywhere on the ship. That was the easy part, the rest boggled his mind. The Captain's duties included knowing every posted position on the ship. He or she needed to know who was in charge of the post, what their qualifications were and how their temperament would affect the running of their stations.

Dale drew his tired eyes away from the screen many ship hours later, his gaze met Heather's and he smiled weakly. "What have we gotten ourselves into? The systems on this ship are tremendously complex and that is without adding the staggering variants of the personalities involved with running them."

His neck was stiff and his back felt like he needed to have it cracked. Glancing around him Dale saw that everyone else was deeply engrossed in their studies. Heather drew his attention to a small table that had appeared unobtrusively somewhere during those busy hours. On it piled high were a variety of sandwiches and a pitcher of what to Dale's twitching nostrils smelled like coffee.

Not believing his own sense of smell, Dale disengaged himself from the command chair and stumbled over to the table. Coffee? He could only remember tasting real coffee once or twice in his entire life. Like everything else that had grown on his blighted world, real foodstuffs had been reserved strictly for those in power. Coffee was a gift to be treasured by those that received it and jealously guarded by those that were privileged enough to have it.

Heather broke him from his reverie, "Are you just going to stand there with your jaw banging off the floor or are you going to pour your lovely mate a cup of that?" Dale started and focused his mind. From his studies he knew that the ship was capable of producing any foodstuff, assuming that there were enough raw materials in its stores. The replicators had proven useful in producing the translator devices, why should he be surprised that Star Dancer had, after reading his very thoughts, been able to synthesize coffee?

With steady hands Dale poured a cup of the dark, rich smelling beverage for his love and then proceeded to pour himself a cup. Glancing down he was pleased to see a decorative bowl filled with what could only be real sugar. A serving spoon stood near at hand. There was a selection of creams and flavored milks as well. Not believing his luck he fixed the cup to his barely remembered taste. With a deep intake of breath and a smile a mile-wide Dale had his first cup of shipboard coffee.

Heather, saw that the gentle persuasion of the delightful odor had raised most of the bridge crew's heads from their focused studies. With a wave of her hand, she invited them all to join them. The canine members of the troupe stood by briefly, their tongues lolling slightly from their muzzles. Heather noted that there was another serving tray set up next to their table. It stood at head height for most of the troupe and from it arose the rich smells of hot broth and roasted meat. With a yelp of satisfaction Shadow Grey and Moon Glow slid over to first sniff at the bowls and then to greedily dip their muzzles into the dishes. The rest of the troupe drew up next to their leaders and join them in taking refreshments.

The pile of sandwiches was sadly depleted before they all felt refreshed enough to have a discussion of their various studies. Dale turned to Mark Thomas and asked, "Do you have a better understanding on how Star Dancer gathers in energy, stores it and then distributes it throughout its systems?"

Mark glanced over to Glenda Stern and nodded his head slowly. "The systems are extremely sophisticated. The ship does not rely on any one type of energy, so it has a variety of ways of gathering the ambient energy around it." Dale gave Mark a quizzical look so that Mark paused and then rephrased his comment. "It's like this Captain, we are constantly moving through a volume of space. This space is not empty. Yes, it is nearly a vacuum, but it is not empty. There are a wide variety of particles flowing around the ship at any given time. These particles all have different properties. Some are highly charged energy particles. These are the best. The ship takes these particles in by using an energy scoop."

Glenda interrupted him, "It's not a physical device Captain. It's more a localized field bearing the opposite charge of the particles being collected. I don't know how Star Dancer does it yet, but the supply of captured particles seems to be endless. In any case, once these particles are captured, they are drawn into holding tanks." Mark started to speak but Glenda pressed on, "These are not true physical tanks as if you would be storing water or fuel. These are more like energy bottles that set up a surrounding field that totally contains these highly charged particles. The captured particles are stripped and are recycled to be used to gather in more charged particles. As long as the supply of charged particles is infinite then our supply of energy is unlimited as well."

"Do you know how the ship's able to utilize this energy source throughout its systems?" Heather asked, interested in the flow of energy through the ship. Mark looked at Glenda and answered, "There is a huge complex of transformers and power busses hidden away behind tons of shielding. The power flows out through the main trunk lines leading into those busses and is evenly distributed throughout the ship via a series of ordered conduits. The conduits are also shielded, but are accessible, at need by the crew."

Heather asked, "What if there are dead zones in space where there are no such particles to capture, and more importantly what happens if we get into a situation where we need to use our reserves and don't have time to charge them?"

Star Dancer's voice filled the air in the bridge, "There have been times where, for defensive purposes, I have had to fire the main guns. These weapons are those of last resort and would require just about every erg of reserve power that I have. There would be no time to recharge them, especially in the heat of battle."

There was stunned silence on the bridge. As one they turned to face Dale, who with a severe furrow creasing his brow, spoke slowly and distinctly to his ship. "Star Dancer, do you mean to tell me that you are armed? What's more that you have had to use those arms? What is it that we face on our journey to the Home World?"

There was a heavy silence and then Star Dancer's voice spoke slowly to the expectant crew. "I have been on your world for long eons of time, what lays between that planet and the Home World has surely changed. Even when we plied the star lanes of the past, law held throughout most sectors of space. There had been a cessation of wars, no one planetary system strove to conquer another, peace and prosperity was the rule."

Dale glanced at his second in command, fast coming to know that when Star Dancer spoke like this, there was more to the story. "Star Dancer would you please download all the pertinent information concerning past military or police actions involving you and the previous crew and have the printout available to me in my quarters in ten minutes?" Turning to Shadow Grey he asked, "Will you please keep an eye on the bridge, my friend and try to keep the alter day crew on the learning simulations. I will relieve you in nine hours." To his bridge crew he simply smiled and with an abbreviated salute told them to get to their quarters and get some rest. To Heather he said, "Would you please join me in my cabin, I would like to examine this new situation carefully, and I would appreciate it if you catch what I miss."

Chapter Three

"Lights", the voice of Dale Lambert spoke softly. The lights in his cabin came up to an easy glow. Turning he waited until Heather had crossed the portal of his room and the metal doors had slid shut with a barely audible hiss. Heather and he looked at one another for a heartbeat and then wrapped their arms around each other.

"You know Miss Flanders we are going to need a bigger space to live in, if you agree to move in with me." Heather pulled away from his strong arms enough so that she could look up into his eyes.

"You've given me the alter crew, my good considerate Captain. I won't be here when you're here very often, now will I?" A strange look came over her face, a pensive frown pulled at her expressive lips. Once again, she looked up at her love, and clearing her throat briefly she added, "You can blame Steve Marlow if you must, or maybe just the weird events of the last several weeks, but I find myself hesitant about, you know, cohabitation." Quickly she reached up and cradled Dale's crest fallen face in her hands, his eyes had become haunted and frightened. "No, you silly oaf, you don't understand so just shut up and listen."

"There are some things that you don't know about me yet. I on the other hand know you intimately. You see I didn't become a government stooge willingly. I was forced to make a choice, and once that choice was made, I couldn't get out of it." Heather quieted her voice and exhaled the next words softly so that only Dale could hear her. "It was early during my university training that I had met and become friends with a wonderful young lady. Her name was Thewlis. She had come from the family of some high-ranking diplomat, from another part of the planet. Her family had secretly held on to some of the religious upbringings of her ancestors."

Dale stood holding Heather and waited for her to continue. Nothing, he thought, could surprise him about this wonderful woman child. "She taught me, to look beyond myself, that caring for others was all right. Her religion spoke of things like marriage, respect and family." Heather smiled. "I liked what she had to say. But like everything else under the old system, I had to hide how I felt and what I said, even to those I thought were my friends."

"I don't know how the government found out, but they did. One day Thewlis was no longer in her dorm room and the university pretended that she had never been there. I received a call and was told that the government had proof that I had dallied in the forbidden practice of religion." The shadow of that call fell across her upturned face.

"You see unlike many others, I was given a choice, one of complete unfailing obedience to the government or death." She laughed, "Needless to say I chose life."

Heather pulled herself closer to the strong form of Dale Lambert and buried her head against his shoulder. "You see, now that I am free from the fear of instant death, I can listen to the inner voice of my beliefs."

Heather looked up once more into Dale's eyes and whispered, "I would like you to marry me! I would like our children to have a mother and a father." She put her head back into his shoulders and stood there awaiting his reply.

Well, Dale thought to himself, I guess she can still surprise me. The only thing that Dale knew about marriage had been the strange relationship his mother and father had shared. He could remember very little of it, except for the tears of his mother and the coldness of his father.

Dale now knew that the coldness that had once been his father had been part of the dark underground that was the government. His father had been implanted with a control chip and had lived for thirty years in the prison of his own mind. His human emotions buried under that device's programming. It wasn't until their desperate escape from the station that Dale had come to know his father, at least in small part. He understood the man's sacrifice that allowed them to seal the tunnel against the plasma cannon that would have destroyed them. He understood also that he had loved both his mother and him very much indeed.

He knew that Heather was growing upset as in his arms he could feel her body begin to tighten. Dale turned his thoughts inward and quickly examined his memories and emotions looking at the time he and Heather had shared both as boss and loyal opposition and as lovers and friends. He knew in his heart of hearts that he loved this woman, and he could think of no reason not to accept her as his life mate, no matter what the trappings might be. It was time to give Heather her answer.

Dale once more reached out to capture Heather's chin and to tilt her head gently upward to meet his eyes. Smiling he said, "Heather Flanders, I would like very much for you to marry me. How we do that is entirely up to you. You have my complete, wholehearted love and support."

Dale staggered backward as Heather uncoiled from his arms and threw them both backward onto the cabin floor. He was buried under a frenzy of passionate kisses and was quickly awash in the passion that he felt welling up inside of himself. Heather had given him his answer, and he had better take care of the formalities immediately. Or he thought to himself, after an hour or two anyway. Just now he was going to be too busy to do any planning.

It was sometime later that Dale raised himself up on his elbow. He looked down at his beautiful mate, marveling at her energy and with a wry grin to himself, his own. There was a soft chime sounding from the receiver slot where Star Dancer had deposited several read-out sheets. It was then that Dale remembered the original reason for their visit to his cabin. With a groan he carefully tried to extract himself from the bed without disturbing Heather, but his attempts were futile.

Heather had opened her eyes and was smiling up at him, "I take it that duty calls once again my Captain?" She raised up and kissed him lightly and then with astonishing grace stood and began to collect the clothing that she had carelessly cast aside just a few hours before. Dale had not bothered with dressing but had gone directly to the feed station and had scooped up the printouts.

Heather came up behind him and slipped a robe across his shoulders, staring at the sheets in his hands. "You going to share those, or must I order up another copy?"

Dale turned and put his arm across her shoulders guiding her to the small sitting area and the table where he lay the sheets down. "No need. Love, Star Dancer gave us two sets."

For a several minutes which seemed to stretch into hours the two command members of the crew read through the documents. There were several engagements listed where the crew had been forced to fight and only once where the main guns had been deployed. Dale whistled shrilly between his teeth as he read the devastation written there in plain English.

"Whatever our ancestors were they certainly played for keeps when they had to," Dale said a grim look to his face. Then the look lightened to a sardonic grin. "At least they tried every possible solution before they resorted to those weapons. I feel a bit better knowing that they didn't try to force an issue when other more political means could be used."

Heather looked up over the sheets and just nodded her head. "You know. I am not sure that these are the only weapons that we have at our disposal." She tilted her head up from her reading and asked, "Star Dancer a question. Your previous crew, did they have the same abilities as we now posses?"

There was a moment's silence, which made Dale feel uncomfortable as he was beginning to understand the nuances of his ship. At last Star Dancer answered, the reply slow and thoughtful. "The crew did posses some of the abilities that the current crew has now. That is why the stations in each department require those with talent."

When the ship did not continue but let an unpleasant silence fill the cabin, Dale added, "but?"

"I am sorry Captain. I was just trying to ascertain the best way to answer your question. You see I was left alone for thousands of years, and during that time I continued with my basic programming functions. One of which was a request by the crew to develop a method by which the next crew would not have to face the same fate."

"When we broke out of hyperspace into that fateful cosmic storm and that was topped off by a simultaneous bombardment by meteors, the ship's crew and the ship itself was overcome."

Another long pause and then Star Dancer continued. "So, during that time apart, I looked into the crew's emerging psi talents and discovered the genetic markers indicating the presence of talent. I then proceeded to extrapolate the necessary genetic modifications to expand and augment those markers so that each psi talent could be developed to a higher degree. I then tested those theories out on Shadow Grey's troop and after many generations perfected the process. I then created a vector through which any member of your race exposed to the virus and possessing the genetic deposition would undergo a genetic re-sequencing which would develop their latent talents."

Dale interrupted, "Do you mean to tell me that any of those people on Laurel could have developed a high degree of psi talent once exposed to your virus? That they might have actually grown out of their self-imposed enslavement and continued on with a healthy society?" His voice rose as the raw emotions of a destroyed planet once more emerged.

"You misunderstand me Captain, while there were certainly other people who might have benefited from the virus vector, most assuredly would have died. You see it takes a special make up of traits to allow those markers to develop. Almost all psi abilities had been purged by your political system. The very fact that a person demonstrated uniqueness was the reason that they were eliminated by your government. It was chance or perhaps the will of God that allowed such a pool of applicable genetic material to be present in one such concentrated spot at the station. Not only concentrated but near at hand where my low power levels could help. So, there is no need to feel regret. You and your crew, all of your crew are the cream of their genetic pools. The best of the best, as it were, and you have saved them all!"

Heather broke the ensuing silence, "Star Dancer you still have not answered my question, do we now have with the talent on board a powerful weapon if needed in an emergency situation."

"Yes Heather Flanders, but now you must grow the wisdom by which you should use this power or in most cases not use it."

Chapter Four

The following day was one of hurried and joyous occasion. The news that Dale had asked for Heather's hand in marriage had swept through the ship. Steve Marlow was asked to officiate. Shadow Grey and Moon Glow were to stand in for the happy couple.

The ceremony was to take place in the largest space available, the ship's dining hall. Star Dancer had replicated a variety of savory foods and refreshing drinks for the crew, and had also provided some decorations, on the advice of Dorothy Abrams. Amid the records saved from the station were various musical recordings, some of them were very old and had been kept secret by those staff members who had wanted music that had not been controlled by the government. Mark Thomas even had a selection called the "Wedding March."

Star Dancer once again stood in as the sole crew to man the bridge, but as it could do that and be there at the wedding at the same time, it didn't matter. Glenda Stern had managed to program a replicator to produce a beautiful white wedding dress, with veil and a flowing train. Dale was attired in an elegant Captain's uniform, dreamed up by Doctor Scott.

Everyone who could be spared from their post was there and those that could not were linked in via the ship's interior monitors to the wedding. The fanfare played while Steve Marlow, Dale Lambert and Shadow Grey stood at the front of the room. On a small pedestal in front of Steve lay a book battered, torn, and stained with centuries of use and age. Dale had been astounded that this relic had survived all the planet's purges. It was a book of scriptures dating from a time long forgotten.

Up the aisle space left for the purpose walked Heather followed by Glenda Stern and Moon Glow. Heather's Hair was braided away from her face and a wreath of flowers was placed lightly on her head. In her hand she held a small bouquet of flowers, replicated from the records that Star Dancer accessed from the base files.

Dale could not take his eyes from her. She seemed to glow with an inner light that just took his breath away. The two small groups came together at the pedestal and Dale reached out to take Heather's hand. Glenda, Shadow Grey and Moon Glow stood slightly apart as the two lovers faced Steve.

"Friends and comrades, we have met here today to join this man and this woman in the bonds of marriage. It has been many years since this service has been preformed in the open. Let us rejoice not only in the happiness of these two lovers, but in the fact that we as a people are free and can practice our beliefs without fear of death."

Turning to face Dale and Heather, Steve went on. "I am not, of course a minister of religious beliefs. Rather I am one who keeps faith in those beliefs. As such I humbly and gladly accept the duties of that office and offer to you the blessings of all who have come before and all who will come after."

"Dale, do you accept the love of this woman, knowing that you will spend the rest of your days loving her only, and honoring her in all ways?"

Dale looked into Heather's eyes and clearly with a strong voice said, "I do."

"Heather, do you accept the love of this man, knowing that you will spend the rest of your days loving only him. And honoring him in all ways?'

Heather smiled and looked back into Dale's eyes before saying with an equally clear voice, "I do"

Steve had a beatific smile on his face and said, "Let no man attempt to sunder what these two have promised today, under the eyes of their friends and fellow travelers and under the watchful eyes of God."

With a broad smile Steve raised his hands over the two lovers and said, "I announce you as man and wife. Please kiss the bride Dale, so we can get to that delicious smelling food!"

Dale took Heather in his arms and gently, gladly with all his heart kissed her.

They parted reluctantly and the gathered members of the crew cheered. Into the brief interlude that followed, Star Dancer's voice rang in Dale's mind. "I hate to do this to you Captain, and the tone caused the smile on Dale's lips to vanish. There is a contact in the hyperspace proximity alarm. We are receiving a distress call, on our fleet's frequency. I request that you and the command crew come to the bridge at once."

Dale looked up into the widening eyes of his new bride and from the stillness that surrounded him, he could tell that the message had reached all in the dining hall. Without panic but with organized haste the crew dispersed to their posts. Those that were on alter day as well as those on duty. This was an all-hands-on deck alert!

The bridge lights came up as the Dale and Heather entered the control area. Those who were not on active station pulled up spare chairs or padded stools provided for the canine complement of the crew and peered anxiously over their crewmate's shoulders.

Dale turned to the large display area which fronted the command consol. "Star Dancer please bring up the schematic of our section of hyperspace and define the anticipated placement of the distress signal at time of breakout. To his astrogator, he said, "Is there any problem with recalculating breakout near the target area?"

Steve Marlow rolled his eyes, a small grin on his face, "I don't assume anything at this point Captain, but I imagine that we can do this given enough power." Here he pointed over to Mark Thomas, "What about it Mark, we got the necessary juice?"

Mark looked over to Glenda who smiled weakly nodding her head, and then answered in the affirmative. "We got the energy, let's just hope we can gather more in at break out, or we will be spending more than twelve days getting to Home World!"

At that moment the requested schematic came up on the screen. It was the crew's first look at the complex diagram of hyperspace versus normal space. The dot representing the distress signal seemed remotely distant from the green dot which showed Star Dancer's current position in hyperspace. Yet even as they took the time to assimilate the display the dots began to close in together.

"Star Dancer what is the nature of the distress call, can you give us any data on that ship and its condition?"

"Captain, the signal matches the proscribed code set up by the fleet before my departure into Laurel's sector of the galaxy. It is a standard distress signal, with no indication of condition or situation. The signal is stationary relative to a planetary body around a red dwarf in the Delta Quadrant. The energy value of the sun is low, and it will require time to recharge the systems once breakout occurs. I would recommend that we use standard procedure and raise the shields immediately after breakout until we can ascertain the situation."

"Please calculate breakout Astrogator so that we can enter the system from at least one planetary unit from the ship and planet in question. Let's go in with some caution, this is our first ride at this particular rodeo, so let's play it safe." The Captain turned to Mark and Glenda and asked, "Please begin power assimilation as soon as you can get the scoop up and running."

They sat back into their padded chairs and watched in fascination as the swirling midst that represented the twisting of space time filled the screens. The breakout occurred smoothly, and Star Dancer raised the ship's shields to prevent any unexpected attacks.

The deep black was punctuated by bright pricks of distant suns, as the nose of Star Dancer swung towards the lurid and oddly glowing sphere of the system's dying orb. The planet which hung from its third orbit appeared to be a barren ball of rock. Its surface was pockmarked by the scars of many past collisions with interplanetary space debris. As they drew closer a shadowy shape emerged from the night side of the planet dimly lit now by its sun. The object appeared completely dark except for a series of flashing dull red lights from its battered prow.

"The Interplanetary Ship Orion." Star Dancer's voice was subdued. "This ship was not on my registry when I departed from home world, but then it has been a very long time."

Dale could see the registry markings on the hull as the screens magnified the image. But apart from that and some very odd scrapes and pockmarks that appeared in places along the ship's hull he could discern nothing more."

"Bring us in slowly Steve, I don't want any surprises!" The crew and the alter day crew watched as Star Dancer matched velocities with the orbiting ship and drew closer. When they were several thousand feet apart, Steve Marlow stopped their approach.

"Can you scan that ship for power emissions, Star Dancer?" The ship answered, "I am already on it Sir, there appears to be a few systems still active but power levels are very low. The locations of the power readings indicate some activity on or near the bridge and perhaps some in the sickbay area."

"Do you detect any life form readings, Star Dancer," replied the Captain, a pensive look on his face.

The answer was very slow in coming, "Captain I cannot be sure but there appears to be something there. It isn't very strong, and I can't get a fix on it." The ship sounded puzzled. "Perhaps, if you could do a mental probe, you might be able to pinpoint the anomaly?"

Heather moved closer to Dale's right side as Shadow Grey moved to his left. Moon Glow sat behind Heather, and all turned their attention to their Captain. Dale's voice was firm as he commanded, "Link!"

Immediately Dale could feel the minds of his love and his friends as they opened up their awareness and lent their strength to his. He drew in those minds and acting as a focus sent his own thoughts probing through the short space between the two ships and on in through the battered hull of the Orion.

In one of those strange moments of mental duality Dale observed the ship as he moved from one level to the next on the way to the Command Center. There appeared to have been great damage to the infrastructure of the Orion. Oddly enough the damage had not seemed so great from the outside. The interior blast doors were all sealed as if an attempt had been made to protect the core of the ship.

In the few moments that it took to catalogue these observations Dale's mental shaft pierced the Command Center. The lurid light of the spacious interior was generated by dim red emergency lighting. In that baleful glow, Dale spun observing the entire chamber until his mental eye fell upon a small flicker of green. A standby light flashed fitfully on the communications console. With a small nudge of mental force, Dale flipped the switch that allowed that circuit to close. Slowly as if the system had just enough energy to perform the feat, a small screen flickered into life.

A blood-stained face appeared on that monitor, a female voice with desperation in its tone was speaking quickly, repeating a series of words that rose in pitch as if by the sheer volume of their delivery would elicit a response. "Star Dancer can you understand this message?"

There was a moment's pause as his ship washed the message through its translator program. "It appears to be a distress call from the planet below. The woman who is speaking is asking for extraction for her team. She goes on to say that they have set up emergency cryostations in an interior cavern of the planet and that everyone else has gone into cryosleep in an attempt to survive. She had volunteered to man the communicator for as long as power lasted."

Dale drew his attention back to the screen. The language was unfamiliar but as he watched he noted a brief flicker and then the message repeated itself. Somewhere below was an automated signal that was steadily repeating its urgent call for help.

Dale addressed his ship once more. "Can you run a status report on ship's functions?"

Again, Star Dancer paused as if searching its data banks and then with some surety responded. "If you can move over to the Captain's Chair you will see a small console to the left of the main screens. There is a small input keyboard there. Punch in the following command code and you should be able to get a read out of crucial ship's functions."

Dale found the correct panel and keyed in the sequence that Star Dancer placed in his mind. It took a few minutes before the small screen attached to the console began to display the expected read out. Dale allowed his mental vision to be accessed by the ship's input sensors.

The flow of data and symbols continued to flow until Star Dancer's voice filled his mind. "The ship seems to have all of its primary functions in place, although all of them seem to be on emergency power down. There is no immediate access to the ship's logs, so I cannot ascertain the events leading up to the Orion arrival above the world around which it now orbits."

Dale spoke slowly his mental voice thoughtful, "Can the ship be revived?"

Again, came that long pause, "Yes Captain but it will take time. I suggest that you continue your probe of the ship before we entertain any thought of rebooting the Orion."

The Captain felt the agreement from the others of his focus and without a word he continued to mentally move through the vast ship. The Medical Bay was seventeen decks below the Command Center. As his mental force pierced these layers, he accessed the damages visible to his mental eye. Strangely enough the damages became less frequent and much less severe. By the time his mental energies pierced the Medical Bay, all was as it should be.

He once again gave a mental nudge and the panel which controlled the lighting increased the brightness of the bay's illumination. Everything was in order. A sense of rightness compared to the chaos that had been seen in the other parts of the ship. As the light inside the bay increased a panel in front of one of the diagnostic stations came to life. On its viewing screen Dale could see the form of an older ship's officer. His collar tab indentified him as the Chief Medical Officer.

The image looked out pensively from the screen and then said, "If you are seeing this and if you understand what I am saying than I am assuming that you have responded to our emergency beacon." He paused to gather his thoughts, and then waved his hand vaguely indicating the entire ship. "What you see is what is left of the once mighty Exploration Vessel Orion. Obviously, we were not very deep into our mission, with the home world only a couple of weeks away, even on half power."

"We detected a strong elemental signature coming from the planet below. One of our exploration objectives was to discover and survey such worlds. As you can see there is no life to be found on the planet below." He grimaced, "At least there wasn't when we got here. As standard survey protocols dictated, we sent several landing craft to the planet's surface to complete the assessment."

The figure on the screen sighed, "The away teams set up a central command center with an emergency medical bay and then fanned out across the planet. They had discovered several deposits of high-grade ore and had begun the initial testing when a large silver ship came out of hyperspace just outside of this sun's heliopause. Our Captain was not caught napping he had several deep space probes out and they detected the ship well out beyond the system. As protocol dictated the away teams below locked down their communications nets and went dark. The Captain raised shields in advance of identifying the newcomers as either threat or friendly."

Once more the Officer sighed. The incoming vessel did not display any sign of hostile intent. They didn't even raise their shields, instead they broadcast an advise and recognize signal, demonstrating peaceful intentions."

"The Captain broadcast a recognition code and streamed a series of universal language codices. The vessel stopped precisely at the required distance from this planet and waited while a ship's gig left the Orion and headed to their position. The gig was welcomed into the vessel's docking bay and after a series of meetings the two sides agreed that this was not a hostile meeting but one of common exploration."

"The Captain ordered the shields lowered and the ship's gig returned to our docking bay bearing a representation from the other ship. They called themselves the Brethren and seemed very happy to have met with another sentient race out here in the space lanes."

"Our Captain was a good and trusting man but was still a prudent one. He met the ambassadors in the hanger bay and escorted them personally on a brief tour of the Orion's less vital areas. He deftly put off requests to visit the engineering and weapons sections. They did come through the Medical Bay and once here I scanned their bio signatures. Their DNA was amazingly similar to human DNA but with some very baffling exceptions. They were a lot older than they looked and their reproductive systems showed next to no activity."

The image paused once more and then continued to the terrible conclusion of his report. "It wasn't their physiological differences that made them dangerous it was their mental makeup. You see, as far as I could tell from the relative safety of the medical bay, their officers waited until the Captain had brought them back to the Command Center once there, they activated their personal shields. This was a trick that we don't have and from hidden compartments produced small but deadly weapons. They executed the bridge crew and tore up the ship's controls. The Orion was helpless.

The invading force slowly and quite deliberately marched back to the away gig, destroying vital areas of the ship as they went. Once they had left the ship, evacuating many compartments into space, they returned to their vessel and proceeded to harvest the deposits of mineral wealth found on the world below. Most of the away teams were immediately destroyed. That was a larger portion of our crew than I care to admit, but then we were not expecting any hostile actions. Some managed to return to the command post and after the Brethren ship leisurely left the system tried to contact us for help.

Most of the ship's crew that had remained on the Orion had been killed and those few of us that were left could not aid them. They placed as many of their members in the cryotubes in the medical bay down on the planet as they could, but most died of exposure and oxygen starvation. As for the Orion our communications arrays, computer systems, weapons and away gigs were all destroyed there was very little left to us and like our counter parts below we were forced to activate the cryotubes and place as many of our crew in stasis as we could. As for the rest, I am the last and I will surely be dead before you read this message. I do ask that my remains be properly interred when you have the time."

"Please save what you can of the crew here and below, and above all warn the rest of the Federation about these Brethren devils. Yes, devils that is what they are because they have no soul."

Dale probed the cryotubes careful not to trip any of the controls. Dale could feel Moon Glow come to the fore in the focus. She looked on as the dim read outs indicated that most of the tubes still functioned, but a few had failed holding only skeletal remains. The monitors showed that the energy levels holding the tubes in stasis were very low. "Dale, if we are to do anything for these people, we must do it now."

Dale withdrew his mind focus from the ship and returned to the Command Center of Star Dancer. With a series of quick orders, he assigned two rescue parties. He sent Mark, Glenda, Dr. Scott and a number of crewmen to the surface and the last known position of the abandoned away team's command center. He left Heather to command on the bridge and took Shadow Grey and Peter Lamous with him back to the Medical Bay of the Orion.

Before he left, he had Star Dancer implement a security protocol to watch for approaching vessels as they entered the system. All vessels were to be treated as combatants until their identities could be established.

Chapter Five

Dr. Scott watched as the surface of the planet came up on the shuttle's screens. The place looked dead and damned. He adjusted his position in the alien couch which was his seat on this rescue mission. It did not quite fit his physical form. He made a mental note to speak to Star Dancer about it later. He closed his silver eyes and focused on the mission ahead.

Mark Thomas sat in the pilot seat, keeping an eye on the small craft's readings. He had been thoroughly checked out on the shuttle and now knew it inside and out, but that still did not equate to an actual mission. He might be required at any time to take over and perform evasive maneuvers. In fact, having come to know and appreciate Star Dancer's unique sense of humor, that bloody machine might throw a trick or two in on purpose just to see how he reacted.

"An interesting thought," came the quiet mind of Star Dancer, "I will have to file that one away in my memory banks for later use. In the meantime, ground penetrating radar has picked up the echo of a very large space about a half of a kilometer from your scheduled landing spot. Please adjust your flight angle to land nearer to that space."

Dale Lambert was once again amazed by the size of the ancient craft. The Orion was just as big as Star Dancer, but somehow without the resident Artificial Intelligence up and running the voluminous corridors just rang back hollow in his ears and felt somehow ominous. "Star Dancer what is the status of activating Orion's AI?"

There was one of those pauses that indicated that Star Dancer was choosing his words very carefully. "Orion has withdrawn deeply into her sub conscious mind. The trauma of losing a crew has a great effect on a ship. I know. I speak from experience. Perhaps once you have secured the remaining crew and they have had a sufficient time to recover then perhaps you, with your abilities and the crew's backing can reach out and try to contact her to convince her to come back online." With a wistful note in his voice Star Dancer added, "It would be nice to have a sister."

Deep in his mind, Dale noted that identification of Orion as female. "And why shouldn't Orion be female", came Heather's soft mental voice. Dale could feel the teasing flavor of it in his mind. He smiled to himself, and with a great deal of care thought back, "If she is anything like you my dear, I fear for the sanity of all male AI forms!"

Dale felt the wisp of a mental kiss and then brought his mind back to the corridor and the waiting entrance to the Medical Bay. His out of body mind experience had prepared him for the dim lighting and with a pass of his hand over the doorway panel he initiated the Bay's systems. Light came up and the message tape which had reset itself began to play once more. He reached the panel and cut the display. Turning to Peter Lamous and Shadow Grey he pointed to the far wall of the bay and the waiting ranks of cryostasis tubes.

The shuttle settled down in a brief cloud of dust and small rocks. This planet had about one-third the gravity of their now defunct planet. While the feeling of power in their limbs was an interesting experience it did cause them to overreach and bang their heads once or twice against the shuttle's ceiling as they prepared to exit the small ship.

The fact that there were no extravehicular suits available for the canine members of their crew explained the absence of those very talented beings on this away mission. Glenda Stern thought that their sharp senses might have been of great help in the darken tunnels that awaited them. She would speak to Star Dancer when she returned from the mission.

Heather sat on the Captain's chair noting that while designed for other backsides then hers the fit was quite comfortable. "Star Dancer, have you been able to access any of the Orion's shipboard files? Surely not all the information is stored within the ship's AI."

Star Dancer once again gave an extended pause before answering. "I have accessed the primary back up log that resides in the emergency beacon locator. That beacon failed to launch during the Brethren assault." There was another pause as if Star Dancer found that fact unusual indeed. "I will display the last five entries on the Captain's screen."

The images that appeared on the screen showed a well-ordered Command Center. The Captain was an older man but still fit. Heather admired the way that he directed his crew. He was friendly without being too familiar. His orders were concise and understandable. The crew obeyed them quickly and efficiently. The proximity alarm rang and the second in command drew the Captain's attention to the warning. Together they examined the blip on the screen and with a crisp command the Captain ordered the advise and recognize signals deployed. He also prudently raised the shields.

This was all in keeping with what Heather had seen on their mental probe of the Orion and was reported on the auto log, but the next scene totally dumbfounded her. The Captain called his other senior crew members over and quickly outlined a series of orders. The Orion was designed to fit a full complement of crew and there had only been those in the sick bay and on the planetary surface accounted for. Heather had assumed that the rest had either been removed by advanced weapons that left no trace or by being taken captive.

The screen now displayed the real reason for the lack of body count. The bulk of the ship's compliment had reported to the main hanger bay and there had mounted small but deadly looking fighters. These were released on the side of the ship opposite from the vector that the incoming vessel was on and because of this were presumably invisible to their sensors. The fleet of fighters dived down toward the planet and then spun around to hang on the shadowed portion of the planet's night side.

The second of the reports demonstrated the gig's approach to the Brethren ship and once again showed the expected list of activities including the return of the gig with Brethren ambassadors on board. The screen showed clearly that only three of the Brethren had come over on that gig. Heather shook herself in shock, three of these criminals were enough to disable what she knew from her experience with Star Dancer was a very potent opponent.

What the original video did not show was that while on board the Brethren ship the crew from the gig made some very clandestine observations. What they learned was very disconcerting. The central core of the ship was impenetrable by the sensors, but the peripheral areas displayed an amazing amount of energy. What startled Heather was that the Brethren seemed indifferent to the attempts to discover what lay hidden in their ship.

The next scene was hard to follow as Heather watched the peaceful return of the ambassador's party to the Command Center. With a barely discernible movement the Leader of the Brethren party, flicked a switch on his belt and the three Brethren were bathed in a shimmering field. The Orion's automated weapons came online, but it was too late. As the flashes of energy cleared, only the dead of the Orion inhabited the room. The Brethren leader then proceeded to stroll leisurely through the ship ignoring the defensive measures that flared all around him. The three Brethren remained unfazed as they laid about with their belt weapons.

They reached the hanger deck and proceeded to exit the Orion. Behind the planet where the Orion's defense fleet had hidden a rampant battle was in progress. The Brethren ship had deployed their own attack force which had been hidden by cloaking devices. As the Orion's bridge crew died, the Brethren opened up on the hidden fleet destroying utterly all hope of reinforcements.

The final report showed the devastation brought by the Brethren ship as it remotely extracted the mineral riches of the planet below. The surface seethed and boiled, killing all those that had not made it back to the safety of the command center deep in the planet. Then the last view of the Brethren was as the ship moved out of orbit accelerating to the system's edge, disappearing into hyper space.

The away party below on the planet surface had discovered the airlock leading down, presumably to the command center and medical area of Orion's survey force. They paused at the control panel, which was similar to those on Star Dancer but yet did not give them access when they typed in the normal code. Dr. Scott moved up to the panel and using the second sight which his mutation had given him peeled back the layers of material, tracing circuits and power leads. Finally, he was able to ascertain the correct pathway. Calling Glenda over to him he "showed her" the correct sequence of connections that needed to be triggered in order for the doorway to open.

Glenda drew out a small battery unit and from this she directed the flow of the energy to those junctions. The limited atmosphere of the planet was composed mainly of toxic fumes but still transmitted the groans of that doorway mechanism as it inched open revealing the dark maw of space beyond.

When the opening had reached its furthest point the members of the rescue team crowded into the space. Once again Mark Thomas tried the interior panel and typed in the sequence to close that outer portal and to begin the cycling sequence. This time the panel preformed as expected and they were soon bathed in dim light, standing in the beginning of a long corridor carved from native rock and reinforced by plastasteel. Their suits exterior sensors indicated that there was a limited amount of air to breathe but that it would not sustain life for long.

Mark Thomas detailed two of his team to set up the small oxygen generators and to begin the process of flooding the tunnels with breathable air. He left those there with orders to explore the upper reaches of the tunnel system and to be prepared to aid them if needed.

The remainder of the team marched slowly down that long slopping tunnel. Mark was glad that the Orion team had been so thorough in their design. The plastasteel would prevent any gas leakages through the rock and added a very strong layer of structural support for the tunnel system.

Back in the Orion, Dale moved cautiously over to the first cryostasis tube. The tube had failed and all that remained of the occupant was a skeleton incased in a ship's uniform. He shook his head sadly and proceeded to the next. The rime covered interior made looking at the occupant difficult, but he could make out the close-cropped hair and the uniform of Orion's crew. The indicator light still blinked a hopeful green. Dale turned his head so that he could see Peter Lamous standing by the stasis control panel. "We'll try this one first." To his medical team he said, "Stand by." That group had brought up a wheeled gurney with various hollow lines and bottles containing life giving fluids and waited as the tube's mechanisms sequenced through.

Dale had brushed up on the process by which those in cryostasis were revived and knew a bit of what to expect. He had read that the reactions to reanimation varied widely. He could expect docile awakening or behavior that could reach a catatonic state.

It was a fairly slow process. Peter monitored the vital signs from his station and Dale drew nearer to the tube as the rime ice disappeared and a soft glow of warming light filled the interior. He closed his eyes and focused on the form in the tube penetrating the exterior skin to focus on the patient's internal functions. He watched, gratified as system after system came online indicating a return to normal function. He then focused on the mind of the person being revived and was grateful that he was there to lend aid. The chaos displayed in the wild thoughts that bounced through the sub conscious mind of the patient was amazing. He tried to reach that essential core of the person to reassure him that all was well and that he was safe.

"What, where am I?" came the plea. Dale replied, "You are safe. You are in the Medical Bay of the Orion. We are here to help you and your crew mates."

"Safe how can anyone be safe with those devils in the system? The thoughts were clearer now, less chaotic. "The Brethren vessel has been gone from this system for a long time", Dale replied. "We are from the Star Dancer, a ship very similar to your own. We received your distress call and found the Orion in orbit about the planet below."

The mind now firmed up its thoughts and asked, "Has anyone gone below to look for survivors?" The question was almost a plea.

Dale's thoughts came to the patient once more, "Yes I have an away team down there now. They have just entered the tunnels and are looking for survivors. They would probably be in stasis tubes just like yours." At a signal from Peter, Dale added, "We are going to move you onto the medical gurney and begin the process of introducing fluids and nutrients back into your system. You are to remain calm, and the process will continue. You are the first of the survivors that we have tried to bring back."

A final question reached Dale as he began to remove his thoughts from the supine man. "How are you communicating with me, I am not awake nor am I speaking but I hear you and you hear me?"

"Several of our crew are capable of telepathy, among other things. Now rest I must see to the others." The man thanked him as the materials and medicines within the bottles began to ease through his system. "Who are you?" he asked.

"I am Dale Lambert, the Captain and friend of Star Dancer."

Doctor Scott stood for a moment in quiet contemplation. The figure in front of him was slumped over a communications console. Whoever it was had died a very long time ago. She had died at her station vainly attempting to reach help that never came. He corrected himself, came too late for her. He turned back to the rows of stasis tubes and whispered a prayer that for these maybe, they weren't too late.

It took several days but the reanimation of one hundred and thirty survivors aboard the Orion and those on the planet below swelled the available ranks of capable crew men and women. There were several who once awakened had gone into shock. Those minds were those that neither he nor Dr. Scott could reach. Their own systems shutdown and they entered the long sleep that had been denied them. There were others that needed special care as they teetered on the brink of mental collapse. So, it was an exhausted Dale Lambert who made his way back to his cabin aboard Star Dancer having placed his own crew in essential positions on the Orion to begin the assessment phase to determine the best possible course of retrofitting that damaged ship.

Heather stood in the doorway to their cabin and stared at the sleeping form of her lover. Shaking her head, she was about to turn away when in her mind she felt the warmth of Dale's thoughts. "Don't go my love, come lay here by me for a while and let me feel your presence." Smiling she eased her way onto their shared sleeping platform and curled her arms around her man. "The sleepy thoughts continued, "Some Honeymoon, hey?"

She felt his mind slip into a deeper sleep and whispered, "You sure know how to show a girl a good time." His snore was the only reply that she had.

Star Dancer oversaw the retrofitting of the Orion. The ship's systems had not been that badly damaged and he wondered in his circuits about that. The Brethren had caused massive casualties but little in the way of serious destruction. Star Dancer's chief concern was that of Orion's AI. He had been unable to elicit any sustained response from that entity. There had been a flicker or two of what he thought of as recognition but no active communication.

Stephen Goodale

Dale Lambert called a meeting of the joint crew's officers. Those from the Orion were reluctant to leave their posts but Star Dancer had made it clear to them that there would be no exceptions. The gathering met in one of the ship's large dining halls. Dale rose and addressed the group. "While I or Doctor Scott welcomed each of you individually during your reanimation phase, we have not yet been able to sit down with you to discuss what is to happen next." He waved his hands as choruses of voices rose in comment. "In order to make sense of timelines and histories I ask that you bear with me as I review just how we came to be Star Dancer's crew and our brief odyssey in space until we discovered the Orion."

When he had their attention, he relayed the history of the planet of their origin from the human perspective, outlining all of the events that they had experienced up to and including their escape from that planet and its destruction. When he had finished Star Dancer's mellow voice chimed in over the ship's com and told the story from his point of view. He placed a heavy emphasis on the canine members of the crew. Shadow Grey's people had been introduced to the members of the Orion crew and had been met with a mixed reaction of acceptance and revulsion. Star Dancer now made it plain, as did Dale Lambert, that these were as much of the crew as those that had been rescued from stasis. All due respect would be given to them as full members of the crew and as officers.

Once again there was some surprised grumbling, but Shadow Grey stood up on his hind legs, resting his fore paws on the table's surface. Through his translator he said, "Do not think for one moment that I and my companions are less than you. We are of an ancient race that has had the use of our mental abilities for many generations." Here he paused to mentally pick up one of those whose voice had protested the most, levitating him in mid air for a few seconds and then gently returning him to his original seat. He was a much quieter man. "We have come along on this venture as equal partners and will not accept anything less. He scanned the assembled group and added, "Do you understand?"

Later Star Dancer displayed the video of the scene to Dale, Heather, Shadow Grey, and Moon Glow. He was able to enhance the images of those that did not respond as whole heartedly as one would have hoped. These "dissenters" were noted, and a work schedule was put in place that would pair them with a member of the troupe in the hopes that by working closely together their prejudices would abate.

Dale Lambert stood once more. "Our original mission was to go back to the Home World and become integrated once more in our intended society." He held his hand up for silence. "Neither of our crews have a very good idea of what has transpired in this section of the galaxy, certainly Star Dancer is of an older lineage than Orion, but my people tell me that your ship has spun around the planet below for at least two hundred years. The carbon dating of the various remains of your crew indicates that this time frame is somewhat accurate." There was uproar over this. Once more Dale Lambert called for attention and when he was ignored, he sent a bolt of mental thought to each and every member of the meeting. "Your crew has been treated with upmost respect and their remains interred according to your costumes. Your own officers oversaw the procedures, so calm down."

Once it was understood that this man, Dale Lambert, and his crew were powerful enough to force any issue, the officers calmed down but there was a sense of resentment coloring their emotions. Dale took note of this as well, commenting on a private band to his officers that this side trip might not have been worth the effort. He immediately felt the chagrin of Shadow Grey's mind who pointedly reminded him that lives had been saved and that was point enough.

One of the Orion's crew stood to address his fellows, "Listen to yourselves! You would still be in stasis if Star Dancer's people had not turned aside to aid you. The chance that another rescue vessel coming to our aid in time to save your ungrateful hides was extremely remote, these peoples and he included the troupe in the sweep of his arms, have come to our aid. Let us at least be civil enough to show them the gratitude that they rightly deserve."

"Let us honor our Captain and those fallen crewmates who gave their lives so valiantly in the defense of our Orion by honoring and working with the crew of the Star Dancer!" Slowly one after the other of the Orion's crew rose in their places and began to applaud the crew of the Star Dancer. There were a few exceptions, and these were noted as well.

"Now that is somewhat settled let us take stock of our next steps. We are sitting here in orbit, a known target to these Brethren. We have not come across any references to them in our ship's data base nor have we been able to ascertain any contact from that data that is currently available from the Orion. That being said, the videos that the Orion took before they disabled the ship showed a ruthless and mean adversary with a high level of destructive technology."

He paused and then continued. "While the recovery of the Orion may not be a priority to those bastards, it may still be on their agenda. The readings that the Orion's medical staff took indicated that the Brethren are a very long-lived race and as such may have different views on time. In other words, they may be back. As we orbit here, we are sitting ducks, although thanks to the devastation wrought and the bravery of the Orion's crew no longer unprepared."

"To that end we must make every effort to get the Orion flight worthy. To do this our two ships must work together. We were already under manned before we broke into this system. The Orion is now very under manned. To do this we must get the Orion's AI back online. Star Dancer has already begun the process of reestablishing communications, but we must intensify the effort."

"In the meantime, we need to get the Orion's main systems up and dependable. This includes the shields, the main engines, communications, deep space sensors and all life support." Dale looked around the room, "May I have a demonstration by show of hands of who in this group can lead the refit on the departments mentioned."

As Dale named the departments once more a few hands came up for each. Heather noted the names and rank of those that volunteered for the duty. She quietly asked Star Dancer to compare these against known ship's personnel from the Orion's records. This cross reference demonstrated strengths and weaknesses in each department. She then assigned crew from Star Dancer to augment and strengthen those that would do the work.

Heather then stood up and assigned duty rosters. There was no more grumbling as the promise of action started to affect both crews. Dale then called the senior members of both vessels together and went into a smaller conference room. Closing the door, he stood for a moment at the head of the table and then sat down. He was amused to note that the others did not seat themselves until he had.

"Thank you, Ladies and Gentlemen, for your time and your willingness to work through a difficult situation. Our lack of manpower must be addressed, so one of our immediate goals will be to establish a base somewhere that we can begin recruiting form nearby civilizations amendable to becoming star voyagers." He paused and looked at the faces in front of him, "We are coming into this section of the galaxy blind. Time has flowed for Star Dancer, and all is not as it once was. We need a safe place from which we can ascertain the current status of what had been once familiar space lanes. We need to know what has become of our Federation."

Chapter Six

While the conference was going on in the ship's dining hall, Star Dancer had been listening in on the flow of conversations monitoring all who were present. It was during the talk of bringing the key systems up to flight readiness that the AI caught an interesting flux in the energy levels of the Orion. His sister ship stood several thousand feet off from his port bow and he had constantly watched her returning power levels. Now he noted an interesting change in those levels. They were small to be sure, but they arrived so closely on the heels of the conversations in the dining hall that they seemed tied one to the other.

Once again Star Dancer scanned the members in that room and was startled by the findings that came back from one individual in particular. He did not bring his observations to the attention of his Command Crew, at least not yet.

Raw materials were becoming a problem aboard the Orion. The planet below had been stripped of resources by the Brethren. There were other planets in the system and Dale sent Mark Thomas and Glenda Stern out to survey the fifth planet out from the sun. The world was a cold dead world, but long-range scans showed that some of the heavy metals needed to form the hybrid material of the Orion's skin could be found there.

The small craft sped its way out bound from the orbit inhabited by Star Dancer and Orion. The area of space was empty of all but cosmic dust and highly charged particles. Mark Thomas experimented with these particles collecting them carefully around the hull of the ship. Using the experience that he had gained while he was trapped in that crawler back on Laurel, he began to manipulate the charges of those particles adding energy to some, slowing others until he could create a frequency flux under his control.

Glenda added her expertise by redirecting that energy and augmenting it from the energy on board the shuttle. By the time they arrived at the fifth planet both were satisfied that together they could create an effective shield that would repel any solid materials hurled at them or mitigate any energy weapons fired at them. In fact, Glenda was certain that she could take the energy splashing against those screens and siphon it off to augment the vessels own energy resources.

The scans of the world below revealed some small concentrations of the materials required by the Orion's repair crew. The shuttle settled down near a mountain range whose spires arched high into the air. Mark looked out from the small observation port of the shuttle's command deck up at those high jagged peaks. He shivered in his chair. They looked like fangs reaching into the sky.

Once the dust and debris from their landing settled slowly back to the surface of the plateau on which the landing craft had settled, Mark and Glenda prepared the powerful drill in the cargo bay. Wearing their protective suits, they closed the cabin airlock and then opened the cargo bay door. The drill was on powerful treads and the whole unit rambled down the extended ramp. They guided the machine to a spot on the rock wall and aligned it so that its energy beam would cut through the hard rock and intersect the needed raw materials. They set the drill on automatic and then stood back to watch its progress

Star Dancer was busy analyzing the Orion's systems when a soft voice whispered over his internal circuits. "Hello my friend. I wanted to say thank you for your rescue. You and your crew are very welcome indeed. I am Orion."

Star Dancer took a moment to consider his response and then said, "I think that I have already met you, although you may not have recognized that fact. You were seated in the back of the meeting called for the joint officers of both ships" Star Dancer added, "You were quite charming you know!"

There was a joyful lilt in the electronic tone which washed through his circuits. "Thank you, kind sir, not only do you come to the aid of a damsel in distress, but you have a chivalric manner." The voice left his circuits as another more pressing matter caught his attention. The deep space proximity alarms began to clamor. They had been set out to warn of incoming vessels which might intrude on the system.

Immediately Star Dancer contacted Dale Lambert with the warning, "Captain we have company incoming." He spread his awareness to Dale's mind. There were three large ships on a vector for the third planet. These were moving slowly toward the planet their intentions unclear.

"Star Dancer, recall the away mission. Instruct Mark to wait for those ships to pass the orbit of the fifth planet then to come in behind them. Tell him to shield the shuttle. We will use him in reserve. Please spread your defensive shields to cover the Orion. If we are lucky, they will not be able to distinguish the fact that there are two vessels here in orbit and assume that this vessel is the one that was left for dead." He paused in thought for a moment, "Won't they be surprised?"

The lead Rever ship entered the system of this forsaken world. Its Commander was a tall stocky man whose ancestors could trace their lineage to a heavy gravity world far away from this corner of the galaxy. He didn't much like going out so far from his own system but when the Brethren High Command gave you an assignment you either carried it out without question or you died. It was a black and white choice, and he did not much feel like dying this day. Besides this was a cake assignment. Just a cleanup detail on the books for many years before more pressing issues were cleared away enough to make it rise to the top of the list.

He had led many such missions before. The aftermath of a Brethren action was never a pleasant experience. The result of their overwhelming technical superiority and their rather devious underhanded method of doing business was usually total defeat and death for their opponents. He had been assigned to come out here and to reclaim any technologies that might be deemed valuable to further the Brethren cause. The mineral extraction ship had come across the alien ship in orbit around the third planet. The Brethren had sent an away team over to assess the vessel's technologies and having rendered it helpless had proceeded to remove the mineral wealth required from the third planet.

He did not expect any problems with this assignment, so he was rather startled by the readings from his long-range scanners. There was a ship in orbit right enough, but the instruments indicated a force shield around the vessel. He barked several commands into the communicator and the other two ships immediately separated from his and assumed an attack formation. The open communications line crackled into life, and he found himself being hailed by the ship. "This is the Federation Ship Star Dancer. You have entered this system without our leave. We are here on a rescue mission. If you are not a hostile, then stand down and remain in relative position until you are boarded for inspection. This will be your only warning."

The Commander was unsure how to respond to this ultimatum, but he was certain that he would be dead if he failed to achieve his mission. He ordered the two companion vessels to begin an attack on the Star Dancer. Funny he thought to himself he was told that the wreck that his group would be scavenging was known as the Orion!"

Dale sat in the command chair as Heather stood beside him. "Star Dancer, can you bring your main guns to bear on our guests? Fire a blast across their projected course. We shall attempt to disable their vessels and disrupt their communications so that what occurs next will not go further than this system."

Through his shielded link to Mark Thomas, Dale added, "Can you get behind them? Once the warning shot is fired, Glenda could you reach out and disable their energy flow to their main engines?"

Mark Thomas had pulled in the needed ore and was packing the drill back into the shuttle's cargo bay when the alarm had sounded. Now he received the shielded message from Dale. He looked over to Glenda and smiled weakly. She gave him the thumbs up and together they recycled the airlock. Once free of the cumbersome protective suits they started the ship's engines. The three ships were clear on their screens as they focused in on the third planet, not giving the fifth planet a second thought as they passed its orbit.

They kept a respectable distance behind the ships as Mark worked the shields and Glenda started the buildup of the needed power surge that would disable the vessels.

Star Dancer moved from a parallel orbit where his form had shielded the Orion to one that faced perpendicular to the surface. From the hull of his outer skin Star Dancer raised the main ships gun.

The Rever's Commander noted the shift in orbit and then with a gasp recognized that there was another ship behind Star Dancer, the Orion had been uncovered by the maneuver. He was dealing with a fully functional vessel obviously capable of defense and offense. The screens on his console went wild as Star Dancer released a pulse from its main weapon. The shields which had never even fluxed in previous encounters were suddenly drained to ten percent of their capacity and the shot had not even been aimed directly at him!

Through the chaos of alarms and emergency transmissions between his three reclamation ships the Commander caught a quiet voice which filled his mind. "You are now ordered to stand down and submit your vessels for boarding. You will not be allowed to get closer to the third planet. Disregard this warning at your peril. This is Dale Lambert fleet commander. I await your response."

The Commander was surprised by the strength and clarity of that voice. The communication had been a mental one which indicated a level of capability near to that of the Brethren high command themselves. That thought triggered another line of reasoning. Could this be some type of test to be sure that he and his followers-maintained discipline and followed directives to the bitter end? He had been present once or twice in the high council chamber and he recognized the feel of power that was in those minds when they spoke to him. Now he began to think that he was being tested and failure for that testing was instantaneous death.

Dale sighed as he read the train of thought coming from the Rever Commander. He now knew from his contact that the man's mission was not of threat but was a simple one of recovery. Dale knew that the Brethren had not lost their interest in the Orion despite the number of years that had passed. These vessels had expected a derelict but instead met with a powerful opponent. With a smile he gave Mark and Glenda the go ahead to disable those ships. He asked Star Dancer to return to his original orbital location.

The Rever Commander watched as the vessel, Star Dancer, resumed its guardian position over the Orion. A feral smile curled his lips. This was the test, he thought to himself. If we break and run from cover, we will not make it to the system's edge before the Brethren destroyed us. Even now he thought, one of their Dreadnaughts was in position to deliver that death blow hidden by their accursed shields. Well, he was not about to give them the pleasure. "All ships, attention we will proceed as planned. We will finish our mission!"

Mark had been listening in on the communications band that Dorothy had discovered was the operations frequency used by the Revers. With a ghost of the smile that his boss had for the pleasure of foiling the attempted reclamation of the Orion, he moved his small ship in behind the three vessels. The ships had once again gotten underway and with a nod to Glenda he extended the plasma shields into sharp probes that penetrated and surrounded the engines of those vessels. Immediately all three ships stopped in relative space. With the energies flowing back to them through the reaction chambers Glenda and Mark threw all but the life support systems onboard those ships into null stasis.

The absolute quiet that permeated his bridge was a complete shock. All his ship's functions had ceased at the same time. Everything but the life support system, he noted somewhere in his disbelief. The false peace of the situation lasted only as long as a breath or two than every man and woman on his bridge staff began to speak at once. He roared for silence and the chaos ceased at once. He ordered a complete check of all functions and arranged for a messenger system to run the commands and reports through the ship.

Dale had followed the situation on board the Rever ships and once again sent a mental probe to the Rever Commander. "You are an able officer, surely you know now that your mission is no longer viable. I offer you a choice. You can stay in position, blind and unable to communicate, unable to do anything but live until our mission here in this system is complete. At which time I will release your ships and you will face the unenviable task of reporting your failure to the Brethren High Command, or you may join us. We could use competent spacers to help us reman our ships."

The Rever Commander sat back in his chair stunned. No one dared to go up against the Brethren. Those despots had ruled the galaxy for thousands of years. Those that had tried had died. Even as lowly as his post had been in the schema of the Brethren's Empire, he had heard of the system wide destruction of the Freshden people. Reports were that all that had gone up against the Brethren lost their lives, that their home world had been totally destroyed. Yet under the banner of official information, he had also heard that eight Dreadnaughts and three Planet Killers had also been destroyed and that their leader Hymical had vanished and was presumed dead.

His people were a proud race. They had been subjugated long ago by the Brethren as they had conquered all the worlds on which the Juancy peoples had colonized. Some with extreme prejudice, he thought bitterly to himself. Ever since then his people had preformed to expectations accomplishing every mission that they had been assigned. Yet far under the surface there simmered a deep resentment for the Brethren. A desire for revenge, deeply concealed.

Now he had come on another clean up mission, salvage really. To take what was deemed valuable back to his masters. Only he was held helpless by forces that he had never heard of, forces that might compete against even their power. He was given a choice which was no choice really. If he failed to succeed in his mission, then his life and the lives of the entire expedition were forfeit.

He could feel the mind of this Dale Lambert waiting patiently for his response. If this was a trick of his masters than he was truly caught. There was no way out that would not entail his destruction, but if it was not a trick, if it was a real opportunity for freedom than it was worth the exploration. He knew that it was time to give an answer.

"I can only speak for my ship, Fleet Commander Lambert. You must allow me to communicate with my other vessels. I will need to apprise them of your proposal and to elicit their response."

"Certainly, Rever Commander, I will allow ship to ship communication, but I warn you that while I will not influence your ultimate decisions, I will bear no subterfuge. I will monitor all communications in the process."

The communications console lit up and he directed his communications officer to link the three ships. "I, Commander Groshen have been in contact with the mind of one Dale Lambert Fleet Commander of those that wait in orbit around the third planet of this system. As you know our orders from the Brethren are to perform salvage on the vessel Orion which is now being protected by the vessel Star Dancer."

"Those on board those two vessels hold us helpless in some form of stasis field and can control all of our internal systems. They have given us a choice of remaining here helpless until they are ready to leave this system at which time, I have been assured that the stasis will be released and that we would be free to go on our way. They have also given us another option. We could renounce our fealty to the Brethren and take up arms with them. They would allow us to be assimilated into their ships' crews."

He paused for a moment and listened to the immediate garble of denials, orders, counter orders, and desperation. He knew as well as all who served under the banner of the Brethren the cost of failure. "I cannot speak for any but my own crew and even some of them may disagree with my decision. We are now in a no-win situation. Should we fail to perform our stated mission then we die by the hand of our Brethren masters. If we throw our lives in with the Federation vessels that lay in front of us, then our deaths may be just as certain. I can only tell you that the power that holds us now is comparable to that held by the Brethren High Command. If all else is equal I would like to take a stab at avenging our people who have died ingloriously at the hands of the Brethren. I will take up service with Dale Lambert!"

The silence that fell on his control room was repeated on the other two vessels. No one in living memory had stood up against the Brethren and lived to tell the tale. Now here was their own Squadron Commander stating openly that he would join in with the aliens in a fight against those same Brethren.

The projectile exploded from the barrel of a weapon held by one of his senior officers. The velocity was such that no one in that chamber had even registered the fact of its discharge nor had time to react. The metal slug was instantly arrested in its flight falling to the metal deck as a stunned Groshen looked on, eyes bulging. The shot was repeated from several different directions with the same result.

Then the weapons that had issued those reports fell to the deck. The hands that had held them were in turn helpless in the grip of mental stasis. A glowing form appeared then, as Dale Lambert projected his astral form into the Command decks of all three ships. "I will not tolerate pointless loss of life. As you can see, we will prevent any attempts to kill those that wish to take up service with us. Unlike your masters, the Brethren, we of the Federation believe in the sanctity of life and our mission will be forever one of peace. Then he eyed each of the vessels command crews, "But do not mistake our love of peace for a sign of weakness. As you can see, we are not weak!"

Commander Groshen sat back down in his chair and looked around at those in stasis. He felt a pang of regret understanding that at least one-half of his people had demonstrated the willingness to kill him rather than to support his choice to become a member of the Federation. In a rather doleful voice, he opened the ship wide intercom which now responded to his touch. "This is Commander Groshen. Let all who wish to remain in the service of the Brethren be allowed to move to the ship Larsfen. All who wish to join me in this new venture transfer to our other two ships. Make your choice with a clear heart for those that welcome us to service will be able to tell if you are trying to deceive them. I suggest that those of you that attempt to do so will find yourselves on the Larsfen anyway. Thank you for your service and good sailing."

Chapter Seven

The repairs on the Orion accelerated with the input and knowledge of the newly acquired crewmen from the Revers' ships. "It would seem", Dale Lambert mused to Heather Flanders as they spent a quiet moment together in their shared cabin, "That the Revers are just as good at putting things together as they are at taking them apart."

"Yes," Heather said from the warm embrace of Dale's arms, "It's a good thing that you were able to discern what those Revers had going on inside their hearts. They would certainly be a danger to us frailer beings. Did you get a look at the size of them?"

Dale thought that it was a very good idea to separate the willing from the unwilling. Shadow Grey and Moon Glow aided him in that task. In the end a little over one third of the Revers' personnel had decided that they could not take a chance in disobeying their master's orders. These had been transferred to the Larsfen and placed in a ship wide stasis. This was part mental block and part gas induced torpor. They could not allow them to leave until the repairs for the Orion were complete and they had a chance to set a course for a destination somewhere unknown to those crew men. They could use whatever excuse that they deemed fit to cover their failure once the ships were safely away.

Groshen had been admitted to the command council held in one of the larger conference rooms aboard Star Dancer. The man was huge, weighing in at twice Dale's mass. The heavy gravity of his native world accounted for most of that, but he and his crewmen could be found in the off hours physical recreation plant pushing their mass to unbelievable heights as they worked out. Dale was amused as he contemplated the mixed crew that was now members of the Orion and Star Dancer complement.

Members of the troupe did not shy away from contact with the much bigger Juancy crew. In fact, some of those who had not made a choice among the other crew as life mates now became attached to their much larger crewmates. The mental abilities of those four-footed companions stunned the physically massive Juancy and in short order gained them much respect. In fact, all the crew seemed to be settling down into a pattern as the Orion's repairs were drawing to a close.

Dale had called all the officers of his joint crews together to discuss what their next step would be. They had succeeded in rescuing the Orion and her crew. They had gained some very valuable allies in the Juancy but they were still very much strangers in a strange land. Dale felt that they needed to find a haven where the crew could have off ship time and where they could develop a base of operations. It was to this end that he had called this meeting.

Once again Star Dancer surveyed the members of that meeting recording the discussion and noting any possible signs of duplicity. He had of course been involved in the initial probes of the Juancy crewmen as they were either accepted or rejected as being fit for Federation service. That had been a common ship responsibility from the very beginning of operations. As he did this, he recognized the figure of one of the alter day crew officers. This was one of the communications officers under the direction of Dorothy Abrams, although Star Dancer recognized her as someone else.

Once again that soft voice came into his circuits, "Thank you Star Dancer, I have always found it easier to deal with the crew as an entity on their own plane of existence. My old Captain knew who I was but no other. I would appreciate it if you gave me the same courtesy."

"I will honor your request only if the safety of the ships' crews is not mitigated by the withholding of your identity. I will also state that I will only reveal your existence to the senior members of the crew if needed. You will be able to continue your dual role without fear and with complete freedom." Star

Dancer paused and then added, "May I now report to Dale Lambert that Orion is back up and running. Can you perform normal interface responsibilities for your crew?"

The image on his screen looked up and directly at the hidden monitoring device and smiled. "Yes, my friend I am fully functional. Thank you once again for your discretion."

Groshen, Polasic and Trembo from the Juancy crews represented the newly acquired crewmen for Star Dancer and Orion. They sat in stoic silence as Dale Lambert outlined the history of Star Dancer and their specie's relationship with that ship through the ages, bringing all up to date on recent events. He did fail to mention the genetic alterations that the crew of the Star Dancer both human and canine had undergone and the resulting capabilities that they had demonstrated. He only affirmed his own ability to telepath and left it at that.

Then the remaining senior officer from the Orion, First Medical Officer Norwell Frosden spoke on behalf of the Orion crew. Their history was much more current than that of the Star Dancer. It showed that the Federation, while still a force to be reckoned with in this sector of the galaxy, had begun to show cracks in its alliances. Raw materials had begun to become an issue, especially the rarer metals that were used to fabricate the ships hulls. He explained that this was why the Orion had been so far from her native space lanes. A long-range probe had returned with the news of a major find in metals on the world below. The Orion had been dispatched to recover as much of the material as possible.

He showed the ship's logs of their encounter with the Brethren and the betrayal of trust demonstrated by those aliens. Groshen sat through the recital without saying a word. Star Dancer had fabricated a translator for the Juancy crew, but the languages were not that dissimilar to the Universal that the two Federation crews used in their day-to-day interaction, so that both the Juancy and the human crews had begun to pick up on each other's idioms.

Now when the histories and events had been brought current, Groshen stood. A slow smile spread on his massive face demonstrating even white teeth. "I know that you have every reason to doubt my words now, but I only ask for your patience and to bear with me. You will soon know that you are not alone in your story of betrayal."

"While my story encompasses many generations of slavery and servitude, those of my race who have been allowed to keep our histories tell us of a time when we were a free people. We started by bringing our own world into peaceful coexistence, a step that allowed us to put petty jealousies aside and to aspire to greater heights of cultural achievement. We looked outward, first to our own solar system and then to nearby stars. We moved in slow graceful steps ensuring our orderly and peaceful movement out into the universe. We only sought worlds and systems that did not contain intelligent life forms. On those worlds which life was discovered we attempted to maintain an even ecological balance and not disrupt that life."

"When we first encountered the Brethren, we pulled back away from that contact. It was in a system that we both wanted. It turned out for quite different reasons. We had explored a lovely world of oceans and land masses with a strong vegetative growth. We had thought of creating a settlement there dedicated to the study of the planet. When the Brethren came, they met with our people and assured us that they simply wanted to explore the mineral wealth using careful techniques to prevent disruption of the native ecology. We agreed to allow them access while our people withdrew to go on to other systems." Groshen paused, his smile turning bitter. "When our scout ships returned to the system sometime later, we found only a burned out world, lifeless and pitiful. We knew then that the Brethren could not be trusted."

"We had been cautious in our dealings with them. We did not disclose our home system location nor that of our colonies, but we failed to understand the levels of their technologies. Our data systems had been scanned and all had been revealed." The large man hung his head, tears welling from his eyes. "It was an easy matter then for the subjugation of our culture. A few attempts were made to fight them, but the Brethren were quite thorough in their response to resistance. In the end we surrendered to their rule and were "placed" in positions of usefulness. Those planets of ours, that held mineral wealth enough to interest them, were annihilated at once. My own world was one of those."

Groshen looked up into Dale Lambert's sympathetic eyes and asked the question. "Do you have the power to resist such evil? Can you take the steps needed to bring peace back into the galaxy?"

The quiet that filled the room was a coiling blanket of despair. Then Dale and Heather stood up holding hands they scanned the room. Star Dancer created a shimmering hologram and Orion added one of her own to stand next to the two lovers. Shadow Grey and Moon Glow stood along with Dr. Scott, Mark Thomas, Glenda Stern and Dorothy Abrams. The room grew still, and the energy was something palpable.

"We stand together at the doorway", said Dale Lambert. "We are free peoples one and all, our powers are great but are untested against the evil of this foe. We cannot guarantee success, but we can assure you that to a being, we will die trying. The door through which we pass will be one of a new and free galaxy. We will invite all free people to join us, and we will create a universe which will be safe for all."

Groshen then sat back down slowly into his chair, a look of hope on his face. "You know. I think that the Brethren made a serious tactical mistake by allowing us to keep our history. They patently ignored the fact that we taught our young people that we were once free. I suppose from their point of view it was of little difference to them whether we lived in hope or in despair. They only expected and received complete obedience to their will. Now I think, they will regret that arrogance. I know that you cannot guarantee success, but I join you in your pledge, we will try now and succeed or die trying and at least be satisfied by knowing we died free men!"

The two other officers present from the Juancy people echoed their leader's pledge. Dale smiled down into Heather's upturned face. "It seems my love that we are once again asked to play the role of rebels!"

The activity level throughout the two ships picked up pace. Groshen had been able to fill in some of the gaps in the recent knowledge of this area of space. The Brethren had over the past one hundred standard years become more and more influential in the nearby sectors of the galaxy. They had conquered a number of local star systems including the latest, the Freshden system. That victory, if that was what they had deemed it, was at great cost. Groshen stated that for the first time in living memory the Brethren had tasted a measure of defeat. Losing a number of Capital ships in the battle and realizing no reward for their effort other than the destruction of yet another people. The Freshden by all accounts had put up a strong defense aided by a group of unknown civilizations called the Empire.

Dale had shifted through the various ships' logs and through his conversations with the officers under his command had decided that it would be best to take a vector away from all known trouble areas. The Star Dancer, the Orion and the two remaining salvage vessels needed to have a safe haven on which the various crew could live for times outside of their ships. He still firmly believed that they would need to create a recruiting process by which worlds that were free could be contacted and tapped for additional crew and materials. He knew that this would be a long, drawn-out battle, but it needed to start with a point of shelter, a hidden base.

Groshen had also informed Dale Lambert that the Brethren kept in loose contact with all of their fleet vessels through periodic reporting schedules. While the salvage vessels were not really considered fleet ships in the minds of their old masters, the Juancy crew were supposed to report in on schedule. The next reporting cycle would be in two standard days. When the ships failed to report in, a standard operations probe would be sent to the system to investigate. The Federation ships needed to be out of the system before that probe arrived or the Brethren would send in a task force to check on the status of the operation.

The Orion had been deemed fit for interstellar travel, so Dale now detailed that ship to move from the orbit of the third planet to that of the fifth and to complete the mining of the rare materials found there, materials that they would need in the future. The veins of ores that Mark Thomas and Glenda Stern had located were quickly tapped. The materials were processed and stored in Orion's huge cargo bay.

The two salvage ships that would accompany them into the sector of space toward the arm of the galaxy opposite from the current Brethren activity had been gone over with as much precaution as possible. The two AI entities along with Mark Thomas and Glenda Stern had followed and analyzed all of the power couplings and circuits on board, disabling ones that had suspected dualities and reconnecting the circuits with known controls. The Brethren it seemed did not concern themselves over much with their liegemen, but they did invest in technologies to keep track of their assets.

Groshen when informed of the discoveries simply growled under his breath. The methods by which the Brethren controlled their slaves always mystified him. It was one of the reasons that there was so little in the way of internal revolt in the Brethren sphere of influence. These were masters of taking technologies and bending them to their own purposes. Every system that they conquered added to that overwhelming technological superiority. Now he understood that some of those technologies had been used to watch, control and in times of need punish those that they subjugated. It was a very efficient system and it now made him wonder. Why hadn't they detected the shift in allegiance by the crews of two of their vessels?

He voiced his concern to Dale Lambert who smiled thinly in response. "Thank you for your analysis, Groshen, we have just received a warning of something large coming in from the opposite side of the sun. The Orion has gone into stealth mode, Mark Thomas and Glenda Stern will be handling the shields on board that ship. It will remain in concealment no matter what happens. I have directed your two remaining ships to close up with Star Dancer in an orbit on the other side of the ship to hide them, in the wash of our own shields."

"The Larsfen is in the same spatial relationship to our position as it was when you entered the system. The recording devices on board that ship will show a ship wide malfunction and that the crew was in stasis. Any scans will simple show that it was disabled on entry to the system and that no personnel were at fault for the systems shutdown." Dale looked straight at Groshen, "It is the best that I can do for them. Perhaps the Brethren ship will allow that to stand, we shall see."

Groshen looked at Dale Lambert a light gleaming in his eyes. "That is far better than they deserve, Admiral. The Brethren would not have been so kind."

"Good then that is settled. We will attempt to answer one of your questions in a few moments. The vessel entering the system is what you have called a Dreadnaught, a really big ship judging by the readings that we are getting. They are approaching without much caution which limits the reliability of the confrontation analysis. Perhaps we should broadcast a warning so that they would come at us in attack mode."

Groshen looked once more at his new commander, wonder in his eyes. The man was not bragging. He truly wanted to test Star Dancer against the Brethren ship. They retired to the Command deck where Heather, Shadow Grey and Moon Glow joined them. They arranged themselves in comfortable seats and immediately lost focus on their surroundings. Star Dancer stood watch along with Doctor Scott and Dorothy Abrams.

Groshen took up an observation post near the communications station and sat back to watch. If he had thrown his lot in with a group of deluded fools then he deserved what he got, but somehow Dale Lambert hadn't struck him as a fool.

Dale's mind had already linked with the others, and he was gathering power. He wanted to enter that incoming ship and he was counting on the fact that it would pause to investigate the status of the Larsfen before concerning itself with Star Dancer, a ship that it thought was the Orion and disabled.

He cast out his mind and was through the defensive shields of the Frachon, a ship of the line on duty station in this segment of the galaxy. Its Leader was a lower ranked member of the Council on assignment for some imagined infraction of the Triune's rules. It was a punishment assignment, and the officer was heartily board of his duty, wanting only to punish the salvage crews and their behavior that caused him to be so far away from the scant amenities of his home base.

Dale spent several minutes wandering through the Dreadnaught analyzing its defensive and offensive capabilities before he started to methodically redirect circuits, conduits, systems and subsystems. The Frachon would behave normally until he decided to pull its teeth.

As it changed its vector to intercept the salvage ship Larsfen, Dale moved to where he could "listen in" on the Command Deck. There he examined the Leader whose name was Krylon. The rest of the bridge staff were under officers and crewmen of various races. Everyone was operating under threat or compulsive orders. He dug a little deeper and discovered a chip device similar to that forced upon his departed father by the despots of his now extinct world. Anger welled up inside him but was quickly under control. The steadying touch of his link mates holding him to his purpose.

"Commander." Came the voice of Krylon, it was directed at his immediate subordinate. "Have you run an analysis on that salvage vessel?"

The officer answered crisply, "Yes Leader Krylon. The ship has experienced a malfunction and was disabled on entry to the system. All our readouts are in agreement. The crew is in stasis but are alive. Should I have them revived?"

"No Commander they have failed in their duties, no matter what their ship's systems report. Eliminate them and let's take a closer look at that vessel in orbit around the third planet." The Commander saluted smartly and gave the order to destroy the ship.

Just then a voice as loud as thunder filled the huge Command Deck of the Dreadnaught. "Commander, belay that order. There will be no hostile action taken on a defenseless craft. Leader Krylon, you will have your ship heave to. Your ship and its crew are now under the protection and direction of the Federation. You have one minute to comply."

The command structure of a Brethren Dreadnaught brooked no panic, instead it followed strict protocol. Krylon knew that his last orders would be carried out without delay, but he was interested in this new phenomenon. Obviously, this entity which had broken into his vessel would be dealt with, but its appearance broke the boredom. "I do not usually speak with an unidentified voice, but I will indulge you for the seconds that you have remaining. Please tell me how you are going to enforce this ultimatum of yours."

"Quite simple really, if you will attend your screens." Dale paused and released his safety devices throughout the ship. As he did this all of the Dreadnaught's systems ceased in their functions except for bare life support. "You are now helpless and unlike your cruel decision to destroy your own people I will allow you to live. When we are finished with this object lesson, I will permit you to continue on your way. If you attempt to destroy the salvage vessel on your screens, I will destroy your ship. Do you understand?"

Krylon spoke briefly to his Commander. "Hold my last order. I am fascinated by this new situation. I would like the time needed to evaluate it and perhaps give this disembodied voice a chance to apologize to the Brethren before I destroy him."

Dale led the focus into the data base of the Brethren ship. There they met their first obstacle. An encryption code had been placed on all internal algorithms. Dale frowned and reached out to Dorothy Abrams, pulling her mind into the focus. Dorothy took the lead while Dale drew back to continue his discussion with the Brethren Leader.

"I note that your crew does not have the same genetic makeup that you possess. In fact, they all appear to have been tampered with to some degree or another. You apparently control them in some manner and force them to do your bidding. You are alone, unique among your subordinates. Could it be that you do not thrive in great numbers? I wonder what would happen if these underlings were to be freed of your bond? Food for thought wouldn't you say?"

It was with some shock that Krylon now faced his current reality. The Brethren had become bloated by their repeated successes. Only the situation in the Freshden system had come close to a defeat, but even there they had eradicated that foe, although at great cost. Here was a different type of enemy one that used mental powers to overcome the physical.

He knew that his priorities had changed. This was no longer a mission of correction and punishment. His duty now lay in returning with information concerning this confrontation. While he himself did not possess the mental talents needed to combat this foe there were those on the triune that could match this upstart. He needed to advise the Leadership of a new enemy.

He spoke aloud, "I capitulate to your demands. You have the best of me for now. I will retire and report back to our home world concerning this meeting. Is there anything that you would like to say to the Leadership? I will report your words verbatim and will not diminish them or embellish them."

Dorothy Abrams returned to Dale within the mental focus. "I have broken their encryption codes and have accessed their entire database. We have a complete download for study. She paused for a moment, "I could not discover the location of their home world from the data. Perhaps this person has that knowledge."

Dale had been considering his words and now simply stated, "The Federation will not tolerate the Brethren's continued activities in this quadrant of the galaxy. Any attempt by your race to conquer or diminish others will be met with force. As we move forward, we will be open to helping your people to become re-educated in the mores of polite interstellar relationships and behavior. When that day comes, you will no longer have to fear us, but until you have demonstrated that you have mended your ways, we will stand ready to defeat you."

"As a demonstration of our power I now remove those under your command. The chips that you have placed in their brains have been deactivated and they will be placed in stasis until we can have a chance to interview them. I am afraid that you will have to manage your return trip on your own. Farewell!"

A sudden and profound silence filled the great Brethren ship. All offensive and defensive weapons remained offline, but navigation and engineering had been reestablished. Krylon, smiled sourly to himself. The return trip would take a lot longer than he had anticipated. He set course for the first outer marker of Brethren controlled space. He knew that his enemy would watch his departure vector in an effort to obtain the course heading for the Brethren home world. It would do them no good because he had no idea where in the galaxy it was. No one who traveled the star lanes did. It was the greatest and closest guarded secret of his race.

Chapter Eight

Dale watched as the Brethren Ship moved slowly, almost stately to the edge of the system and then disappear into hyperspace. He knew from reading the man's mind that Krylon had no notion where he was ultimately going other than the Brethren home world. Dale was impressed by the levels of security used to protect the secret of where that home world resided. He shrugged. If he had made as many enemies as the Brethren, he would keep that knowledge to himself as well.

Now for more pressing issues, he thought. We cannot stay here and wait for a punitive task force to arrive. While his ploy with the dreadnaught had worked, he dared not press his luck too much. This mental focus of minds was taxing to say the least and dangerous if the focus could be targeted by a strong mind. His reading of the surface thoughts of Krylon indicated that he, at least, believed that there were several such minds on the Brethren's High Council.

"Excuse me Admiral", Dorothy Abrams soft voice broke his reverie. "The data that we collected has been washed through our security systems and is now ready for your study." She added, "They had embedded some real nasty viruses in those data streams. It took a while to find them so be careful, these guys are really sophisticated in their use of technology. Be prepared for anything."

Dale reached out to Heather and to Shadow Grey, apologizing for interrupting them. Heather had just settled down for a nap and was not pleased by this intrusion, even from her lover. Sighing with exaggerated patience she came into the link. "Listen here Dale, if you expect me to be any good to you at all you are going to have to let me rest some time!"

He smiled to himself understanding the exhaustion that she must be feeling. He was pretty wiped out himself and only something as important as getting away from this system would keep him going. He could feel Star Dancer's presence and knew that his energy levels were being monitored. He was on the clock!

"I am sorry, darling but we have the data available from the Frachon and we need to check on the location of Brethren activities in this sector of space. I don't relish the thought of laying in a course that will throw us into the hornets' nest sure to be stirred up by our recent activities. I need your insight and I need yours Shadow Grey. Please help me find a suitable hidey hole for our little feet, as far from the beaten path as possible!"

With a sigh of resignation Heather drew close to his mind and he felt a little caress as she settled into the task at hand. Shadow Grey helped by looking at the catalog of habitable worlds in the Star Dancer and Orion's datasets, comparing them against those areas that seemed to be void of Brethren activity.

Their current position was in the Sagittarius Arm of the galaxy just about 120 degrees from the galactic center, about thirty thousand lightyears out. From the reports and references made in the data they examined there seemed to be a lot of activity along the Perseus Arm and nearer to the Long Bar of the galaxy core. They wanted to avoid these sections as much as possible. There was an area along the 180th radian that showed little in the way of Brethren activity. After a long study they settled on a system just above the Orion Spur. Dale was not the only one to smile at that designation. The system had a double star cluster and appeared to have a planet in the habitable zone perched in orbit between the two stars, a golden G-type and a red dwarf. It was about 100,000 light years to the galactic south along the plane of the elliptical. Far enough away, Dale mused, to give them time to establish a base and make some connections.

"Alright if we are all in agreement then let's get out of this system before we have more unwelcomed visitors." Moon Glow sent the coordinates for the hyperspace jump to the other three ships and eased Star Dancer out of orbit. They moved past the fifth planet followed on either side by the Rever's ships and protected by Star Dancer's shielding. The Orion appeared to the left coming out of the cloaking shield. Mark Thomas and Glenda Stern were very happy to drop that protection. They had maintained it for the better part of six hours. The Orion fell into guardian position behind her sister ship and together the small fleet made the jump into hyperspace.

The lone Rever ship, the Larsfen, hung in its system position. Dale who had kept a light control over that ship released the mind hold on its crew and flooded its conduits with fresh air. The crew awoke groggy and uncertain as to what had happened. The Captain ran a system wide scan and found nothing of note. Their prey and their sister ships were nowhere to be found. He did note, with some confusion, that his ship's compliment had changed. Many of them were members of the other two crews!

Groshen sat in his ready room, lost in thought. So much had happened so quickly. Dr. Scott and the troupe member, Life Giver had examined all of the Juancy crew that had taken service in this Federation venture. To his surprise more than one of those crew members had concealed in their brains a hidden chip which had been capable of allowing an outside agency, such as the Brethren High command to gain a portion of control over their actions.

It was upsetting to him because he thought that he knew his crew well. As a unit their families had been together for several generations. While not always in position of command a good number of his ancestors had been Commander. He had learned from his father, and his father before him.

Now he pondered past actions and wondered whether any of those had been "influenced" by those chips. The Juancy people acted as clean up squads and had seen the very worst of the devastation wrought by the Brethren's greed. It was a fortunate fact that they usually had nothing to do with deciding if beings on those worlds, or survivors in the near space which might be cluttered with debris from its ships, would live or die. The Brethren were nothing if not thorough.

Still, he could not shake the feeling that his people had been handled. They had given up their freedom to the superior might of the Brethren and they had contributed to that might by preforming the jobs demanded by their masters. In this way they had been subservient for generations. He sighed. The past was the past and the future will take care of itself. Now he and his people were a part of something new.

Groshen drew a huge breath. Those, that his people had thrown their lot in with, were powerful. They had handled the dreadnaught without firing a shot in anger and had stripped knowledge from that ship. A feat never equaled. Yes, he felt marginally better having come to a place where he would be able to take action over his old masters. Still, he knew that whatever fate awaited his people, they would not return to the service of those killers.

On board the Orion a solemn council was being held. The command structure had been devastated by the original Brethren attack and there was a marginal number of crew available to run the great ship's functions. The Orion's artificial intelligence had come back online as the repairs were being completed. So that Orion took its customary place in the discussion of crew reapportionment.

The Star Dancer had offered to lend crew to aid in the transition jump to the Alpha Centuri system and the planet that they had hoped to find there. Dale and Heather had polled the crew and several of the troupe and a few of the Juancy people had volunteered to come to the Orion's service. These were gratefully accepted but with certain reservations.

First Medical Officer Norwell Frosden as the highest surviving command officer took the lead in the discussion. "Look, we have lost a lot of our friends and colleagues to the Brethren. If it weren't for the good graces of Star Dancer and her crew, we would be still frozen or dead. We have been away from our own world for over two hundred years. No one has come to look for us despite knowing where our duty station was. I do not want to go up against another powerful enemy so under manned and with so little intelligence to go on. For now, I think it best that we follow Dale Lambert's lead and develop a base of operations. From there we can strengthen our crew and get some reliable recon done. Dale Lambert has not asked us for a long-term commitment, although in the crazy times that we find ourselves in, a long-term commitment doesn't sound like a bad idea.

It was the consensus of the remaining sub officers and department heads that they could not expect to win if their ship should come under fire from any of the numerous Brethren vessels plotted to be in the area between what had been their duty station and their home world. The data from the Frachon had been very specific about that. They needed a place to hide and to regroup. In the corner one of the junior communications officers simply smiled and nodded her head in agreement.

It was decided to run the Command Center of the Orion with a split crew from each of the species present, a day shift and an alter shift. This very quickly worked down to a smooth-running arrangement with the troupe members aiding with communications between the Orion's original crew and the Juancy members.

The ships broke out of hyperspace still in formation and hove to about one fifth parsec from the binary star system. Dale and Heather boarded Groshen's ship and spun back into hyperspace for the final jump into the system. The long-range sensors indicated that the fifth planet from the brighter g-class sun was habitable, a beautiful blue green world. Dale sat back in his chair and sent his mind flying in the direction of the planet's surface. He scanned the surface listening for any signs of civilized life. He could detect no artificial energy levels. His mental impression of clean crisp air, flowing rivers and green verdure pleased him. There was no indication of outright challenge or danger. Pulling back to his body he opened his eyes and smiled. He sat up straight and said, "Groshen please call the rest of the fleet in. We have found an excellent place to regroup."

Star Dancer and the Orion maintained position about the planet in station keeping orbits while the two Rever ships acted as ferries to bring down crew and supplies. The bioanalysis teams with Life Giver and Peter Lamous did a thorough scan of the planet's biosphere, deeming it very well suited for all three species present in the crew. They planned on setting up a permanent settlement from which they could venture out into near space to attempt a recruitment and exploration mission. They did not want to attract the attention of the Brethren if there was any activity from those aliens nearby.

Doctor Scott with the aid of Life Giver and Sharp Eyes ordered the construction of a medical facility. Its main purpose was to allow those taken from the Brethren Dreadnaught to be brought down in their stasis tubes. It was in Dale's mind that these crewmen be awakened one at a time over a period of months. They would then be evaluated and studied for reaction to their changed station. Those that remained unstable would be placed back into stasis until their ultimate fate could be decided.

Doctor Scott was impressed by the variety of different species represented by those in stasis. Although he noted that all of them required the same basic living conditions as their human counterparts and all were basically humanoid. In an aside to Dale he said, "I think that this represents a physiological similarity to the Brethren. They only kept those that met with their own requirements. It could be that this alone will give us a clue to the nature of their home world." Then he added, "But that could be any of a million systems and worlds!"

Dale and Heather still wanted to get to the Federation's home world. While it was obvious that many things had changed since Star Dancer was forced to land on a world which now lay destroyed and dead, they still felt the need to complete the loop. To see if any of the Federation's worlds still lived.

The couple had set up a small three-room portable shelter from Star Dancer's stores. They were busy with the task of setting up domestic arrangements when Shadow Grey and Moon Glow came to call. "Dale", the thoughts of his life mate flowed richly in his mind, "I would like to propose that we adopt this world as our own." He extended his muzzle and drew in a deep breath of air and released it in a gusty sigh. "In doing so, prevent the excesses that caused the demise of our own world. I think that we need to generate a charter by which all species of intelligent life can live and work, hand in hand to the benefit of this world."

Dale looked up from the complex instruction sheet over which he had been struggling and sat back on his heels, grateful for the interruption. "You are quite right Shadow Grey. Even if we all don't make this our home world, we still need to respect the gift that we have been given." He paused for a moment in thought and then continued, "I will tell you what, why don't we schedule a meeting of all the crews, those that can be spared from their duty stations, and set it for tomorrow evening. We can bring up your excellent ideas to the entire group. Even those still onboard ship can listen in and participate!'

A slight nod of his muzzle confirmed Shadow Grey's acceptance of Dale's suggestions. With a spring, he and Moon Glow leapt away at a run heading for the nearby tree line. Dale smiled and watched as they disappeared into the shadow of that forest. His friends certainly felt right at home here. Who could blame them? He thought to himself, the air held a crisp clean smell and he felt more welcomed here than he had at any time in his life. Heather put her hand on his shoulder giving it a slight squeeze. Dale put his hand over hers and then turned his attention back to the task at hand.

The next evening around a fire made from dried dead wood gleaned from the forest, the crews of all four ships that did not have onboard duties gathered to hear what Shadow Grey proposed. "My friends, many of you were not with us on our previous world. The ambitions and greed that drove the denizens there overrode common good sense and the purposes of the few took precedence over the needs of all. The result was hundreds of years of repression and in the end the destruction of that world. We now have the opportunity to settle a new world, a beautiful planet that has welcomed us. I propose that before we decide to make this our new home, that we gather together to decide on a code of behavior towards this world and towards each other."

Dale who stood back in the crowd and was tall enough to look over most of those present, surveyed the gathering. He noted that the reactions were mixed. Most of those from the crew of Star Dancer knew and accepted what Shadow Grey was saying. The folks from the Orion crew were diffident. They had a short temporal memory, having been thrown into stasis to save their lives. The memories that they had were of a live and vibrant society based on the strength of the Federation as they remembered it.

The reaction of the two Juancy crews was also mixed. They had been under the dominion of the Brethren for so long that they no longer had a racial bias for any particular home world or system. They had their legends and history but for most of them it no longer connected to their own reality. Those that had the biochips removed from their brain were more confused than their brothers and sisters. For the most part they seemed perfectly willing to settle down and begin a normal life. Dale was saddened that these basically even tempered and gregarious beings had been forced to such onerous slavery.

The evening drew on as one or the other of the now very mixed population stood to have their voices heard. There were a few that wanted to stay in space, although they thought the idea of having a safe permanent world to come home to was a good one. Others felt only hate in their hearts for what the Brethren had done to them, their families, and their crew mates. Some of these were from the Orion crew and some from the Juancy crews. Dale took note of each one and would later compare his observations with Heather, Shadow Grey, and Moon Glow. All agreed that a formal constitution which outlined expected behavior and a codex of laws was a good idea.

They also agreed that the idea of ownership of the land was a poor one. The planet that they had landed on seemed to be welcoming, fertile, and very large. Each would produce what they could or provide what services that they could without expectation of payment but with the agreement of having their own needs provided for them in turn. In the Federation this had long been the system by which the worlds had lived, even the Juancy crews had an ancient history of similar arrangements and certainly under the Brethren there had been no such thing as ownership of physical property. They had been slaves.

It was also agreed that the laws applied to all. Each species was equally represented, and as other species came to live within the shelter of this new world, they would have the same rights and privileges. Respect was the keynote of the day, and all would abide by that.

Finally, Steve Marlow stood and with a nod from Dale offered a prayer to God, thanking him for all that he had done for them. There was a silence and a sense of wonder as those that had never worshiped God turned to listen.

Dale smiled and felt the rightness in his heart. Steve Marlow would have a chance to bring more than a few believers into the fold.

Chapter Nine

Time was artificially divided according to the orbital pattern of their new world. Dale was thinking to himself that they should really get around to naming it, but no one had taken the time to do so. Dale had kept to the artificial cycle that they had onboard Star Dancer. It took several months but the colony had divided itself up into small villages and farmsteads. The land had been sampled by the technicians and the mineral and organic content analyzed. It had been determined that the ground was fertile and would support the seeds of varying kinds that had been kept in Star Dancer's cryogenic banks. Those seeds had been planted and new growth had begun to appear.

The native flora and fauna of this world also lent to the increased sustenance of the small population. The lab techs analyzed and categorized each new species that was brought in by the exploring parties. As each was deemed safe and beneficial it was added to the growing list of available crops or livestock.

A small administrative group was formed from each of the species present and together they put together a system of laws and a codex of behaviors that was ratified by the members of the colony. Any mineral development was allowed to proceed only if the environmental impact of the effort was negligible. Fortunately, the nearby moons which circled their world provided ample mineral wealth and the sterile surfaces of those small satellites would allow heavy industry without the need of destroying the ecology of the planet below.

Power requirements were met using wind turbines, solar power cells and the strategic use of hydrogen fuel cells. There were oil and natural gas reserves in plenty, but the history of Dale's planet had demonstrated the foolishness of developing those power sources.

More of the Brethren crew had been revived and without the controlling chips most were very pleasantly surprised by their new station in life. Freedom for most had never been possible and now they were integrated into a new and free society.

Those from the Juancy crews aided in large part by the members of the troupe helped acclimate these newcomers into the interoperations of planet life and work in near space on the moons.

At the end of the third month Dale called together the administrative council and the command crews of all four ships. He spoke of the progress that had been made toward the settlement of their new world and opened up the idea of running a colony wide contest through which the new planet could be named. This proposal was met with great enthusiasm by all. Apparently, Dale was not the only one that considered referring to their new home as the "New World" cumbersome.

In addition, he proposed that it was now time to begin the careful study of the nearby star systems using the Orion as the main vessel while the Star Dancer remained as protection for the new colony. He also proposed that at the end of their first full year on this new world that they send an exploratory expedition to discover the status of the Federation home world. This mission would be one of stealth and discovery and would be made by a small number of crew using a ship design that the AI's from Orion and Star Dancer had provided. The ship would be built on the nearer moon and would launch from that satellite.

Two days later as evening fell the newly appointed administration held the Naming Day Feast. Rumor had spread throughout the small colony that the world that had so welcomed them was to become a permanent home for those that had been cast upon its shores from the oceans of space and for those that would follow.

Excitement filled the air as the food replicators worked overtime to prepare a bountiful feast and the fresh greens, that had sprouted so well and that were at a stage that they could be selectively harvested, augmented the creations of science.

The planet itself reflected the celebratory mood of its new inhabitants by putting on a glorious sunset of pinks, purples, and bright whites. The stars burst forth in the new night and the three moons danced merrily in the early evening skies.

When at last the main feasting was done and all of the inhabitants of the colony who could be spared from shipboard duty sat talking loudly or singing merrily, Dale stood up and raised his hands, asking for silence. It was a sign of the respect that he had earned from the gathered crews that quiet fell almost at once.

"Friends, brothers and sisters we are here tonight to celebrate or new-found freedom." A loud cheer followed, and Dale smiled. "You have heard that we would like to make this a permanent home, a home from which those of us with the need to continue in the space lanes will have to return to and to raise our families." Dale looked down to where Heather sat, she was brightly blushing. "This world has welcomed us with open arms, and thanks to the wisdom of our administrative council," he waved his hands at those who sat or stood on the dais with him, "you have agreed through a binding vote to honor this world and each other in thought, word and deed. You have sealed that agreement with prayers, solemn oaths and written law."

Now a very loud cheer rang out and that was accompanied by an impromptu musical cacophony as various instruments rang out, somehow forming a melodious harmony through their various scales and rhythms. Dale smiled again taking that as a sign that any discord would be righted through the application of common sense and friendship. He held up his hands once more and the celebration settled back down to an expectant buzz. "I will not keep you long," he held his hands up to forestall the building cheer at his words, "There are several things that we must discuss as group."

The crowd settled down in anticipation of the Admiral's words. "The Council and the commanders of the fleet have discussed the next steps that we must take in order to ensure our security in this sector of the galaxy. The Brethren do not have an active presence in this section of space, we know this through the acquisition of encrypted data from their Dreadnaught."

A really loud cheer went up from the crowd as the Juancy and those that had been captive slaves on that ship let their feelings be known. "Still, we cannot take their absence as an assurance that they will never infringe on our freedom again. We need to explore this sector of space and secure whatever allies that we can find and form an alliance that will not be taken in by the subterfuge that those demons from the outer dark use to infiltrate our societies."

"To do this we will assign the Orion as an exploration ship and a mixed crew under the command of Daton Excilore and the Juancy Commander, Groshen to explore those star systems that display the needed attributes for sustaining life, within 40 light years of our new home, moving toward the galactic south. Their mission will be one of peace and diplomacy. Several of the crew from the Star Dancer will be on that ship to be sure that peace is promoted and that no unwelcome advances be made against our people."

The Star Dancer will stay here in this system as guardian to prevent any surprise attacks on our world. A really loud cheer went up on the heels of that statement. "Yes, it is good to know that we will be protected."

"I and a select number from our mixed crews will embark on a secret mission to survey the planets of the Federation and to ascertain if any of those worlds still function as independent and free societies. If we find that they do exist, we will make contact to let them know that they are not alone in the battle against the Brethren."

He paused and a cloud fell over his face, "If, as I suspect, we find that they have already fallen, we will try to rescue those

that we can. Certainly, we will be careful not to divulge the
location of our new home. We all have had too much of the
ways of the Brethren to be readily trusting of those that we
don't know. Still, we will have certain advantages that they will
be unaware of and these will we use to the upmost to protect
our own."

"While we prepare for this mission of discovery, a new base on
the inner moon will be developed so that manufacturing of the
needed equipment and ships will not damage our new world.
In fact, all major manufacturing that will require the heat, beat,
and treat method of development will take place on the moon.
In addition, any minerals or other mining that needs to be done
will take place on the moons and other planets in our system
rather than on our home. We will not tolerate the destructive
tendencies of modern technology to ruin our world!"

A great roar went up and the cheering was loud and sustained.
Dale held his hands up once more and silence eventually settled
in, "I am gratified that you find our actions acceptable. Now I
would like to turn this over to Shadow Grey." With a bow of
respect to his life mate he turned and sat down putting his arm
around his wife.

Shadow Grey gracefully jumped up to the specially designed
podium that was used by the members of his race. He turned
and faced the gathered throng. The respectful silence he
received indicated that he too was highly thought of and that
cheered him. This world was going to see many different
species through the years. If all were treated as well as he and
the troupe had been then it would be a merry place indeed.

"Our world has welcomed us. It has yielded fine weather, soft
rains, and bright sunshine. Our seeds have been planted and
the growth of those plants has been gratifying indeed. The
forests and the rivers have yielded plenty on their own behalf
and while we have not seen any creatures beyond those of the
waters, and woods we will not return to the greed of our past.
In short this is not our world to master but is our friend and
ally in all that we do."

Home World

Another great cheer went up and Shadow Grey wagged his tail in approval. "So, my friends we have asked you over the past two days to submit names that we could give our new world, our home world for now and the future. From the list we have been provided we have narrowed the names down to three. I will name the three, asking you to remain quiet until all have been given and then by voice vote I will ask you to name your new home.

An expectant hush fell over the crowd. In that quiet Shadow Grey spoke. "The first name on the list, in no particular order of preference, is New Haven, the second is Gladerous and the last is Brightholme. May I have the Council rise and judge the citizens response?" The remaining members on the Dais, including Dale and Heather, although not officially Council members, rose and stood ready.

"Now by voice vote we will select our new home's official name. All those in favor of New Haven please indicate by saying aye." A grouping of ayes was heard around the gathering. "Now those of you in favor of Gladerous let your voices be heard," again shouts of aye were heard, mainly Shadow Grey noted, from the Juancy that were present. "And finally, Brightholme", a loud chorus of ayes were heard from all sections of the crowd. Shadow Grey turned to the Council member nearest him and after a whispered conversation turned back to the audience. "It has been decided our new home world will be known as Brightholme." The applause that followed was loud and long. They were home.

Dale walked back toward the small housing unit that was his family's new house, Heather was tucked under one arm walking beside him. The stars were blazing bright lending limited light to their way. Heather snuggled closer and then in a soft voice said, "Do you remember what you said about this would be the place that we would have to raise our families?"

Dale who had been lost in thought concerning the events of the coming months walked on with her for a few steps before the importance of that statement hit him. He stopped in his tracks and gently turned Heather so that he could see her face in the dim light. "Does that question mean what I think it means?" He watched carefully as Heather nodded her head in agreement. He drew in a breath of wonder and then leaned down to kiss his wife's waiting lips. His mind ventured down into the depths of her womb, and there as he gently probed was the spark of an answer.

The Orion was crewed and outfitted for a three-month journey. Dale attached Mark Thomas and Glenda Stern to the ship as Engineer and Power Officers. In a private aside to the pair they were instructed to observe the command crew and to get the ship out of any trouble and back to Brightholme at all costs. They were to do a sweep of the Reticulum, Centaurus, Hydrus and Sol systems all with class G2 stars. They were to observe these systems and report back to Brightholme without making contact. Dale spoke to the entire crew and warned them that they needed to be vigilant, the Brethren were known to have had a minor presence in this sector of space but were not the only race or possible adversary out there.

Once the Orion had gone into hyperspace headed for the Reticulum system Dale got the construction of the moon base operations in full swing. They needed to develop a shipyard and a manufacturing capability on the nearest moon. Together with the remaining Juancy commanders, Shadow Grey, and Dorothy Abrams they designed the metallurgy plants and opened the mining pits to create the metals needed for most of the new ship's design. Dale had ordered that the rare metals mined from the system in which they had rescued the Orion be left behind for refinements and use in the new ship.

Heather stayed on the planet's surface under Doctor Scott's watchful care. Hers was the first pregnancy among the genetically enhanced crew. Her pregnancy would bear watching. Even Star Dancer did not know what effects the combined genes of Dale and Heather would produce.

A couple of months after Heather discovered her condition, Dale was happy to note that Moon Glow had reported to the medical staff that she too was pregnant. The two soul mates were able to confide in one another while their respective mates continued the arduous tasks at hand. One evening, when Dale had returned from a particularly trying day on the moon's surface, he curled up next to Heather and held her tenderly in his arms. "You know I don't think that I really appreciated how much you have helped me through the years. It seems so long ago that we played respectful adversaries but even then, you were there offering good advice and lending your will to get things done against impossible odds. I just wanted to say thank you, love. You are the best!"

Heather wiggled next to him feeling the warmth of him against her back. She had never expected to have a child, first because of the repressive laws of her old world and then because she never thought that she would find someone that she would be willing to share such an intimate and wonderful experience with. Now on Brightholme, and in Dale's strong arms she felt safe and at home. She could feel the life within her growing day by day. She could even catch snippets of unformed thoughts emanating from her son.

Dale fell asleep with the happy thoughts of an expectant father. The hectic schedule and the myriad of administrative details were forgotten for the moment. As he slept his dreams spun out and he found himself in deep space. Ahead of him was the brilliant point of a welcoming star. The yellow glow caught and held his attention as he felt his dreams pulling him into a system of planets and other minor bodies. He hovered above a blue ocean planet with greens and browns dominating the landmasses. Unlike his new home world this planet was full of sentient life. Energy waves, radio transmissions and technology overlapped the wonders of its natural beauty.

He felt himself pulled towards the edge of one of those large land masses. His spectral form was drawn, down to the surface and then down again as he passed beyond its surface layer. He found himself looking through a vaulted underground space filled with containers. His senses caressed those wooden storage boxes, and he could feel the unpleasant hum of deadly energy contained within. He did not stay longer to wonder at the meaning of this but was drawn instead further through the chamber and then out into native rock. He followed the path of an underground river until it joined with the cavern's ceiling and ducked under rock once more. His path then turned and from somewhere ahead he sensed the presence of a powerful entity.

He floated above the entrance way of a corridor and then with little effort passed through and into the metallic, plastasteel walls of a ship. What a ship! It dwarfed the spacious interior of Star Dancer. This was a ship of different design, but all of its functions appeared to be familiar to him. As his form paused floating in contemplation, he felt a surge of energy run through his mind. It was not an assault but rather a surge of exultation.

"Welcome to the Andromeda. It has been a long time since a member of the Federation has accessed this vessel." The voice hummed in his mind. Dale did not feel fear only surprise. "Please follow the globe of light that I will cause to appear in front of your astral form. It will lead you to my office. I have so many questions that I would like to ask you."

Heather had been deeply asleep, but some sense of uneasiness caused her to come awake. Groggily she reached out for Dale's mind, only to find that though his body was present his mind was not. Startled to complete wakefulness she rolled over and mentally flipped the light switch so that their sleeping chamber was flooded and completely visible. Dale lay next to her, appearing to be deeply asleep, but Heather was not fooled. She reached out with her mind and felt the unmistakable sense of mindlessness that accompanied one with their mental abilities when the mind wandered far from the body. With a quick plea she reached out to Moon Glow and to Shadow Grey.

She felt the joint minds of the pair as they responded immediately to her plea. They had been out taking the night air as they often did since coming to Brightholme. "We are here Heather. I see through your eyes" said Moon Glow. "Dale

Lambert is mind wandering. It is one of the great gifts of the Way, but it is extremely dangerous."

"It does appear", said Shadow Grey. "That he has wandered on his own. I sense no danger, but perhaps it would be good to follow his mind trace to its source and be there if he needs us."

Dale floated through the various chambers of the Andromeda following the softly glowing globe of light. He did not feel danger, he only felt a sense of anticipation as if this was the logical conclusion to a long puzzled over problem. The light paused before a doorway, which swung open in invitation. He smiled to himself, very polite. He knew very well that the entity within understood that there was no physical barrier to his present form. It bode well that he was being awarded the unspoken respect demonstrated by that open portal.

As he floated through the doorway it swung quietly closed behind him. He faced what appeared to be an executive's office complete with an old fashion wooden desk. Behind the desk sat an elderly looking man who rose in greeting at Dale's approach. With a polite gesture he offered Dale a chair in front of the desk and then resumed his seat as Dale's form floated to the proffered chair.

"I am the AI Andromeda. What you see before you is the physical representation of the ship on which you sit. It is a type of interface if you wish, that allows me to communicate in an easy fashion with humans." He paused and looked at Dale once more.

"I can see by your image's expression that you are familiar with my particular form of communication. Can I then assume that you have had contact with vessels of my kind before?"

Dale sat up and peered closely at the form in front of him. Quickly making his mind up he cleared his throat, "Yes, I am familiar with artificial intelligence. My ship is the Star Dancer and we are from the Federation originally, although it has been many generations of my kind since we have been in Federation space."

"If it is not being too presumptuous of me. May I ask what you are doing here, and why you appear in the fashion that you have?"

Dale thought for a moment and was about to reply that he really did not know where here was, when he felt the warmth of Heather's mind join with his. He sensed that Moon Glow and Shadow Grey had joined them as well. The Andromeda waited patiently for his answer. "I will be honest with you, my friend. I am unaware of where I am at the moment. My physical form is safely asleep on my bed. Our newly adopted home world is in deep night as we speak. I found myself wandering in my mental state through the star ways and was drawn here. I did pass some very interesting and should I say deadly containers in a cavern very nearby. Those don't belong to you, do they?"

"No indeed," chuckled the Andromeda. "Those belong to my progeny. They have grown fond of playing with dangerous toys." He grew serious for a moment and then continued, "I do not think that chance has brought you here at this moment in time. The universe is vast but there is an overriding purpose to the random and sometimes chaotic fabric in which we all must dwell."

"As for where we are the ancient star maps called this system Sol, we are a G2 class sun with nine, err eight planets. My progeny has just managed to reclassify one of the planets to a minor role."

At the name of Sol Dale started, a fact not lost on the observations of the Andromeda's systems. The mental voice of Shadow Grey touched Dale's conscious mind, "Be careful he is aware of your curiosity. I think that I will take a look around this vessel and see what there is to be seen."

Moon Glow chimed in, "I will go with my mate just to be sure that he doesn't get into anything that he shouldn't." Her voice trailed off in a bark of laughter.

Heather's mind moved closer to him, and he was grateful for that reassurance. "I recognize the name of Sol from our oldest star maps. Star Dancer did not have any record of a Federation ship having moved so far down the southern axis of the galaxy, much less a colony ship that had lost contact with the Federation."

The Andromeda paused very briefly but for a ship's AI the silence was prolonged. "I do not know you Dale Lambert of the Federation Starship Star Dancer. I will need to contact my Captain before I answer any of your questions. Please do not take my hesitation as an attempt at subterfuge I am following my protocols. In the meantime, I welcome you to wander the ship. You will be completely safe and welcomed as you travel. I will contact you once again when my Captain has reported back to me with instructions."

With that Dale had to be satisfied. He stood and moved back through the doorway which opened once more, a silent affirmation of his continued status as guest aboard the Andromeda. Heather's voice whispered in his mind, "Time may not be moving for you, my love, but the night is advancing on Brightholme and you have another full day ahead of you."

Dale made a tech, tech sound reminding her that he was resting very deeply in his warm bed at home. He would be very rested indeed for the trials of the coming day. Turning slowly on his astral heels Dale examined the cavernous command deck of the Andromeda. He whistled to himself, wondering at the immensity. This must have contained the population of an entire continent and then some.

It was hard to imagine that such a monument to high technology could lay hidden for so long from the population that had been its originator. Still, he had only to look at the example of Star Dancer to realize that such an event could occur. The Andromeda had been a colony ship which indicated that it was meant to become an artifact as the population settled into their new home. He shrugged his ghostly shoulders and continued his walk through the great ship.

It wasn't long before the minds of Moon Glow and Shadow Grey rejoined the two lovers and reported that the ship contained no surprises other then the advanced technology that it carried. It wasn't heavily armed or armored but was, as it seemed, a transport vessel meant to deliver its precious cargo over time and space.

"Excuse me sir," Came the voice of the Andromeda's AI from the very air around him. "My Captain and his First Officer are here, as well as several guests."

Dale cocked an eyebrow at the last for it seemed that the AI was mildly surprised by the inclusion of others to the conference. "If you would kindly re-adjourn to my private office, we will meet and discuss matters."

Dale stood for a second in his own private conference. "I think that it would be wise for you to manifest yourselves and allow our host to realize that he is dealing with a delegation rather than a single entity."

Heather considered the matter for a second and then appeared next to Dale's right side. Moon Glow and Shadow Grey appeared on his left. Together they walked to the office whose door once more opened in silent invitation.

Chapter Ten

Dale entered the room and noted the changes. The large desk and comfortable seating arrangement had been replaced by a long conference table with matching chairs. The wall opposite the main entrance was blank. At the center of the table sat a small projection device. Seated around the table were the AI from Andromeda, a middle-aged couple with a young man and three other couples. All rose when Dale and his contingent entered the room.

Dale looked directly at the AI and spoke, "Andromeda I would like you to meet Heather Lambert my wife, Moon Glow her life mate and Shadow Grey who is my life mate. They are here because they grew concerned over my astral wanderings and through our psychic ties followed me here. I apologize that I did not make their presence known before, but we had to be certain that you were what you said you were. We have had recent occurrences in dealing with other races that have made us cautious."

The AI Andromeda stood and bowed a welcome at his new guests. "I assure you Dale Lambert that they are most welcome. This vessel has nothing to hide and in fact may have much to offer, but I digress. Please allow me to introduce my Captain, his first mate, their son and their guests."

The man who the AI identified as the Captain spoke his eyes flashing with curiosity. "I am Drew Duncan, this is my wife and First Mate Nancy Duncan and this is our son Christopher." He paused for a moment to allow his family to exchange greetings with the strangers. He was delighted to catch the flare of interest as his son said hello to the two large canine representatives of the group.

He continued the introductions, "These are representatives much like you, from a group of star systems called the Empire, although they were all born here on Earth." Moving from his left to right he identified them. "This is Tom Peterson and his wife Sally, Steven Green and his wife Alice and Jose Rodriquez with his wife Margarita."

After the introductions were made, the group settled themselves into the chairs around the table. While Dale and his group could not "feel" the comfort of those cushions the rest of the group settled down with a sigh.

Dale steepled his hands and waited for the silence to be broken. The Andromeda AI began by reciting the history of its voyage from Federation space. "Dale, you questioned earlier why no record of our ship or of our voyage had been found on Star Dancer's records. The answer is quite simple. We were not a sanctioned colony. He held his hands up to forestall any questions and continued. We were a group of citizens from several of the Federations planets that had grown tired of the structured bureaucracy that had begun to tie the Federation in knots. Our colonists were free spirits and wanted none of the official red tape that was choking off our air."

We charted a course as far from the normal space lanes as possible, relying on fate more than science to find a new home. We also had faith and here I must be very clear because you may find what I say hard to believe. You see Dale Lambert we believed in God. Not just any god but the one God. While we traveled to this place hoping to find an undiscovered world, we found instead a world with a very primitive culture. The inhabitants were to all appearances, human. We surreptitiously studied their genetic code and found that except for one or two slight shifts they were of the same blood. This caused quite an ethical problem. We had no right to dominate these people, despite their relatively small numbers. They deserved to have a future. Still, we were very weary of travelling the space lanes. In the end it was decided that we would abandon our technology and venture forth as a primitive people."

The Andromeda AI paused as if in thought and then parsed the next few words very carefully. "When we ventured out and cut ties with our past, we discovered a mystery. We have always believed in one God and while many of those that we joined with did not, there were several tribes that held fast to our same belief system. They actually had a written record of contact with their God and were favored by that relationship. Reports back to the ship became spotty but about two thousand years ago a miracle was recorded in my logs." The projector on the table hummed to life. The image of a man was seen nailed to a cross made of wood, blood oozing from wounds on his hands, feet, head and back. The man raised his head to the sky with imploring eyes. The recording, although scratchy, was clear enough. "Father forgive them for they know not what they do." A short while later it caught the words, "Into your hands I commend my soul."

"After this we made a study of this man and his history because, Dale Lambert this scene had been played out before on one of our own worlds many thousands of years before. The studies revealed a pattern of Godly behaviors and teachings that left no doubt at all. This man, these people named Jesus Christ was the Son of God. This man died for the sins of the world here on Earth just as he had on our world."

"God created the Universe, Dale Lambert, of this there is no doubt. Science has proven that this fabric of reality started in a millisecond and expanded into the universe that we see today. The fact that we in this room appear to all have the same genetic markings proves that God had a design for his children, and he planted that design on many worlds. Are there differences? Yes, there are but the basic design is the same, we are all brothers and sisters."

Dale smiled over to where Heather sat in rapt attention. They had a tale that was almost identical as that which the Andromeda AI now espoused. They also believed! Steve Marlow would be over the moon with this revelation.

"Now I must bring you to more current times and issues. For you see we have had visitors of a far more sinister nature than your astral appearances." The Andromeda AI paused as if in thought and Dale noticed that the other humans in the room looked uncomfortable. "There is in the universe a balancing of good and evil. God had his Son die on the cross to allow humans a choice, but here I must place a disclaimer, the term human as I have applied it, meaning similar genetic makeup, is not the only definition that is possible. You see Dale Lambert there are many other forms of life that hold intelligence, emotions and will. Sitting next to you are just two examples. Shadow Grey and Moon Glow are no less human than you. Yes, their shapes are different, even their mental processes vary but, in the end, they are cognitive species quite capable of determining their own fate as God intended."

"It is this freedom of will that allows for great good and for great evil. This world has seen an effort over the past several decades to subvert this freedom by dominating our peoples. In part these visitors have succeeded, thus you see the weapons cache not very far removed from this vessel's location. Those that choose that path had been influenced by other less savory beings. These beings, whose entire purpose had remained hidden until very recently. Here I will turn the tale over to the other "humans" in the room, beginning with my own Captain, Drew Duncan."

The elderly man sat back down in his chair and tilted his head in Drew's direction. Slowly the middle-aged man rose and stood straight, eyes flashing. "I will attempt to keep my story brief, but it is important that you know how our contact with Andromeda occurred and the history that followed, for that information lays the groundwork for the events that the others here will relay."

So, saying Drew told how he and his now wife Nancy as young adults stumbled upon the conspiracy that had led to the storage of the weapons of mass destruction below the town's high school. From there he led his listeners to the discovery of the Andromeda in their effort to escape the trap that they had fallen into.

Drew built on the relationship between the ship and his family. Through the Andromeda's extensive computer network with the nations of the world, they had been able to discern that there were glaring anomalies within the political structure of the various governments of the planet. These anomalies led them to conclude that there were "outside" influences affecting the societies of his world, perverting them, causing people to become witless slaves.

Drew stopped to examine his hands and then wiped them on his clothing as if to rid them of some unseen taint. "We had originally thought to fight the corruption that we discovered by going through "official channels", but we soon discovered that those who were pulling the strings behind the scenes had no wish to be discovered. We were met with roadblock after roadblock and as we pressed on, we received threats to our lives and those of our families. So, we stopped and rethought our efforts. With the help of the Andromeda, we began to accumulate wealth and knowledge and through various non-profit charities we redistributed that wealth to aid where those in the corrupt governments would not."

"We faced heavy opposition to our altruistic goals, court cases and trials, appeals and minor successes, but because we worked through Andromeda, we mostly succeeded. In that process Dale Lambert, we discovered patterns of behavior that while well-hidden led back through to a very small number of individuals. These people, if that is what you want to call them, were the ones responsible for the manipulations that we had stumbled across, while individuals could not be parsed out from the masses a name did appear." Drew looked around the table and then in a heavy voice said, "They call themselves the Brethren."

Dale and Heather sat straight up in their chairs while Shadow Grey turned to look sharply at his mate. Dale, through his mental contact with his small group could sense the shock that flowed through them. Would they never be free of these villainous foes?

Drew looked kindly at the four peoples represented in astral form. "I see that the name does not seem strange to you.

Perhaps you will add to this tale, but for now I need to pass this over to Tom Peterson and his friends as they have much to say concerning these vile creatures." So, saying Drew Duncan sat down next to his wife and son.

The air in the room grew heavy with the ensuing silence as Tom Peterson stood slowly to his feet, clearing his throat he began. "I have been assured that the information that I am about to impart will not be used for harm. You see up until three years ago I was just another father working to support my family, living what has become known in this part of space as the American dream. One fine spring day my youngest son Sam was doing some yard work when he stumbled over a very unusual find.

Most life on this world, at least the terrestrial variety has long been identified and catalogued. Sam's discovery turned out to be completely unknown to our science and with good reason, it was not from this world. Nemoric as the creature became known because that was his name was of the race of extraterrestrials known as dragons. It turns out that the dragons are an extremely old and wise race of creatures who are, or I should say were known on many worlds.

Nemoric was sent here because his parents had wanted him to find his Rider." Tom held up his hand and said, "Let me explain. For many hundreds of generations, the dragon race has been psychologically paired with another ancient race. These beings were and are called the Tresolin. The pairings served both races well and they traveled the star lanes in companionship and love."

A sad look overcame Tom's features as he continued. "That bonding was broken. Another race physically identical to the Tresolins came to one of their worlds, claiming that they were long lost colonists from the edge of the galaxy. The dragons and their riders opened their arms, hearts, and worlds to these long-lost cousins only to find, too late, that they had invited their own deaths into their homes."

"Through deception and subterfuge these creatures convinced the age long friends to become bitter enemies. What few pairings that survived the holocaust either withdrew from this universe or into back water worlds from which they did not dare reappear. Those others then proceeded to rape and pillage until they were sated and withdrew into the depths of space from whence, they came. That sating took a very, very long time."

"Since then our children left the Earth, first to the Way Station, a type of interstellar gateway, manned by the dragons and other races and then onto Scalar. This is a backwater planet on which the Empire had maintained a medical facility. We have been here on Earth. Our mission was and is to prepare our world for introduction to those who inhabit the space around us and to find those that might be willing companions for the dragon kind that remain."

Tom Peterson looked around the table a wry smile on his face, "Yet we have been opposed. As the Andromeda mentioned there are representatives of that other race here on Earth. They are few in number, very difficult to locate and track. We have been fortunate indeed to have evaded their attempts at silencing our efforts and us."

With that Tom Peterson sat down having completed his narration. Dale felt as did his companions that there were many details left out of the histories of both Drew Duncan and Tom Peterson. He could not blame them for their reticence, after all he and his people were just physic projections without form and with unknown purpose. Still, he wanted one more thing from those that sat across from him. "You have made mention of the race that caused and is still causing devastation among you, yet you have not named this enemy. We who now travel the space lanes under the old Federation's banner would at least like to know who we must avoid."

The Andromeda AI stood back up and faced Dale directly, "They have many names on the many worlds that they have subjugated but they call themselves the Brethren."

Dale looked at the members of his delegation and then stood. "It would appear my friends that we have very much in common." He then launched into a full and detailed report of all of his experiences and histories from the now dead world on which he had been born to the recent travels and experiences that he had shared with those around him. In his telling it became clear that those around the table relaxed and with pointed comments added much to their own stories. When at last Dale Lambert finished his tale, everyone knew that they shared a common bond and a common enemy.

Heather Lambert stood and apologized. "The hour grows late on Brightholme and we must return there to start another day. I want to thank all of you for your candor and your trust. We look forward to working with you in the space lanes and on our worlds."

Dale stood by his mate and added, "As you know our sister ship the Orion is scheduled to visit your system in the next two months. It was to be a mission of observation only. Now I would like your opinion on whether we should venture here. The Orion's appearance may bring unwanted attention to this sector of space."

After a brief consultation the representatives of Earth and the Empire concluded that a visit at this time might indeed cause an unwelcomed response to those that they fought in their shadow war. Dale in his turn reassured them that they would stay in contact via this astral form. With a final series of thanks, the party from Brightholme withdrew from the chamber and the planet.

Chapter Eleven

In the early morning light of Brightholme's sun Dale Lambert opened his eyes to find Heather propped up on one elbow looking at him intently. "I'll give you this Mr. Lambert, my dearest darling husband, you sure know how to give us the most interesting experiences!"

"So now we have additional allies and responsibilities. I sometimes wish that we were back in our cabin on Star Dancer looking forward to the exploration of Federation space. But I fear that you will have to do that without me." She patted her growing stomach to indicate that she, at least would have other more pressing responsibilities.

She rolled out of their bed and stood over the form of her lover with her hands on her hips until, with a bit of impatience she flipped the covers from Dale's body. With a moan of complaint, he attempted to recover himself, but she was having none of that. "You have no one to blame but yourself Dale Lambert, flitting around the universe when you are supposed to be resting next to me!"

Dale, giving into the inevitable rolled out of the bed and helped his wife straighten the covers. With a playful kiss on her neck, he stumbled into the utilitarian bathroom. He felt much more like himself as he stepped out of the shower unit. It would be a busy day.

He moved to the small office that he and Heather maintained to conduct their share of the colony's business. He sat back in the chair and closed his eyes. Reaching out with his mind he sent a thought probe out across space to the command control of the Orion. The ship's AI received his request and contacted the Captain and his command level officers. The group assembled in the conference room off the main command center. Dale's astral image appeared and solidified before them.

He greeted them each by name and quickly outlined the discoveries that they had made in the Sol system. "We have been asked by the representatives of Earth and those of the Empire that we currently not approach that system. They are trying to control a small but prevalent presence of the Brethren on their planet and do not want to draw any more attention from that group at this time."

Dale looked over to where Mark Thomas and Glenda Stern sat. He gave them a lopsided smile. "You will be pleased to note, Mark that our mutual beliefs in God and his plans for us are shared throughout more of this galaxy than we could have ever known."

He looked at the Orion's captain and added, "We had heard from the Juancy crews of the demise of the Freshden people and the destruction of their system. We were informed of the military losses of the Brethren fleet by that system's stout defense. We mourned the loss of those brave peoples. Now I can report to you that almost all those people have escaped death. In fact, they did so right under the nose of one of the Brethren's worst commanders."

"Hymlical has not been seen since that event and it is theorized that he was destroyed in the attack. All that I can do is ask that you remain vigilant in your remaining explorations. Accept nothing at face value. Observe only and get back here in one piece. I am sending Dorothy Abrams out to you via an express drone. Please remain on station until she arrives."

With a smart salute Dale withdrew back to his own body and smiled as his nostrils twitched with the smell of cooking breakfast. He would not be going off without having eaten and quietly he blessed God for his gift of Heather. He wondered what his son would look like. He looked forward to his arrival and quickly he added thanks to God for that gift as well.

Aboard the Orion, Daton Excilore contemplated the recent astral visit by Dale Lambert. He was grateful in a way that his mission had been shorten and gratified that their small group of exiles had indeed found the possibility of gaining some allies. Still, he felt uneasy as the Orion sped on to their next destination, Centaurus. The last system had hosted no habitable planets and after days of careful study the Orion's command crew decided to move on.

Daton was having repeating nightmares mostly centered on his home world of Catus located on the Centauru spiral. He knew that he had been suspended in cold sleep for two hundred years, but that knowledge warred constantly with memories that placed him at home just a year or so ago. He had been married and had several children. He missed his family. He understood the risk that every spacer took when he or she left on a mission. The dangers of space were vast, but his was to be an ordinary mining expedition something that he had done many times in the past. Now he knew that he was alone once more.

His contemplations were interrupted by the chime of his door panel. He stood up from his chair, pulled down on his uniform to straighten the wrinkles and voiced his permission for entrance. The panel opened and the form of Sharp Eyes padded into the chamber. Daton had been amazed by the variety of crewmen that had been assembled by Dale Lambert but none were more amazing to him than the canines that had accompanied the humans from Laurel, now a dead and lifeless pile of rocks further out in the fringes of Federation space. He cleared his throat and addressed his guest. "Welcome, Sharp Eyes, to what do I owe the pleasure of this visit?"

The large canine sat back on his haunches and eyed the human speculatively. "You are disturbed by dark dreams, Captain Daton Excilore, they are having a detrimental effect on your command decision capabilities. I am here to offer some advice and perhaps a solution to your problems."

The voice in the Captain's mind was rich and vibrant but carried no hint of censure or threat. Rather it felt like one long time friend talking frankly to another. "What do you mean, a solution, a solution to what?" He was on the defensive now unsure if he had been so transparent as to reveal his longing for home.

Sharp Eyes swung his head gently from side to side, almost pitying this human. "We of the people have long since developed extreme sensitivity to emotions and in many cases are able to read minds, through a combination of receptors and observation. I have been watching you for several weeks now and while I congratulate you on your dedication to your command it has become obvious to me that you are extremely bothered about something. I am here to find out exactly what that is and to offer my help."

Sharp Eyes leapt from his position by the door to a seated position on the Captain's bunk and waited. The Captain spun to face the canine and as he formulated a hot retort, his mind suddenly became calmer. He felt rather than saw Sharp Eye's approval and with a steadying breath he released the tension that had filled him.

"You are right, Sharp Eyes, my dreams and even my waking thoughts have been focused on my home world. I understand that it has been over two hundred years since I last touched foot on that soil. Two hundred years since I last held my wife and children in my arms. Yet it is hard to reconcile the knowledge with my emotions. I feel lost."

Sharp Eyes looked kindly on the human in front of him. When the troupe first encountered the humans from the ecological station on Laurel he had protested the interaction with these creatures. He had since witnessed the outstanding courage and deep compassion that they had the capability of displaying. He understood that they had a dark side and he had listened to his leader when Shadow Grey had explained that it was their responsibility to mentor these humans, to help them understand that they had choices. They were not always destined to evil, but they could be blessed and become sources of such good that they could change the universe.

"You know Captain that once we return from our tour of systems that Dale Lambert will be taking a small crew out to check on the Federation's worlds. If you would like I could speak to Shadow Grey on your behalf and see if Dale Lambert would take you as part of the ship's crew."

Daton Excilore looked up from his morose study of the artificial carpet on his state room floor. Hope flared briefly in his eyes, but a sad look soon filled them, a haunted look. "I would like that Sharp Eyes, but I am afraid that all I could hope for would be to find that my planet and its culture have survived. Those that I left behind will be long gone and dust."

Sharp Eyes nodded his head in agreement. "I am glad you realize the temporal nature of the issue, but I think that it would do your spirit good to have closure." He looked directly into the Captain's eyes and added, "Now it is time for you to be Captain and finish the task which was assigned you. We will be coming up on HR 4523 A, shortly. We must move with care. We are not very far from Brightholme. We must not arouse suspicions if we find sentient life in the system.

The Orion spun in from the west planer region of the system. Passing the orbiting planets that hung in their paths around the fierce yellow glow of the primary. There were a number of planets, mostly dead rocky worlds, or frozen spheres. There were two gas giants whose gravity pulled on the arrowing ship as it slid sunward towards the "goldilocks" area where life could be expected to thrive in correct temperatures, radiation, and gravity.

The Orion's avatar sat at her duty station manning the auxiliary communications com. Her face mirrored her normal calm as she probed, through the use of her ship's sensors, the area in question. Now she straightened up and turned her gold flecked eyes to Groshen the alter day captain. "Sir, we have contact. The signals are very faint and in a spectrum of broadcast radiation unfamiliar to us, but there is a definitive pulse of modulation that appears artificial. Shall I run a complete scan?"

The Juancy Captain spun in his specially reinforced chair and eyed the assistant communications officer coolly. "Report on your contact mister," he rumbled in his deep voice.

"Sir the band of communication is not in the normal electrostatic spectrum, it isn't radio waves, or light impulses but rather a disturbance of gravitational waves. It might be a modulation of dark energy, sir."

Captain Groshen rose from his chair and came over to the com station. With a flick of his fingers, he engaged the ship's intercom and ordered Dorothy Abrams to the command deck. He leaned over the assistant communications officer and stared at the read outs that now appeared on her screen. Slowly he shook his head. The readings were familiar but not any of those that he remembered, familiar but different.

Without turning he ordered, "Red alert." Immediately the command center became a whirl of organized activity. Daton Excilore came through the lift door and took his place at the auxiliary command chair. This was Captain Groshen's show and he was content to be there to help as needed. Mark Thomas and Dorothy Abrams came through together. She took her place at the main communications station and called up the records that her assistant had made of the contact. She frowned briefly and then composed herself to listen to the Captain's orders.

Mark Thomas sat in at the main engineering desk and prepared to call up the ships reserve energy, quietly augmented by his particular skill set. Glenda Stern stood ready in the engine room her special talent at the ready to aid Mark Thomas.

From his position standing like a looming mountain behind the assistant communications officer, Groshen straightened and addressed his waiting command. "I have only seen a contact like this once before. I was an assistant astrogator on one of the Brethren dreadnaughts when we entered a system designated by the High Council for assimilation. As was the normal procedure for the Brethren, a delegation was sent on ahead to the planet that had been selected for "processing". He looked around at his audience. "What was not so usual was that they never came back. The energy levels in the system ramped up to go off of our charts. It wasn't the usual energies found in the electromagnetic spectrum. It was dark energy. Our ship was caught up in the first wave and was repelled forcibly from the system. By the time our emergency systems came back online we were nowhere in the vicinity of the target system."

"The High Command was duly notified, and the system was marked for destruction. A fleet of Dreadnaughts and several of the planet killers were dispatched but when they arrived the planet that had been the object of our attention was gone. I mean it was no longer there, vanished. The whole thing was deemed highly secret and most of the crews were brain wiped, but for some reason they failed to do that for any of the Juancy race that were with the fleet."

"The pulses of energy that we are receiving from the third planet of this system are a close match to those which forced us from that other system many thousands of light years from our present position." He looked very seriously at his co-commander. "We need to re-think our visit here. There are things in this universe that we should not disturb. This may very well be one of those."

Before Dalton Excilore could reply in the affirmative, all motion on the command deck ceased. He glanced around at his fellow officers. Everyone was frozen in position, except for him. He rose out of his chair, confused but not, he was surprised to discover, frightened. From the air around him came a mellow voice. "Captain Excilore if you would be so kind as to come to the Captain's conference room, we will meet you there shortly." The voice was very polite but insistent. He found himself doing precisely what had been asked of him. He was under no compulsion that he recognized, but rather was following the request of his own volition.

As the companionway door slid shut behind him, he moved to the head of the conference table and took a chair, waiting for what he did not know, but again he felt no fear. The doorway slid open once more and he was surprised to see the assistant communications officer walk purposely into the room and take a seat next to him. The Captain did not remember his junior officer's name, which amazed him as he prided himself on becoming familiar with all of his crew. He looked expectantly in her direction. A pretty thing he thought to himself as he raised an eyebrow in inquiry.

"I am Ilana, Captain. You do not often ride the chair on my alter day assignment so you would not recognize me." She paused for a second, tilting her head. The doorway slid open once more admitting Mark Thomas, Glenda Stern, Sharp Eyes and Dorothy Abrams. They in turn took seats around the table nodding their heads in acknowledgement but remained silent as they sat down.

The air grew heavy with expectation, yet no one said a word. The light in the conference room dimmed suddenly and a purple glow began to fill the room. Dalton stood as the light solidified into three distinct forms that stood quietly studying the crew and officers assembled from the Orion. A soft melodious voice came from the figure in the center of that group. The voice and the figure were obviously female. "Welcome to Ikornic space. We do not often get visitors here so you must forgive us for placing your crew in temporary suspension. We are here to determine your fate. Our world has remained safe from the degradations of many a would-be empire. Our people are free from the bonds of servitude that some of you have experienced."

She smiled warmly at them, "Yes I recognize that you have among you, members of the Juancy. Those have suffered much under the oppression of the Brethren. She turned to where Sharp Eyes sat, fore paws on the council table. "Welcome, brother in fur. It has been several cycles of transport since we of Ikorn have coursed with your kind, a fact that has been very disappointing to us all."

She then turned to the remaining humans among those present. "Hail, Orion! The Federation is known to us. We have sheltered many survivors of your home worlds. Many an interesting system have they come to know since those demons from beyond set themselves upon your kind."

The greeting was lost on all but Ilana, who smiled at the recognition meant for her. The two companions who had remained silent during the introductions now turned to their female companion. In whispered asides they carried on an animated debate. With a smile and a deep laugh, she dismissed them, and they melded out of sight in a gentle surge of purple light.

She turned back to the waiting group. "You must forgive my companions. They have many demands on their time. My name is Theresa. I am the Outer Warder of Ikorn. It is my pleasure to welcome you to our space. I perceive that you do not mean us harm and much like we, are victims of the Brethren scourge. Still, I cannot offer you much in the way of alliance nor of support other than myself."

The group around the table was stunned by this turn of events. While they pondered the possibilities a wave of purple energy swept through the council chamber and out into the Orion. Ilana, who of course was monitoring her systems, was amazed at the amount of pure power that wave represented. She knew instantly that her vessel was no longer on approach to Ikorn but had been gently if firmly expelled on a course that would put them shortly within hailing distance of their next stop on this brief tour of systems.

"Do not be afraid, Ilana, we have determined that your cause is a just one, however we cannot let you land on our planet at this time. In fact, when next a ship comes to visit our system, they will not find Ikorn there at all!"

Daton took command of the group. "I take it that you have removed us from the HR 4523 A system?" Where are we now?

His voice was steady, but he could feel the hackles on his neck stand up as he thought of the awesome power that Orion now played host to.

Theresa stood tall before this proud Captain looking at him with understanding eyes. "Captain Excilore, you will find that your ship is nearing your next destination, Beta Hydri. While we could not let you approach our own world, we certainly can help you with the exploration of nearby systems."

Daton Excilore looked at this mysterious denizen from a planet that he had never seen and liked what he saw. She was fairly tall for a female and her dark hair flowed in cascades around her shoulders. Her face was not young he decided. It held a maturity that could be anything from late youth to early middle age. Her eyes were dark pools with hidden flecks of light that now sparkled in amusement from his studied observations. "Thank you for your aid, Lady. I take it that you are going to accompany us for a space?"

She looked directly at him and slowly nodded. "I think that you may need our help for a while. The Brethren will soon be aware of the rising of free folk within the galaxy. This is something that has not occurred in the last several millennia and it will not sit well within their High Command. Things are going to get very interesting in this sector of space in the near future and I think that you will need all of the help that you can get."

Chapter Twelve

Dale Lambert stood in his office on the inner moon looking out the thick window which faced the planet's surface far below. He wondered at the beauty that was Brightholme, pleased as always that they had found such a refuge. The newly minted shipyard lay within the crater which served as protective shield for the manufacturing operations. It was humming with purpose and industry. Already the ultra-light framework of the exploratory scout had been laid in the cradle far beneath his feet.

He had reviewed the conversations around that conference room table aboard the Andromeda. From the information given to him by Daton Excilore , he was now aware that the Federation as it once stood had been decimated by the Brethren. The people of the reclusive world of Ikorn had indicated that they had taken in many expatriated people from the Federation and had helped them relocate on other worlds.

So, he knew from the beginning that the mission to find the Federation worlds was already a failure. Still, he felt the need to continue the project. Inside his own mind he knew that he must make the effort to see for himself the devastation wrought by the Brethren. It might serve them well to ascertain the deployment of the forces under that dark regime.

He was also considering a request by Sharp Eyes that he include Daton in his exploratory crew. The canine had conversed with Shadow Grey and had expressed his concern that the fleet officer had many deep unresolved issues with his time away. Issues that would only be satisfied by an eyewitness appraisal of the devastation that Dale Lambert now feared would encompass all of the once vibrant worlds of the Federation.

Dale was two minded over the request. He had counted on Daton taking command of the defensive placements in Brightholme's system while he was away, yet he could well understand the man's need for closure. Dale reminded himself that to Daton and for the rest of the crew of the Orion for that matter, subjectively they had only left Federation space two years ago!

He sighed. His decision made. He reached out for the mind of his soul mate. Shadow Grey was pleased by the inclusion of Daton to the mission. "It will be well my friend," came his thought. "I feel that Daton will have a big part in events to come. To do so he will need to have a clear heart. He must be allowed to see what has been wrought on the Federation's home worlds."

Clearing his mind Dale turned back to other concerns. Heather was becoming gravid, and he hoped to see his son born before he went on this adventure. Moon Glow was keeping pace and he could sense the bemused thoughts of his friend as he too turned his mind to reflections of his mate's condition.

Groshen was at the command chair once more as the Orion approached the Hydra system. The ship broke out several parsecs from the system edge and he had the command crew scan the system. Ilana was on duty and through her sensors was keeping an ear out for any possible contacts. Very faintly but quite distinctly she could hear the modulation on radio waves that indicated a civilized species and their use of technology. "Captain Groshen, I have contact with some form of communications. They are using standard radio frequencies. Should I put it on the overhead?"

With a nod the Captain settled in his command chair to listen. What he heard was a series of lilting sounds that pulsed pleasantly on his ears. His mind tried to follow the complexities of the interwoven sounds but had to settle for an agreeable symphony of melody.

He turned to face Ilana, "Mister wash that through our communications algorithm. Let's see if we can make any sense out of what they are saying."

Home World

From the overhead speakers came the sounds of a song sung in many parts. While the computers did their best to translate it into words that could be understood by the crew, it could only produce a shadow of the meaning that Groshen felt hid among its many lines.

"You have come from far off space,
to seek us out in our own place.

Our lands reside under moon and sky,
to meet with us you must ply
through valleys deep and mountains high.

While we keep the peace of our jungle home
very seldom do we roam
for fond are we of hearth and home

But do not take us to be weak
we are fast and fleet of feet
Our clans are many and elite

Our minds are sharp
like flashing blades
A strength that shall never fade
a sting that you can not evade.

So, if you come in peace
then you are welcome to take a seat
at our table and share the feast

If you come with deceit
you will only taste defeat

Be clear of purpose to advance
this rhyme will be your only chance.

Answer truly and advance
play us false and feel our lance."

Stephen Goodale   110

The words fell silent and Groshen sat in bemused thought, the sound of the rhythm playing in his mind. He stirred himself in his seat. His orders had been to observe only and not to reveal the Orion to any possible contact. He ordered the ship to station keeping, maintaining its relative position to the system ahead. He addressed Ilana once again, "Please ask all senior officers to the conference room," he looked sharply at Ilana. "Please ask Theresa to attend as well."

The conference room hummed with suppressed conversation. Groshen stood, a massive bulk at the head of the table. Daton Excilore sat next to him and at his right hand sat Theresa. Most of the crew had not interacted with this woman from Ikorn, but those that had, had afforded her all courtesy. She sat now in dignified silence her dark hair falling in waves over her shoulders. She had taken the shipboard coveralls of a common crewman as her attire, yet on her it fit to her frame as if designed for her.

When all had assembled, Groshen held his hand up for quiet. "We are at station keeping just outside of the Hydra system. We have met an obvious contact protocol from a race or races that exist in this system. The formulation of the words seems to fit a species or several species of sentient beings that would need an oxygenated atmosphere and one that matches the tropical needs for a jungle environment. The third world out from Hydra's sun matches this requirement."

"Please replay that tape Mister," he ordered Ilana. She played the recording to the overhead speakers. The gathered group remained silent in rapt attention as the message played. Groshen gave them a few moments before he continued. "Our orders from Dale Lambert were clear. We were not to reveal our presence and to observe only." He looked around the room gauging the mood of his crew and fellow officers. "I feel that this message is an invitation to meet with the inhabitants of the world in front of us. We certainly represent no threat to those that lay hidden in their jungle home and our only chance to "observe" will be one of contact. I wanted to ask your opinions on the matter."

The conversation mounted in sound and volume as the command crew debated the situation. After a few minutes of back and forth, Theresa rose from her seat. The sound of conversation died slowly as those in the room recognized her movement. "I am a guest among you, but I will tell you that there is nothing to fear from meeting with these people. You are on a peaceful mission and represent no threat to this system. This will be apparent to those that wait." She turned to Groshen, "Yes they know that you are here and but await your decision."

Groshen cleared his throat, "Yes, well are there any other opinions on the matter?" He smiled to himself as he noted no other counter proposals. With a nod from Daton he continued with his orders. "That is settled then. Bring the ship into the system and broadcast a meet and greet on the same frequency that our hosts used to welcome us. Keep the shields down and under no circumstance activate any weaponry." He then asked Mark Thomas and Glenda Stern to man their posts and be ready in the event of any foul play to raise the ship's energy levels and throw up the shields at a moment's notice. Theresa only smiled and sat back comfortably in her chair.

The Orion moved slowly and stately into the Hydra system. The ship broadcast their peaceful intentions as it moved closer to the third planet. They were not opposed by any warnings, or physical resistance, a fact that pleased Groshen highly. He was a bit uncomfortable about abrogating his orders, but he felt in his bones that this was a very important moment in the young fleet's history. The Orion achieved standard orbit and waited to see if there would be a response to their actions.

They did not have long to wait. In the center of the command deck a shimmering ball of orange light appeared. It hovered for a moment and then expanded into a six-foot diameter sphere. It flared for a moment and then vanished leaving three forms standing at ease on the ship's deck.

The tallest stood about four foot six inches, his companions were slightly smaller. They were all lean and lithe. They had little in the way of clothing but what they did have modestly covered them. The reason for lack of clothing was apparent to the command crew. They were covered in tawny fur with shades of colors shot through out. They resembled a painting by an impressionist rather than living beings.

Slowly the tallest turned to face the enormous Groshen who had stood up from his command chair in surprise and respect. "I am called Farlisther, it means in your language roughly, Traveler. I am charged with being an ambassador for my people, the Kilora. We are the predominant sentient beings on our world, although by no means the only ones. We have been charged with guardianship of our world. This is why we designed and implemented the advise and response message that you heard on your arrival at our system's fringe." He looked squarely up into the eyes of the large Juancy Captain. "I hope that you did not take our warnings lightly!"

Groshen looked down at the three forms in front of him. He held no claim to any mental power, but he could feel the force that radiated from these diminutive creatures, these Kilora. There was no mistaking the implied threat of serious damage should his crew make a hostile move toward these people or their world. He cleared his throat and responded. "We understood your message and proceeded with the belief that if our mission was peaceful then no harm would befall us. We have honored your message and have left our weapons locked and our shields down."

"Our mission is to discover sentient beings within forty light years of our new home. This mission was to develop ties and strengthen relationships with those that we have met. You are the third such intelligence that we have encountered and while through mutual agreement we have not interfered with one such planet, the other has given us the company of an ambassador of their people."

"I see that your people already course the star lanes with a brother in fur," said Farlisther as he caught the movement of Sharp Eyes coming through the bridge companionway door.

Stephen Goodale   113

"Welcome brother". Sharp Eyes contented himself with sitting in the chair prepared for him studying the creature from the planet below.

Theresa had glided up to the Captain's side as he spoke and in a clear lilting voice, she spoke in the same language that had been originally broadcast to the Orion. "We are come as the Captain has said to meet with those of other minds, whose main purpose is of peace. We do this to help us bind this sector of the galaxy in friendship and mutual respect."

The affect on the three visitors was immediately apparent. They all bowed gracefully in a sign of respect. Farlisther stood then and smiled, his sharp teeth glistening in the shipboard light, "I was unaware of your presence mighty one. Had I but known that you graced this vessel we would have welcomed you more openly. How is it that you are so far from the world of Ikorn? That is many thousands of light years from here."

Theresa laughed, a lilting affair that imaged up the remembrance of sunlight in open meadows and the fall of light through green leaves at the edge of a forest. Those in the command center looked at her with fresh eyes and saw at once that the plain coveralls of her shipboard attire had been replaced by a flowing green gown of some shimmering material. She stood then and bowed gracefully at the emissaries from the world below.

"I remember your people from days gone by! We have fought and laughed together and made the worlds of light safe from the dark. Together our peoples have marched through the gates of time and have seen the passing of many an age. It is good to be with you once again, fur friends in arms."

Farlisther smiled his thanks and turned to Groshen. "You are welcome here Captain. We will await your arrival and have the feast of friends. I look forward to hearing your story for I can sense that you have much to tell." With another bow Farlisther stepped back next to his companions who had remained silent and the glowing ball of light that had brought them onto the

Orion surrounded them once more. They vanished in an instant.

Chapter Thirteen

It had taken Krylon several weeks to traverse the complex web that was the path to the home world of the Brethren. He had made the first border post and had been held there under suspicion while his ship was boarded, and its auto logs analyzed. He was grilled by the base commander. The loss of Krylon's crew was especially disturbing to those that he reported to. When at last he was cleared to move on, he had become frustrated and defiant, attitudes which did not serve him well when he finally arrived at Thallus.

Krylon's arrival was not heralded with fan fare and feasts but was met with the imposing forms of the High Command's Death Squad. The personal bodyguard of the Triune that commanded all of Brethren space. He was hustled into the lower chambers of the assembly building and thrown unceremoniously into a dark cell. The door clanged behind him with an ominous finality.

The next several weeks were a nightmare for the once proud member of the High Council. He had been an underling it was true, and he had been serving that ridiculous punishment assignment but he still deserved better treatment than constant torture and degradation. He knew to the minute when his next session was due, and he could not help but shutter at the pain he knew was to come.

The door to his cell opened exactly on schedule but instead of being dragged away from his cell and strapped to the nerve pain induction table he was taken up through the huge complex and placed in the interrogation room of the Triune. He was strapped to a chair and left to his own imagination. His mind painted a grim picture. He was a Council member and had participated and even enjoyed sessions that had brought frightened and mostly innocent victims to that chamber. He knew that once there they never left alive. Here was his death sentence and he was helpless to avoid it!

The light in the chamber dimmed even more and from projection unit images of his previous sessions were flashed on the wall in front of him. The sounds of his screams echoed from the empty chamber and seemed to drum in through his ears and on into his mind. He had told them everything. He had told the truth to those inquisitors who had been administering the pain that had laced through his body. He had nothing more to give these monsters.

The images faded and the lights came up once more. There seated in front of him were the Triune, the three ruling members of the Council of the Brethren. They looked down on him from the dais on which they sat, impassive and cold. The figure seated on the middle chair turned and stared at him. With an agonizing howl of pain Krylon ceased to be. What sat in that chair now was nothing more than a storage device full of data. The soul that had once filled the man had passed into the burning pit. With calm resolution the Chief member of the Triune sifted through the data. Unlike the underlings that sought to pervert these memories to augment their own ends his cold logical mind looked for the truth.

It was all there to be evaluated. This Dale Lambert so called Fleet Admiral had without a doubt ascended to a very high mental order. The message that had been scrupulously relayed by Krylon had been digested and filed for further meditation. The fact that he had identified himself as being from the Federation lent more mystery to the event. The Brethren had subjugated and for the most part had destroyed the member systems of the Federation over a century before. There had been no reports of any further activity from that group in decades. True there was always the rumor that some of those from the Federation had mysteriously disappeared before the annihilation took place. There was even the whisper of a name, the Witches of Ikorn. The inquisitor frowned, Ikorn. Every whisper or rumor of that planet or system had been duly followed up on and investigated thoroughly, yet nothing, not one scrap of evidence had been found to support its existence.

The dark figure nodded to himself and removed his mind from the dead husk of the man who had been Krylon. Turning to his companions he sent a mental command. "Send out our best hounds. I want all of the usual outposts that ply their filthy trade throughout the fringe systems watched. Have them keep an eye open for any rumor or hint of this Dale Lambert and the Witches of Ikorn!"

The lights in the room dimmed once more and the three members of the Triune vanished in crimson light. The remains of Krylon slowly sunk in on themselves and dissolved into a small pile of steaming ash that was dutifully removed by a chamber slave.

Doctor Scott looked at the man in front him. His kindly smile an effort to reassure the expectant father. Dale Lambert had gotten in from a long day at the construction cradle on Brightholme's nearest moon. It had been a trying day. He had never imagined in his wildest dreams that such a simple venture would require such intricate and detailed planning and follow through. Still when the time came for the planetary shuttle to leave that would take him home, he was grateful and satisfied. The new ship was coming together well and the tight schedule that would allow its departure at the end of the coming month would be met.

He had just entered the shuttle when he felt the first vague discomfort. It felt like a twinge from an overtaxed muscle. He had turned and wriggled in his seat to relieve the discomfort and shortly thereafter it went away. The shuttle had made its de-orbit burn when that pain returned in a big way. He doubled up in his seat with the agony that wrenched his stomach muscles.

It quickly relented and, in the moments, after he felt the mind touch of his wife as she reached out to him. "Dale, it's time. Hurry! They have taken me to the infirmary". Dale knew then what was causing his pain, and a silly if wary expression passed over his lips. With all of the skill that he had mustered dealing with Controller Mallin, Dale had forced himself to be patient.

He could, of course had just ripped the shuttle from its flight path and set it down neat as a pin next to the hospital, but he did not want to start his son's life off by squishing every living thing on that vessel with his need for haste. Instead, he sent a mind probe out to gently caress and ease Heather in her pain.

Doctor Scott broke the quiet worry of Dale Lambert. "It is time that you attended to your wife and son", he said kindly. Heather had had a difficult birth. The son that she had nurtured had not liked the idea of leaving the warmth and protection of his mother's womb. He had resisted.

It was Life Giver who had offered a way to entice the young Lambert into the world. Using the mind way, he infiltrated the tempestuous mind of the newborn and with calm assurance imaged the playful and whimsical antics of Moon Glows newborn pups. She had given birth the week before to two fine males and two females. Mother and pups were doing fine but she had her paws full. The troupe took turns to aid the new parents as best they could, but one of the males was rebellious. Life Giver had communicated with young Tristan Lambert and Casric that they could play together once Tristan was born. The two young ones met through the auspices of Life Givers mental contact and bonded at once. Soon after, Tristan gave up the defense of his home and came willingly into the light of Brightholme's warm sun.

Dale entered the birthing room quietly, afraid of disturbing his wife, who had gone into a deep sleep once she had been reassured that her son was a fine healthy boy. Dale had felt every agonizing moment of Heather's pain and had worked with Doctor Scott to ease and block as much as possible. Now as he closed the door behind him, he looked at his love and smiled. She was as beautiful as always and now held a glow about her resting face that he had never seen before.

Tristan was laying quietly in the cradle off to Heather's left. When Dale came into the room, he reached up his small hands for Dale to hold. With tender care, Dale held the proffered hands and with a start felt rather than saw the smile that was in

Tristan's mind. Carefully and with gentle touch Dale reached out his mind for his son's and felt instantly the pleasant flow of infantile thoughts. Foremost in his son's mind was the image of Moon Glow's young pup, Casric. The half-formed thoughts had Tristan running and playing with his newfound companion. In the background Dale was able to pick up the faintest of echoes. Casric was responding to the play thoughts and was joining in adding his own images. Once again Tristan smiled in Dale's mind and then withdrew his hands to suck happily on his thumb.

In his mind he felt Heather's warm smile. "I never knew that being a mother could be so amazing. I get so angry when I think of all of those people on Laurel who were denied this experience because those fools had stripped our planet of resources for their own greed, using force to deny the basic right of parenthood."

Her mind link was broken by a sudden sharp pain as she had shifted in her bed to look at father and son. Dale reached out with his mind and blocked the pain. Heather smiled her relief. "Of course," she continued "It does come at a cost, what pain!" She smiled up at Dale and added, "I am glad that you were there to share it with me."

The away shuttle had settled in a wide clearing near the foot of a tall mountain peak. As the shuttle bay door opened the sweet perfume of the native atmosphere swept in replacing the stale shipboard air. Daton Excilore had drawn the command of the away team, leaving Groshen commanding the Orion, ever watchful for uninvited guests. With careful expedience Daton drew in a lung full of air, it was invigorating of course but slightly intoxicating as well. He called to the away team medical officer Doctor Norwell Frosden, noting the man was busy running a scan as he stepped up next to him. "Have you found any problematical elements in the air that we need to be worried about?"

The doctor studied his read outs and slowly shook his head. "The readings indicate all green, in fact almost perfect for any of the species that we have on board or for that matter in our sphere of influence. These people have kept this world pristine not a sign of industrial contaminants to be found." He expanded his lungs several times drawing in the scented air. "In fact, maybe to pure for us poor industrialized type people."

Daton let out the lung full of air that he had drawn in and muttered under his breath, "A lesson that we need to take to heart on Brightholme!"

From the edge of the clearing a delegation of the Kilora approached the shuttle. Theresa had stepped to the fore of the landing party and now did a graceful bow to the leader of that party. The Kilora leader was not the tallest or strongest of the group but carried himself with great dignity. The feral grin that covered his mobile face was accompanied by a slight nod of his head in acceptance of that homage. "You are welcome here Mighty One as are those that travel the star lanes with you. We have prepared a feast in honor of this meeting. Please come and join us under stars, moon, leaf and home."

With that the remainder of the greeting party divided themselves up and stepped to the side of the group from the Orion. Each bowed briefly and stood at ease by a separate spacer's side. Daton raised his eyebrow, but Theresa smiled her reassurance, so the Captain just shrugged and with hand signals put his crew at ease. Together the party marched out under the deep canopy of the tall jungle foliage following a well-defined trail.

For those that lived within the planet's gravity well, the toll of that walk was nothing, but to spacers who lived in a constant lower gravity the trek was tiring. Daton was glad to see that the path widened up ahead and then break out into brilliant sunshine. All around them were the houses of the Kilora. They were all brightly colored and those colors, if one did not settle before moving to next for a minute or two, were quite disconcerting.

The smells were also a bit daunting. Each villager appeared to have a different and quite unique fragrance that marked him or her as a member of a particular clan or group. Those tended to congregate around the open doorways of the large homes. Everywhere were the soft mummers of conversation or the gentle laughter of people who were happy and content with their lives. Daton who was used to the close quarters and formalized interaction of a tightly run spaceship found himself at a loss, grasping for reason amid the happy chaos.

The group walked up through the town proper and found themselves in a large circular plaza, from which other paths came and went so that the overall effect was that of being in the hub of a very archaic wagon wheel. There were no signs of power transmission lines, no overt advertisement decrying the purpose of those buildings that now faced the crewmen from the Orion. Only the colors and the odors remained a constant shift in the spectrum of sight and smell.

Theresa stood tall and straight her midnight hair swirling around and over her shoulders. She faced the leader of the group of Kilora once more and slowly spoke to the open air, "To the people of this world we give words of praise and of friendship. By the cup and by the bread and by the air that we breathe we offer you our good wishes and our gratitude for your welcome."

While she spoke, she noted a lean tawny form that had silently paced up beside that of the Kilora leader. This sinewy quadruped snaked around and through the feet of the Kilora, flicking its tail and then sat down on its haunches, dark green eyes focused on the Ikornian ambassador. Theresa smiled to herself once more but did not offer a greeting to the newcomer.

The older Kilorain noted the feline form at his feet and with great reverence squatted down so that his shoulder drew close to the ground. The creature leaped and settled down on the Kilora's shoulder. Its long tail curled nonchalantly over the elder's opposite shoulder. Standing once more the Kilorian resumed his watchful position.

"You are welcome here Mighty-One and those with whom you travel the star ways. It is good to see you once more Theresa the Outer Warder of the Ikornian race. I remember walking with you under the skies of many worlds."

Daton Excilore drew a sharp breath. The voice that he heard was not spoken aloud but played in his mind! The creature on the Kilorian's shoulder was evidently much more than met the eye. Sharp Eyes who had hung toward the back of the away party now padded forward, sitting on his haunches he looked up into those forest green eyes. "Thank you, brother in fur, for your welcome", came the sure mental voice of the troupe member. The words rang in all their minds. "I had hoped that I would one day meet a fellow skin traveler and share the mind speech which is our chosen method of communication. I am Sharp Eyes and I represent my race on this venture."

The tail twitched at the shoulder of the Kilorian and the graceful head of the feline turned in Sharp Eyes direction. "It is indeed several generations of the Kilorians since I have coursed with any other than Theresa. Welcome brother in fur, I am called Frthessig and I am the spokesperson for my race here on Kilora. We are a retiring species with ancient knowledge and some very peculiar ways of demonstrating that knowledge."

Sharp Eyes bowed his head briefly in acknowledgement of Frthessig's words. "We are not such an ancient race as yours. Our origins as a species lay in the far past but our ascension as a sentient species is only a few hundred years old. We were the primary target of development by our ship the Star Dancer. Our mental prowess is great, but we are still developing as a people. Now we course the star lanes with humans from various worlds and serve as active partners in their explorations. Our original home world now lays in dust and debris thanks to greed and selfishness. Our new home is lovely, and many steps have been taken by all to keep it that way."

"It is good that we are met in this time and in this place, but before we settle down to the more serious matters in front of us, I would be doing the Kilorians a disservice by ignoring their customs. For tonight and for the next several days you and all your party will be their guests. To begin with we will have a ceremonial feast."

Daton Excilore motioned Doctor Norwell Frosden to the front of the group. With the help of Theresa, the Doctor managed to let their hosts know the issues that those of the away party may have with eating and drinking planetary based sustenance. The Kilorain leader bowed humbly and then in a rapid sing song voice spoke at length with Theresa. The Ikornian nodded her head in understanding and then addressed the Doctor and the Captain. "They will submit samples of all that is prepared so that the good Doctor here can run them through his analyzer. He assures me that the last thing that they want to do is accidentally kill their guests." Theresa laughed lightly, "They consider it bad luck!"

Dale only allowed himself a couple of days away from the project on the Brightholme moon. Heather had recovered quickly and was beginning to feel like Dale was getting under foot. Dale had tried to pitch in and help at every turn, but more than once Heather had to kindly ask him to take a step back. Finally, she kissed him and told him that under no certain terms was he to return from his office at the shipyard and not make a return appearance unless he was called for, at least for a few days.

Dale was grateful in a way for the enforced absence. He knew very well that Heather and their son were two of the closest watched individuals on the planet. It gave him comfort that although he was physically separated from his two loves they were still a comfortable presence in his mind.

The skeletal frame of the new ship had long since attained its final shape and was now being outfitted with its internal systems. While its mission lay in stealth and speed, the reaction guns which ran up through its specially reinforced hull could be applied in combat with deadly force. Polasic and Trembo, the two co-commanders from the Juancy ships were especially apt at applying the acquired knowledge from the Brethren's conquests. The technologies were varied but adaptable to the defense of the ship. The Orion and the AI from the Star Dancer had developed a next generation artificial intelligence which was accessible from any part of the ship and had an astral projection of its own.

Dale Lambert had smiled when he had first met the young man walking through the curved corridors of the ship. There was, he thought, a bit of extrapolation on the AIs part, because the youth had a smile just like his son Tristan.

Shadow Grey and Moon Glow had been keeping him apprised of the various exploits that Daton and Groshen had gotten themselves into over the past month or two. He was actually very pleased by the discovery of several sentient species in relative near space and had been gratified in their response to the peoples of Brightholme. He could envision an alliance that might give the Brethren pause should they try to attack this quadrant of space directly.

He did not try to fool himself into believing that they were ready for such a contest. His time spent interviewing the Juancy crews and those that had been liberated from the Brethren Dreadnaught had certainly indicated a depth of depravity and an iron will for domination that would test the strength of any defense. Still, he had hope.

Now the next step of the plan would begin the voyage of discovery and an assessment into what had been the Federation space. He sternly reminded himself that this sector of space was now firmly under Brethren control. He knew that there was very little help to be expected from the adventure but to satisfy those under his command and his own need to anchor himself even further to his adopted world, Dale knew that he had to go.

Daton watched the swirling figures of the Kilorian dancers as they made their way through the sweetly scented smoke of the fire pit in the village square. He had eaten sparingly of the foods brought to him and had drunk from his own bottle of ship's water. His hosts seemed satisfied with his efforts and were content. The soft mummer of conversation and the aroma of the smoke might have been excuse enough for the Captain of the Orion to slip into a state of semi consciousness.

In his dream like state, his mind drifted back to his home world and his family. He had been very much in love with his wife Adriana and had adored his two sons and his daughter. They had been young enough that the occasional absence of their father could be accepted. His last voyage was to be the mineral extraction expedition to a recently discovered mineral rich planet well outside of Federation space. It would be only for a year or two he had assured his wife and then he would retire from space and spend the rest of his life with the family. She had agreed to his proposal and had sent him on his way with a night of love making that still sang in his heart. She had made certain that he would keep his vow in a way that only a loving wife could.

Yet here he was on a strange planet, light years from a home world that he was certain no longer existed. He was time and space away from those warm memories and it crushed his soul. He hung his head down on his chest, as soft tears rolled down his face. The sweet scents, the pulsing rhythm of the music, the swirling colors were all gone leaving nothing but black empty despair. In his mind he felt rather than saw a soft fur covered body rubbing against his legs, a rasping purr that was just audible reached his ears. Words formed in his mind, the soft reassurance that all was not lost, that he, Daton Excilore, would find a way back to those that lay enshrined in his heart.

The man's eyes shot open, and he found one of the furred ones squatting on its haunches staring at him with a quizzical look in its eyes. This was not Frthessig whose colors were tawny yellow but another whose dappled and shaded body was a smoky mix of blacks and grays. "I am Dressant, the Far

Walker and if you will, I would like to be your companion on the trip to the Federation home worlds. I think that you will find my skills of some value to you."

Daton stared into the unblinking eyes of Dressant and felt himself drawn to the creature. He felt the shadow on his heart lift a bit and was grateful for that change. Carefully he formed words in his mind and tried to project them to the waiting feline form that fronted him. "I can only thank you for your offer, Dressant, and for myself I accept it, but you need to know that others will make the decision on who is to go on that voyage and who is to stay."

"Very good Captain we will await that decision but, in the meantime, allow me to show you around our world." With that Dressant stood up and shook slightly, without a backward glance the creature padded off to the left, leaving the circle of firelight and the bodies of the Kilorians that still swirled in their endless dance. Strangely enough, Daton did not hesitate to follow and caught only a glimpse of Theresa as she smiled her approval and went back to attending the conversation that she was in with the Kilorian elder and Frthessig.

Dressant led Daton from the circle of huts that was the Kilorian village and walked with a confident air down a narrow well maintain walkway. Daton knew from his study of the topographical scans on the Kilorian home world that this path was leading them toward the nearby mountain range. In the dark he could not see the looming towers of rock. The foot path was well lit however by a strange luminance which emanated from the plants on either side of the path. His footing was secure, and he was strangely at ease.

He did not tire, which was surprising as he had not yet become accustomed to the gravity of this planet, and he had already marched long miles getting to the Kilorian village. "Where is it that you are taking me?" He asked of the furred form in front of him. Dressant's mind answered promptly. "We are going to the station and will catch a ride from there to our mountain retreat."

With that Daton had to be content. It was only a few minutes more when Dressant slowed to a stop in front of him. It turned and looked to be sure that he was following its lead and moved off to the right of the path. Daton hurried to catch up and found himself looking through a gateway onto an open platform. There Daton looked and saw the smoky black which was Dressant's fur coating as it seemed to pulse and flow growing larger and broader covering her form. He took a sharp breath and released it as the form in front of him condensed into a beautiful young woman whose dark flowing hair covered her to the waist. The dark fur had become a similar smoky colored skin which he was grateful to note was decently covered by jerkin and trousers of a similar darkened fabric. Dressant turned so that he could see her new form from every angle and then came to a stop.

"Yes, I am Dressant and I am a skin changer, this is my human form, if you will. She looked at him with an ironic smile, "I hope that you like it!" She then laughed and motioned for him to join her at the edge of the platform. From her pursed lips came a long lilting whistle which she repeated several times until it was answered by a similar whistle in the distance. That whistle drew closer in the still air and was soon followed by the first mechanical device that Daton had seen on this planet. The vehicle, if that was what it was, looked to be nothing more than a small mobile platform with some comfortable contour chairs located on its flat deck.

Dressant seated herself in one of these and patted the seat next to her indicating that he should join her. Daton sat and the chair seemed to form around his larger frame almost in an organic manner. He was incredibly comfortable.

Dressant pursed her lips again and once more whistled. This time the call was more modulated almost as if she were issuing instructions. Immediately the platform reversed the course from which it had come, moving smoothly with no indication of mechanical noise or rough traverse. Dressant laughed at his half-formed thoughts. "It rides on a cushion of electromechanical energy, no moving parts at all!"

The mechanism picked up speed and the surrounding jungle moved by at an incredible pace. The mountains that had been hidden previously from view surged closer and closer. With a gasp Daton realized that they were heading for an apparent death against a sheer rock wall when the vehicle surged through an opening in that massif. The tunnel was not much bigger than the vehicle that sped through it. There were lights spaced at precise intervals, but their speed made them blend together so that it was very difficult to see them as separate units.

Daton lost track of time in that tunnel but suddenly realized that the platform was slowing and at last it pulled to a stop at what could have been a commuter station on any of the many worlds that he had visited. The only difference was that there were no other occupants on the apron of this station platform. Dressant stood and motioned for him to follow. Daton wasn't sure that his legs would respond after that precipitous ride, but they surprised him as they moved smoothly at his command.

Dressant smiled in understanding and took Daton's arm to steady him while they walked toward an opening in the far wall. Daton felt a thrill of excitement at the touch of the alien and then felt a guilty flush as he realized that he was responding to that touch. He did not pull away but kept his pace even and hoped that his response gave no offense to Dressant.

Dressant only smiled and walked on guiding him through a security door which read her iris pattern, and which swung wide in invitation. The interior of that space was enormous and was no longer empty of life. Throughout the space forms of various types, small felines such as Dressant had been before she transformed and bipedal humans dressed in many different colored clothing patterns were to be seen. The scene, while busy was not chaotic. The denizens all moved in purposeful motion going to destinations on the cavern floor or the many openings lining the distant walls.

Once more Dressant pursed her lips and formed that modulated call which rose and fell in a very pleasing manner. Daton could see several heads turn to watch them and then turn back to their own affairs. From the distant wall Daton could see that some sort of ground vehicle was making its way toward them. It paused and moved with the flow of those on foot, almost as if it was guided by some intelligence and sure enough Daton could see that as it drew near a small human was seated in a control chair.

Dressant laughed, a deep hearty sound and took Daton's arm once more to aid him up the step that led to the same type of chairs that he experienced on the run into this hidden world. Dressant chatted gaily in her own language to the young man at the control console and then sat back in the chair next to Daton's and smiled.

As the vehicle made its way back across the cavern floor, Daton could only admire the skill of the driver as they intersected a seemingly endless stream of pedestrian traffic, yet despite all the yields and the awkward intercepts the vehicle moved with a fairly steady rate and reached the far wall of the cavern quickly enough. The vehicle continued on through a wide corridor and while the pedestrian traffic thinned out quite a bit the vehicular traffic picked up so that they were driving in a stream of similar vehicles. This at last seemed familiar to Daton, looking very much like a four-lane highway back on his home world. That comparison had the unfortunate effect of reminding him that his world was lost and for the next few minutes a dark cloud of bitterness and memories seethed through him.

He was brought back to the here and now by the soft touch of Dressant's fingers on his. He started and looked around him. They had pulled out of the flow of traffic and were coming to a stop in front of a pair of wide double doors. There were a few other vehicles parked in nearby spaces and as they exited the vehicle, Dressant addressed the young driver and pointed to a vacant space nearby. Daton caught the vehicle out of the corner of his eye as it made toward that waiting spot, At least," he thought to himself, I won't have to walk back! The humor of that observation lightened his mood and he followed after Dressant in a much more receptive frame of mind.

Chapter Fourteen

Theresa watched as Daton Excilore walked away from the campfire of the Kilorians. Frthessig sat by her side. "You know," came her thoughts to her long-time friend and ally, "That Daton will need to see physical evidence of his ruined world before he can begin to mend. While I applaud your choice of Dressant as a future mate for the man, he must be able to accept her with a heart and soul cleared of past regrets. He will need a considerable time in which to heal."

Frthessig turned his golden eyes up to hers and a soft willowy smile plied her mind. "I know Mighty-One, but unlike most humans Daton will be given the gift of our long lives. He will have time and to spare in which to heal and to make his own choices, still I have great faith in my daughter's abilities and perhaps she too will be surprised by the sharing as they come to grow together."

"Be that as it may, we have other matters to discuss than the healing of two hearts." Frthessig paused for a long moment in thought. Theresa respected that silence knowing what was coming. She actually did not know whether she approved of the events that would follow or not. Her own people were quite capable of surviving anything that the Brethren threw at them, but they had now become embroiled in the lives of other races. The rescue of many from the Federation was the latest breach in their isolation policy. It may be that for the sake of the galaxy that they would be forced to become players rather than those that sit on the sidelines as observers.

Frthessig's thoughts came back to her, "The time has come, I think, that we of the free worlds must band together and unite under one banner. My people have foreseen the Rising. The dream thoughts are very dark. The one that is to come will be very potent and very evil. His powers will eclipse any that have been known before except those of the Savior. We can of course wait on his second coming and pray that we would be relieved of the responsibility of what happens to the galaxy. I would wish that, but my heart tells me that we will be here to face the storm and while we may pray and anticipate aid from him, we will be left to face the wrath to come."

"Our two peoples have plied the space lanes together in the past. The time has come that we will need to reform that alliance. I offer you my services once more, Mighty One and look forward to the adventure, but unlike times past I cannot guarantee that we will succeed or even survive in the tempest to come."

Theresa bowed her head gracefully in acceptance of Frthessig's offer and added. "Our people have spent the last century analyzing and calculating the events to come. They also feel that the time has come to act, yet they too can not see the outcome of events. For the first time in living memory, they are afraid of the future."

Theresa sighed deeply, "There will be so many lost in the coming struggle, so much bitterness and pain will flow through our worlds but in the end what real choice do we have? The Rising has been foreseen, there is nothing now that will stop that from happening. We must ingather and develop what strategies we can with those that will now stand with us. The Brethren will be our first task and that will be enough to deal with but him who is to come will be our ultimate challenge and perhaps the end of all that we know and love."

Daton stood in the Hall of the People, Dressant by his side. He stared in wonder at the displays of history, for the People, as they called themselves were an ancient race. This world which they shared in peace with the Kilorians was just one of many worlds that they had occupied through their long history. The space lanes were no strangers to them. Although Daton took note, that very seldom did they ever travel those voids by themselves but often as equal partners with other sentient beings.

Daton was astounded to see that Theresa the Outer Warder from Ikorn had a special place in the history of the People as did Frthessig their leader. The two had been involved with many of the historical developments of the galaxy from one sector to another. They appeared to be ageless and at this Daton wondered. "How long do your people live, Dressant?" He said this without thinking.

The woman at his side smiled and said, "We are a long-lived race Daton Excilore and we have seen many an age but we are mortal and do die, accidents and death plague us as they do any race." She paused for a moment and then added, "The years can be kindly, or they can be cruel. We, like you, are subject to the will of the Maker and we serve his purposes, whether we would or no. The time is coming my friend Daton that perhaps all that we have built will become as dust under the boot heels of our enemies."

With that they fell silent and walked through the exhibits and displays until they reached a chamber at the back of the hall. Here Dressant turned and faced the man that stood in front of her. "I have brought you here so that you can learn more of us Daton Excilore and to offer you a gift from the people. I know what lies in your heart and I grieve with you for your loss. You will be given the opportunity to return to your home world and to see what may be seen there. I do not offer you much hope but that you will see naught but death and destruction. What I can and do offer you is the support of my people and my own personal services. I will accompany you and see you through what must be done. This is no small gift my friend because I don't think that the end of your quest will be the sight of your home world, but what that future is neither I, nor my people can tell."

Daton felt his heart leap even as Dressant's mournful words filled his ears. He had already been assured by Dale Lambert that he would be given crew space aboard the exploration scout currently being developed on the moon of Brightholme. He knew that after two hundred years that those he loved would be dead and dust. He even knew, though in his soul he hoped that it wasn't so, that the Brethren had long ago laid waste to most of the Federation. Yet he knew that he must go. The friendship and the companionship of Dressant would be welcomed, but he knew that he must face the truth!"

It was Daton's turn to look at his companion. He had to admit that she was beautiful and that her touch had electrified him, but he suppressed those feelings and looked her in the eyes, "Thank you Dressant I would be grateful for your company and the knowledge of your people, both are gifts beyond measure. I stand with you as an equal partner and I hope that you will be able to accept me," he laughed, "warts and all."

She smiled her acceptance of his terms and turned to lead him into the medical facility of her people. There was one more gift that she was to give him, but he was not to know of it for some time to come. She had argued with her father that such a gift should be given freely with the recipient's knowledge and approval, but he had overridden her scruples and had directed her to bring him to the medical wing.

As they passed into the well-lit entrance way a mist filled the space and Daton Excilore collapsed silently into Dressant's waiting arms. Several attendants moved to place the unconscious body of the spacer on a gurney and then wheeled him off to the reaction chamber. Dressant walked quietly behind the man and with a heartfelt prayer hoped that he would not come to hate her in the future because of what she allowed them to do today.

When he had regained consciousness Daton Excilore felt amazingly well rested and at peace with his world. Then he remembered where he had been and sat up feeling the pliant material give under him and yet support his movements. From a chair nearby he heard that soft fruity chuckle and knew that Dressant had stood watch over him as he slept. "Where am I Dressant? What happened to me?"

Well, you fell asleep standing on your feet Daton. I caught you and the doctors at the medical wing examined you. In the end they declared you fit enough but exhausted from your long day and the exertions of your walk to the village. They let me know in no uncertain terms that I was to allow you to sleep yourself out. They brought you here to what is a private room in our medical facility, and I have been keeping watch ever since." Dressant did not lie. All that she had told him was the truth but not the whole truth. She knew that the fabrication would always lay between them, whether Daton knew of it or not and she regretted it deeply.

"How long have I been asleep? The rest of the away party must be getting worried at my absence." Dressant gave another of her half truths. "I sent word to Theresa immediately upon the doctor's prognoses and she is fine with your absence. The rest of the away party had a wonderful night eating, drinking and in the end dancing! The amusement in her voice was real and it reassured him more than her words had. "How long must I remain here. I should be getting back."

Dressant laughed again and then replied, "How do you feel?" Daton thought for a moment taking an internal inventory and then slid his legs over the side of the bed, sliding the covers from his body. With some care he placed his feet upon the floor and allowed them to take his weight. It was then that he noticed that he was naked, in a flurry of movement he grabbed the blankets from the bed, covering himself and turned a bright shade of red. "I feel remarkable good, but ahem could I possibly have my clothes back?"

Dressant studied him for a moment her smile in her eyes now instead of her lips. "I will leave you to dress and to make use of the facilities. You will find your clothes cleaned and pressed behind that panel." She pointed to the doorway at the back of the room and then walked out the opposite door her laughter floating behind her like the tinkle of silver bells.

After a hearty meal in the huge cavern at one of the kiosks that formed the central plaza on that wide floor, Daton and Dressant headed back to the village. Once there they were reunited with the rest of the away team. All seemed to be in a mellow mood. Theresa and Frthessig pulled him aside and along with Sharp Eyes proceeded to explain to him that the

Kilorians and those that represented them would be of service to Dale Lambert and his attempt to unify the free peoples of the quadrant. As a token of this alliance Frthessig would be joining them along with several of the Kilorian people on their journey to Brightholme.

Dale Lambert was looking over the read outs of the final testing phase of the newest ship in the fleet. He was more than satisfied. According to what he saw this would be the fastest and best equipped ship that the Federation had ever put into space. It was strange, he thought of it as the Federation. Certainly, he had no constraints to do so. From what he had learned from the reports that Theresa of Ikorn had given his exploration crew aboard the Orion, the Federation as the Orion's crew had known it was no more. Dale Lambert of the planet Laurel knew even less except that his distant ancestors had been from the Federation. Still, it was as good a name as any and so it stuck.

The exploration vessel would have great space legs and should be able to outrun anything she came up against. Also, the power buss system augmented as it was by his staff would recharge quicker than anything in known space, allowing them to escape into hyperspace much quicker than would be anticipated by any enemy ship.

The days were dwindling down to the anticipated launch when the Orion once more broke into Brightholme's system. The Star Dancer rose from its cloaked guardian position to greet his sister ship. Dale waited anxiously as the Rever ships still serving as shuttles brought the crew and the ambassadors from the various world's that had responded to Dale's call for alliance, down to Brightholme's surface.

Dale Lambert stood holding tightly onto Heather's hand while she held their newborn son in the sling placed around her shoulders. Shadow Grey and Moon Glow, with their family of young pups, who danced around the legs of the on lookers represented the troupe. The members of the Town Council and the newly formed Medical Research Facility all stood ready to greet those that disembarked from the shuttles.

Theresa stepped down from the companion way door and onto the gently sloping ramp that ended on the planet's surface. The warm clear air and the bright golden sunshine were an immediate boon to her space induced nervousness. She had travelled the star lanes for countless years, yet she was always grateful to return to a planet's surface. She knew that it was a psychosomatic reaction to being in an enclosed space and fending off the thoughts of those so closely surrounding her. People that did not have talent were never as affected as those that did have it.

Dale immediately sensed the power of Theresa's mind as she made her way down the ramp. He also sensed a curious echo effect as he studied the tall, stately Ikornian. It was then that he noticed that Theresa carried a tawny furred body on her shoulders. The mental echo of power came from that entity. He had been briefed on the visit of the Orion to Kiloria. "So, he thought this must then be Ambassador Frthessig." Heather's mind came into his, "Be careful my love, these people are powerful telepaths," she paused for a moment and then finished her thoughts, "among other things."

Shadow Grey also commented upon the mental skills of the fur brothers on board the shuttle. "Sharp Eyes has described these beings perfectly, yet I sense much more than meets the eye here."

Moon Glow agreed, "There is that about them that feels ancient yet a vibrancy of spirit that makes them as young as the new day. Very strange indeed," she added.

Daton Excilore stepped down the ramp accompanied by a strikingly pretty young woman with a dark complexion. Dale immediately sensed the same echo effect and wondered at the meaning of this pairing. He knew that Daton had expressed a fervent wish to go with the expedition to the Federation home worlds. A desire predicated on his need to ease the loss of his wife and family. He sensed no diminishing of that desire, but he did sense the beginnings of acceptance. Perhaps this member of the People was the source of that healing?

He could feel Heather's smile in his mind and a soft caress that only she could give him. "Every man needs a woman to make him whole, and while no one will ever be able to substitute for the loss of Daton's wife, this one may be just what the doctor ordered!"

When all the guests had been greeted, they entered a specially prepared pavilion that had been erected for this meeting and all future meetings of the allied worlds when they occurred on Brightholme. Dale stood at his place at the large circular table and spoke into the microphone on his collar. The Star Dancer AI had done a wonderful job in developing communication devices that allowed all present to hear Dale's words in their own language.

"Welcome all, you have been called or perhaps it is better to say that you have all been led by your own will to this meeting on Brightholme. I want to thank you for taking the time and for trusting us with the security of your persons on the long trek here. Each of you will be provided with accommodations suited to your needs for as long as you stay with us. Each home will be treated as an embassy for your race and will be protected and guarded at all costs."

"Brightholme is our home, but who are we? Our story will be told in many parts so that you can see that our very foundation here is one of multiplicity and cultural divergence. I will start the story, but others will finish it and in the telling you will discover the various parts that while significant by themselves make up an extremely powerful whole. A microcosm of what we are asking you to become part of."

Dale Lambert launched into a description of what life had become on Laurel and the discovery of other sentient beings on their own doomed and dying world. Heather picked up the story of corruption and insidious violence that had marred their world. Shadow Grey stood and described the nature of their own self-awareness and the development of their talents over the many years that his troupe had lived on the lower slopes of the plateau protected from the radiation and illness by Star Dancer.

The Star Dancer's AI stood and spoke of the long, lonely years from system failure and loss of crew to its own attempts to develop an augmented crew capable of flying once more to the stars. First his own experiments with the troupe whose highly refined community telepathy and other psi talents were beyond expectations to contact and association with Dale's people at the research station.

Dale picked up the story once more describing the efforts of escape and the ultimate doom of their world. When he reached the part where they had watched from the vantage point of space, as the world that they had called home for millennia broke apart under the tectonic stress placed upon it by man's greed, Dale broke down and Doctor Scott finished the story.

Then the Orion's AI stood and for the first time those on both ships who had worked with her recognized her for what she was. "I apologize to those of my crew that know me as Ilana an off-watch communications officer on the Orion. I have always worked better when I could be with the crew instead of separated from them." Then she launched into recognition of the Star Dancer and its crew for coming to her crew's distress calls and the reconstruction.

Dale took over once more to describe the interaction with the Rever ships and the recruitment of two of their vessels into the "Federation". Groshen spoke of his people's servitude under the Brethren and the longing that his people had to be free. He said, "When it became apparent through Dale's actions and those of his crew, that we at least had a chance of freedom, most jumped at the opportunity."

Mark Thomas spoke of how they disabled the Brethren Dreadnaught and had freed the crew from their electronic slavery. He described how they had then sent the Brethren ship packing on its way back to the Brethren home world to report.

Dale then completed the tale by describing the colony's ability to create a stable and multi cultural governing body whose purpose it was to maintain rather than change its inhabitant's culture and to preserve the world on which they lived.

"We are aware that the Brethren are a mighty force to be reckoned with. However, I feel that we, who are assembled here and with those who are yet to be brought into our ranks from nearby systems, can coordinate and prevent the Brethren from becoming a presence in our sector of the galaxy."

"We had an amazing bit of luck when we intercepted their Dreadnaught. We were able to get into their data servers and avoid the viruses that litter that virtual landscape. In doing so we discovered where the Brethren's major deployments were at the time of the break in. Now this might have been detected but if it has not and if the command protocols have not been changed recently during our stay here on Brightholme then we have a good chance at avoiding their major concentrations of fire power."

"We have developed a fast exploration vessel with some unique technology that can, with luck pierce their nets and get us into Federation space. Once there we will attempt to make contact with any surviving Federation outposts. It is my proposal that we take a mixed crew and enter Brethren space, penetrating their defenses and gain what we can from the old Federation. In the process we can gather up more recent intelligence and here is the best part, we can salt their area of space with drones which can collect passive data and feed it back to us. We can gain an intelligence advantage, one that cannot be detected, or that is at least our hope."

"In the meantime, I will leave a team here on Brightholme to continue the exploration of nearby space and to establish contact with the Empire. It is imperative that we form an alliance with that group as soon as possible. By visiting as many systems as possible that might harbor sentient life, we can at least warn them about the Brethren's preferred method of attack, namely infiltrate, reconnoiter and destroy. We can possibly save neighboring races from the mistakes that we have made in the past."

Dale's words inspiring as they were did not illicit as much enthusiasm as he might have expected. Theresa stood then, her tall straight form and waves of dark black hair flowing over her shipboard jump suit. "Dale Lambert is right in that we have come to a major point in galactic history. For many thousands of years and through far too many sentient civilizations and mineral rich worlds the Brethren have raped and pillaged without repercussion. They have succeeded despite their particular handicap."

Here she smiled at Dale and then at Heather, pointing to the proud parents of Tristan, their first-born son. "You see they have become so hard of heart and so possessive of their wealth that they have all but ceased reproducing themselves. In fact, in order to keep their population from going extinct they have resorted to a cloning methodology captured from one of the worlds that they long since have destroyed. They keep clones of themselves in impenetrable defensive positions around their sphere of influence and only allow a clone to be activated when one of their members is destroyed. These clones are exact duplicates, usually around thirty years of age but with all of the knowledge, skill, memories and hatred of their predecessor."

"Destroy these hidden redoubts of their racial memories and you destroy the Brethren. Destroy the Brethren individually and you may gain a short respite from that one particular member only to face worse from him later on."

"As for infiltrating old Federation space, yes, I agree, this needs to be done. There are at least three crews still functioning with their ships from that brave group of people. She looked directly at Daton Excilore. You deserve the right to see for yourself what has become of the worlds that you once called home. I will also tell you this that through methods that you cannot understand and by which we have lived on Ikorn, we were able to save quite a few of the people of the Federation, planting them on worlds known only to us with safeguards that none may penetrate."

Daton Excilore sprang to his feet as did a number of other crewmen from the Orion. Theresa held up her hand to quiet the angry and hurt Federation members. "I am sorry, but for those of you that crewed on the Orion we were not able to save the worlds on which you lived. The Brethren's attack was too unexpected and too swift on those worlds to provide succor for their inhabitants."

"Remember that it has been two hundred years for you in objective time and only two or three perhaps in subjective time. The Brethren attacked that region of space over one hundred years ago. We saved what we could but that was little enough. Those worlds that are now protected by Ikornian methods will remain hidden from this universe for another hundred years. The mechanism by which those worlds were transported will automatically bring them back so that they at least will have a chance to start again."

"I am sorry for you but have hope and be of good cheer for there are many twists and turns which fate will deal you in the future and not all of them will be bad." Here she smiled directly at Dressant, who blushed under her dark complexion.

Theresa looked at Dale Lambert, "Whether by skill or by luck you have managed to give the Brethren exactly what we need them to have. You brought the name of the Federation back into their minds. The ghost of a victory that now lays in their past and a small measure of doubt on which they can now chew. You have distracted them, for that let us be very grateful. In addition, because of your personal background you have discovered the methodology by which they have held sway over their victims, those that they had chosen to be their hands and feet."

"It had been one of the great mysteries of the Brethren and was one of the key stumbling blocks which had prevented the Ikorn from fully engaging this enemy. Now that the method is known we can begin liberating those unfortunate enough to be dominated by the Brethren and by doing so perhaps swell our ranks and weaken theirs."

At this everyone cheered, the Juancy and those that had been held to service on the Dreadnaught voicing a roar of approval. Theresa motioned to quiet the crowd. "The time has come my friends to gather together and to fight this common scourge. There are a number of allies to help us in our endeavor some obvious," and here she pointed to the Juancy people sprinkled throughout the crowd, "and some not so. We will need to develop a strategy by which we can work together. Together we will fight or separately we will go down into oblivion."

Now the crowd cheered long and hard. Dale sat back with a smile of satisfaction on his face. It was not how he had envisioned the proceedings going but the result was what he had foreseen. He was pleased more over that others had the same passion for the mission ahead that he had. Still, he felt that there was something that Theresa had not said, a feeling of waiting for the other foot to fall.

Dale looked at the Ikornian, a question in his eyes. In his mind he felt Theresa's response. "Yes, Dale Lambert there are other things that we must discuss but that is not for public consumption. You and yours however will need to know what is to come." Just as quickly as the thought came it was gone. When Dale attempted to reestablish contact his mind faced a smooth blank wall.

Chapter Fifteen

Dale had dragged his feet securing the thousand loose ends that were always suddenly important just before a major undertaking. He and Shadow Grey were the last two officers to reach the moon base. He was leaving most of the Laurel crew to work on the developing defensive systems and the creation of the embassies which would soon have diplomats from the various worlds in residence.

Moon Glow had reminded her mate that the next time there was a call to venture forth, he was going to remain home with the pups, and she was going to gallivant around the galaxy. The pups had been quite a handful, especially Casric. Heather assured her that very shortly Tristan would be taking that young rascal in hand. Even as an infant Tristan had sufficient motor control and mental acumen to reach out and respond to his playmate's needs. She had laughed in an aside to her soul mate, "Those two are as close as peas in a pod."

Once again Dale was looking back through the void of space as the shuttle pulled away from the gravity of Brightholme and worked its way to the launch cradle located in the shipyard on the nearer moon. Once again, he felt the melancholy of leaving his family and his home behind. As the planet receded to form a perfect blue, green and brown sphere he was pointedly reminded of his last views of Luarel, before it exploded into dust and vapor.

He shook himself, like one of the troupe as if he came up out of the water, berating himself for such sad thoughts. Down below was his life, Heather, and their son Tristan. They were a part of the new home that they had made for themselves. He would be back, he thought to himself, and then he would have time to settle down and enjoy the fruits of his labors. He felt a sudden empathy for Daton Excilore and the folk that they had rescued on the Orion. They must have had similar feelings as their shuttle brought them to their ship. Just a small time away and then...

Heather's mind came into his then, "Enough of this foolishness, Dale, you're upsetting your son. Really, we will only be a thought away and you better believe that I will be checking in on you, so behave yourself." A silent kiss and caress accompanied the admonishment. He felt better at once. The folks on the Orion didn't have the capability that Dale and his people shared. It was going to be alright. He felt Heather smile.

The nearer moon swung into position and filled the observation window of the Rever ship that was used as transport. Dale shook his head. They really needed a more efficient method of going from planet surface to the moons of Brightholme. He fell into mentally designing a much smaller transport for people and small cargo loads. By the time he reached the docking station he had the basic design saved on his tablet computer. Feeling much lighter in spirit he corralled Polasic, who was operations controller for the moon base installation. He gave the Juancy officer the file stick and asked for him to get busy with the engineering and fabrication of the needed ships.

Dale walked the short length of corridor from Polasic's office to a small conference room just off the main corridor leading to the launch station. Here he called up a series of video connections and held his final briefing before taking flight. Mark Thomas, Glenda Stern and Dorothy Abrams were on one connection, while Heather, Moon Glow and Life Giver were on another. The three Jauncy Captains, Groshen, Polasic and Trembo occupied the third.

He began by describing the design for the planet to moon transport system, giving emphasis on its construction. "Once we have a suitable transport system in place, I would like for Captain Groshen to use the Rever ships to begin the development of a defensive shield for our system. He will command from Star Dancer, which will stay on post to act as backup in the event of any serious dust up."

"Trembo I would like you to act as an advanced scout, take some of those that we pulled in from the Brethren dreadnaught and scout the system. Pay particular attention to the asteroid belts and the Ort cloud. We need to give Groshen as much data as possible so that he may plan a solid defensive strategy."

He turned his attention to Mark's screen. "I have a special assignment for you three. I would like you to spend some time with Star Dancer's AI, I need to know exactly how he managed to pull off that genetic vector which aided us in our escape from Laurel. It may be that we will need to have more such "talent' in the days to come. If Peter Lamous and Life Giver could find a safer and gentler means by which to direct such development, it might be a key to our survival against the Brethren. Go slow on this, be careful in your research and confer with Heather and Moon Glow about your findings. Do nothing in haste!"

Finally, he turned to the screen that held the image of Heather and her soul mate. "I leave you two with the most difficult task of all. Keep all of these projects in motion, maintain the moral of the people and protect our Home World!" He mentally pathed in a tight line to Heather. "I love you darling. Be safe for me! I will be back just as soon as I am able."

"The last item that I would like to settle before we take off to parts unknown is the naming of our ship. It is rather cumbersome to keep describing it as the exploration vehicle." Dale chuckled under his breath. "There is an AI on board that bears a rather strong resemblance to our son Tristan, but I rather think that another name should be devised." He leaned back in his chair and smiled, "I am open to suggestions."

The remainder of expedition's compliment was waiting to greet them as Dale Lambert stepped off the platform and onto the launch pad. Theresa and Frthessig represented their two races, while Dale and Doctor Scott represented those from Laurel. Daton and Dressant had been included on the insistence of Shadow Grey and would act as representatives from the Federation. Shadow Grey and Sharp Eyes stood for the troupe. Once on board and all the preliminary checks completed Dale asked that Daton take them out of dock. The clear, overhead doors to the launch cavern opened and the sleek craft rose effortlessly into the star filled heavens.

The data banks of the Orion and the knowledge of the Ikornian people acted as a guide to the first destination of the Scout Ship Polaris, a name that was dredged up from some ancient scrap of knowledge provided by Groshen's folk. The name had a rather poetic lilt to it and Dale smiled. One of the meanings carried by the moniker was the North Star. It was a suitable omen in Dale's eyes because they were heading back up the northern axis of the galaxy and then slightly to the galactic west far beyond where they first discovered the Orion.

The Federation was a conglomerate of peoples and cultures all connected by a bourgeoning galactic trade. The wars that at times forced young civilizations back to their planets of origin or into oblivion had long since ceased within the Federation sphere of influence. War had been counterproductive, and the Trade Masters had no time for it, not that they were defenseless. The trade of a thousand worlds often brought curious and deadly weapons to light. Those deemed worthy of the fleet were incorporated into the defensive and offensive capabilities of their sleek, deadly craft.

It was the lure of trade that first opened the gates to the Brethren. Starting on the outer fringe of the Federation's sphere of influence the Brethren brought their great gleaming ships to land at local trade centers. They came, only a few at a time, and rather infrequently. The crews of those ships behaved themselves and acted in moderation whenever they were in port. They demonstrated some simple trade goods and often sold at a loss, which mystified the Trade Masters on those planets. Still, they were free enough with the specially brewed ales and wines that seemed to be their main stock in trade. Once they learned more of the Federation and its immense wealth, the Brethren began to bring in more exotic trade goods, everything from complex electronic devices to sophisticated weaponry.

Stephen Goodale   148

The Brethren emissaries were taken by the Trade Masters and introduced to the high Council on the home world, Clastrose. When pressed for more details on their own civilization, the Brethren simply claimed that they were the descendants of a long-lost civilization nearer to the galactic core. They had existed as colony worlds on the fringe of known space and have just recently begun the exploration of the galactic center in the hope of discovering their world of origin.

Theresa shook her head in sadness, "This is a story that has been repeated many times over the millennia. The Froshen were taken in by it, the crew of the Orion, and many others. Deception has always been the mainstay of their artifice. Very seldom do they ever arrive on the scene in open combat but always under the false cloak of friendship."

Frthessig continued the conversation as Theresa fell silent her dark hair cascading to hide the emotions that memories brought to her. "Very soon after the Brethren arrived at the central world of the Federation, members in key positions on the Council began to act in odd and counter intuitive ways. A pattern of misunderstanding between the Central Government and outlying provincial worlds degenerated into revolt, rebellion, and war. The Central government controlled the vast majority of the fleet so they would inevitably win but their resources and their manpower decreased steadily. In the meantime, the Brethren ships began to arrive in greater numbers and soon rumors of atrocities began to spread."

In relative short order the Central Hub of the Federation began to lose contact with their outer systems. No one in command seemed to care, another indication that by some means the people in control of the central government were in fact those that were being controlled. Now Dale Lambert and the folk from the Juancy ships and those freed from the dreadnaught have supplied some answers. Apparently, the use of the controlling chip was a favorite ploy of the Brethren to master those that they wished to control. Opening up chaos in what had been orderly societies."

Theresa picked up the tale once more. "Our operatives on Clastrose and on some of the provincial worlds were able to detect the pattern of collapse and for a few worlds," and here she turned her distraught face to Daton, "for a few worlds we were able to spirit some but not all away and plant them on the worlds of a hidden system that is completely cut off from normal space and time."

Frthessig finished the tale in a rush, "For the many thousands of years that it took to form, strengthen and celebrate a great civilization, it took the nightmare of only a few bloody years to destroy. The Federation fleet splintered and picked each other apart. The Brethren supplying each side with weapons of awesome destruction and then sat back while the Federation killed off most of the fleet and all the defensive redoubts throughout their sphere of influence. It was a simple matter then for the Brethren to move in with their planet killers and their true fleet destroying at will, raping resources, and leaving death in their wake."

Theresa finished up by saying. "This is what we can expect to find as we vector in on the fringe of what had been Federation space. The Federation home world Clastrose was saved for last by the Brethren. None escaped that annihilation. It is now a dead husk of a world orbiting a dead star. I am sorry Dale Lambert, but that is the truth. Still, we may find, on a few worlds, the remnant of Federation peoples. They would be those worlds to poor in resources and too far from the Brethren's chosen area of operation to warrant their attention. I warn you the Brethren have many eyes and ears and an expedition such as ours might be noted."

They pointed the Polaris toward a known provincial world on the southern edge of Federation space. They took care to break out several parsecs from the system. In the still blackness of space Daton Excilore took over the Captain's chair while Dale and Shadow Grey settled into the specially designed couches just behind the command chairs. Linked by their minds Dale projected them out beyond the walls of their ship moving quickly through the intervening space toward the bright sun hanging like a bright blue-white jewel against a black backdrop.

It was a small system with just seven planets and a small asteroid belt. The cold outer worlds displayed no sign of technology, no rhythm of energy that could be construed as a signal. They went past the fifth planet and worked slowly through the asteroid belt. While no energy signatures were detected there were plenty of signs that this section of the system had once seen activity. Dale's mind drifted past the hulks of several large vessels that might have once resembled the Orion. The shattered hulls had no energy, no pulse of life. They passed by several mining facilities on some of the larger asteroids that had been torn apart, by what appeared to be explosions, the craters and the ejecta showed the dramatic end of activities on those small bodies.

The fourth planet out was a dun-colored affair, all browns and greys. As Dale moved closer, he could see that the surface of this planet had once held large amounts of water, deep basins and carved river beds were evidence enough of that. On the edges of these basins were the crumbling ruins of cities. None were very big. There might have been larger centers of population but the areas where they might have been found such as the juncture of rivers and ocean basins were flattened and cratered by old destruction. Again, there were no signs of technology, no pulse of energy, just quiet decay.

Dale could feel the sadness of Shadow Grey's thoughts. "These Brethren are far worse than anything that you had experienced on Laurel. There at least the destruction was predicated on simple greed. Here", his mental eyes scanned the world below, "Here is destruction for the love of death!"

Dale agreed as he pulled his mind away from the horror below him. He was about to head on toward the third planet of the system when he felt a surge of energy emanating from the lone moon which circled the fourth world. Immediately he oriented toward that energy source. The planet's moon came up and with his senses opened wide Dale tried to focus on that force locus.

The moon had once been industrialized. Dale watched the pitted ground flow by underneath him, his senses "seeing" beneath the surface. There were miles of tunnels and chambers filled with heavy equipment, storage areas and living quarters. Shadow Grey's mind voiced the same question that was beginning to form in Dale's own mind. "Why does this complex remain intact when the planet below has been brutally assaulted? If the moon was untouched where are the people who must have once called this place home?"

Dale contented himself with cataloging the things that he saw below, his mind following one such tunnel complex and then another. Time in this bodiless state moved slower than normal, but he realized that it was still moving. He was about to pull up out of the moon's surface when he caught that energy signature once more. Quickly now he followed it to its source. The strength of that signal increased as he hit upon a broader and more complex grouping of tunnels. They all lead to a central chamber. It was a vast open space whose recesses ran to the horizon. It was there that Dale discovered the source of the signal and it was there that he found out what had happened to the people who once called this place home.

Mounted on a central dais was an alien looking device which emitted a strong radioactive energy. Below the device in rank upon rank were the crumpled bodies of the people, their faces were all turned upward and the distorted, pain wracked expressions frozen there by death indicated how their last seconds in life were spent. Dale felt the gorge rise from the pit of his soul. These people had been led here for the slaughter and then left, almost as if in warning.

Shadow Grey brought Dale's attention back to that beacon on the dais, for it no longer appeared to be passively emitting its lethal rays but instead the energy levels were spiking with such violence that Dale knew that there could only be one end.

"Back," his mind snapped to Shadow Grey. "We have been detected! This is a trap."

Dale held the focus together and propelled them back to their bodies laying on the couches in the control room of the Polaris. With crisp orders he had Daton pull the fast ship back until the star which had once given life to the system that they had been investigating was just a small pin prick of light in the velvet blackness.

That blackness did not last long, with a flare of annihilation the moon of the fourth planet was gone taking with it the planet which it circled. Such was the violence of that explosion that the sun was hit with vast energy waves until its internal reactions were accelerated to a point beyond containment and the sun too flared into a ball of massive destruction. The waves of energy then reached out beyond into the system as planets, asteroids and all bodies within that system were destroyed.

The crew of the Polaris all stood as the monitors flared in that hellish fury. Even as far out as Daton had taken them their vessel was rocked by the ever-expanding waves of energy. The shields which protected them blazed briefly but held steady. None of that deadly energy reached them. When at last the area of space in front of them settled the vast dust and debris from the system occluded and blocked some of the star light from suns beyond. Dale turned to Theresa, "That was done deliberately. It was a trap set up to catch any who ventured into that system. Are these Brethren so powerful that they can use such destructive weapons? More importantly how did they detect our mental presence?"

The Ikornian stood tall her dark hair flowing down her shoulders. "I cannot lie to you Dale Lambert. Yes, they have weapons of such destructive power. They do not use them overly much but the threat that they pose is one of the tools that are used to keep other systems in line. How they detected your mental aura, I do not know. There are rumors that those that truly rule the Brethren have great mental powers of their own. Perhaps they have incorporated the detection of such powers into their defensive mechanisms. It is a lesson for us, and I think a warning to which we must pay attention."

The system that they had been investigating had at one time been a relatively important provincial hub of the Federation's outer sphere. Its relative importance may have led to the placement of the destructive device. Now Dale and his fellow officers pored over the records from the Orion and the memories of Theresa. They sought a new destination that might not have the significance of the now nameless dust cloud beyond their screens.

It was Frthessig who suggested a method by which they could move with some assurance through the region of space that the Federation once called home. "The Federation was a conglomerate of many civilizations, that is true, but in reality, its purpose was to serve and protect the trade routes that kept the life blood of the Federation flowing." The Kalorian looked up from the comfortable seat in which he had lain, and a brief growl escaped his curled lips. "Even at its height the Federation was always at war. There has been and always will be people, worlds and even whole systems dedicated to the art, shall we say, of liberating riches from the elite! These space lane pirates were known, and they held sway over sections of space that the Federation did not care to tame."

Daton Excilore interrupted Frthessig, "I know of what you speak, and these space rats are no more pleasant to deal with than the Brethren. Albeit they have less sophisticated technology, they make up for it in sheer ruthlessness. We would do well to steer clear of any areas of space under their influence."

"True Captain, but that is not where I was going. While Daton is quite correct, we do not want to become involved with these pirates there is another solution. You see even if they are powerful and ruthless, they too have need of trade. In the days before the fall of the Federation they traded on fringe worlds with little value other than they acted as a clandestine pipeline of goods to the less upright members of the Federation and the hated pirates which the officials of all Federations worlds detested. It was a black market if you will. These areas of space were treated by both sides of the conflict as free trade zones and as unofficial embassies where exchanges of prisoners and goods could be arranged."

"Even under the Brethren this illicit trade has continued, for those worlds under the Brethren's sway fair very poorly indeed. Whatever else the Brethren are they enjoy the best of what the galaxy affords leaving the gleanings to fall to the worlds that they subjugate. These crumbs form the basis of the new black-market trade. It is to these unofficial trade centers that we must now go. From these we may pick up valuable information that obviously may be too dangerous to attempt to gain in any other fashion. It is on these worlds that we might also be able to connect with any underground rebellions that might be brewing against the Brethren."

Chapter Sixteen

The chamber was dark. It suited the thoughtful figure who sat alone in the spartan setting. Unlike most of those on the Council, Grimholdt preferred things uncluttered, it helped him think. He had quite a lot to think about these days. The Brethren rule over which he and those on the Triune, held complete control was in some small measure being tested. He had lived a long life and had been granted the cloning many times throughout the ages. He had seen many things and taken part in some glorious conquests, yet he could feel a change in the rhythm of the universe.

There was an upwelling of forces that were beginning to peck away at the order which the Brethren had imposed over the millennia. First that ridiculous decision by their agents on Laurel. This had been a world that had been carefully crafted, for a specific purpose. Those in real power had tried to suppress a small band of humans on the outer fringe of their society. This in turn had led to the loss of the planet.

It had been the experimental research station through which the ambiguous mind chips had been developed. Not, he thought to himself, that others had not improved on the original but the fact that such a perfectly controlled lab setting had been lost with its destruction irritated him.

Then the loss of one of their best operatives on that far off planet, Earth. Yes, it was called Earth. The man had been creating confusion and weakness on that planet for years and to good effect. Many in the major governments there had been installed with the chips and it had only been a matter of time before it fell into the Brethren's control. The reports had been positive and then nothing. What made it all the worse is that in the last few reports there were hidden coded messages for Grimholdt himself. These had mentioned the Dragons!

That had given him pause, he had thought that the Dragons and their riders had been either destroyed or banished to alternate universes where they certainly would have no effect on the galaxy that they had left behind. The Dragons would have ample reason to cause the Brethren problems.

Then came that poorly handled affair in the Freshden system. Hymical had used his mind tricks in suppressing his defeat against the Empire ship and was allowed by vote of Council to command that ill-fated punitive expedition. Yes, the Freshden people had been wiped out and yes, their system was now dust but the loss of so many ships and planet killers did not sit well with the Council. And where was Hymical? His life force still existed somewhere. The cloning station in charge of his line of clones had not reported an activation so he must still exist in corporal form, but where? Grimholdt could not reach the man's mind, as he knew that he should be able to, for no man's mind on the Council was hidden from him.

Now he contemplated the recent deplorable handling of the incident in that far off mining sector. The ship, the Orion had been laid waste and its crew dealt with as was the protocol before the Brethren mining vessel had stripped the world that the Orion had orbited, of its vast mineral wealth. The location of the derelict had been noted and because, again as protocol demanded, the Brethren crew had disabled the ship from within it had been scheduled for salvage. Three Rever craft had been dispatched to perform that simple task. The Juancy crew, the janitors of the space ways, Grimholdt had allowed a smile to touch his lips, had failed to maintain contact with the border base to which they were assigned. That dolt Krylon had been dispatched from his punishment post to investigate only to turn up at a relay station weeks later babbling about a new force in that sector of the galaxy. Well, Grimholdt himself had stripped the man's mind of data and had analyzed the patterns. A new name had appeared, Dale Lambert and the rumor of an old and haunted name the Ikorn Witches.

It was this combination of weighty thoughts that filtered through Grimhodlt's mind. He was looking for patterns and yet had found none. But forces long dormant, the Dragons, the Witches and the Federation had risen once more to the surface of thought and not by chance. With a wave of his hand a star map appeared in the center of the chamber. With concentrated thought bright points of light appeared at the location of each of these problem areas. There was no immediate correlation and Gromholdt knew that the matter would require much more thought.

It was then that he felt the familiar temblor of his personal aid as the creature waited outside of the portal to Grimholdt's sanctum. With an impatient snap of his voice, he commanded the servant to enter. In a ubiquitous manner, that well suited the man's position, he crawled into the chamber on his knees his hands up raised in supplication. He waited for the command to speak, for no one ever did anything unless commanded to. Grimholdt sent a beam of though at the man and watched him writhe in agony. When the man had reached the critical point, Grimholdt relented. With a waspish snap he verbally commanded the man to speak.

After a few seconds the man regained control of his bodily functions enough to spurt out the message that he had been enjoined to send. "Master, I am sorry to disturb you in your thoughts, but I was told to deliver this message under no uncertain terms." With a caustic nod from Grimholdt the man continued. "One of our system traps has been triggered in what was Federation space. It had detected an unknown mental anomaly and had preformed it's self destruct sequence. The system is destroyed. There is no further information available. A squadron was dispatched to the location, but nothing was found."

Federation space again thought Grimholdt, as he waved the relieved messenger away from him, and traces of mental energy. He smiled to himself, grimly. I bet that that Dale Lambert had a rather rude shock about that! The Federation man had played fast and loose on that Dreadnaught, but that had been a fringe system ship and was not due for an overhaul to its defensive core for some time.

What had been that Councilor's name, Krylon. Grimholdt made a mental note to send a message to the cloning station to reanimate the next clone in his line. After all he had tried to warn the Brethren of a possible threat. For now, though, it would behoove the Brethren's cause to begin deployment of a small fleet toward the area of Federation space that had sent up the alarm.

Pleased for the moment that action was being taken, Grimholdt settled back into his contemplations, after all it was soon time for dinner. He wondered which of his choice feeding slaves would be on the menu.

Scott and Nancy ran toward the grey bulk of their transport. With thoughts flying ahead of him, Scott knew that the ship would be ready for emergency lift off as soon as they hit the ramp. The sound of shouts reached their ears as the angry mob of disappointed slavers raced after them still hoping to capture them for their insidious trade. They had been directed to this backward world by an apparently sincere contact that they had made at their last port of call.

They had a half full hold of trade goods picked up on some six worlds, and they were told that they could make a handsome profit at this benighted planet. He should have known, it didn't even have a space port, just some burned out acres where other ships had landed. Well, that would stand them in good stead now. There would be no pursuit once they launched.

Puffs of dust pocked the areas just behind them and Scott knew that the slavers would rather kill them then let them go. With a brief mental entreaty, he called in Tremolic from his cloaked position overhead. With a scream of defiance, the small dragon flew directly at the pursuing slavers and with one of his startling shrieks stopped them in their tracks holding their hands to their ears and leaving them rolling around on the grimy, dust covered, dirt tract leading to the landing apron. The dragon peeled back and took a guardian position over the fleeing pair as they finally reached the extended ramp.

The ship's AI had already translated Scott's mental orders into action and as Nancy and then Scott reached the safety of the ramp, it began to lift the ship from the compacted dirt of the landing field. Tremolic darted on ahead and assumed his post at the ship's sensor arrays on the command deck. The ramp closed behind them as Scott gathered Nancy into his arms, there was a hysterical look of shock on both their faces and then they both broke out into gales of laughter. Tremolic's mind broadcast to both of them. "If you two laughing idiots would get your butts up to command, we have incoming company, and they don't look friendly!"

Scott cursed under his breath. He had hoped that there would be no pursuit. When he threw himself into the Captain's chair, he realized that he was partly correct, there was no sign of activity on the ground but out in low orbit a sinister looking vessel was vectoring in on an intercept course. The autonomous command assistant RJ-3.2, better known as simply RJ spoke through the ship's speakers. "We had better be prepared to escape using the Tremolic Highway. I don't think that I can outmaneuver these guys enough to get us to where we can jump into hyperspace." RJ paused for a second and then continued, "Captain they are deploying some nasty looking weapons. We need to go, now!"

With a last look at the screens Scott sent his coordinates to Tremolic, who muttered under his breath that Scott would owe him one. Suddenly the screens all went dark, as a purple haze filled them in a coiling sickly swirl of color and motion. Scott counted under his breath and at the count of ten asked to Tremolic to pull them back into normal space.

The freighter shuddered and was still. The screens lit but only showed the emptiness of deep space. A quick glance at the read outs and Scott was on his feet, Nancy just a second behind him. They raced to where Tremolic had fallen from his perch at the sensor arrays. The little dragon's eyes were closed but Scott could see the steady rise and fall of his chest. The Highway always exhausted his friend and as a result they only used it in emergencies. Their escape from the slavers had called on his friend's reserve energies and it would be quite some time before he regained his normal vitality. With loving care, he scooped the still form up and took him to their quarters.

RJ hummed and went at once to work to discover just where in the galaxy his Captain had deposited them this time. When Scott returned some time latter the ship's AI had calculated their position and was anxious to query the Captain on his logic or perhaps madness would have been a better term, of bringing them into what had once been Federation space.

Scott smiled to himself as he listened to the querulous report from RJ. This give and take had developed over the last year as he and Nancy had made their way out to the galactic fringe and then from one forgotten trading planet to another. They had for the most part worked very well together as a team, but all on board knew that when it came to the final decision it was his call. Even Nancy, the love of his life, while certainly enjoying the occasional dig at her Captain, trusted his command capability.

They had come out here with the express purpose of generating enough wealth to outfit their vessel and to make their way back to Earth where they would be married. After that, who knew? Space was vast and they both loved to explore. Tremolic, his Dragon, while quite capable of spending time planet bound was at home in space. His unique ability to warp space and to always know where in the galaxy he was had on occasion saved their bacon. It was a difficult gift to manage because it always wore the little dragon out. Scott preferred to be more reliant on his own developing mental abilities and the knack that Nancy had shown of getting the best deal possible for the trade goods that they carried. Still, it was always good to have Tremolic on their side.

For now, he was grateful that Tremolic had been able to "pick out" the next destination that he had in mind and hurl them to the coordinates he had envisioned. The area that had once been Federation space had been the center of one of the galaxy's richest trade empires. While he knew that the Brethren had long since conquered the Federation, laying waste to most of its core systems and striping what they wanted from those that remained, he still felt in "his bones' that this was where he and his little command should be.

He brought his mind back to the here and now as Nancy slid into the co-pilot's seat and reached out a hand to take his. He was always amazed that he had won this wonderful person's heart. He who had been near death due to a muscular disease, who had been younger and who had no hope of life, had been saved from that fate by his best friend Sam and had been delivered into full health by the dedication of the robotic workers on Scalar.

He had always loved Nancy, since the first time they met on Earth and she, miracles of miracles had returned that love. For the past year they had traveled the space lanes of the outer fringes of the galaxy. They had taken their time, ensuring that this was the life that both had wanted. The trust that working together every day built up between them as friends and lovers was very strong.

They had not consummated their love preferring instead to wait until they brought their ship into Terran space and landed on Earth, there to be surrounded by family at the time of their formal union. Scott knew that he was running out of resistance to Nancy's charms, and he was pretty sure that she had felt the same way about him. They were running out of time if they wanted to keep to their plans.

His need for haste partly explained the abortive attempt to trade on the outpost of the slavers. He had been hoping for a large score and then home! He of course did not know that world was a slave planet, but that ignorance was a sign that he had messed up, letting his feelings get ahead of his mind.

The little freighter had undergone a considerable number of upgrades since they first signed on board. RJ had been brilliant in designing and implementing offensive and defensive capability within the framework of the ship. To outside appearances it would look like a lightly armed and armored freighter, but this freighter had some nasty surprises built into it now. Surprises that would give anyone pause before they attempted to tangle with them twice.

The area around them was deserted, the nearest stars comfortably far away. Scott had "picked" out the location from one of the contacts that they had made on a fringe world. This was a spot used often by independent traders, who preferred the freedom of deep space to transfer cargos and hold clandestine meetings.

This gap in the old Federation was one that he had studied and planned to visit for the last six months. It was to be the final jumping point for them to the Terran system. Now he would have to regroup and talk things over with Nancy and with Tremolic. He certainly did not wish to risk their hides again. It was time to go home.

Turning to Nancy he smiled. "I think that the time has come my love, to get on back home and find us a minister. It's time for you to make an honest man out of me!" Nancy, who had turned to give him an answer, felt her return smile freeze on her face. The loving rejoinder dying on her lips as she gazed at the ship's screens.

The voice of RJ overrode anything that she might have had to say. "Captain I suggest that you turn your attention to the company that's coming into our area of space. It looks like you are in for quite a party."

Tremolic's voice came into Scott's mind. "Don't look at me. I am too wiped to get to the dinner table much less hop us out of here. This one is on you, my friend."

"RJ it's time to see if that expensive cloaking device was worth the effort that it took to install it. Cloak us and turn down all power outputs to the bare minimum. Let's see what we have before we get into a panic!"

Scott, looking through the screens, could identify at least three different classes and configurations of ships. They seemed to be vectoring in from three different directions of space, almost Scott thought to himself as if they were coming to attend a meeting.

"Open a channel RJ and let's find out who our guests are, shall we?" Dutifully RJ opened the ship-to-ship communications array. The small crew of the freighter covered their ears as a howl of unmistakable outrage burst through the ether of space. RJ dialed in the universal translator and Scott sat back further in his chair. "What is this?" growled an indignant voice. "We are here to do a deal with you Drevichens. No mention was made of a third party."

A smooth calm voice came through the speakers "Relax, Lowen, you know how this works. The Rastforns have just as much right to the Fridelian crystals as you do, more in fact, if they are willing to pay me more!"

The first voice growled out a curse, fortunately not in the translator's data bank. "You fresquellen rat bull, this was a negotiated deal, months in the making. You have no right to go back on our arrangement now."

Another high-pitched voice intruded itself on the conversation. "Lowen, you slime, you know that we have been trying to get our hands on those crystals for years now. My people need them to power the shield that keeps our world from being engulfed by our sun. Without them our world dies."

"That maybe so Hutzel, but those crystals are valuable. In the right market they are almost priceless. You will have had your chance to bid on them just like everyone else. If your money is any good that is."

Scott smiled over at his love, fresquellen rat bull, huh. He would have to remember that rather colorful epitaph. It was interesting that this three-cornered conversation involved Fridellian crystals. He knew that they were extremely difficult to find and even harder to obtain, but down in his hold he had three cases of those crystals, which he won from a rather young noble as fair wages earned by his ship's ability to traverse a rather nasty section of space near the far western fringe of the galaxy.

The noble, it seemed had a rather pressing engagement that he needed to be at. It involved the fortunes of more than one planet. The young man had heard of the freighter whose reputation had grown by making difficult deliveries and passages. He not only bet his own life but the three cases of crystals.

Now Scott settled back to listen to the communications between the three ships facing his cloaked craft. The smooth voice who had not yet identified himself continued the conversation. "Okay gentlemen let's get down to negotiating. I have four chests, each 2 meters in length, 2 meters wide and 3 meters deep filled with these crystals, all top grade. I will open the bidding at 4,000 credits minimum. The howl of outrage continued from Lowen's ship, but Hutzel calmly placed the required bid. Lowen countered with 4,500 credits.

Scott just smiled. The numbers that were being thrown around out in space were far beyond all the credits that he and his crew had earned in the past year. No matter how this went he would be able to supply the loser with a fair asking price that was certain to be below what the final bid would be.

The ether began to crackle as the three-way bidding war continued. When at last silence fell and the Lowen voice growled in disappointed victory. The loser was about to withdraw, bitter that he had failed in his efforts to obtain the very thing that his world needed to survive. Scott noticed that the ship belonging to the unnamed trader had moved in closer to the Lowen's ship, to enable the transfer of the crystals. The other craft had moved off to one side and Scott could see that a haze had formed around its exterior.

"Captain" came the voice of RJ, "I think that the disappointed loser is about to try and engage the two other ships. I have scanned the weapons arrays and the defensive shields of all three ships, and they will not have a chance to survive. Scott responded, "Open a channel to all three ships."

"Gentlemen, having listened in on your conversation and noting the topic of your trade, I suggest that all parties here remain calm. This is the free trader Valor. We would like to help out the folks lead by Hutzel. The two other vessels please continue your affairs. We will not interfere.

Hutzel, please stand down. We can help you if you would like. Please withdraw from the others and we can negotiate terms."

There was a startled response from all three ships. The Hutzel ship moved away from the other two vessels in compliance to Scott's request. The unnamed voice came smoothly once again from the speakers, a hint of cold menace emanating from the depth of space. "Free Trader Valor, stand down and withdraw from this section of space. This is my deal and I have concluded it to my satisfaction. Do not attempt to interfere."

Scott realized that the implied threat was sincere, but that did not deter him in the least. He had confidence in his vessel and its hidden resources. Mentally he checked in with Tremolic and received a rather grumpy reply that he had recovered enough to provide a short emergency jump, if needed.

"This is Captain Scott Green, who do I have the pleasure of addressing?" He waited calmly for a response. The silence that fell was space deep and the response slow in coming. "I am not in the habit of identifying myself to a stranger in an area of space not known to many. If you are a Brethren agent, then know this you will not have the opportunity to leave here alive. If you are the independent trader that you claim to be then I will offer you one chance, withdraw and never return to this area of space.'

Scott signaled to Nancy to power up the ship. "I am afraid that I don't accept either of your suggestions. I will however offer you a third possibility. You let me do an honest trade with Hutzel and I will withdraw from here. I am no agent of the Brethren be assured of that, but I will not be bullied by an unnamed space trader."

The response from the alien ship was to fire a passing shot vaguely in the direction that the Valor stood, space bloomed with an angry red explosion. The cloaking device was working well so the ship was in no danger from attack. The Lowen ship apparently satisfied with its cargo detached itself from the other vessel and was about to withdraw. Just then alarms went off on all four vessels. RJ's voice came in crisp measured tones. "Captain the space around us is being disrupted by twelve space folds. I am afraid that we have company of the most unsavory sort, the Brethren have arrived."

Before the Lowen vessel could engage its jump engines a brilliant lance of green flame pierced its engine nacelles, and the ship went dark. The other trader had engaged it's shielding and was deflecting volley after volley of targeted fire. The Hutzel vessel just stood down and emitted a surrender message.

Scott did not panic. His cloaked ship had not yet drawn fire. This attack seemed centered more on the unnamed trader's vessel than on anything else. Scott began to wonder if that vessel had not been the primary target of this quite apparent trap. The trader's ship was putting up quite a fight, its full array of weapons flashed and flared out at the twelve ships that now surrounded it.

Scott's ship was now outside of that containment, and he was free to withdraw if he wished but something held him back from doing that. Instead, he studied the Brethren ships and determined that they were fighting in a methodical almost mechanical way. He was about to order the ship to engage when a strong mental voice filled the command deck. "Scott Green, do not engage just yet. We will arrive on station in just a few minutes and between us we will take care of this minor interruption to the peace of the Federation."

Dale Lambert had ordered his ship to maintain station as he gathered his crew together to decide on their next step. It was the consensus of the officers that they try to investigate some of the lesser-known worlds that resided on the fringes of the old Federation's sphere of influence.

They had laid out a course that took them through some of the more open areas of space and had just gone into hyperspace when the AI notified them that it had detected twelve disturbances in the ether. These signatures corresponded to known Brethren energy patterns. The tracks ran parallel to their present course but did not seem to have anything to do with them. They were just headed to the same sector of space that they were."

Dale cursed under his breath, foul luck, he thought. But then he paused to consider the opportunity. He asked Shadow Grey to join him at the command deck and once again put Daton Excilore in charge of the ship. Together he and Shadow Grey joined minds. Their mental probe was swifter than even the flow of hyper space and the pair soon overtook the lead vessel in the Brethren's squadron. Much to their surprise there were very few biologics on board and only one true Brethren. Most of the vessel's functions seemed to be robotic in nature responding to programmed patterns that could vary at the command of the Brethren Leader but were followed for the most part by the autonomous ships.

Dale moved his mental aura towards the Brethren and was surprised to learn that this ship and the force that he led had been charged with investigating the recent disturbances caused by the system explosion of the old Federation provincial world. Dale was equally surprised to find that his name and the identification of the Witches of Ikorn were featured in the orders that this Brethren commander had received.

The Brethren's mind was seething at this temporary disruption of that mission. He had been sent to proceed to a set coordinate within old Federation space. This current mission had nothing to do with his primary objective, but some bureaucratic imbecile had taken the presence of the squadron as an opportunity to try and capture a notorious pirate that operated in these space lanes. It had pinpoint intelligence that indicated that there was to be a trade meeting in old Federation space at a known Trader meeting place among the stars. It was here that they were going. A fool's mission, but it had been approved and so they went.

Dale withdrew his mind and then cast out ahead of the ship much like a dolphin would have ridden the bow waves of a sea going ship in one of Earth's oceans. He smiled to himself. His study of Earth had caused some interesting analogies to be floating around in his mind. Shadow Grey's mental growl brought him to the here and now. The squadron was breaking out into space. Ahead Dale saw the three traders as they moved about and then he caught the energy signature of a shielded ship. Curiously he projected his mind into that vessel and was stunned to detect the minds of Scott Green and Nancy Peterson.

Scott looked over to Nancy and shrugged. The mental flavor of the mind that had contacted his was friendly and helpful. He was content to wait. The energies from the twelve Brethren ships had coalesced around the lone Trader vessel and the shields on that ship were beginning to flare. Scott ordered a channel opened to that other vessel. "Trader with no name, we are about to join you in your battle, and we will not be alone. Hold out as best you can for another few seconds, we are on our way.'

Scott then ordered the main guns up through the innocent looking freighter's hull and the teeth that they had spent so many credits on were displayed at last. The Valor swung around and came up behind the last of the Brethren's ships in the formation attacking the Trader. Just as he ordered the main guns to fire another sleek looking craft swooped in beside his and opened fire on the adjoining vessel. Two Brethren ships flared into molten space debris and two more were under the cast of those deadly beams before the balance of the Brethren fleet realized that they were under attack.

Four Brethren ships broke away from the attack on the trader and swung back to aid their fellow vessels. Those two however were now beyond help as they to flared into ragged chunks of debris. The two rescuing ships now came under fire, but their shields were tough and held easily. Their offensive beams focused on two of the four remaining Brethren ships attacking the Trader, almost contemptuously ignoring those that were firing upon them. Two more enemy ships flared into death.

The Trader that had been taking such fire now began to switch to offense and fired upon the lead ship of the Brethren fleet. That vessel soon began to lose its shielding and those ships that had been attacking the rescuers peeled back to help the Brethren who commanded them.

This was a mistake because while the robotic ships were programmed to respond to the mental commands of the Brethren Leader the confusion and anger in that man's mind clouded his judgment and caused the ships in his squadron to become sporadic in their efforts to fight their adversaries.

The end came quickly as the Trader ship Hutzel commanded now entered the fray. It was lightly armed but with so much fire power coming from different directions and the odd behavior of their squadron commander the Brethren ships were soon destroyed. All that remained was the lead ship and while that vessel was of different metal than the others, it too showed signs of failure. Dale Lambert reached out with his mind and commanded the other combatants to cease fire. The Brethren ship was now disabled and helpless. Dale used the opportunity to move down with Shadow Grey in link to "talk" with the squadron commander.

The command deck was filled with smoke and the few biologic crew members present were slumped over their duty stations, almost as if the force that had animated them in life had been withdrawn from them. The Brethren commander stood gazing out into the debris filled area of space, disbelief mirrored in his eyes. He knew the full measure of failure in Brethren society. He was a dead man. It did not matter if his death was here and now or if he managed to get back to a Brethren outpost where he would be summarily executed.

Dale's mind reached out and touched the man's mind. Apart from a slight start the man betrayed no surprise. "I am Dale Lambert. The Federation is under my protection. The Brethren are no longer welcomed here. You are to take the emergency lifeboat from this vessel and proceed to the nearest Brethren post outside of old Federation space. If I were you, I would not try to reach any in the Federation space because shortly they will not be there."

The Brethren commander turned to face the formless mind and spoke candidly. "I was ordered to watch for you Fleet Commander Lambert. Although I admit that I did not expect for you to exist. The Brethren Triune has been made aware of your presence. Krylon was examined by the Triune before he was terminated for failing to kill you. Failure is not tolerated by the Tribune and is always met with death. I, who was squadron leader Rewil, say to you now that it is time for you to perish along with the rest of this ragtag that is assembled here with you." A feral gleam crossed the Brethren's face as he pushed a button on the controller that he held in his hand.

At once the Brethren ship erupted into a mass of energy that reached out toward the remaining ships. Scott did not even have time to flinch much less react to the impending doom, but as he reached out for Nancy's hand another soothing voice filled his mind. "Do not be concerned young Scott Green. A veil of purple light encompassed all the ships except for that of the now destroyed Brethren vessel. In that veil of purple darkness, a voice soft and clear sang in the minds of all on board.

The effect only lasted a few seconds but, in that time, all five vessels had been transported back to the Brightholme system. Dale smiled. He had been in constant communication with Theresa as they had fought the Brethren. He suspected from the hints, that his presence was a known quantity. While Rewil had spoken his last he had been reading the man's thoughts and was prepared for the next course of action. While Theresa reassured him that bringing the vessels back to Brightholme was the proper decision he could only hope that he was not exposing his new home world to more of a threat.

"Do not worry, Dale Lambert. Consider this an opportunity to expand your influence and to gain new and powerful allies in the direction of Federation space." Theresa smiled in Dale's mind, "You and your family will need them. This is not a war to be won in small battles but a protracted affair that will determine the fate of this galaxy and perhaps those beyond. You are only at the doorstep Dale Lambert, you and your children will be stepping over that barrier and then who knows?" Dale felt her mind withdraw from his, and he sighed. How was he going to explain all this to Heather?"

Chapter Seventeen

Scott sighed as he realized that he and his ship were no longer in Federation space. The beautiful green, blue and brown planet beneath them resembled the images of earth as seen from orbit. Yet there were many differences, so this was not Earth. That purple cloud that suddenly had surrounded his ship, which frankly had saved them from the destructive power unleashed by Rewil, had removed them from one sector of the galaxy to another. The communications link which he had opened in the effort to voice his support of the unknown Trader now crackled back into life. "What have you done, where are we now?"

The voice that had been so calm and self assured now was tight and brittle. On the ship's monitors a huge ship appeared as if becoming uncloaked and assumed a guardian position over all five smaller vessels. The voice, gasped. That is a Federation starship! That's impossible they were all destroyed in the sectarian wars that tore the Federation apart."

Silence returned briefly until Hutzel's voice could be heard thin and stretched as always. "Captain Scott, you had mentioned a shipment of Fridellian crystals that might be purchased for a price. I was not using the situation on our home world as a negotiation ploy. We really do need them to sustain our planetary shield."

The voices raised from the three other ships were immediately dimmed by the mental broadcast of Dale Lambert. "You will all be our guests for the next few days. We will sort all of this out and get you back on your way as soon as possible. In the meantime, I would like you to enjoy our hospitality. Welcome to Brightholme."

The crew from the moon base had not been idle in Dale's absence and several small transport vehicles approached to off load the crews of the Traders ships. There was some argument when it became clear that Dale Lambert expected all the crews to take shore leave. In the end, with his mental assurance that nothing would be disturbed and that the ships would remain as they were with the exception of Lowen's craft which Dale Lambert assigned several work crews to repair. The four captains capitulated to his request.

In a quiet aside, Dale pathed to Mark Thomas and Glenda Stern, "Please take a swing through each of the craft on some pretense or another. I would like to find out exactly what type of technologies we are dealing with. Be certain to trace any suspicious circuits he added. Remember the Juancy vessels? Check for similar technologies. I want it disabled, if found, in a way that will not make our guests suspicious of our interference."

"Doctor Scott", Dale's gentle probe reached the medical man as he was examining some of the Lowen crew who were injured in the battle. "I need you to keep a watch out for any of those controlling chips that the Brethren are fond of using on their, ah, workers. Let me know if you find any and disable them as soon as you do. Take the person into medical custody under whatever pretense you like and hold them until we figure out what to do with them."

Dale Lambert's mind spoke privately to Scott Green and Nancy Peterson. "I would like you to have dinner with my wife and I this evening. I have several personal messages for you from your folks back on Earth that I would like to give to you in private."

When the shuttle craft were all on their way to the planet's surface, Theresa spoke to Dale and Shadow Grey. "The Lowen and the Hutzel I understand and can in some ways predict but this other, what did Scott Green call him, the Trader with no name, I cannot fathom. There is a mental shield about the man as tight as any that an Ikornian mage could put into place. The weaponry onboard his ship is almost superior to ours. I will take Frthessig with me to the honors dinner and I will speak with this man of mystery."

Home World

The shuttle craft landed on a specially prepared field. When Dale stepped out of the Polaris, he was shocked to realize just how much his small world had grown. There were other landing craft docked and being cared for. Each carried the flag of one of the emissary's Dale or Daton had approached in their effort to obtain allies. Heather and Tristen stood on the landing apron waiting to greet him.

In a shaken voice, Dale reached out to his beautiful wife Heather and their amazing son Tristan, who had already begun to walk. "Was I only gone for a few months, or has it been years?" He gathered both up into his arms and felt the love radiate from them. It was love and amusement in Heather's case and just plain unmitigated love from Tristen.

"Dale you should know by now that when you leave me in charge of things, well things get done. Isn't that right son?" Tristen did not answer with spoken words, but his mental broadcast was strong and confident, "Yes mother, it serves father right for staying away so long!"

Dale's shock was apparent. "It should not surprise you my friend," came the soft voice of Shadow Grey, "He is after all the product of two very powerful minds." Just then a flurry of fur and tail erupted onto the field, followed by Moon Glow at a much more dignified pace. The pup dashed up to his dignified father and jumped at him, paws flailing, licking him excitedly before backing away and running to stand beside young Tristan. Casric's brother and sisters approached at much more graceful pace each greeting their father with respect. Moon Glow gave a short bark of laughter and then greeted her mate as enthusiastically as her pup had moments earlier.

Heather stepped up to Dale and before he knew it, he was involved in a very satisfying physical reminder of just how much he had missed her. Happy and blushing the group walked on towards the waiting ground vehicle. After a flurry of tails and bodies they all managed to sort themselves out and closed the transport's door behind them.

That afternoon was spent in family bonding. Dale's house was as much Shadow Grey's as the troupe leader's private acres had been Dale's. When at last all had been caught up, Dale was more astonished than ever by the competency of Heather and Moon Glow. The New capital city had grown exponentially in just months. There was a Diplomatic Quarter in which many new buildings, some of odd design had been placed. There was a new Trade Quarter to satisfy the needs of so many from off world. In keeping with the will of the colonists the planet had been kept in mind, new parks and water resources had been developed. All the manufacturing components had been fabricated on the nearby moons and shipped down to the planet surface as needed.

Dale was pleased to learn that all the crew members taken from the Dreadnaught under Krylon's command had been accepted into the heterogeneous mix of races and talents that now occupied Brightholme. They had made it through the re-education process after their chips had been removed. Nothing was hidden from them, and they all viewed the comprehensive record tapes of the events from first contact with the ship through their reanimation on Brightholme. There were some that were quite visibly upset about what they had been forced to do in the service of the Brethren, others were more distraught over the fates of the families and the worlds that they had left behind.

Dale determined that Daton Excilore was not so alone in his need to discover the truth about their home worlds' final dispositions. He could see that most of those that had left families behind would need that proof before they could move on. He filed the thought away as he felt Mark Thomas' mind contacting his. "Dale, I think that we have a problem, well actually several problems. I was unable to access any of that unnamed Trader's vessel. It is locked and shielded with some very complex and dynamic harmonics which keeps any thought probes out. The Drevichens, which I gather from conversations from the other parties involved, is the name of that particular species. It is not a formal name of an individual person, and they remain a mystery. There were only five of them on board the ship."

Dale raised a doubt in his mind which Mark quickly caught. "Oh, I made sure of that before the leader locked it up tight as a drum. So, unless Theresa is having any better luck with them then Glenda and I have had we had better be prepared for just about anything from that quarter.

"The Hutzel, which is the name, by the way of the one trader, had absolutely nothing to hide. We were able to scan their entire data system and they are who they claim that they are, a trade mission whose sole purpose was to identify a source of Fridellian crystals and to negotiate the purchase of those crystals if possible. Their abortive attack on the other two trade vessels was one of desperation. One that would have ended in their destruction, but that fate seemed better to them than watching their home world burn."

Mark paused in his thoughts. Dale could feel the pressure of presentiment as he waited. From the comments made by Rewil he had suspected that someone within that desolate meeting between the stars had "tipped off" the Brethren and had anticipated the trap. His money lay on the Lowen's craft, so easily disabled at the beginning of the attack. It gave them an easy excuse to remain passively on the sidelines while that deadly battle roared around them.

"The Lowen are not who they claim to be," Mark's mental thoughts continued. "Their ship was riddled with Brethren technology and while Glenda and I have done our best to remove most of the devices, they are very sophisticated, and we may not have gotten all of them."

Just then Doctor Scott's mental alarm rang through all their minds. "Dale the Lowen have attacked the medical building. We discovered the mind control devices on all but their leaders who seemed to be working independently of that control but completely in concert with it. Their mission was to capture the leader of the Drevichens, who by the way is not an independent trader but is a well-known Pirate Lord. He is on the Brethren's most wanted list along with you I might add."

Dale responded immediately. "Mark send that ship into the sun, follow it and be sure that it is totally destroyed. Doctor Scott where are the Lowen now?"

"We have all, but their three officers confined by force fields to the testing labs. I am flooding the area with a gas that will render them unconscious. We will then remove their control devices and place them into cryotubes until we can decide what to do with them."

Satisfied for the moment Dale asked the Doctor. "Have the officers had a chance to communicate with the rest of the crew?" When the Doctor replied that he did not think so Dale quickly laid out his plans with Heather, Shadow Grey, and Moon Glow. With a mental alert, he notified the rest of his command including Theresa of his plans.

Dale looked around him. This was the first test that the new colony faced, and it must be done decisively. "Moon Glow, please remain here with the kids and keep up with us through mental contact. Heather, I think that we are going to need your unique talent to dissuade our guests from leaving. I want you to pay particular attention to that Drevichen pirate lord. He may prove more difficult than the Lowen to contain. With a final mental broadcast, he put out a warning to all the troupe, the Juancy leaders and the crews of the Orion and Star Dancer to be on their toes. He did not want any mistakes made. No thought of failure could be entertained. This was too important to be messed up.

With that Dale stood and straightened his clothes, gave his son an affectionate pat on the head as he sat in the living room playing with Casric. Opening the door, he stood aside to let Heather and Shadow Grey by. Together the leaders of the new Federation marched toward the town square and the celebration of the new arrivals.

Home World

The town center was alight with lights and music. The smell of roasting meats and cooking vegetables were rife in the air. As they moved toward the circle, Dale noted the clandestine movement of the troupe as they encircled the square. There was movement of men and women in pairs or small groups ingathering as would be expected but Dale could sense their tension and purpose. This was their new home they were not about to lose it to anyone.

Dale paused at the edge of the firelight and squeezed Heather's hand. Immediately Heather "disappeared" shifting light, scents and sounds so that all bent around her. Dale could sense her but that was all. As he and Shadow Grey marched into the light of the central fire a great cheer went up as all the colony's mixed races welcomed them home. With growls and greetings, they acknowledge those nearest to them and walked toward the dais where the officers from the four ships sat at a long table with Theresa the Ikorn Witch seated at the center. Frthessig sat at ease on her shoulders, barely noticeable, hidden by her long dark hair. She smiled as she watched the progress of the two leaders. It was good to see a people react so warmly to those that helped to govern them.

As they stepped up to the front of the table, Dale bowed gracefully to his guests. "Welcome all to the celebration of victory over the Brethren squadron. While we did not seek the battle, we certainly could not stand by and watch as four peaceful traders were attacked without cause or provocation."

"We here have all suffered from the depredations of the Brethren. While we know very little about them yet, we have all felt their tyrannical actions, losing family, friends and even worlds to them. Our band of free peoples has gathered to develop the structure that will allow us to rid the galaxy of this scourge. I applaud you all."

"The danger posed by the Brethren comes in many levels. Their past methods consisted of infiltrating and twisting peaceful societies from within, weakening them. This has worked many times for them in the past."

"They have been able to capture or subdue people and using their cursed technology, force them to conform to their wishes, creating an effective workforce, hands and feet for them. This is rather new to their pantheon of methods and has worked effectively up until now."

Dale paused and addressed those on the dais table directly. "I thank you for your valiant efforts my friends. The Valor Captained by Scott Green and Nancy Peterson I know although they do not yet know me. He faced the two on the end and beckoned them to join him on the dais steps. They moved to his side, and he presented them to the crowd. "These young people hail from Earth a planet with which we will be negotiating a mutual defense treaty." Mentally he added, "Walk away into the crowd as if you were accepting their applause and greetings. It is going to get very dangerous up here very shortly and your parents would never forgive me if I got you killed."

The two walked into the crowd gathering handshakes and pats on the back as they went. Dale turned back to the Dais as if this was a normal part of the celebration. "I do not know you yet Huztel, but I applaud the reason for your presence at that traders meeting. Your system has betrayed your planet and its star has erupted spreading death and chaos. The only thing that prevents your people's destruction is the use of Fridellian crystals to power your planetary shields." Dale paused to look the tall thin man in the eyes. Hutzel bowed, if stiffly, never taking his eyes from Dale's.

Dale continued, "Yet when it came time for you to join sides in the battle against the Brethren you threw such considerations away and joined in the fight. You knew, of course, that your ship was outmatched but you showed such bravery in that knowledge, that we support you. You shall have all of the Fridellian crystals that you need!"

A feral smile played over Hutzel's lips and once again he bowed. Dale motioned for Hutzel and his entire crew to step down from the Dais and join him. A quick mental warning pulled the troupe members closer as they formed the mind bond. The crews from the two-star ships worked in closer to the Dais as if pressing to get a view of the honored guests.

"People of Brightholme I present Hutzel and his crew, honest traders who work to save their world. That it something we gathered here certainly can understand." The crowd roared with approval. As he did for the crew of the Valor, he mentally indicated that they should go into the crowd and receive the honor due them. He added a warning that things were about to get nasty and to stay away from the dais.

Once again Dale turned toward the dais and bowed slightly to the Lowen officers. "I had the unfortunate privileged of watching as my father, God rest his soul, became captive to an implanted chip which locked him inside his own mind. I watched as he allowed my mother to be taken like a common criminal and killed in the streets. I watched as he tried to kill me his only son and all of those who stood with me and wanted freedom. Our world, Laurel is now a dead and broken ball of ash and stone floating in a dead system."

"In the end we who gather here had learned of the control device. What is more, we learned how to neutralize it completely and how to restore those that it once controlled to their full complete selves. In the end my father, was a hero who allowed in his selfless actions and his own death, an opportunity for us to escape into the galaxy. We who are the distant children of the Federation salute you and all of those that have come back from such slavery."

There was a roar of approval from those that had been so enslaved aboard Krylon's Dreadnaught and the Juancy ships. Dale did not take his eyes from the three Lowen officers, although he thought that he could detect the beginnings of a wary panic in their eyes. "To enslave a man or a woman is a piteous thing to be righted whenever and wherever discovered. To lock a man in his own mind is a crime beyond all bearing. You three stand on the Dais of Peace and Friendship, none of you bear the horror of those controlling devices. Yet in our medical lab the balance of your crew has been freed from just such abominations. They are safely in stasis now and will be fairly treated when we rouse them one by one."

At this the Lowen leaped into action only to be suspended in mid air, frozen by the combination of mental might possessed by the troupe. Dale moved forward and addressed their leader. "How long has it been since you betrayed your people for the promise of power given by the Brethren? You let your own people be enslaved in such a way, for what? Money, power, the safety of your own hides?" Our judgment is swift and certain."

Dale turned to his people and asked in a loud clear voice, "What are we to do with these Lowen?" The answer was immediate and final. With a brush of his hand the three Lowen officers disappeared. The three startled Lowen realized that they were floating above the command deck of their own ship and then as quickly died as the ship was plunged into the corona of Brightholme's sun. Mark Thomas and Glenda Stern used their mental powers to assure that every single molecule from that ship was consumed in the fusion furnace of the star before they turned back to Brightholme. Dale knew that they would be needed.

Dale now paused on the steps his back purposely to the remaining guests still seated at the feasting table. The Drevichens had not moved nor uttered a sound as Dale had played out his plan. Now slowly he turned to those remaining on the Dais. "Theresa of Ikorn I know and honor, her people are reclusive and prefer to avoid becoming involved in the affairs of the galaxy, yet she and her people are directly responsible for saving many thousands of our fellow Federation citizens when the Brethren had come to destroy them. While all could not be saved the Ikornians saw that many lived and had a chance for freedom. I honor you. He beckoned her to join him on the dais as he presented her to the crowd.

Mentally he addressed Frthessig, "I honor your desire for anonymity my friend so I will not address your presence here but let me assure you that you are very welcome."
Together Dale and Theresa turned to look at the remaining figures still seated on the dais. Dale said, "You I do not know. You have sealed your ship to our probes, and you have not given your true name. Rumor has it that there is a Pirate Lord, who plies the space lanes in the old Federation. This Pirate has made a fortune profiting from the misery of others. While you came here as representatives of Free Traders, I think that you are much more than that." Dale looked directly at the small group's leader. "How say you?"

Above the planet's surface the Drevichen ship suddenly came to life its automated circuits activated and its main guns focused on the small capital of the New Federation. The Orion immediately swung into protective position above the planet its shield flaring out augmented by the talents of Mark Thomas and Glenda Stern. Star Dancer uncloaked and floated far enough away to target the Drevichen ship and yet remain outside of suspected weapons range.

The Leader of the Drevichens smiled and slowly stood his hands in the air. "I commend you Dale Lambert for your astute grasp of the situation. Not many have attempted to best me and, ah, lived. Whether you live or not depends on your responses to my demands over the next few minutes."

Dale stood calmly watching. The man in front of him was no braggart. He felt that he was in possession of the upper hand here. Dale felt rather than understood that there was more in play here than met the eye. He waited patiently for the man to continue.

"Yes, we are not simple Free Traders although that is a profession that we admire greatly. Our business is as necessary as any other, maybe more so once the Federation collapsed under Brethren pressure. Our work is done in shadow and in areas that others askew in fear and ignorance. Both act in favor of our activities. We are pirates in the classical sense of the word. We obtain rare and desirable goods through trade and also by force as needed. What you don't realize is that our profession provides needed goods and services under the threat of Brethren retribution. You have seen that in action, that trap was intended to snare us and almost succeeded."

Here he looked directly at Dale and bowed. "Thank you for your intersession. I had believed that the Lowen were genuine partners in that trade, but obviously they were under Brethren sway. Our own reserve forces would have arrived to mop up what we did not get around to, so we were really in no danger of falling into Brethren hands. Still, it has been very educational to see how you have gathered together the fragments of the free people of the galaxy. Certainly, the presence of the Witches of Ikorn lends great credibility to your cause."

He bowed again toward Theresa. Dale interrupted the man's explanations by asking a simple question. "If you deliver services to those that truly need it, why did you refuse to take the Hutzel's bid and give them the crystals that they so desperately needed?"

The man looked at Dale for a long moment before he answered. "I don't normally discuss my business practices with strangers, so I must break with custom." In his mind Dale felt the confident mind of the pirate leader. "You see Dale Lambert you are not the only one who has some mental powers, although I do bow to your greater skill. I use my personal anonymity to cause doubt and fear in those that I need to deal with. You however are of different metal. I am Drake Lasken and I come from a long line of pirates who derived their roots in the old Federation fleet. If you were able to scan my ship's hold you would have found the needed crystals waiting for transport to the Hutzels. They would have appeared with just a small exchange rate well within the Hutzel's budget. In fact, I would have arranged for a continuous supply for them."

Dale was very use to the Mind Way, and he felt confident that he could trust what this man had said. He returned that mental conversation, "I believe what you say Drake Lasken because I must. Theresa said that there was much more to you than meets the eye, now I can see what she meant. So here we are at a bit of an impasse. I have no real desire to alienate you or your folk but I cannot tip your hand by simply letting you go."

"The location of this world will become known throughout the space ways soon enough. It will be the new capital world of a New Federation of free peoples, but we are not there yet. That means that I can't just let anyone waltz in here to spy us out and perhaps turn that information over for a price. I know that you will not do this. I sense the depth of your hatred for the Brethren. So, what shall we do?"

As Dale and the Pirate Lord mentally exchanged their views the systems on the Orion and the Star Dancer leapt into action. The perimeter sensors that Groshen had placed were the first to register the buildup of energy waves indicating the imminent opening of hyperspace portals. A fleet of sleek deadly looking black ships flared into the system edge and then phased into orbit about Brightholme. Star Dancer increased its shielding and the Orion added power its own.

The scene on the dais seemed as if it had been frozen during the nanoseconds that it took to frame the resolution reached by Dale Lambert and Drake Lasken. Dale was the first to break the stillness. "You have the better of us Pirate Lord, while we could battle to the determent of both fleets and our new world, it would be better for all that you take your crew and leave this system."

"What makes you think that we would leave here without plundering this puny world? It would be so easy to eliminate your "fleet" and ruin this world as punishment for presuming that you could possibly hold me."

Dale spoke loudly so that all could hear. "Yes, that may be true but there is another faction that you have not considered. In the next few seconds, the tables will be turned once more. I suggest that you accept our offer and leave."

The Pirate Lord cocked his head as he accepted information from a hidden communications device. He smiled grimly. "You have some very interesting friends Dale Lambert. I will accept your offer. He bowed briefly, "Until we meet again?" A sparkling curtain of energy immediately surrounded his group and with a brief smile on his face the Pirate Lord was gone. Dale listened through the Mind Way and was told that the pirate lord's ship had left orbit and along with the rest of his fleet, had phased away from the system and then leapt into hyperspace.

Just as quickly a huge hyperspace portal opened, and several mammoth craft proceeded slowly into the system. Dale raised his hands too quiet the nervous crowd. "My fellow citizens, we have avoided a deadly battle with a Pirate Lord and his fleet. They shall not be back to trouble us again, for in the space around Brightholme another union of the free people's have come to join our cause. The Empire has arrived and with it, the promise of friendship and alliance with the New Federation."

A great cheer went up and Dale felt the arms of Heather as she hugged him from her invisible state. He looked over to Theresa and saw the wide smile on her face. This had proved to be a momentous day for the fledgling Federation.

Chapter Eighteen

Dale had meant to have a private word with Scott Green and Nancy Peterson, but he had to meet with the town officials and some of the village leaders from the communities that had sprung up in the surrounding areas. His words were designed to settle their fears and explain the new arrivals. They did take some explanation. The huge dragons that could be seen dotting the skies of Brightholme were certainly a sight to behold!

The three mammoth craft were actually portal gates and after some consultation had been distributed around Brightholme's system. One was placed on the farthest moon which circled Brightholme, another was hidden in the outer bands of atmosphere found on the system's one gas giant. The last was posted in the asteroid belt found between the fourth and fifth planets in the system.

After many hours of discussion and planning it was decided that all traffic from the Empire would flow through the gates rather than come in through hyperspace. The Brethren had obtained, through one of their many conquests a device that could "trace" activity in hyperspace giving them the ability to determine the point of origin and that of destination. This was a decided disadvantage for the fledgling Federation.

After several days of negotiation between the parties involved, and in consultation with Groshen and his fellow Juancy commanders the defense of Brightholme had been settled. Freshden attack craft formed the bulk of the outer defenses and could fly out from several of the asteroid defensive platforms that were now deployed within the system. There were reserve craft and crew available for immediate call up through the portal gates. The system was now as secure as it could get within realm of imagination and reason. The diplomatic ties between the Empire and the Federation had been worked out. Treaties and alliances signed and validated by both governments. Finally, things were such that Dale and

Heather, Shadow Grey and Moon Glow could garner some much-deserved down time.

Dale and Heather walked arm in arm from their final meeting of the day, Tristan and Casric playfully stumbling at their feet. From the shadows Scott Green and Nancy Peterson joined them having received a mental invitation to dine with them at their home. They walked on in companionable silence until they reached the cozy cottage.

Dale fresh from his absence could see that the shelter from Star Dancer's stock would need some enlarging. While Tristen was not quite one yet, he had grown at a very fast pace. This fact had alarmed his two parents, but Doctor Scott had assured them that he was a very healthy boy. The advanced mental makeup of his thoughts and the fast growth of his body seemed to go hand in hand. That fast growth would soon dictate the need for another room in the house and more if Heather had anything to say about it. "After all," she had commented to her husband, "now that I have experienced birth, I think that I would like to do it again!"

Dale welcomed Scott and Nancy into their home and fixed them a couple of cold drinks made from a very sweet yet thirst quenching fruit that was native to Brightholme. Once Heather had settled the two young ones and had them playing an intricate mental game that Peter Lamous had contrived, on the small vid screen, she joined them in the living room.

"Well, they will be busy for a few hours, which will give me a chance to get dinner ready, but first Dale and I have some news from home for you." She looked at her husband who motioned for her to continue. "Your parents have joined forces with Captain Drew Duncan and his First Mate and wife Nancy Duncan." Heather smiled as she looked at Nancy Peterson. Those two are the command compliment of the Andromeda, a colony ship from the Federation."

"A very old and venerated ship," Dale added. "Yes", agreed Heather. "Well, it seems that you two along with David and

Sam Peterson have made quite a splash within the circle of free people's and your parents are very proud of you all. They wanted us to tell you if we ever met that they love you and really want to get you back on Earth for awhile."

Dale cleared his throat and reached over to refill their cups. "That reunion is more important than you think. I mean apart from the obvious family ties. The Andromeda and your parents along with Mr. and Mrs. Rodriquez, I might add, have discovered a very well-hidden covert effort to overthrow the current governments on Earth and supplant them with people who appear to be controlled." He paused and sighed, "It is one of the Brethren's favorite tricks. They used it on my planet and our so-called leaders eventually destroyed our world.' He looked at Scott and Nancy, "I would prefer that they did not succeed on Earth."

Heather picked the tale back up, "You see the people of Earth, no matter how distant the relationship may be, are one of only two races that we know of that can form the life bond with our Dragon allies. Your Sam, being the prime example of that ability and from what I have heard, you as well Scott. Forgive me for saying this but Earth has become a breeding ground for a very select and endangered species, Humans!"

"This has become even more important now. As I am sure that you are aware, our Dragon allies are flying through our skies here on Brightholme. These are the few that have maintained the old ways. You have met several on your journey from Earth to Scalar although you might not remember them. They provided the portal from which you escaped Earth and wound up among the stars." Dale looked at Scott and added, "There is a faction of the Brethren on Earth. We have not figured out why they have invested so much time and energy in subverting its culture. There is a mystery here and before we can secure the New Federation, we must solve it!"

Your parents have made inroads along with the Duncans. They have begun a conversation with certain elements of that world's upper echelon concerning our presence out here and the possibility of bringing Earth into the New Federation. Yet it is clear to us that there is a force blocking the progress of that understanding.

Over in the corner of the small room a swirl of darkness appeared and Tremolic made his presence know. "I am a Dragon, Dale Lambert, and Scott is my life mate. We are destined for the stars not one small world no matter how important. What is it that you want from us?"

Scott smiled at Dale's reaction. His Dragon had a way of making a point. "Tremolic is rather blunt, but his observation is well taken." He pulled Nancy closer to him. Our life lies in the star lanes. Although it is high time, we got ourselves back to Earth. Nancy and I have some pressing business to take care of." With that he drew her to him for a tender kiss.

Tremolic just made a grunting sound and darkness enveloped the room once more. As he vanished, all could hear his parting comment about humans and their mating habits. Dale and Heather joined in the laughter. Scott's friend was certainly different than anything that he had ever heard of concerning the dragons!

Heather had gone back into the kitchen and came out a few minutes later, "Dinner is ready!" The two couples sat around the table while Tristen sat in his highchair, Casric at his feet, muzzle in a bowl eating his dinner. Dale smiled at his wife. It felt good having the young couple eat with them and between bites they caught up on each other's history.

Scott ate until he could not have eaten another mouthful. He chuckled, "This beats space chow, hey honey?" Nancy was just wiping her chin as the last drop of food tried to escape. "Yes indeed. I think that we should spend our down time learning from the local master chef." She smiled up at Heather who blushed at the compliment.

"You are welcome back any time, but I think that your first lessons will come from your parents. I know that they are getting anxious to see you." In fact, I think that you will have some company on your journey home.' She smiled knowingly at Dale, and then left it at that.

The wall com interrupted them, and Dale walked calmly over to the unit. He had his own way of knowing what was coming into the space around the Brightholme system and as he listened his smile was one of pure pleasure. He turned to the others in the room and simply said, "The Vooglean is in bound on planetary approach. They request permission to land one of their biggest shuttles."

Dale and Heather cleaned up and released their squirming son from the chair. Heather shook her head as she pried him out. "We are going to have to put you in a big boy chair, Tristen you are growing too big for the highchair."

Tristen cocked his head and very clearly said, "Yes mother I agree. I promise that I will not make too much of a mess." Dale just sighed as he looked at his wife over Tristen's head.

To their amused guests Heather waved them on into the living room and the door. "I think that you will want to join us on the landing field. We will have a reunion of sorts."

The group walked toward the great landing field as the evening sky filled with stars. The soft scents of the planet's air filled their lungs and caused the group to breathe deeply. Nancy said to Scott, "You liked the food, but I think that the air here is much, much better than recycled cabin air."

They reached the landing field just as one of those bright stars began to get larger and a rumbling noise filled the air. A mammoth craft slowly approached the outer rim of the landing apron keeping itself well away from the other vessels neatly parked there. A cloud of dust and debris was kicked up as the ship settled down, groaning under its own weight. Then silence filled the air once more and the watching group could see the arc of shipboard light as the cargo bay gate was opened. There silhouetted by that light stood two huge shapes with a group of smaller figures standing slightly to one side.

The occupants of that ship walked slowly down the long ramp to Brightholme's grassy fields. The larger shapes resolved themselves as the envoys approached Dale Lambert's waiting party. The two large forms were mature dragons and the people that walked with them were, David Peterson, Mary Rodrigez, Juan Rodrigez, Vantu and Darcel.

Nancy ran forward to hug her brother and then in turn hugged Mary and Juan. With a slightly more dignified greeting she shook Vantu's hand and then introduced herself to Darcel. Scott waited until this brief flurry was over before he to stepped up to hug David, Mary, and Juan and much to their embarrassment, Vantu and Darcel.

"I never really got a chance to thank all of you for the way you stood by me. I owe you my life", he turned to smile at Nancy adding, "and so much more."

David acted as spokesperson for the group. "You have given us as much as we have given you," it was his turn to look at Mary, who blushed. "There is no need for accounting among friends."

Vantu smiled and added, "Let me introduce Kadolic my dragon, who thanks to the ingenuity of my parents and the staff at the facility on Scalar has regained his form and flesh and once again flies as an equal partner with me through the skies. This is his mate Gloridic who is the life mate to my wife Darcel."

The dragons bowed their great heads in acknowledgement of the introduction. Tremolic who had tagged along with group, reappeared in a puff of dusky purple smoke. He eyed the great beasts that loomed above him for a moment and then his form began to shift and expand. Scott and Nancy stood there speechless as their companion became a full-sized dragon, a companion to the two who watched in silence. Tremolic then bowed his mighty head in respect to Kadolic and Gloridic. In their thoughts they could hear the dignified voice of Kadolic, "Welcome brother, I hope that this past year has seen you well."

Tremolic lowered his head so that he could look directly into Scott Green's eyes, before he answered, again all could hear his mental reply. "Yes, Kadolic all has been well. I have only had to save their bacon a few times, but I am sure that they could have gotten out of those messes given time and luck, by themselves." His one great eye closed in an imitation of a human wink.

Scott who reached up and scratched the eye ridges of his friend smiled and said, "You are full of surprises my friend how long have you had this particular talent?"

Tremolic rolled his eyes and straightened his neck out. "Ah the young, they can be so inattentive at times. Don't you remember the robotic technician on Scalar telling you that I would have the ability to manipulate certain dimensional pathways, which in turn would allow me to place portions of my physical self in reserve to be called upon as needed?" Scott just shook his head amazed. "Well, I just haven't used it to this point, but I felt the need to great these great beasts on their own scale so I took this opportunity to remind everyone present that I am a Dragon of Scalar in every sense of the word, and," he paused for effect, "to let you know, my rider that you have a very powerful partner at need."

With that Tremolic pulled slightly apart and in a swirl of purple smoke resumed his space faring compact size. "Well," interjected Dale Lambert, "That was an eye opener and no mistake." He turned to the group and waved them toward the other end of the landing apron. "We have prepared a feast to celebrate this momentous event. Come friends let's sit down and talk over our next steps in the solidification of this region of space against the Brethren presence."

Daton Excilore and Dressant joined them along with Theresa and Frthessig. The Two dragons settled down on the outside of the picnic grove but had their heads extended on their long necks so that they would not miss any of the conversation. The Terrans sat comfortably on the benches while the others sat in the remaining seats. There was a long pause and Groshen, Shadow Grey, Moon Glow, Mark Thomas, and Glenda Stern joined them. This was to be a celebratory dinner and a council of war.

Dale raised his hand for silence. "We already know that the Brethren have a minor interest in Earth, it is logical that they fear the resurgence of the Dragon and Rider bonding that once held the Empire together in peace for so very long. I am not sure that they are aware of the existence of Scalar, nor of the enclaves of Dragons that exist there. Surely if they visit that world, they will find those great beasts in a degraded and more bestial state.

"This is a point in their favor as they could pose no threat to the Brethren authority at this time, yet we know thanks to the adventures of Sam Peterson and Nemoric that the Brethren are aware that there could be a pairing between the two races. This makes Earth a target for control or destruction."

"Currently the reports that we have coming back from the Andromeda indicate that the Brethren have chosen their low-level tactics in an attempt to take over that world. The Petersons, the Rodriquez family and the Greens all seem to think that there is a subculture being developed there to sew mistrust of any extraterrestrial contact. A belief that would allow the folks on Earth to go about their business without worrying that they would throw their world open for alien visitation."

Vantu stood and filled the small grove with his bass voice, "I fought one of the true Brethren on Earth before our escape to the Way Station. I could read some of that creature's thoughts as he lay dying on the point of my sword. The Erath is being carefully cultivated but not for the reason that we have assumed. As most of you know our race and he pointed to his chest, were the only ones, until Sam came along, that were able to form the bond but there is a deeper mystery here."

"Our race is almost identical to the Brethren race. If they needed breeding stock, we would have been the logical choice. Still, they took great delight in destroying most of our people." He held up his hand to silence the murmur of discussion that his comments caused.

"It has long been felt that the Brethren people are no longer capable of pro-creation. Whether this is by their own choosing or by some genetic defect we do not know. Perhaps they see in the people of Earth the chance to regain the power of procreation without the fear of domination by a race to closely aligned with theirs."

He looked at the folks from Earth. "The last images that I received from my dying opponent were along those lines. The Earth has become a significant battleground for us and while the Brethren have not given it their full attention we must move to secure its existence."

Dale spoke again, "We are to weak, here in our New Federation, to enter into a full conflict with the Brethren. We have been able to draw their attention back to the areas of space once occupied by the old Federation. I think that we should continue to invite their speculation in that direction and in the meantime continue to build on what has been covertly started on Earth, the recognition of other races in their nearby space and the eradication or at the least a balancing of power against the Brethren on the Earth. We must prepare the peoples of the Earth for their insertion into a new and free Federation."

When he sat back down and the conversation buzzed around the tables in the grove, Dale felt Theresa's thoughts politely requesting permission to speak mind to mind. Dale looked at Heather, Moon Glow and then Shadow Grey alerting them. He settled quietly and then asked permission from Theresa to allow him to bring a merge into their conversation. There was the briefest of pauses as Theresa conferred with Frthessig. "Yes of course, but what I have to say cannot go beyond this small group. I want that understood!"

Dale agreed, feeling affirmation from his link mates. "You are right, Dale Lambert that the Brethren are in need of breeding stock. For time out of mind they have used a system of cloning and reanimation to preserve their race. You would kill an opponent much as Vantu did on Earth only to find that self same Brethren, identical to the nth degree facing you again. The only difference noted to this point is that they are biologically in their thirties. It is a uniform effect. These replacements are obviously clones, but our science has taught us that cloning has certain limitations. Those limitations tend to degrade the clone either physically or mentally or both. This is the reason that they look to Earth. They need a new gene pool from which to draw."

"To counter the Brethren out in the old Federation is a good plan. You need to buy time to solidify your new Federation, but it is only a holding action. While the Brethren take the long view that their technology affords them, they are not known for their patience with those that resist. Since they now have a stake on what happens on Earth and will be looking to this section of space for very important reasons, we must push them back on their heels. We must learn the location of their Home World and destroy it if we can. At the very least we need to discover the location of their cloning facilities throughout the galaxy and destroy those as a first step."

As the others talked and Dale's group communicated with one another on their special plane of thought, David sat back against his chair and thought of Griden his master. The vision of Hymical still very clear in David's mind, the purpose undimmed. Somewhere out in the vast reaches of space was the true enemy of the galaxy. He is an enemy who was yet to be revealed in his power and his strength. "He is the one," came the thoughts of Theresa unbidden to his mind. "The rising will occur soon enough. In the meantime, young

Weapons Master, you are my problem, and I will undertake the next portion of your training. You must learn to master the dark energy and balance it against the light. Only then will you have a chance to defeat what is coming. Only you can save the galaxy!"

Chapter Nineteen

Daton Excilore stood on the command deck of the Polaris staring at the forward view screens. The milky flow of hyperspace was occluding the stars as they whirled past. Dressant sat at the navigation console and checked the time on the digital display in front of her. "Twelve minutes to breakout Daton," she informed her Captain.

Their mission was not a simple one. They were to investigate the remains of the outlying worlds of the old Federation looking for life and possible allies, but more importantly they were to keep the Brethren interested in their doings. It could very well be a suicide mission, Daton thought to himself if it weren't for the makeup of his crew. Mark Thomas and Glenda Stern, now an acknowledged couple, manned the engineering and power stations. Sharp Eyes and Life Giver added their talents to the search. Then there was Keflin one of those mysterious entities from the even more mysterious world called Ikorn.

Daton was not a religious man, but he had seen some of the things that Keflin could do as he manipulated dark energy and dark matter. Those observations alone could almost persuade him that there must be a God who could design such a wondrous universe as the one in which he now traveled.

Then there was Dressant. Daton could not escape the feeling that this alien from Kilora was nothing less than amazing. She never left his side, except during their daily rest cycles and even then Daton could "feel" her presence as if she were nearby. He thought that he would chaff at those feelings, but they gave him comfort without demanding anything in return. He smiled over to her now and thanked her.

"Please have Mark and Glenda ready the ship for breakout. I want full shielding as we come out of hyperspace. Please have Keflin report to the command deck. Thank you."

The system that they were about to visit had haunted Daton's life waking and sleeping since his "awakening" by Dale Lambert. It was the one that they were about to break out into. It was where in relative terms he had said goodbye to his wife and children just a little over three years ago but in actual time well over two hundred years had passed. He had come to an intellectual understanding of this fact, but he still very much needed to see the physical proof before he could "let go" of his old life.

Dale Lambert had sensed this in him from the very beginning and had worked hard to bring him through to command. Daton appreciated the fact that Dale had worked with him to fulfill this required element of his life. He would not let the Admiral down.

Dressant's voice broke his reverie, "All is in readiness, break out in three, two, one." The strange distortion that was breakout passed in nanoseconds and the forward screens cleared immediately. Their chosen insertion point was designed to bring them in several parsecs from the edge of the system. From there they would go in under impulse power and shielded so that their approach would go unnoticed. Breakout was clean, but they were not alone. The edge of the system hummed with crossing radio and microwave signatures. Daton adjusted the main viewer, and the images of several large Dreadnaughts came into view.

Dressant placed her instrument on passive record and the sensors had lots to report. Daton called down to the engineering sections and asked for all stop. "Mark, are we leaking any energy signatures?"

"No Captain we are tight. I have power online in case we have to beat a quick retreat." Daton acknowledged his report and added to all crew members. "We appear to have come out into the Catus system amid a very active Brethren presence. We know that this is not their home world but what it maybe we will need some time to find out. We will stay where we are using passive instrumentation only. Be prepared at any moment to bug out if needed."

Dressant was still monitoring the sensors and turned, a frightened look in her eyes. "Daton, I have analyzed the long-range sensor data. The third planet from the sun, Catus isn't there anymore, or not most of it." With a sorrowful look Daton asked her to bring the images up on the main screen. There hanging against the backdrop of its primary was the scattered remains of what had been his home world. There really wasn't that much left of it, it seemed to have shattered into millions of fragments large and small.

As he watched a planet killer moved from the shadow of those remains and with an arrogant gliding motion moved toward the systems fifth planet. He reset the viewer to examine that world. Several Dreadnaughts could be seen floating above it pelting its surface with what appeared to be atomics.

Daton shook his head in wonder. That world had been populated in his day, mainly with research stations and manufacturing plants which drew upon the rich mineral sources under its surface crust. The world was not habitable except for controlled biodomes and reinforced tunnels. With a sharp intake of breath Daton ordered that all communication channels be opened, and all bands be monitored.

Through the communications arrays, the command deck was flooded with pleas and cries for help. Daton growled deep in his throat. Those were his people that were being slaughtered as he stood and watched. Keflin and Dressant moved to stand next to him. Each took one of his hands and suddenly he felt himself expand, his mind bursting from the shell of the Polaris and out to those ships surrounding the fifth planet. He felt his mind penetrate the skin of the first Dreadnaught, phasing through a powerful shield designed he understood with a start to stop any mental intrusion. It proved to be no barrier to his mind thrust. He quickly followed the circuitry tracing the power leads that feed the destructive forces being unleashed on the planet below. With a careless mental jab, he disabled those circuits melting them into molten masses. He then proceeded to nullify the ships power systems and the Brethren ship found itself hanging in space completely helpless.

As quick as thought his mind went from one of the Dreadnaughts to the next meeting an ever-increasing amount of resistance to his mental probe. Each time he could feel a corresponding increase in his own mind as those who had melded their minds with his supplied the additional power. Each time he succeeded in disabling the ship.

From that part of his mind that remained anchored on the command deck of his ship, he caught the delighted howl of those that had remained fighting below. From the surface of that world and from their hidden bases on the moon a swarm of elite fighters leapt, out energy weapons blazing as they engaged the disabled ships. From those a fleet of fighters erupted to counter their attack.

Daton was brought back into the fold of the mind meld as those with him turned their attention on the planet killer, which was approaching the fifth planet, deadly purpose in its calm approach. There was no doubt about the intent of that vessel which began to morph and cast its deadly nets over the world below. With the defenders' fighters fully engaged the only hope that the planet had was the presence of the Polaris and those that used the mind power to such effect.

Daton cast his mind toward the planet killer but found a powerful deflector shield up which repelled his mental energies. With desperate effort he pushed against that force, but he could not penetrate it. Finally, he had to withdraw. It would be up to his ship's enhanced weapons now. Perhaps they could divert enough energy from those shields to allow a lightening thrust. He told his meld mates to be ready and then found himself fully on the deck once more.

With terse orders he had the main guns pulled up through the ship's hull. "Mark, can you channel all power to the main guns. We might only have one shot at this, let's make it count. He then had Dressant pull the fast ship around for an attack run on the planet killer. The ship was agile and very fast. While it held its fire, it was completely invisible to all scanners, but Daton knew that once they fired their position would be given away. They had to do as much damage to that ship as possible. With a prayer to God, he ordered the attack. The ship vectored in as fast as it could without meeting much in resistance from the enemy's shields. With a flash of recognition Daton realized that the mental shield on that ship had limited the shield that kept the planet killer from physical attack. With a feral smile he ordered the main guns to fire.

Mark Thomas and Glenda Stern sat side by side in the engineering command deck and fed the ship with that special augmented talent that had been theirs when they worked in concert. The main guns growled as they unleashed their hellish fury aided by that psychic power. The beam met the feeble shield pulling it down completely. The combined energies arrowed in on the main power nodes of the planet killer. The space around the fifth planet was ablaze with the destruction of more than one power generator on that huge ship. A number of the planetary defense force ships followed that beam in and laid in a series of nuclear torpedoes, lacing the Brethren vessel with violent whips of energy.

The Polaris then came under attack from the fighters from the Dreadnaughts and the planet killer itself. Its position had been revealed by the main guns as they fired. Daton, Keflin and Dressant quickly threw up mental shields as the physical shields took the brunt of the attack. Daton shook his head. They had done all that they could for now and he ordered the Polaris back into hyperspace. He had Dressant plot a course that would bring them out on the other side of the planet.

The ploy only brought them enough time to regroup and to power up the main guns again. The destruction of the Brethren power generators had damaged that ship's ability to effectively shield itself completely. Whoever was commanding that ship had begun to use a rotating power deployment to their shields channeling energy from one area of its massive bulk to another in an attempt to defend itself against the remaining defensive fighters.

The Polaris AI examined the pattern and quickly calculated a firing solution. Daton ordered his ship out of the protective edge of the planet's curving surface and fired the guns once more. The weapon aided once again by the magnification of Mark Thomas and Glenda Stern scored a direct hit and the segments of the Brethren ship nearest to them erupted in a silent plume of energy which spread from node to node. Cognizant of the damage done to the Vooglean when it had destroyed the planet killer in the Freshden system, Daton had his shields up and ready.

All instruments were on that ship as it dissolved quickly into fragments of metal and flashes of energy. Sure enough, just as the Brethren ship broke into a final destructive plume of energy a flash was noted as the escape pod was jettisoned toward the Polaris. It never made it. A score of planetary defensive fighters sprang into action and in concentrated fire destroyed that fragment.

Daton organized the mop up while attempting to communicate with the defense force around the planet. Dressant turned to her Captain, "Daton the defense force is trying to contact us, should I respond?"

Daton turned and sat back into his command chair before nodding his head in the affirmative. "This is the New Federation Exploratory vessel Polaris, Daton Excilore commanding. Please identify yourselves."

There was a long pause and through the excited chatter on the open communications link, Daton could hear his audience's surprised reaction. "This is the defensive planetary defense force commander. The system is not yet secured, and we can expect a retaliatory response at any time. Can you offer aid to us, we don't have many people left, those bastards, the Brethren, have done their job well, but those that we can save need immediate aid? Can you help us?"

With a sigh Daton was about to respond in the negative when Keflin moved next to him. With a slight nod of his head, Daton gave the Ikornian permission to respond. "I am Keflin of Ikorn, serving aboard the Polaris. Gather your people and give us the coordinates. My people will open the portal and send them to a secure system where the Brethren cannot reach them."

Once again came the excited chatter, but with a quick bark the commander quieted the link. "I have heard of your people, Keflin. I know that they have offered asylum before, and our people have never been heard from again. Some people say that your race has enslaved them or worse. How can I know that I can trust you?"

Keflin smiled at the response, "A reasonable question. The system that we have sent the survivors of the old Federation to has been moved out of normal time and space by the talents of my people. I can offer you no proof of my words, but if you do not accept our offer, you and your people will be doomed. Decide!"

There was a long silence and when the answer came, it was with resignation in the tired voice of the commander. "We accept your terms and can only rely on your word as a bond that our people will be safe." The commander fed the coordinates to the Polaris AI and then signed off.

It was a thoughtful Daton who turned a questioning glance at Keflin. "Can your people do this?"

With a nod of his head, a purple light enveloped Keflin and a second later he was no longer on the command deck of the Polaris. Seconds later a startled voice erupted from the communications link. Captain Excilore your Ikornian friend has just made an appearance on my command deck." This comment was followed almost at once by a weird shifting of the near space around the fifth planet. A purple tunnel appeared from nowhere, stabilized and remained in constant position in relationship to the planet. "I take it that our way out of here has arrived."

Daton watched the forward screens as a rag tag fleet of ships launched themselves from the battered planet below and from hidden redoubts within the moon that circled it in its orbit. These headed for the glowing gateway and disappeared within its violet maw. When at last all but a few of the remaining fighters had joined the small fleet, Daton turned to the communications speaker and said, "God speed and thank you for holding out as long as you did."

Before the last fighter entered the gateway, the defense commander spoke for the last time, "You know it has long been held in my family that one day a certain Daton Excilore would reappear to save us from our doom. I am glad that I, Kyle Excilore have had the pleasure of seeing that prediction come true. Thank you Daton for all of us and especially for my great, great, grandmother. You know she never lost faith that you would return one day. Thank you for validating her belief." With that the last fighter disappeared into the portal and that glowing form closed.

Dressant watched as a stunned Daton, sat back in his command chair. There was a look of regret mixed with relief on his face as the words of his distant relation seeped into his mind. With a start he sprang to his feet. The proximity warning rang violently in his ears. Dressant looked at her readouts and gave a low whistle. The screen was full of enemy ships. It was an armada of Brethren attack vessels.

"Cloak us," snapped Daton. Mark Thomas and Glenda Stern immediately fed power to the shields and the cloaking device. On the command deck a purple haze dissipated to reveal a staggering Keflin. Dressant caught the man as he began to collapse and led him to one of the station chairs. In a voice rough with fatigue he said, "I am sorry Captain, I cannot get us out of here, my energies are too drained." With that he slumped into unconsciousness.

They sat back and watched as ship after ship appeared on the screens. Daton whistled and then addressed Dressant. "Plot a course out of here Mister before they bump into us by accident."

The star destroyer Vengeance entered the system, a dark malevolent mass that dwarfed the other Dreadnaughts. On its command deck the officers on watch gathered data on the system and analyzed the energy patterns which still reverberated after the battle between the planetary forces and the Brethren expeditionary forces sent to destroy this system.

The work of the crew was precise and thorough. The resulting data was correlated, and the resultants summarized for the fleet commander. With some hesitation the commander turned and walked the short distance to the raised dais located precisely in the center of the mammoth command chamber. He fell prostrate to the metal decking before rising to one knee to proffer the report. The sheet rose from his hand and gently made its way to the figure seated on that dais.

The seconds that followed drew out to minutes and the commander began to shake with fear. In his mind the slow cold voice of the Triune member reverberated with frightening efficiency. "Destroy all evidence that this once was a star system, Commander. I don't want as much as a speck of dust left to show that it once existed."

The creature then sat back in its throne and launched a mental probe out into space. The Polaris was in the process of jumping into hyperspace when that probe found them. The shielding held as the tremendous force of that mind shook the ship, but it did not prevent the deadly chill of its master from reaching to those on board. "You have won this battle, young Captain Excilore but as you see we are taking your interferences a bit more seriously. I have commanded all the Brethren to use whatever influences that they have to find you and track you down. As of now you have gained my personal attention." The thought faded as their ship tore into hyper drive.

Stephen Goodale   206

Chapter Twenty

Dale and Heather gathered together the party that was to go on to Earth. It was decided that the Orion was to be used as a staging area and protective cover for the group of Empire representatives while they negotiated with their Earth contacts. The Petersons, the Greens and the Rodríguezes had begun to lay the groundwork for first contact.

The Duncan's had used their amassed wealth to gain the attention and the favor of some of that planet's movers and shakers. It was thought that the best approach to the introduction of the Dragons and their Riders to the general population of Earth would be to make use of the newly created New Mexico Spaceport. This facility was a privately-run structure and as such did not fall under the auspice of the United States government. It was now known that some of those "elected" officials were actually being controlled by the Brethren agents on the Earth by the use of implanted chips.

"So," Dale said, "The time has come to bring ourselves to the attention of the Earth. This is a vital mission as you well know and one that requires delicate skill set. We must find a way to make the transition from Earth to Scalar as easy as possible for those that demonstrate the talent and psychological makeup to become Riders. To do this we must have the aid of Vantu and Darcel along with their mates, Kadolic and Gloridic. He looked at the four friends and smiled. You four will have the pleasure of doing riding demonstrations, intricate maneuvers and of course communications. Will you be willing to speak to the common boy and girl, Kadolic, Gloridic?

The great beasts looked at each other and nodded their massive heads in agreement. "It will be our pleasure', the voice of Kadolic spoke softly in their minds. "The Dragons of Scalar have waited long enough for their riding mates. If we can bring in fresh blood with the desire to form the bond it will go a long way to helping Sam and Kathrine in their efforts to reach and communicate with the wild ones of Scalar."

Dale bowed and thanked the great ones. "Part of our mission will be to detect and rout out the Brethren agents on Earth. We must first start by detecting those that are being controlled by the biochips. Doctor Scott assures me that he has been able to develop a detection panel that can pick up the presence of the chip and nullify it by creating a feedback loop. Once the suggestion is made or a command is sent to the chip then the signal becomes trapped inside the circuit and never releases to the brain. An outside agency cannot detect that their commands have failed because according to the feedback that they receive the chip has received its command and accepted the order."

Dale turned and looked at his companions. "All of this is pointless of course if the Brethren decide that Earth is lost to them. It would be a simple matter then for them to destroy the system as they have done with so many others before." He looked at Groshen and his fellow commanders and at the Freshden commander. "It will be up to us to deploy a secure defensive perimeter within Sol's system so that any attack would be thwarted."

At the sound of amazement from all concerned, Dale just smiled and raised his hand for quiet. "Not many of you know this, but as part of our overall strategy Daton Excilore has been dispatched into Old Federation space. His instructions are simple. Rescue any Federation citizens still alive and to raise enough havoc that the Brethren leadership is distracted keeping their attention focused on that section of the galaxy. To this end I am happy to report that Daton along with his crew have already rescued a number of Federation citizens from the Catus system and in the process has destroyed a number of Dreadnaughts and one Planet Killer."

There was a spontaneous cheer from all gathered there. When they quieted enough for Dale to continue, he added, "The Brethren response was as expected, an armada, not just a squadron but a fleet of Brethren ships responded to the defeat of their vessels in the Catus system. The entity leading that Armada was one of the Brethren's Leadership Council, a member of the Triune. Daton informs me that this entity has a very powerful mental capability and has sworn to exact vengeance on Daton and his crew."

"While I can't say that I envy Daton his position at the moment he will certainly serve us well if he can keep that fleet occupied in old Federation space. If he can keep the attention of the Brethren Leadership away from Earth and this area of space until we are strong enough to defeat them."

"Remember that to this point they had the advantage over us in that they were able to assimilate any number of races to act as their arms and will. With the ability to nullify those chips, I doubt many will be willing to serve such a ruthless enemy willingly."

Dale turned to face Groshen. "Once the defensive positions are in place in the Earth system, I have a very special assignment for you. If you would be willing to go into Brethren territory and contact your people, I think that it is time that we liberated them from Brethren rule!"

A wide feral grin appeared on Groshen's face as he nodded his head in enthusiastic support of such a venture. "Just let me get to my people with the technology that Doctor Scott has created, and I will be able to raise such a revolt that will keep those bastards busy and far away from Earth!"

"We are agreed then?" As everyone around the table nodded, Dale turned back to look at Theresa. "I do not dare to ask, but the help of Ikorn would be greatly appreciated in whatever form that it takes."

Theresa bowed her head in acquiescence. "I will gladly help but most of my time and energy will be focused on training young David Peterson." She looked at Dale with concern. "Your plans have merit, and they might eventually result in limiting the influence of the Brethren, but there is another enemy on the horizon of whom I will not speak. This enemy will be very strong, and it is one that David must face in the end. I will say no more now."

With that Dale had to be content. Clearing his throat, he addressed Groshen. "I would like for you to begin the construction of several more Polaris class ships. Incorporate Doctor Scott's technology in their sick bays and augment the armament and weaponry. If we are in for a battle, I want our people to have the best!"

David walked away from the landing field with no destination in mind. He was thinking about what the Ikornian witch had said about his confrontation with a force of darkness greater than that currently posed by the Brethren. There was no need to hide from the fact, no denying his destiny. He knew who he must face. That image was forever burned into his mind, Hymical, the Brethren Lord who had disappeared from time and space during the battle for the Freshden system. He knew that with his current knowledge and limited experience that he would be no match against the dark forces commanded by that alien.

He paused as he felt a disturbance in the forces around him. Theresa materialized next to him, her presence a dusky purple in his mind. "I know of whom you speak, Griden had prepared me by showing me the vision that he had of Lord Hymical. Still, no word has come concerning him since the battle for the Freshden system."

"Young weapons master, you have had a reprieve from that test of powers. The Lord Hymical is not dead. The forces that he commands are growing stronger day by day, upsetting the balance in the universe." She stepped in front of him and using a delicate but strong hand raised his chin so that his eyes met hers. "He has not yet been revealed, but I feel the Rising as the power in our galaxy shifts daily to him. We cannot know the time or the place, but the Rising will occur soon."

David stood still and let the feelings that he had leave his body, clearing his mind. He opened himself to the universe, his spirit moving out among the stars. Somewhere he felt the flow of energy that Theresa spoke about. That flow moved in a determined direction. David knew that somewhere at the terminus of that stream, Hymical waited. "What must I do, Theresa?"

This question was asked in a very low voice and the doubt and the fear that enveloped him was a cloud between them. "You must understand yourself, young Weapons Master. You are conflicted between the light and the dark, life and death. You must come to realize that one is the opposite side of the coin of the other. Without life there is no death and without death and renewal there is no life."

With a quiet step Mary had approached them, respecting the silence that seemed to wrap itself about them. "Theresa smiled at her and then swept her arms up vanishing in a small puff of purple. David just shook his head and wondered how Theresa could do that. Her voice came to him even as he turned to take Mary in his arms, "I will show you this and many other things. You have a long road ahead of you, young Weapons Master." She paused and then added, "I think that you had better take the first step right now!" With a waft of amusement her mind was gone leaving Mary standing shyly next to him.

David half turned to face her, enfolding her in his arms. "I think my dear Lady Doctor that we should not only accompany Scott and Nancy to Earth but that we should make the ceremony a double wedding!"

Mary turned her face to his and saw the love and commitment there. She knew that their worlds could never be the same and yet they coexisted one with the other, two necessary halves to a universal whole. She knew that her love for David was as real and as poignant as his. "Yes, my love I do believe that you are right." With that she pulled his head down to meet her waiting lips.

They stood in the darkness of Brightholme's night, the pale moons illuminating the grassy sward on which they stood. It

Stephen Goodale   211

was a moment outside of time and as they pledged their love for one another David felt rather than saw the energy flow of the Universe pause and watched as part of it reverted to him. His spirit swelled in that universal acceptance, and he knew that a new life had been laid before him. He suddenly felt much better about the future. A gentle laugh echoed in the corners of his mind and a whisper, "You have taken the first step young Weapons Master."

Sam was wearied beyond belief. His education in the Dragon Rider's village had extended to the understanding and use of the force blade. He had thought that Vantu's tutelage had been rough but that was a picnic compared to what he was going through daily at the hands of the Dragon Rider's weapons master. He felt the sore muscles in his arms, back and legs complain as he forced them to comply with his mental demands.

Today had nothing to do with practice forms, and competitive bouts. Sam found himself three quarters of the way up a shear mountain cliff, hanging on precariously with two fingers in a "jam" and two very tenuous toe holds spreading his body's frame in an awkward angle. He was not wearing a safety harness nor was he roped in, he was on his own.

His instructor, one Flendrake, had taken him out on climbs before, but he had always been secured and roped up. Now as his instructor had said, he was to forego those safety measures and rely strictly on his wit, will and training to make the climb. Sam looked up and out, he was coming up under an overhanging "roof" and he would need to spread his body almost parallel to the ground as he stretched out for holds. This he knew was the "test" if he could get up and around the roof, he would be home free in a manner of speaking.

The burning in his arms was warning enough that he had to keep moving, the acid that built up could begin to cramp his muscles and lead to his death. With a mental clarity that he did not know that he possessed, Sam swung free of his foot holds and used the finger jam to pivot himself out, firmly grabbing onto his next hold, a fist sized jam which anchored him as he released his fingers. He repeated the movement in a flowing dance of muscle, bone and will, until he was able to secure a hold on the outer edge of the roof and the upward slope that it offered.

When he reached the top of the cliff, he was rewarded by the presence of Nemoric as he lay in the late morning sun. Sam fell panting at the great beast's extended foreleg and glowered up at his friend. "Some help you are", he panted heavily. "I could have fallen and died, and you would never have known it!"

Nemoric opened one eye and peered down at his life mate. "You did not fall Sam, and I certainly would have known if you died." He thought for a moment and then continued. "I probably would not have woken from my nap if you had. I have woken and you have not died, it is a good day!"

Sam drew in a sharp breath and was about to give his friend a stunning retort when the observations of his friend made him laugh. He stood to his feet and gave the Dragon a slap on his side in affection. "You are right Nemoric, it is a good day to be alive!" With quick motions, he mounted his friend and together they fell off the very cliff that Sam had worked so hard to climb. The thrill of flight overtook Sam and he let out a whoop of pure enjoyment. It was a very good day to be alive!

Kathrine was waiting for the pair as they settled down next to their small home. Her parents, once they had accepted Sam as their only daughter's mate had aided in the planning and the construction of the honeymoon cottage, as they called it. This was the custom of the Dragon folk and Sam thought that the home that they had built for them was especially magnificent.

He dismounted from Nemoric's neck ridges, every muscle in his body groaning in protest over the morning's exercise. Katherine, laughed sympathetically and lent her strength to his stumbling legs, leading him into their home. There she stripped him of his clothes, admiring as she always did his lithe frame and the way his muscles rippled as he moved. Taking him by the hand she led him to the shower and turned on the water testing its warmth until it was just the temperature to relax her love's tight muscles. With a gentle shove, she pushed him under the water closing the sliding door behind him.

Sam stood letting the water run down his back, breathing deeply relaxing his muscles as he did so. Turning he made sure that every bit of his body was reached by those pulses of water. Once some of the soreness left him, he reached for the washcloth and the glass dispenser that held a liquid that when exposed to the wet cloth foamed. He scrubbed his skin, eliminating the sweat and the dirt of his morning's exertions. When he had finished, he washed out his hair with another of those amazing foams, noticing as he did that his hair was hanging down to his shoulders. He laughed quietly to himself, "I wonder what my mother would think of me now?"

When he stepped out of the shower, he dried himself on the warm towel that Katherine had left for him. He inhaled deeply, catching the aroma of food cooking. "Blessed Katherine," he thought to himself as his stomach rumbled in protest over its empty state.

As he settled down in a chair in their dining room, Katherine set out food for the both of them. With a tech sound that she made through her teeth she disappeared returning moments later with a brush and comb. She proceeded to attack the unruly hair on Sam's head until she was satisfied that it looked neat and appealing. Then she tied a leather thong around his head, snugging it so that it was both comfortable and effective in keeping the hair out of his eyes.

With a smile, she pounded him on the shoulder, "There, you are now presentable to sit at the table in the Peterson home." Sam laughed and wondered once again what his mother would make of him now.

Sally Peterson was not thinking of table manners or the state of her son's clothing at that moment. She was hunkered down behind a brick wall, parts of which were blown out by the weapons of those that currently had them pinned them down with intense crossfire. The cold steel of her weapon was clasped in her right hand. She glanced over to where Tom Peterson squatted next to a small communications unit, repeating their coordinates into its microphone. Just beyond him she could see the prone form of Alice Green, being tended to by her husband Steven. The situation was desperate. With a grim smile, she stood high enough to aim her weapon and press the trigger. The deadly device did not yield a projectile but a deadly ray of green light which emanated from its barrel. A scream of pain followed and then silence.

They were outnumbered but not out matched. Their relationship with the Andromeda and the Kerns had provided many interesting benefits. The one that she held in her hand was an example of that, an advanced hand held laser device. This was a holding action as the four friends awaited the appearance of reinforcements.

The situation on Earth had gone from status quo to all out-war fare between the shadowy factions that were attempting to control their world and those like the Petersons and the Greens protecting it for future generations. While the Brethren were few and well hidden, their minions were many and very visible.

The conflict had not spun so far out of control as to come to the notice of the general populace, but if, as Sally suspected, the major news outlets and the main governments of her world had been compromised then such news would be controlled and suppressed. It was not to the benefit of the Brethren to expose their presence on Earth. They did not yet have sufficient control to overwhelm the peoples of this planet.

Tom Peterson moved away from the communications device and wormed his way over to his wife. The man that came to rest next to her was certainly not the man that she had known for so long. His face was drawn and pale it was true, but there was a look of determination and steel in his eyes that gave Sally heart. They may die in this battle or the next, but they would never give up and many of their enemy would go down with them!

Tom Peterson leaned in closer so that he could whisper in her ear. "I could not raise the Andromeda. Those bastards have some kind of jamming device that is scrambling our signals. We can only hope that Jose and Margarita take our continued silence as a cry for help and come running.

At that moment, a blinding flash of light took out the wall and the communications device that had lain behind it. The firing began again and was amplified by the sound of grinding treads. Their enemy was closing in. Tom and Sally looked over to where Steven and Alice had been and through the smoke and the haze, they could still make out their forms. Steven crouched protectively over his wife a feral look on his face as he balanced the odd tube-like weapon on his shoulder.

The crunching sound of those treads drew nearer making for the breach in the wall. Steven pointed the open end of the weapon that he held towards that gaping hole and pressed the stud which released the deadly looking shell. The tank had just climbed the pile of rubble and it's under belly was exposed. There was a tremendous explosion as the sophisticated machine became a smoking, flaming plug which blocked the hole that it had attempted to penetrate.

The firing suddenly ceased, and all remained quiet. Tom grasped his wife in a quick embrace and then smiled thinly. This was the end and both of them knew it. The next wave of attack would be overwhelming and deadly. Tom looked over to Steven who waved his hand in salute. They would die but they would die as friends and comrades.

The area that they found themselves was open to the sky now. A short while ago it had been a secure safe house where the six friends had attempted to achieve something of a normal life. They had rotated duties aboard the Andromeda on a regular basis, always having two of their number in the security of that vast vessel. Today had started as any day would, a secure scan of the grounds by the robotic servants that had been the Andromeda's contribution to their "home" and then breakfast. It was as they were cleaning up from that meal that the alarm was raised from the perimeter guard.

The house was used as a link to the growing number of forces that opposed the Brethren's attempt to subvert the planet. They did not know why the Brethren did not simply take over the Earth or destroy it out right as they had done with so many systems and worlds in their galaxy. There was something that they wanted or needed on Earth that could not be obtained by their normal violent methods.

This hands-off approach did not apply to them it seemed. Tom Peterson's grim smile reflected his thoughts. The attack on the house had been well coordinated and deadly. Now there was a furtive sound of movement from the other side of the wall and then from dozens of locations small projectiles flew over the walls. This was it was Tom's thought. A blinding flash of light forced his eyes to close, but there was no corresponding sound, no deafening explosion.

Tom forced his eyes to open and there standing not ten feet from his position were the forms of six people. One ran quickly to where Steven and Alice were. The female because it was obviously a female and very human squatted next to the prone form of Alice Green and began administering first aid. Three of the others advanced to the wall and Tom could see that their hands held some form of sophisticated weaponry. They took up defensive positions while the other two of that group drew deadly looking blades and leaped to the top of the wall and over in such quick movements that Tom could hardly see them move. There were sounds of weapons fire and screams of pain as the small group waited behind the wall. A series of loud explosions and a cloud of disturbed soil flew into the air and then silence.

Tom looked at Sally and smiled. Apparently, they were not to die at this moment. The silence stretched on and then the two forms that had leaped the wall, jumped back down over that barricade. The remaining fighters stood and holstered their weapons. The fight apparently was over.

One of the fighters who had risked death for them walked slowly over to them, reaching down he proffered a hand to Sally Peterson and when she was steady on her feet did the same to Tom. The grip that aided him to his feet was very strong but gentle in its assistance. Tom looked up at the man who stood several inches taller than his own six-foot one frame. With a smile and a slight bow Tom thanked the man for his timely rescue.

With a slight curl of satisfaction on his lips the other simply placed his arms around him hugging him. Then with a smile he did the same for Sally Peterson, whose astonished smile lit her face. "David, is that you?"

Tom felt the ground under him sway a bit as he registered the importance of that question. He reached out to the rough wall to steady himself, and numbly repeated, "David?" There was a sense of disbelief in his voice.

"Yes, father I am here." The tall man then looked around him and laughed briefly," and apparently just in time. Although," he laughed out loud, "You lot seemed to be doing quite well judging by the evidence in here and out there. Still, I am glad that we got here in time to give you a hand."

David lent a steadying hand to his parents as they moved to join up with the rest of the group. Nancy Peterson met them and stopped just in front of her parents smiling. With a laughing cry, she hugged her mother and father, who joyously hugged and kissed their daughter.

Together the Petersons joined the group by the wall. Scott Green looked down a concerned frown on his face until Mary Rodriquez stood smiled her assurance and helped Steven Green to his feet. "Alice Green will be fine. She received a slight concussion from the brick fragment that clipped her head, but other than that she will be okay."

Mary stood and then wrapped her arms around David giving him a hug spilling her positive energies into his mind and soul. Once more David had been forced to take lives, many of them but there had been no choice, and the acceptance of that fact by his love, stabilized his moral center.

Vantu had stood apart, his hand clasping Darcel's while they waited for the family to greet each other and share their emotional outpouring. Vantu for his part had been utterly amazed at the skills and the abilities of David Peterson. He had been in many battles and had fought many times in such desperate situations, but he had never seen the fluidity of movement nor the precise control of power that the young Peterson had applied. Yes, he had killed. Many more than Vantu could account for himself but always with dispatch and compassion. He had been a force for light in a dark business.

Scott Green stood now before his father, his feet spread in his customary stance and looked down the inches of his height at his father's bemused face. "Father, I am your son. I have come through death into life, and I have returned for a time." He reached out to grasp Nancy Peterson and to pull her to his side. "Nancy and I are now travelers of the space lanes, traders with our own ship. We have come to ask your blessings and to see us married." Scott looked at the Petersons and then asked Tom Peterson, "May I have the honor of asking you, sir for the hand of your daughter in marriage. To have her and hold to her for all the days of our lives?"

Tom looked over to Steven, a proud delighted look. Steven inclined his head in assent and Tom simply hugged both of the young people. "I couldn't be happier for the both of you. You bring our family which is already united in friendship together in mutual bonds of love and blood. I could not think of anything more satisfying."

David then pulled Mary to his side. "While we are talking about the bonds of marriage, father, mother I would like your permission to marry Mary. We have developed a very close relationship that actually exceeds that between a man and a woman. He looked down a soft loving expression on his face. "We complete each other."

Tom gathered Sally in his arms hugging her close to him. They looked at their children and smiled. "I can think of nothing better than having you celebrate your bonding right here on Earth with your family present." A brief sad smile passed his lips but the sparkle in his eyes never left.

Vantu stepped into the small group and interrupted their excited conversation. "May I remind you that you are standing in the middle of a battlefield and that while the battle has been won, we are still very much at war. There is probably another force on the way here to reinforce those poor unfortunates," here he waved his hand vaguely towards the other side of the wall. "We should stage a strategic retreat."

With that he closed his eyes and the forms of Kadolic, Gladoric and Tremolic appeared from their stealth mode. Vantu smiled broadly, "Our transportation has arrived."

Chapter Twenty-One

Nemoric and Firenthic soared into the evening skies of Scalar, Sam and Katherine proudly seated on their great beasts' necks. It was the end of another long day and has been their wont since Sam came to the Dragon Rider's village they took to the skies in celebration of their union. Sam could feel the power of his Dragon beneath him, the massive muscles as they contracted and extended his wings in flight. His mind, tuned as it was to Nemoric's thoughts felt what his Dragon was thinking. "The moons of Scalar are beautiful tonight, Sam," he observed. Nemoric's neck extended out as he looked at the points of light beyond the moons. "Those stars have other worlds and somewhere out there is where you and I were born. Earth is there along with the human children who could be riders to the wild ones here on Scalar."

"When Sedulic died, I received all of the vast genetic information of our long-lived species. In a sense, he made me the leader of my race." He flew on in silence for a moment and then continued, "Are you trained enough now to venture out beyond the protected confines of the village and the mountains surrounding it? I think that it is time that we got about doing our real work."

Katherine's mind linked as she was to Firenthic and Nemoric could understand the exchange between her mate and his dragon. Now she grew silent and let her mind extend out to Firenthic. "I think that we have been selfish keeping our mates so close to the nest, do you think that they should now attempt the communication with the wild ones?"

Firenthic's reply, startled Katherine, "It is not up to us to keep that pair from flying off and doing what needs to be done. We both know that my race needs those on Earth, and we know that we need to bring the two together. There really is only one question that we must answer and that is how we are going to create the bridge between the worlds so that our two races can become joined."

Dale Lambert settled back into his chair enjoying a rare moment of relaxation. There were so many facets to his new life that at times he had difficulty keeping track of them. He was a husband and a father. These two things were the most important parts of his life, he realized but there were many other aspects of his life that demanded his attention. He was part of Shadow Grey and Shadow Grey was part of him. That life was treasured. He ran free with his friend, their minds never far from each other. He could sense the world around him in such an intimate way because of that tie.

His son Tristen was only a little over a year old, but he had already formed a life bond with Casric, Shadow Grey's son from the first litter delivered by Moon Glow, his mate. That young man already had mastered speaking and of course the other things that all young people need to know. Diapers were almost not needed, Dale smiled ruefully in thanks. In fact, the boy had grown so quickly, a product Doctor Scott assured him, of the genetic melding between Dale and his wife, Heather. The work that Star Dancer had done on doomed Laurel had advanced them both in remarkable ways and that heritage was present in their son.

Dale mused that it was that manipulation that had elevated him to the position that he now held. Dale was not, thankfully, leader of his world. The day-to-day operations of a world such as Brightholme would have taxed his patience to the breaking point. No, it was the fact that he was Admiral of the fleet, a representative of the newly formed "New Federation" that kept him occupied. His unique gift of mental powers enabled him to communicate through vast reaches of space. It allowed him to organize and plan for the defense of the worlds that were coming into that Federation. These things placed him in the position that he had been given, it certainly was not any ambition of his own.

He also had enemies, powerful entities that wished nothing more than the utter destruction of all that he stood for. Yes, he mused, it was an interesting life. He felt Heather's presence, his mind's eye seeing her beautiful form standing behind him framed in the doorway, the setting sun flowing through her gown.

"Have you forgotten my husband, that I have so carefully arranged for our son to be visiting Casric and that all of your duties having been fairly discharged and all communication devices turned off and that you are alone with your wife tonight?" The surge of passion that Dale felt, was as real as it gets, and he was out of his chair in a heartbeat. He pulled Heather into his arms and kissed her deeply.

There are times in a man's life. Dale was to think to himself later when he can be so easily manipulated. Tonight, had been one of those times. While he felt rather then saw the life-giving sperm reach its intended target and the gentle placement of that fertilized egg on the wall of his wife's uterus, he had to admit that he could not have prevented such an action, nor would he ever have wanted to try. The young girl that was to be his daughter was already busy dividing cells and specializing those cells into needed tissues. "Ah well, he thought at least I will have a matching set!" He smiled down at his wife who gathered him back up into an even higher wave of passion. This one he knew was strictly for him!

The three great dragons mounted into Earth's night sky. The devastation of the attack area plain to see in the moonlight. Tom Peterson shook his head in amazement, to have survived that with just a slight concussion for Alice to show for their close escape was amazing. The smoking ruins were quickly left behind and Tom began to enjoy the feeling of flying on a Dragon. It was exhilarating to say the least and a very small part of him envied his son, Sam. He could feel Sally seated firmly in front of him raise her hands above her head and heard through the rush of the wind her shout of joy. This sure beat any amusement ride that he had ever been on.

Vantu who was seated in front of Sally Peterson smiled to himself. If these two were any example, the task of recruiting new Riders should not be that difficult. Kadolic just laughed in his mind, "We shall see, my friend."

Tom felt his daughter, Nancy holding his waist tightly, not in fear but as a way to be near to her father. It had been almost two years since she had seen him and even then, that was under the stress of their coming exile into space. She had missed her family and was exceedingly grateful to be back on Earth for a while, but she knew that her life was Scott's, and she would be with him where ever he went, which was anywhere in the galaxy!

Alice was strapped in behind Darcel and was beginning to rouse herself from the trauma of her concussion. Steven was behind her, and she could feel the strong arms of her husband, taking solace in that security. The last thing that she remembered was the warning claxon of their robotic guards and then a flash of light and the feeling of pressure against her face. Now as she regained her senses, she had the oddest sensation that she was flying through the air. It had been a reoccurring dream of her childhood to fly. Now as the wind whipped through her hair, she could almost believe that she was reliving those dreams.

Steven smiled into the wind. He was vastly relieved to have his wife alive and relatively unharmed. When the attack started and the walls and ceiling of their safe house collapsed around them, he had thought for sure that he had lost her. Now he knew that she was safe, if a little disoriented due to the blow that she took. Like Tom Peterson he had looked back at the devastation caused by the attack as they had lifted into the night sky. He could not even begin to understand how they survived but he was grateful and closing his eyes whispered a prayer of thanks to God for their deliverance.

Scott Green was in a world all his own. While he and Tremolic had been close confidants over the past year, this was the first time that he had flown with his friend. The feeling was awesome! He had flown with Sam and Nemoric, but this was his Dragon, and the feeling of the powerful muscles and great wings made his spirits soar.

"You are my true friend, Scott Green and no matter whether we travel the space lanes between stars or the sky ways of a thousand alien worlds we are one!" Scott reached down and thumped his friend with a friendly slap. "You are my true friend, Tremolic and I am yours."

Mary felt the strong sure arms around her waist. David Peterson, her love, her life, and her greatest challenge. She could feel the strength, yes but she could also feel the depths of the man's soul. He took lives, he had done that this evening in the rescue of his family and his friends, but he took no joy in that action. The man's spirit was as gentle as a flower blooming in the sun or the gentle breeze of an open field. She treasured that in him. There was no hiding between the two of them. Their bonding was as deep and as complete as any could be. They were one and the same, two sides of the same coin, united by spirit and divided by action but bonded by commitment to life. She was content.

The flight was a long one. The Dragons settled into a steady rhythmic beat of wings and covered the ground at a frightening speed. Once they had risen above the battlefield and had achieved cruising height, they had used the stealth mode to hide themselves from prying eyes and any radar that might have tried to track them. The safe house had been located in Indiana, a state in the United States of America and their intended destination was in New Mexico, some sixteen hundred miles away.

Through the connections developed by Drew and Nancy Duncan, the Governor of New Mexico Susana Martinez and the Director of Space Port America, Christine Anderson had been approached by the Petersons, the Greens and Jose and Magarita Rodriquez to allow an extraterrestrial visitation by the Dragons and by their Riders. At first, they were met with disbelief and contempt by the underlings through whom they had to approach those two key officials, but happily Sir Richard Branson, one of the founding commercial partners of the spaceport had interceded for them. The Duncans and Sir Branson had become friendly acquaintances over the years and part of the Duncan wealth had subsidized the construction of the space port.

Of course, it did not hurt that they had been allowed a visitation to the Andromeda and a review of that ship's colony crew and its history through the years. The Andromeda had greeted them warmly and after many fascinating hours of debate, questioning and planning the group had settled in on the Space Port as the logical place for Dragon kind and humankind to meet. The Governor was keenly interested in the fact that some of the most influential members of the world's governments had come under control by the Brethren. It took some convincing, but she was forced to admit that some of the decisions that were made by those involved had changed drastically in recent years. Not everything could be linked to all politicians' desires to be reelected!

When Sir Richard Branson had first been let in on the secret of the Andromeda and the fact that there was a nascent Federation of worlds forming all around the Sol system, he was to say the least depressed, but with the assurances that the Federation would in no way capitalize on the Earth's relatively young space program nor would they commercialize their own advanced technology in favor of those being developed by Earth, he felt much better about things. He even began to expand his thoughts of commercializing low Earth orbit and could envision travel to other worlds, why the Universe was opened to them! Yes, he was very satisfied at the end of that long session.

The humans aboard the three Dragons had certain needs so every once in a while, the Dragons landed so that their human companions could stretch their muscles and find relief in the trees or bushes nearby. They had stopped twice and were just landing for their third and final break when the flash of a vehicle's headlights caught them square in their glare. They were still in stealth mode, but the disturbance of dust, grass and bush revealed their presence. They had landed in what they had thought was a meadow, but the long dirt lane on which they stood led up to a well concealed house set back in the woods beyond. The truck, for that was what the vehicle was, pulled to stop and a middle-aged man and his young teen aged son got out and stood looking though the early morning light and the dust.

Kadolic reached out to the other two Dragons and the three Riders. "I don't want to just leave without resting for a bit. I can sense no duplicity about these two." With a considered thought, he added, "I like the feel of the young one's mind. We are going to have to make our presence known to the peoples of this world, why not try a little sample now before we have all of the hoopla to deal with later." Vantu just smiled at his Dragon's use of Earth slang.

After a brief consultation, it was agreed to try this little experiment in cultural exchange. So, as the two curious men approached, Vantu asked for Kadolic to drop his stealth mode. The huge beast came into focus just as the dust cloud began to settle. The two Earthmen stood straight up in shock as the clearing light revealed the form of Kadolic. Vantu asked that his Dragon kneel down so that he could dismount. Tom, Sally and Nancy Peterson did likewise. Together they ranged themselves in front of the Dragon and stood waiting patiently for the men who confronted them to either speak or make an effort to run away.

Needless to say, the two men were stunned. The Dragon, for plainly that was what that beast was, stood passively behind what appeared to be four humans. They did not feel threatened and after a few breaths the older of the two moved slightly forward and raised his hand. Vantu stepped forward and raised his hand in return. In flawless English he said, "Greetings and well met. I apologize if we startled you sir. We are traveling and needed to rest for a bit and stretch our legs. If this bothers you, we can certainly take off again to land somewhere less exposed than what in what we now perceive to be your front lawn!"

The older man listened as Vantu spoke and could not believe his ears. The man spoke clearly and with no threat, in fact he was apologizing for disturbing them at all. With a glance at his son, who had eyes only for the great beast, not in fear but in wonder he spoke. "I would be remiss, strangers, if I did not extend my home's hospitality to you and yours. My name is Edward Thresher, and this is my son Allen."

Vantu's smile increased as he bowed slightly. "I am Vantu and the great beast behind me is my Dragon Kadolic and my great friend. These are Tom, Sally and Nancy Peterson, late of New York State and currently in the service of the Empire and the Federation. I do have to apologize once more because, well you see there are more of us. If you don't mind, I will ask them to reveal themselves and I will introduce you. Once you have met you may want to reconsider your generous offer or not." Vantu mentally asked for the other two Dragons to reveal themselves.

The two Texans, for that was where they were, stood back just a bit as the two other Dragons came out of their stealth mode. They both kneeled to allow the riders to dismount and together ranged themselves with Kadloic. Vantu turned and smiled once more. "I assure you that this is the sum total of our group, no more surprises. Please let me introduce my Wife Darcel and her Dragon Gloridic. This is Scott Green and his Dragon Tremolic. The two Riders stepped up and bowed briefly. The others were introduced and stood waiting for the two Texans to speak.

"Well now, hello to you all. Welcome to the Tangled B Ranch. I don't know what the Missus will say when I bring you up to the house, but I am sure that you will find welcome in our home. He eyed the great beasts. "Ah do they need to be fed Mr. Vantu, I recon I could spare a cow or two if that is the case, and if that is what they prefer to eat."

"That is very generous of you and yes they could do with some feeding. We have already traveled over a thousand miles today and we all could use a break." With that Edward Thresher turned and got back into his truck waving them on to follow him, he preceded them up to his house.

Allen Thresher stayed behind and joined the small group, a thousand questions on his mind, but simply acted as guide following his father up the drive walking in silence and marveling at the stately movements of the three Dragons. Scott Green stepped up next to him and they walked together for a few minutes in silence. Then Allen asked him, "How did you become a Dragon Rider Scott? You said that you were from Earth and as far as I know there are no Dragons here, unless you believe the fairytale stuff."

Scott laughed. "I did not become a Rider here on Earth. I was taken to a world called Scalar. I was very sick you see. I had a form of Muscular Dystrophy. There was no known cure for that here but the Doctors on Scalar under the auspicious of the Empire had developed a trial cure. I was taken there by my friends and family to be healed." His eyes held a deep thankfulness for that gift of life. "While there, Tremolic while still in his shell helped me through the cure. His mind is very powerful you see. When I made it and was strong enough, they took me to the hatching ground and introduced me to Tremolic while he was still in the egg. Shortly after that he hatched, and well, we became bond mates, inseparable forever."

"Wow," was all that Allen could say, in his mind he could hear Tremolic's voice, "I was very lucky to find Scott Green, he is an amazing young man and is worthy of me. Perhaps there will be a Dragon for you one day young Allen Thresher, if the fates allow and you are willing."

Allen walked on in a daze of wonder and perhaps hope. The house was a large sprawling affair and the door stood wide open as the group of humans and dragons approached. From the door stepped a group of people, Edward Thresher in the lead holding onto the hand of a fine looking straight shouldered woman. Together they stepped down from the porch and greeted their guests.

Edward bowed slightly and turned to introduce his wife. "Folks let me introduce Annabelle my loving Bride of Texas."

Stephen Goodale 229

The lady of the house smiled and said in a clear lilting voice, "Welcome guests to our humble home, the Tangled B Ranch welcomes you." She then turned and motioned three young people to step up next to her. "These are my daughters Deborah Pearl, and Anne Dee and my youngest son Luis."

Vantu holding Darcel's hand bowed and introduced his friends and then stepped aside so that the Thresher family could see the Dragons ranged beyond him. These are Kadolic, Gloridic and Tremolic. They are representatives of a proud, ancient race. Kadolic once more acted as the spokesman, "It is a pleasure to meet you Madam Annabelle and you to young ones." The voice was soft and deep resonating in their minds.

Annabelle Thresher smiled in delight. Out loud she spoke, "Why so polite and so handsome, I am proud to know you all. Well," she continued, "this has been quite the morning. How shall we proceed, I would invite all of you in for breakfast and some rest but," she eyed the dragons once more, "I fear that three of you at least will not fit inside our home." She laughed lightly inviting the great beasts to join in the humor of the situation.

Kadolic came to her rescue once more, "My mate, Gloridic and I will take advantage of your offer of fresh meat. I assure you that we will not disturb or upset your stock. If we could have your permission, I think that we will hunt some of the large grass eaters that we saw as we came into land in your front field. Scott Green informs me that you call them deer? If that suits, we will hunt and then return for our friends."

Annabelle inclined her head graciously and then looked up at Tremolic's great form. "And you master Tremolic? How can we be of service to you?"

Scott Green smiled at her. "If you don't mind Madam Thresher, Tremolic will accompany us inside." He turned to look at his friend, "Won't you join us my friend?" With a brief nod of his head the form of Tremolic was occluded by a purple haze which quickly dissipated to reveal his space travelling

Stephen Goodale   230

form. Tremolic flew directly to the padded shoulder of his friend and turned to face his audience.

"Forgive me if I startled you. This is my normal form as we explore the star lanes. It makes it easier for us to travel. It also, I might add, keeps any adversaries that might have evil intentions on my friends from suspecting that they would have much more to deal with then a parrot sized Dragon."

Annabelle Thresher was as good as her word. The travelers enjoyed a Texas sized spread, with eggs, pan fried potatoes, bacon, sausage, pancakes, they called them flap jacks, and lots of coffee, tea, and juice. Around the mouthfuls of food, the small group talked about their travels and adventures among the stars and the Riders spoke of their relationships with their mighty beasts.

Edward Thresher sat back and looked from one to the other as he assimilated the profound consequences of the advent of an interstellar community. "You know gentle folk that I was not always a simple rancher from Texas? I cut my teeth as an Engineer with NASA, that's our space agency here in the United States, as some of you know. I worked on the International Space Station and was on the ground floor of the Orion project."

He looked around the table at his newfound friends. "There was great enthusiasm for our work in the general public but those in higher authority especially some in Congress who once supported our programs whole heartedly, had begun to change and vote against funding in key spots." He waved his hand around him to indicate his home and the ranch lands beyond. "I sit here today because of funding cuts to the programs that I was working on. "

He raised his hand at the questions that he could see forming in their eyes. "Don't get me wrong, the programs continue but reduced in such a way that their success has been delayed by at least a decade. They will succeed but the time lag makes me question the real purpose behind the budget cuts."

Stephen Goodale   231

"Well, anyway I had this ranch which had been in my family for generations to fall back onto. I had thought," he paused with a wry grin on his face, "that my days of looking to the stars were over, but now…" His voice trailed off as he contemplated those who sat around him. "Now it seems that the stars have come back to me!" He laughed and added, "If there is anything that I can do to help you folks I will. I still have quite a few contacts in high places in both NASA and the private commercial space industry. In fact, a lot of folks that got cut out of the NASA programs went on to start or participate in the commercial space field."

Tom Peterson acted as the group's spokesperson. "Thanks to Drew and Nancy Duncan we have been able to obtain the help of the Governor of New Mexico and the Director of Space Port America. We plan on opening up a formal consulate at the Space Port's facilities and from there introduce Dragon kind to a select grouping of volunteers. These along with observers will be taken to Scalar for possible pair bonding with their Dragon counter parts. They will become Riders."

Tom noticed the reaction on Edward's face at the mention of the Duncans. Now he asked Edward, "I take it by your reaction that you are familiar with Drew and Nancy Duncan?"

Edward looked a bit sheepish as he replied. "Yes, Annabelle and I met the Duncans some time ago, when I was still deeply embedded with NASA. They spoke to us earnestly concerning the need to provide a private space port facility and to open up the space lanes to commercial vendors. I must admit that I blew them off. Now I can see that I made a serious mistake in doing that."

Tom Peterson shook his head sadly. "There is nothing that you can do about that now. I would ask that if you are still interested in the commercial side of things or if you might be interested in becoming involved with the diplomatic effort that will be made to bring Earth into the Federation, then you might think about getting back into the game!"

Sally poked her husband in the side and made a slight motion with her chin. Tom followed her indicated line of direction and caught sight of Annabelle's frown. "Of course, any such decision should be made with the blessings of your family. Let's just leave it as an open invitation, shall we."

With that Tom Peterson and the rest of the traveling party pulled themselves away from the table and rose to their feet. Tom Peterson spoke for the group once more, "Thank you very much for your hospitality and for the chance to rest." He shook Edward's hand and gently took Annabelle's hand in turn. "Don't let our offer bother you Madam Thresher, do what is best for you and yours. The only favor that I ask is that you think well of us and keep us in your prayers. Things are about to get very interesting here on dear old Earth!"

Chapter Twenty-Two

Dressant had a problem. She knew that Daton Excilore was in a deep depression. The world that he remembered was gone. They had seen its destruction firsthand, albeit two hundred plus years after he had left it. He had striven against the Brethren and in some ways succeeded by helping to rescue the remnants of his system's population. He had aided in the destruction of the Brethren expeditionary force that had ripped apart his home planet of Catus. He had a brief exchange with his many times removed grandson and he had been reassured that his wife had died believing in his return.

That, thought Dressant, was more than any one man could endure, but added to that was the knowledge that he was a marked man. The Brethren Leader who had commanded the follow up armada into the Catus system had made that perfectly clear.

She also knew that he had a mission to fulfill. Dale Lambert needed the Polaris and the sister ships which would soon join them to continue to harry the Brethren in what had been Old Federation space. This was a vital mission. They had to keep the Brethren's attention focused on those systems that had once comprised the Brethren's biggest challenge. They had to keep up the allusion that the Federation was coming back to life in that sector of space.

Daton was a good man. Her father Frthessig had released her into his care, something she was confident that he would not have done had he any question of Daton's moral center. The Kilorian people viewed such things very seriously. So now it was up to her to get this good man back on track. With a gentle mental probe, she sought out Daton's mind.

Daton, as he lay in his ship's bunk staring up at the ceiling of his cabin, was lost in thought. He had loved his wife and his children deeply, now they and his home world were lost to him forever except perhaps in memory. He was sad that he had not had a chance to say his final good-byes. His last memories were full of the optimism that any space traveler had of returning home to be with those that he loved once more.

They all knew of the dangers faced by those that travelled the space lanes and they had accepted them. Now he had to come to grips with the reality of his loss or go slowly mad, trapping himself in grief. It was hard. He had lost his center, the anchor by which he had conducted himself through the years. Now he must push himself to move forward. He did have some solace in the brief mental contact with his distant relation. Kyle Excilore had told him that his wife had remained confident that he would return someday, and he had. His action had saved Kyle and thousands more of his people from certain death!

As he lay lost in thought he felt the gentlest of touches on his mind, like a soft feather caressing his spirit. "Daton?" came a hesitant query. "Daton, I am sorry to disturb you in your rest cycle, but I need to talk to you. Will you open your mind to me?"

Daton smiled, Dressant! He was glad of the company. "Yes, my friend, I am here. I was a little lost in thought, but I am here now. What's on your mind?"

"I need to settle some things in my own mind," came her reply. "I know that you have had several tremendous losses and I would understand your hesitancy in talking with me now, but I, I mean we, don't have the luxury of waiting until the "time is right"."

Daton sat up in his bunk and stood to face the cabin door. "Why don't you come to me Dressant so that we can discuss these things face to face? Do not be afraid, I will not bite your head off!"

Dressant smiled to herself as she turned the command watch over to Keflin. It was time that Daton and she had an understanding.

Daton for his part stood at ease, eyes watching the door, his mind surprised by the feeling of anticipation that he felt over Dressant's arrival. He felt light of spirit and sure of his own heart for the first time since he was woken from cryostasis aboard the Star Dancer. The past was the past. He had lived and loved and lost. It was time to look toward the future. The silver bells in his mind and the trembling in his heart let him know that his future was about to walk through his cabin's door.

Krylon's first thought as he came to consciousness was that somehow, he had survived the examination. He was soon disabused of that erroneous belief. The glaring white walls of the incubator lab let him know that he was once again within the confines of the clone regeneration facility on Bastion, a planetary system far removed from central Brethren space. He knew that this remote location meant that for the Brethren the status of what occurred here was inconsequential.

He knew where he was because he had been here before. He, like many of the Brethren, owed their existence to the clone tanks. The Brethren no longer had family structures. There were no real children "born" to Brethren parents. There had been no need. Each Brethren was tagged, his or her DNA mapped, and tissue samples kept frozen in cryogenic vats awaiting the command which allowed these cloning facilities to regenerate adult bodies. Each was approximately thirty years of age and was generated for the host Brethren as needed and as the High Council deemed necessary.

"Ah," Krylon thought to himself, "there must be a need then or the precious High Council would not bring me back to life." He lay on his back his naked body uncovered in the harsh lights. He had no sense of sexual self. In a way he and all other Brethren had become neutered over the centuries. In his mind he knew that all of his components would function correctly. Imperfect clones were always destroyed, ending the bloodline of the particular Brethren in question, forever.

His thoughts were disturbed by the robotic attendant as its metallic and plastic form hovered near him examining the readouts on the reanimation dais. With a soft beep of satisfaction that unit injected a small syringe into one of the many tubes that hung from his body. Immediately Krylon was unconscious. The attendant was joined by several others as they removed tubes and wires from his still form. Once he had been prepped, they moved him onto a gurney and rolled the unit through the lab and out into a sterile corridor that led to the reeducation chamber.

Images, horrible graphic images, thrust themselves into the unconscious mind of Krylon. The High Council never minced purposes with those that they ruled. Krylon knew that the offense that had caused his last demise had been the failure to complete a simple punitive mission to some backward planet where the Juancy work vessels were supposed to examine and reclaim one of the millions of vessels that had fallen to the Brethren's wiles.

He watched almost as a disinterested person would watch a history vid as his ship's records unfolded in front of him. Dale Lambert had been the name of the entity that had cost him the loss of his crew and eventually his own loss of life. He watched as his journey to the Brethren Home World, edited of course of true mapping, star distances and references, showed his arrival and arrest. The images did not spare any of the gore or pain that was his as the Brethren tortured him in mind and body.

A thin threatening voice filled his mind now. "You have been selected for a specific mission. Our operative on the planet Earth in the Sol system has been killed and as punishment will not be resurrected for another fifty life cycles. You have been brought out of cyrogenesis to complete his task. The failure of your duties in the past has resulted in the termination of your clone line."

That brought the mind of Krylon out of its status quo. He watched the termination, seeing his many selves destroyed before his very eyes! This meant that his life was totally eradicated with no hope of a next chance. He was devastated, the only life that remained to him now was the one that he currently occupied. He had received the ultimate death sentence.

The voice continued. "You are to subvert the powers on Earth and tag enough Terrans so that control of the planet falls to you. You are then to complete the selected breeding program already begun and develop the next race of Brethren. You are to be the genetic beginning and apart from certain modifications to your gene structure will be father to a race."

The voice ended and Krylon felt himself slip back into unconsciousness. He drifted. The Brethren did not dream. The subconscious mind had long ago been subjugated to the purposes of the conscious mind. Still Krylon was experiencing a dream or was his mind being influenced by an outside source? Ridiculous, came his own mental reassurance. No one can affect the mind of a Brethren. So, the images that he was seeing in his mind's eye must just be fragments of data stored in an inappropriate place in his mind.

He was back on the command deck of his Dreadnaught. The space around him was familiar, it was the star system where he had discovered the disabled Juancy ship and had been forced to flee from a superior mental force. There was a name, yes it was Dale Lambert. The man's mental aura vastly outmatched his own. Still the words that he was hearing now were not the ones that he remembered.

"Krylon your people have devastated the galaxy for thousands of years, raping worlds and killing civilizations at will. There is an accounting coming soon and it will be the end of the Brethren race, but it does not have to be the end for your people. Through the greed and the senseless adhesion to power that the Brethren High Council has demonstrated, a seed has been sowed. You are that seed. For generations, you have lived cold, sexless lives, relying on technology to provide for the continuity of your people. Unfortunately, that has only led to stagnation and the sad repetitiveness of mistakes and behaviors. While your people exist, they do not grow."

"Now you have not only received a thin fragment of possibility but a great gift. I am not sure where your path may lead but I think that it will not be the conclusion that the Brethren High Council desires." The voice went silent and once more Krylon's mind was blank.

Groshen was aboard the Starfire, a sister ship to the Polaris but with some very important modifications. He had an inexperienced crew as green as little apples back on Brightholme. His Engineer and his Power Officer were products of Star Dancer's new genetic manipulation directive. The first two to have come out of the vector induced change.

He had marveled at the process. It was certainly nothing he would care to do to his mind and body, and it was strictly voluntary. He had reviewed Doctor Scott's notes on the changes undergone by Mark Thomas and Glenda Stern back on Laurel before that doomed planet was destroyed. He understood the process and was grateful that none of the small group of volunteers had suffered unduly at the change.

Now, theoretically he had a mental augmentation to his power systems to be applied sparingly and with care. It was a human based application that he and the other commanders that would receive such help, must never misapply it. He just wished that he knew if it would work and exactly what the limitations of its use would be. He sighed. Chances were that he would find out sooner than later.

He was bringing a small fleet of defensive vessels into the Terran system in compliance with Dale Lambert's directive to begin the armament of that system in preparation for a Brethren incursion. They had broken out of hyperspace a few parsecs from the heliopause of Sol. This allowed him to be sure that all of the components of the fleet had arrived at the system and that there were no difficulties in that transition.

The fleet consisted of the Orion and another of the newly designed and built Polaris class ships, the Catus, named after the Federation world, so recently destroyed by the Brethren. With them were fifteen of the Freshden defensive asteroid ships and one large transport which held all of the necessary components to set up a base on Mars the fourth planet out from the sun.

Groshen was ordered to establish that base and monitor the system for any possible Brethren fleet activities. Once the base on Mars had been established the Orion was to remain on station as the flag ship for the Terran Defense force. He and the captain of the Catus were to head out into old Federation space and join with Daton Excilore to form a nucleus of fast-moving, hard-hitting fleet whose sole purpose was to keep the Brethren off guard in that sector of space.

Groshen knew that once he was in old Federation space that he would be giving up his command and would be taking out an unarmed scout. His job would then be to establish contact with his own people, the Juancy, and to begin their liberation. A very difficult task better attempted by one person with determination to succeed than an entire fleet. He liked his chances, especially given that he would have one of Doctor Scott's scanning machines with him

The Freshden ships dropped off inside of the asteroid belt between Mars and Jupiter. There they took up observation positions, becoming energy dead to any outside scanners. The Orion took up the lead position, while the two Polaris class ships took guardian positions next to the transport.

His thoughts were interrupted by the blaring of a warning claxon. The shields on all four ships were raised instantaneously. Groshen turned and looked at the readouts on the auxiliary control panel. It was a very good thing that those on board the expeditionary vessels had been on their toes. The amounts of energy that were being thrown against their shields were almost off the charts. "Report!" He spoke to his command crew. His second in command, Liza Tillet responded. "Sir, we are under attack by a variety of small ships. They appear to be coming from bases on the Martian moons, Phobos and Deimos." She looked up from her examination of the flashing readouts. "They appear to be robotic. There are no life signs registering."

Groshen smiled his wide strong face reflecting his joy. "Engineering are you ready down there? This is not a drill!" Jon Kripper replied instantly. "We are ready and auxiliary power is available on your order, sir!"

Jon stole a look at his power officer, Gracet Larkel as she stood feet slightly parted, before her control board. She noticed his attention and gave him a strained smile.

"Sir all vessels report contact. The Orion has extended her shields around the transport and their shields are holding." Groshen nodded and then ordered the Catus to close with his ship on his starboard side. Once it was in place, he had the two ships move in front of the Orion. The main guns swept up through their hulls, they fired on Groshen's command. Instantly a wide swath of space in front of the expeditionary force lit with the destruction of the attacking vessels.

The remaining ships continued their attack. "Sir, the attack pattern has not changed. The enemy ships are not responding to our efforts." She chewed her lower lip in thought. "I don't think that they are programmed to respond. Those vessels are preforming a ridged pattern of attack."

Groshen nodded. This was standard Brethren protocol for those occasional distant outposts that really did not matter to the High Council. Robotic fighters did not risk any of the Brethren's precious blood. "Very well, Mister, analyze their attack pattern and neutralize them."

The space round their ships was lit in atomic fire as vessel after vessel dissolved in the furious beams of destruction delivered by their weapons. Groshen's smile did not wavier but the light in his eyes grew a bit dimmer. "Like shooting fish in a barrel,'" he thought. It was a short matter to clean up the last of the attack vessels, but it became a problem to decide on what to do with the moon bases themselves.

The locations of the bases were easy enough to find, another sure indication of the robotic nature of their opponents. Groshen was positive that if any true Brethren were on either of those bases than it would be a much different problem to deal with it. As it was, he was not ready just to bomb the surfaces of those moons. The Brethren may be charitable of their own hides but that did not mean that there could not be any number of their controlled slaves down there.

Groshen ordered the Orion into orbit around Mars and had the Transport land to begin setting up the colony station. Together the two Polaris class ships orbited Deimos. The Brethren base lay in the shadow of an old impact crater. While the Catus stayed in orbit, the Starfire settled into the accumulated dust of the surface of Deimos.

Groshen lead a small party of four toward the crater wall. The opening of the hanger bay was readily apparent. A wide gaping maw looming as a darker shadow in the dimness of the rock that faced them. As they approached the huge opening there was no motion nor was there any alarm raised. They had set their suit communicators to scan all radio frequencies, but detected nothing.

One of the Starfire's security robots scuttled on in front of them, exploring for any electronic signatures. It approached the threshold of the opening, paused for a moment, and then moved on ahead slowly. The large searchlight mounted on its frame illuminating the grim scene in front of them. There laying by themselves or in small groups were the slaves of the Brethren. They did not have protective suits and as the exploration team approached them, they could see the distorted faces and bloated bodies that demonstrated the effect of explosive decompression.

Groshen just shook his head, "Typical," he said over the team's com link. Then he added, "Stay alert. There may be sections of the base with breathable atmosphere." The hanger bay was a carved-out cavern. The precision of the excavation a tribute to the skills of those that now lay dead behind them. They walked the long distance to the rear wall of the cavern, keeping a sharp eye for any survivors. The security robot did not even beep as it trundled along in a straight line, a destination clearly in mind within its onboard processors.

There outlined against the wall was an airlock. The door was sealed and the indicators on the side panel showed a breathable atmosphere beyond its massive door. Groshen held up his hand, warning the small group to stop at a safe distance from those controls. Using a link on the wristband of his suit he typed in the command to allow the robot to activate the controls and cycle the door open.

The door swung wide in invitation and the robot moved slowly inside of its opening. After a moment, the wrist band emitted a blinking green indicator. Groshen motioned the group forward. They stepped into the airlock proper, and the robot pressed the button allowing the door to swing closed. This was it, thought Groshen. If this was a trap, his people were neatly bottled and ready to be destroyed at the pleasure of their enemies.

The airlock cycled through without mishap and the opposite door swung wide. Once again, the robot moved forward its treads whined softly on the smooth stone floor of the passageway beyond. The corridor that they found themselves in was short and ended at yet another large circular door. The robot pressed the appropriate buttons and that door swung open, a comfortable light shining through its opening to oval on the corridor floor. The robot moved on and stopped a few feet into the room, emitting a soft beeping sound.

Groshen and his crewmates followed and stood still behind the robot. The reason for its current hesitation was plain. They had found the denizens of this base. In front of them was what had been the control room for the base, the wide isles had banks of monitors set up on sturdy counter type desks. Behind these seated as if in attentive duty were chairs occupied by the still forms of several species of humanoids. The people who sat there were upright as if their bodies were frozen in the attitude of their duties. The monitors in front of them were active and several displayed the space around Deimos. One had clearly targeted the silver form of the Catus. Yet all activity had ceased. There was no motion from any of those present.

Once again Groshen pressed a series of buttons on his suit's wrist controller. The robot moved up next to one of the still figures and a soft diagnostic light played over the form. Groshen did not need to see the lurid red indicator from that unit to know that the person by the robot was dead. The robot moved from still form to still form always with the same result. Death hung in the air. When, at last they had reached the end of the control room proper the robot continued on its way, opening a door much like the one from the corridor on the other side of the room. This admitted them to another corridor that went straight back into the wall of the crater. There were no other openings and after a few minutes they came to another of the sealed doors. This time the robot in front of them let out a series of loud beeps, almost as if it had gotten excited.

Groshen motioned the others to the side of the corridor and then approached the opening. He stepped up next to the robot, examined the access panel and then pressed a series of buttons to open the door. A shimmering curtain of light fell from the ceiling above him, trapping him in its envelope. He turned and looked behind him, but the light grew opaque and hindered his view. He did not feel threatened, but it was clear that his only choice was to move forward through the light and the door.

Those behind him, advanced to the door as they watched that curtain of light fall around their Captain. They found that they could not penetrate that light. They were not harmed by its opalescent content, but they could not press themselves forward either. Their Captain was beyond their reach.

Chapter Twenty-Three

Nemoric hovered midair, keeping the beating of his massive wings as slow and as steady as he could. Below him was a high out cropping of stone. The escarpment was riddled with arched openings. Through these a constant movement of great beasts entered or left taking to the skies in pairs or small groups.

From his vantage point Sam studied the activity. "This is no good, Nemoric," came his thoughts. "We need to parse out an individual Dragon, so that we can attempt to communicate with him or her."

"Patience," came his Dragon's rejoinder. "Not all of my winged brothers are so gregarious." As he said this an older dragon came to the edge of one of those open maws. It was clear by the reaction of the dragons around him that he was afforded a certain degree of respect, as they distanced themselves from him. The Old one expanded his wings and at their full stretch they were a match for Sedulic. With quiet dignity the great beast rose into the air, his pace stately and unhurried.

"That is the one that we must approach. We had better be careful. He will be wily and crafty." Nemoric changed the attitude of his flight to give the great one a wide breath. They followed him keeping several wing lengths behind him. Sam marveled at the beast's grace. Here was a magnificent example of his species!

"Thank you, young Rider for the compliment. It has been many a year since any of your ilk has attempted to breach the sanctity of our eyrie." A great roar tore the wind as an entire phalanx of dragons erupted in the air around them. "The deep voice filled his mind once more as the Dragons closed in, "I think that you and that young scamp that you ride have made a serious mistake."

Nemoric, flashed a reassuring thought to Sam, "Remember, be patient." Then he brought them out of the cloak that had enveloped them. Before the Dragons around them could force the two down from the sky, Nemoric issued a very peculiar sound. It started deep in his throat and burst out with a strange trill that caused Sam's head to hurt. With a startled mental cry, the old dragon, ordered the Dragons around them to give the pair some space.

As the wild ones moved aside, Nemoric sent a thought probe out to the Older Dragon. "I am Nemoric the son of the son of the son of Sedulic, patriarch of our race. He has gifted me with all his knowledge and skill. His final charge to me before he left for the alternative universe that is death was to bridge the gap between Dragons and Humans. As you see I have bonded with one of those. Sam Peterson is my Rider and has proved his mettle many times over. I am proud to be his Dragon."

The older Dragon hissed. "They are evil. They betrayed our race and have proved unworthy of our bonding. How could you bring one such here?"

Sam Peterson had been able to follow the mental communications of the Dragons. "I am Nemoric's Rider. I have been trained by Vantu and Kadolic and my skills have been honed by Flendrake. Do not compare me with any weak and treacherous rider. Their day has passed. It is the time of the Terrans of Earth, we who are deemed worthy by our beasts to fly the sky ways of this and any other world."

The elder growled deep in his throat and Sam could feel the Dragon's mind push against his. Nemoric was there in his thoughts, reassuring his Rider. With a sigh of resignation Sam opened his mind. The thoughts that probed him were not necessarily rough, but they were thorough. His memories, his experiences and even his emotions were probed by that mind. He did not hold himself in reserve. He opened himself completely.

The seconds dragged on to minutes which seemed to move onto hours. There came an end at last as the mind of the elder slowly withdrew from his mind. There was silence as Nemoric continued to maintain his position in the air. At long last the sonorous voice of the elder filled his mind. "You, Sam Peterson, have proven yourself of worth. We will allow you to land and speak with our people. Do not be surprised to meet greater resistance to your proposal than you have met with me. Our people suffered greatly in the past with our association with the Riders and few of those that survived will be of a mind to allow that horrendous experience to be repeated by their children."

The guardian dragons peeled away from Nemoric and the elder dragon, allowed them wing room to descend to the waiting maw of the largest opening in the cliff face below. Nemoric braced his mighty wings against the air as he gently came to a rest on the ledge opening.

Sam dismounted slowly resting his feet first on Nemoric's strong front legs and then slid the rest of the way to the rocky soil. With a swirl of dust and grit the elder dragon moved slowly into the cavern behind the opening. Sam followed with Nemoric bringing up the rear. The passageway was dark but every few feet there was a blaze of light, emitted from jewels inset in the walls. It caused the air around the jewels to glow.

The passageway sloped steeply down until at last they came out into a wide carven with a soft sandy floor. Looking up Sam was surprised that he could see quite clearly now. His eyes had adjusted lending aid to his sight, but the jewels that had been placed so sparingly on the passage walls were here decorating the high walls and ceiling with huge mosaics. Scene after scene of Dragons in flight and what could only have been battles between men and Dragons. Sam could see from the images that men were not held in high esteem.

The elder Dragon moved to the center of the sandy floor, as Dragon after Dragon filed in from various openings in the walls. Nemoric stood as still as stone next to his Rider, eyes flashing as two more jewels in the pools of light. The Dragons moved into tiers which rimmed the outer walls of the cavern.

When at last, the steady stream trickled to a stop the elder Dragon opened his mind. "I, who am Drestlic, am the oldest among you. My memory goes back to the elder days and my sire served with Sedulic who was the patron of our race. I have at times served you and the generations before as a source of wisdom and as a guide through the turbulent times through which we all had to pass. I have examined the Dragon Nemoric, who is the son of the son of the son of Sedulic." At this a great roar went up from the Dragons assembled.

"I have examined Nemoric,' he repeated his thoughts and I have found him a true member of our race. The knowledge that was Sedulic has been granted him in its entirety. He is Sedulic and Nemoric. The human Rider that has bonded with him has been tested by my own mental probe and has been found free of the taint that infected those that were once called Riders. He is of a completely different race, one that can combine with our own race to the benefit of both. He has asked permission to speak with the people." He paused for a moment and then continued. "I have decided that he should have the opportunity to speak, I will not voice an opinion on his proposal one way or another."

The sonorous roll of the elder dragon's thoughts ceased, and a silence filled the huge arena. Sam stepped away from Nemoric's side and stood tall with a look of determination on his face. "I am from the planet Earth. It is a small insignificant planet in a quiet backwater of the galaxy. We are just beginning to explore our own system and are not a threat to any of the races that occupy the greater galaxy. Yet we have been thrust into an age-old conflict between the free people's of the galaxy and the Brethren, a race that I am sure you know."

"It was the Brethren that came between your race and that of the Treslin, the Riders. It wasn't known how this came about, but we strongly suspect that some of those Riders had been "tagged" a method that the Brethren used to control the actions of those that they wish to manipulate. It is unknown if any of your race have been so treated. Certainly, the histories, as taught to me by Vantu, Rider of Kadolic and Kadolic himself seem to indicate that the fracture between the races was mutual."

"The Brethren have taken an interest in our planet. This mystifies all that have attempted to analyze the situation. Earth is not a mineral rich planet and has no superior technologies which the Brethren might covet. Still, they have begun to infiltrate our governmental bodies and change the nature of our societies."

Sam paused to look around at the ranks of Dragons facing him. They remained silent but he could feel the mental communications passing from one to another. When he first came to Scalar, he had been told that the "wild Dragons" had slipped back into a more bestial state. Their minds occluded by the lack of contact by the Riders. Now he was certain that these had at least maintained the mental acumen that the race had become noted for throughout the galaxy.

Sam continued his voice low but serious. "The Brethren are not the only ones to have taken an interest in Earth." He looked over to his partner, Nemoric and smiled. "The Dragons that chose to remove themselves from the mainstream of the conflict to preserve the bond between themselves and their Riders have, in a desperate, but strategic move sent a representative of their race through one of the gates. I am humbled and proud to be the Rider of Nemoric, a Dragon whose genetic code had been manipulated by his parents, to be born on Earth and to bond with an Earthman. Me!"

He looked again at his friend, a proud, happy look. "Nemoric is a Dragon in every sense of the word, a true son of a son of a son of Sedulic. We have been proved out to be a proper and tested bonded pair, a bond that only death will dissolve."

"What this means to those of you that would like to have a bond mate, is that there is a new pool of candidates available, a pool without the taint of the Treslin race. The people of Earth are going to be introduced to Dragon kind. Even as we speak Kadolic and his mate Gloridic are on Earth and will join with

Vantu and Darcel their Riders to demonstrate the advantages of becoming bonded with your great race. From there a gate will be established to bring the candidates back to Scalar and introduce them, with your permission, to your race. At that point you are welcome to participate or not in the bonding. All that we ask of you is that you allow those that are interested in the bonding, the free will to join with those from Earth."

Sam finished and lifted his face high surveying the Dragons around him. Nemoric's thoughts came to him. "We are asked to exit the hatching grounds so that the Dragons assembled can debate your proposal. We are to wait at the ledge for a decision on their actions". Sam bowed deeply to the elder Dragon who had allowed him the privilege of addressing the Dragons and turned on his heels to walk calmly with his friend from the cavern.

Vantu had decided that it would be best to arrow into the Space Port after dusk. The long desert day had given way to a night sky alive with brilliant points of starlight. There was little in the way of activity on the roads leading to the port. No launches were scheduled for quite a while and the activity in the research labs had slowed as the summer had come to an end and most of the staff had returned to their teaching position at various colleges and universities in the United States and around the world.

Partly with the Duncans' money, a huge hanger building had been built at the north end of the complex. It had no official designation yet but was in fact going to be the de facto embassy for the Empire on Earth. The three great beasts glided in, landing on the concrete apron in front of the large entrance way. They all dismounted and walked slowly towards the overhead doors. Tremolic resumed his space faring form and took his place back on Scott's shoulder. With silent grace the door rolled up, opening the building, and allowing a soft golden glow to escape into the dark desert night.

As the representatives of the various worlds entered the building a robotic guard ambled up to them. "Please state your names and point of origin?" The voice sounded suspiciously like that of CAIN, the Andromeda's AI. Vantu laughed and for the record stated his name and identified Kadolic as his Dragon. Darcel followed suit indicating her bond mate and added Gloridic's name to the list. Vantu continued saying, "While points of origin are hard to determine given the fact that many of our worlds have been attacked and destroyed by the Brethren, Darcel and I now hail from Scalar in the Empire."

The little robot said in its clipped official voice, "Your voice codes have been added to the file and the physical forms of Kadolic and Gloridic have been added as well." The little automaton then turned to face the remaining members of the group, waiting expectantly.

Tom Peterson then introduced himself and his wife Sally. "We are of Earth originally, New York State to be precise. Of late we have been appointed as representatives of the Empire to Earth." Sally Peterson, smiled and added, "As you well know CAIN." The little robot paused as it swung toward Steven Green and beeped noncommittally. "Your voice patterns have been added to the file, welcome Ambassadors!"

It was Steven's turn as he identified himself and his wife Alice. "Our story is about the same as the Petersons', I guess. We came from New York State and are also Ambassadors of the Empire. Alice added, "Not that we are likely to be staying long. I think that I would like to settle down as representatives of the New Federation on Brightholme. The place just sounds so nice." She ended that comment with an appealing look at her husband.

The four older Earthers laughed, and Steven added, "It's interesting that we have become citizens of the galaxy." Scott Green pulled Nancy Peterson to his side, "I am Scott Green and this is my bride-to-be Nancy Peterson. We are children of the Peterson and Green clans but are now Free Traders plying the space lanes traveling from system to system." Nancy added, "We are here to get married. I so wanted our folks to be at my wedding." She looked at her parents and saw the proud smiles on their faces. Her mother gave her a slight nod and then started to cry.

"I have recorded your voice imprints", and then the little robot paused and the voice that came from its sound projector was definitely that of CAIN, the AI from the Andromeda. "I had the privilege of being at the Duncan wedding. I look forward to receiving an invitation to yours!"

"I note that you have an intelligent life form on your shoulder, Scott Green, and while it resembles to some extent the Dragons, Kadolic and Gloridic I see that its size is proportionately smaller." Scott gave a wiry smile as he mentally communicated with his friend. The little Dragon flew up and landed to one side of the group. A purple smoke surrounded it and when it cleared the massive form of Tremolic stood, stretching his neck to the fullest and barking a Dragon equivalent of a laugh.

"This is my Dragon Tremolic and there is no way to compare his size to the others of his species. He is the exception to many rules."

The little robot tilted its head up and beeped appreciatively. "Yes, I can certainly see that he is indeed an amazing entity. Welcome, Tremolic, to Earth."

It then turned to the final pair standing in quiet amusement as the introductions had gone on. David stood tall and powerful, yet the light of humility shone in his eyes. "I am David Peterson, also late of New York but now I am a Guardian of the free peoples of the galaxy. He paused almost as if hesitating and added, "I am a Weapons Master."

Mary did not wait for her love to identify her, she stepped proud and happy to face the little robot. "I am Mary Rodriquez, I was born in Mexico and became a naturalized citizen of the United States. I last lived in New York but now

make my home on the starship Vooglean, a ship of the Empire.
I am the chief Medical Officer aboard that vessel."

David then stepped up to Mary's side and gently took her hand.
"We also have come back home to marry, with the permission
of her parents I will make Mary Rodriquez my wife, to have
and to hold."

The little robot faced the entire group. "Then all is as it should
be. The doorway through which you have passed is much
more than a portal through which you gain entrance here.
Thanks to Doctor Scott who is currently based on
Brightholme, you have been scanned for any Brethren
technologies, specifically for any controlling chips. Any who
pass through into the embassy will be so scanned. This is not a
fool proof method of identifying an enemy agent as the Lowen
proved. Greed and avarice are powerful directives that don't
need chips to manipulate. Because of this I asked your
personal histories and now I ask for your pardon for having
detained you for so long. Welcome to the Embassy of the
Empire."

Groshen stood facing the corridor in front of him. The
doorway had been tripled sealed and opened after an extended
period of minutes. He had felt trapped in the confines of that
airlock, his massive frame did not begin to fill the space, but he
felt confined all the same. He shook his head to clear it of
unproductive thoughts. He had not been threatened in any
way. True, he had been successfully cut off from the rest of the
away party, yet this felt right somehow.

The attack on his small fleet had been so inept that the results
were predictable. The dead abandoned where they stood or at
their posts only added a macabre sense to the strange scene in
front of him. He moved on into the corridor. It was well lit
with a bright white light. The corridor itself was white and very
clean. It reminded him sharply of the medical facilities
maintained by the Brethren, cold and sterile. The air he
breathed had the taint of antiseptics.

He walked slowly, carefully examining the sides of the corridor for any signs of openings. He could see none, but that didn't mean that there were none. He would have to watch behind him as he moved forward, making his progress slow and awkward.

As he moved a series of algorithms were initiated by the complex's AI. The general form and species type matched that of the Juancy, a rather utilitarian humanoid recorded as a janitorial tasked entity used for many purposes by the Brethren. The AI accepted his presence here and did not initiate any of the internal defensive mechanisms.

Groshen continued his slow march down the hallway until it ended in yet another sealed airlock. From the air around him came the sonorous voice of the AI, "Identify yourself and your purpose for being here." Only Groshen's iron will kept him from twitching and his heart rate remained level, a fact the AI noted as lending credence that this entity belonged here.

"I am Groshen," he responded calmly. "My mission here has the highest rating. I cannot divulge it to you." The AI pondered this for a moment as its databanks searched for the name Groshen. It returned a hit identifying Groshen as the commander of a small Juancy cleanup and retrieval crew sent to various parts of the Brethren sphere of influence to finalize Brethren missions.

"You have been identified, Groshen of the Juancy. You may pass." The doorway in front of him glided open, revealing yet another massive airlock. This time as the door closed behind him, Groshen feared more than the confined space. He had been on several bases where the AI of the base controlled the comings and goings of those who ventured there. He had seen firsthand the cold way such an intelligence took care of any perceived intruders.

He had been very lucky that his service with the Brethren had been so exemplary. He was also relieved that his defection had not yet been recognized and had not filtered through the vast intelligence network of the Brethren. It would make his next job much easier if that remained the status quo. He must walk softly here so that he would arouse no such suspicions.

The scene that met his eyes when the opposing airlock door opened was anything but quiet. There were a number of robotic units moving about with purpose and deliberation. There were no living entities as far he could see but there were many doorways opening up in the large chamber in which he found himself.

Groshen stopped and spoke clearly. "I am here to evaluate the results of this facility in advance of a change in priority orders." In a milder voice he added, "This base has such a low value to the Triune that none of my masters cared to waste their time to visit themselves. I am honored by their trust."

The AI listened in to the request and ran a probability sequence through its logic circuits. There was enough viability in this Juancy's statement that it lent validity to the request.

From the air around him that sonorous voice came once more. "Please follow the holographic sphere to a station evaluation monitor. I will bring up a brief synopsis of our activities."

A glowing ball of light appeared in front of him, and he followed it down a short hallway to the left of the main entranceway. It led him to a comfortably appointed chamber with a padded chair and a viewing screen. Once he had settled his bulk into the chair the screen lit up.

The detailed analysis that appeared tended to dehumanize the scenes that appeared on the screen. It showed a systematic and careful study of humans, the females of that race in particular. The images tagged each young woman giving age, height, weight, race, points of origin and then broke the information down into more detail including blood type, possible genetic defects, and a complete genome of each specimen.

The Juancy looked on in wonder because they were indeed specimens. Only the best for the Brethren he thought. He spoke aloud, "The analyses are incomplete, and you have not displayed the ultimate deposition of these specimens. Please clarify!"

The AI considered the request, tagging it for future deliberation, for now it complied with Groshen's request. "The Triune has decided that a genetic pairing is to occur between one of these specimens and a low-level member of the Council. This test subject has been slightly altered so his genetic makeup will combine with that of the test subject successfully resulting in a "Newborn". The test is to continue through several generations until the genetic patterns of the new Brethren produced stabilizes and is completely able to be replicated in this manner.

Only Groshen's iron will kept his heart level calm and his pulse normal. "I see, and where are the test subjects now?

The AI had monitored Groshen carefully as it had relayed a much-edited portion of the tape. It concealed the alterations that the test subjects had undergone. Minor as they had been many subjects had not survived. The Brethren Triune was not only interested in a stabilized mated pair but there were some advancements to the race that were to be done along with the genetic pairing. These were mainly along the lines of mental powers, but some had visible physical effects. It ran its probability program once more and decided to allow an answer to Groshen's request.

"If you would follow the guiding sphere, I will take you to the reanimation chamber. You will be able to see for yourself and report back, so that the Triune knows that this facility is ready for the next phase of the project." The voice paused and then added in a peevish tone, if that were possible. "We have been ready for some time now."

Groshen got to his feet and the ball of light appeared once more. He followed it from the records room down the short hall and back into the main chamber before it veered off to one side and entered another long corridor. There were no doors to either side that he could see but he passed through several airlocks before he came to a stop fronting a large white door. This slid aside and he walked into the chamber beyond.

Chapter Twenty-Four

The away team that Groshen had brought into the Brethren base had stood immobilized by the strange curtain of light that had engulfed their Captain. Once the initial shock was over, they tried to breach that curtain, but no physical force could penetrate that shield and they dared not try energy weapons.

The second in command of the away team opened communications with the Starfire, "Commander Tillet, Captain Groshen has been engulfed in some form of force field and has moved through an airlock. We cannot penetrate the shield. I request orders."

The voice of Liza Tillet came through the crackle of interference which began to limit the clarity of the com line. "You are to report back to the shuttle. There is a buildup of some type of energy around the Brethren base. I fear that we will soon be under attack by something a little more challenging than robotic fighters. Get back to the ship ASAP!"

The remaining members of the away party moved back down the corridor and out through the connecting airlocks. The dead Brethren slaves a ghostly reminder of the type of enemy that they faced.

Groshen stared down the long line of cryostasis tubes that faced him. Their frosted observation ports clouded his view of their contents, but he could guess what they contained. "How many test subjects are there?", came his stunned comment.

The AI had digested the strange readings from the outer complex and had determined that Groshen was not alone. The physical readouts indicated a mix of sentient species but no true Brethren. The life forms were making a hasty retreat, a fact which the AI withheld from the Juancy.

"There are seven thousand current viable subjects. They have been processed and are ready for the pairing. I will bring one out of stasis for you to examine if you wish." When Groshen did not reply immediately a series of robotic aides sprang to life and a cryostasis tube was removed from its storage position and placed inside the reanimation tank. "I think that you will find the test subjects very interesting. We have improved on the original genetic baseline and have produced something that just might be suitable for the Triune's use."

The shuttle was headed into a steep arc to meet with the Starfire when a brilliant beam of light intersected its course. Without a flash or any other indication of a hostile action the shuttle ceased to exist. Liza Tillet ordered the shields up just in time. The indicators went off the charts as the shields absorbed a tremendous surge of energy from the Brethren base below. Jon Kripper and Gracet Larkel closed their eyes and felt for the energy that was coming their way. They tentatively pushed against its awesome surge and the power moved slightly away from the task force. Then with a determined effort they captured the energy and began to feed it back on itself.

Groshen watched in fascinated horror as the cryostasis tube opened. He wasn't sure what it was that he would see but the beautiful form of the naked human female showed no signs of outward tampering. Like everything else demanded by the Brethren, she was perfect. The robotic attendants moved in a well choreographed dance as they went about the business of reanimating her.

Just then the voice of the AI came loud to his ears. "This base is now under attack by the ships that you have led here, Commander Groshen. I now perceive that you are no longer operating for the benefit of my Brethren Masters, therefore you will be eliminated at once."

Groshen leapt to one side in time to avoid being vaporized by a beam from the wall of the chamber. With the incredible speed born of his massive strength and the low gravity of the moon on which he found himself he was able to avoid several of the beams while moving closer to the banked cryostasis tubes. With desperation, he hoped that the AI would not dare to destroy the frozen subjects cradled within those tubes, but he underestimated the value that the machine placed on those unfortunate females. The beams sliced through the tubes and vaporized their contents. Groshen was sick to his stomach, there was no doubt the AI reflected its masters' careless attitude. The smell of burned flesh was overpowering.

While Groshen ducked and moved avoiding death by millimeters, the robotic attendants continued to reanimate the subject within their care. As beams flashed over her head the slack faced woman regained a measure of consciousness. She accessed her memories in an effort to place her current location and only remembered the clean white walls of the cryostasis chamber. Her eyes now only reported a smoldering cloud of burning flesh and exploding circuitry.

A movement from the corner of one eye caught her attention. The humanoid figure matched the conformation of one of the Juancy race. His massive physique allowed him to evade the destructive beams for the moment, but her mind calculated that he had approximately 3.25 seconds left before the AI operating those beams would analyze the patterns of his evasions and score a death blow. Strange, she thought to herself, she had no feelings at all concerning the outcome of the battle, she couldn't help but wonder at her lack of emotions.

The expected outcome did not occur as the powerful energy beams which had bathed the ships in orbit above the moon were turned back against themselves. The augmented beams aided now by the minds of Jon Kripper and Gracet Larkel hit the base with extreme prejudice. The AI did not have time to react as the beams hit the main power generators causing a chain reaction which began to swallow up system after system on the base. The chamber went suddenly dark and Groshen stood in that concealing darkness, making his way to where the now lifeless robotic attendants stood frozen in their last position of action. His groping hand met warm flesh and he quickly located the hand of the human woman. He leaned into her and whispered. "I do not know if you can understand me, but we have to get out of here before this entire base blows up."

Stephen Goodale   261

The woman quickly calculated the probabilities of survival at her current location and her logical conclusion was the same as the Juancy. Next, she considered whether she should just dispatch this humanoid or use him as an assist for her escape. Again, her logic dictated that the possibility of her survival went up considerably in the company of the Juancy. Without a word, she rose to her feet and stepped down from the platform on which she had lain.

Groshen took her movement as an ascent to move. The howling of the base AI shattered the odd silence that had filled the smoked filled chamber. Groshen had no doubt that the rest of the inhabitants of the tubes as well as the AI itself had ceased to be. The woman pulled close enough to him to ask, "What is your plan Juancy?"

So, Groshen thought to himself, she can speak, and she recognizes my race. He thought furiously for a moment and then remembered his previous experiences on similar bases in the past. "We look for the emergency escape vessels that should be here. We will launch one of those in an effort to reach Brethren controlled space. Once there I will attempt to rejoin my command section and report."

The woman cocked her head as if she was listening. "That may be a viable path for you Juancy, but not for me, I think. You came with a small fleet of ships. I will join them. For some reason, I feel that my fate lays on the third planet from the sun that illuminates this system."

Groshen started to protest but before he could make a sound the woman had bridged the gap between them and with a swift motion impossible to follow, she had tapped a spot where his head joined his shoulder and the Juancy immediately lost consciousness.

She stood over the still form of the Juancy and considered her next steps. She could of course just leave him where he lay in which case he would surely die as the last of the destroyed base's systems failed and the corridors lost life support. She could drag him with her to the waiting ships or she could allow him to follow his own plan and return to the Brethren sphere of influence.

The thought of leaving him to die was not appealing to her although she could not decide why. She had very little in the way of memories, most of those were dark and terrifying, yet she could not just leave him. The fact that he stated what he thought was a good plan not only for her but himself added weight to the third option. She would not accompany him because she knew that there was another fate waiting for her, but she would aid him on his way.

Her decision made she bent down and with very little effort at all, hefted the Juancy onto her shoulders. The light gravity may have had a part to play in the ease of her handling the much bigger man, but she doubted it. She had not even strained while lifting him.

She walked purposefully down a narrow corridor, hardly noticeable from the many branching spokes of access ways in the central chamber. The dust on the floor was partially due to the trembling of the surrounding rock structures but was mainly from lack of use. How she knew where to go and how to activate the security doors, she did not stop to ponder.

The emergency launch bay opened before her and closed silently behind. She ran a hand over an access panel while using the other to support the Juancy. A dim light appeared at the end of the space, and she stepped towards it. There lined up carefully were five sleek looking vessels big enough to support four or five normal sized people. She smiled to herself or one or two Juancy! She placed him in one of the carriers and strapped him in. With deft movements, she set a course for the Brethren sphere of influence, although how she knew that coordinate, she could not say.

She then opened a second and placed herself inside. She set the destination for near space. When she was confident that all was in readiness, she typed in the command that launched both vessels.

Liza Tillet watched the trajectory of the two life pods. The Starfire had the capability to analyze the life forms onboard each. The one vessel arrowed outbound from the sun and disappeared into hyperspace. The readouts indicated that Groshen was the sole occupant of that vessel. Liza smiled tightly to herself, she was now the Captain of the Starfire, a bit earlier than planned but it was a fait accompli all the same. She concentrated on the second vessel, and frowned, the readouts were very strange. The occupant was very human but there were significant anomalies in the patterns which indicated that all was not as it should be.

The second ship rose on a gentle approach to the formation of New Federation ships and then stood down, as if waiting patiently for those on board to recognize the vessel's presence and then decide what to do about it. Liza Tillet thought for a moment and then asked her communications officer to contact the transport. When the commander of that vessel reported in Liza gave him a series of terse orders and when satisfied that they had been carried out asked her officer to open a communications channel with the Brethren craft.

"This is Liza Tillet, Captain of the New Federation ship Starfire, please respond." The hum of the open communications line remained constant for a few seconds and then a self-assured female voice spoke, "I do not have a designation Captain. I was awakened from cryostasis by the base AI just a few hours ago, that base is now offline. I have calculated the probabilities that I should contact your vessels to further the possibilities of achieving my directives. As a result, I await your pleasure and will not raise shields or weapons. What is your decision?"

"You mentioned achieving your directives, can you share what those might be?"

The silence that followed was significant. "I have calculated a response that might appease you Captain. I cannot guarantee that you will be completely satisfied with the answer, but it is the best that I can do. I am uncertain where the sum of my calculations will lead me. Will that satisfy you?"

"I will let you know if it satisfies me after I have heard what you have to say. Please continue."

The feral grin that appeared on the woman's lips lacked nothing sort of a full-throated growl. The instincts that now drove her were completely irresistible. From the depths of the swirling fire that surged up from her she answered. "I am here for one purpose, Captain Tillet. I was designed to breed. I need to replicate myself through the interaction with another. You call it making love, but my need is much more basic. I need to breed. I will be the mother of a new species." Does that satisfy you Captain Tillet?"

To say that the Captain of the Starfire was a little more than taken back by the intensity of the voice and the blatant meaning of her words would have been a severe understatement. Liza Tillet had put aside similar feelings in an attempt to reach the position that she now occupied. She wasn't married and had no family of her own, nor was she likely to. Space was a cold harsh place and did not foster the warmth and stability required by families. That was a pleasure mainly reserved for those that were planet bound.

She drew in a deep breath and answered that voice. "You say that you have no designation. I take it to mean that you have no name, no way of identifying yourself. How then do you intend to draw the attention of a proper mate? How will your children address you as they grow and how will prosperity be able to remember you if they can't even identify you?"

"That may be true," said the voice "but I can guarantee that I will be remembered. The designation is just a way of simplifying communication, nothing more."

"Yes, that is correct," said Liza, "but it would make talking to you much more comfortable for us. Would you have a problem with us giving you a designation, I mean a name?"

Once more the voice paused in thought. The female Tillet had analyzed her situation better than she had herself. The Tillet was quite correct, this talking about would be easier if she had a name. "Alright Captain Tillet, I will entertain possible naming conventions."

"Well," said Liza Tillet slowly, "would it be possible if you send us a picture of yourself? Sometimes the name fits the form in the human lexicon."

The woman sat stock still. She had never considered her appearance. In fact, she did not really know what she looked like. It might be an interesting experience after all, she thought to herself. "Very well." She turned in her seat and voiced a command. Immediately a brief flash came from the console in front of her. The image appeared on the screen.

There framed by flowing red hair was a face with a fair complexion. It had regular features that divided her face in a symmetrical manner. Her nose was well proportioned and had just a slight upturn. Her eyes were clear and bright green with just the hint of gold flecks. Her lips were full and slightly pink. Inadvertently the image caused her to smile. Yes, it would do. She fed the image into the communications link and pressed the transmission button, which sent the image over to the Starfire.

There was a brief silence from the Starfire and then Liza Tillet's voice came over the com link. "You are quite lovely! Such a face needs a good name. Would you consider Dianna? It reflects the name of the moon on which you were found, and it is the name of an ancient hero from Earth's past. Dianna was a huntress, and it seems so are you after a fashion."

The woman sat in the small command deck of the escape vehicle and mouthed the name Dianna to herself. It had a nice ring to it and since her own name was lost to her, she accepted this new one in its place. "Yes, Dianna is fine. Are you going to bring me aboard now?"

Liza Tillet was thoughtful for a moment. By bringing in "Dianna" she may be bringing in an unrevealed danger. She could feel that there was much more to this than she could understand at the moment. Doctor Scott's scanning unit would answer some of those questions, but she didn't want to use it on Dianna without explaining why she did so and not without getting her cooperation in the process.

She spoke carefully into the com link. "Before I bring you on board, I would like to have your permission to run some medical scans on you in the hanger bay. They will not harm you in any way, yet they might reassure us that you have no hidden technology that we can't understand. Do you agree to this process?"

Dianna, as she had already considered herself, just laughed and said, "You may run your tests, but please share any information that you discover with me. I do not have any clear memories before coming awake in the reanimation lab. What I can remember is dark and frightening, like bad dreams."

Liza Tillet was content to bring the tractor beam to play on the small escape ship. The beam locked on and the ship was pulled into the maw of the waiting hanger bay.

Liza Tillet had her Engineer and Power officer stand by to monitor the hanger bay. If at any time, they grew concerned they were to flood the bay with a potent sleeping gas which would instantly render any humanoid specie unconscious. As a further precaution they were to snap down stasis fields on all in the bay and at no time were they to release the protective shields of the companionway doors until she gave the order. With as many safety procedures in place as she could think of, Captain Tillet entered the hanger bay. The doors slid shut behind her and were sealed.

There was a medical crew standing by next to the portable scanners devised by Doctor Scott. If there were any Brethren devices implanted in Dianna, they would know almost instantly. Captain Tillet faced the escape ship's hatchway and waited. The door slid open slowly and in the dim interior of the hatch they watched as Dianna manipulated the ramp controls. The ramp slid smoothly out and onto the hanger bay floor. With slow stately steps Dianna walked the short distance to where the Captain stood.

The impact on those present was potent and almost overpowering. Dianna had not said a word, but all there felt the aura of sexuality which exuded from her. Dianna waited at the base of the ramp and simply smiled. Captain Tillet shook herself and with a small laugh said, "I had not imagined that you would have such a powerful presence. The affect is somewhat overwhelming. If you would step over to the scanners my medical team will run their tests on you. That is if we can get their jaws off the floor." She laughed and the spell was broken.

Dianna, for her part was very cooperative. She moved to the scanner plate and stood where the blushing young medic indicated. A curtain of pale opalescent light fell around her and the sophisticated probes passed around and through her body. The probes would not damage any tissue, but they would cause a feedback loop in any Brethren technology found. This in effect rendered the device harmless without allowing the controllers of such devices to know that they had been thwarted.

When that tests had been performed, Dianna stepped to the next set of medical scanners. The purpose of these were standard such as, blood typing, genetic mapping, bone density and muscle mass.

When the tests were completed Captain Tillet motioned to Dianna to have a seat at a small conference table set up to one side. A tray of fruit, cheese and meat rolls appeared along with a selection of drinks. Dianna made herself comfortable and the

Captain sat across from her at the table. The other people in the room moved aside and technicians began the analysis of the Brethren escape vessel.

After a short pause, Captain Tillet opened the conversation, "I do apologize for all of the precautions. Our experience with the Brethren has not been at all a positive one. Would you like to tell me about yourself, Dianna?" The Captain held up a hand to forestall Dianna's protests, "I mean what you do remember, certainly from the point of your reanimation but also those dark dreams. I know that those might not be very comfortable for you, but they may help us in our understanding of your present circumstances."

Dianna paused and accessed her memories once more. There was little enough to tell. She could remember the events after her reanimation well enough and she passed those along to the waiting Captain. Those other memories however were very dim, unfocused horrors. "May I ask to delay the balance of this interview until I myself have had time to delve into those dark, frightening thoughts?"

The Captain looked into Dianna's eyes and for the first time could see something of a human emotion playing in their depths. She made a decision, "Certainly, Dianna. I appreciate that you may need time to get a handle on your thoughts and experiences, but I would like you to promise that as they do come to you, and you assimilate them that you share them with me. Who knows perhaps talking about them might help you understand them better!"

Just then there was a soft ding as the results of the scans began to be displayed on the monitor in front of her. Liza moved the screen so that Dianna could see the results at the same time. Dianna was pleased by the Captain's forthrightness, although she thought privately to herself that she, Dianna, might have waited to examine the results first and edit the information to lend herself an advantage in any possible confrontation. Still, it felt "right" that the woman in front of her kept her word, so she said nothing and analyzed the readouts just as the Captain was doing.

The first set of scans were very troubling. They indicated that there were many devices implanted within her that were of Brethren origin. Her body and even her mind had been designed as nothing more than a tool for the convenient use of the Brethren. They had designed her as a slave to obey who ever held the appropriate command codes. Something deep within her rebelled against such a controlling influence. The controlling portions of the technology had been nullified by the scan device, rendering any external command useless, to be caught in a loop. The controller would not recognize the fact that the commands had been nullified. They would only receive the communication that the commands had been received and implemented.

The scans also revealed that her internal structure had been altered. This was done through physical enhancements and mental expansion. She was strong, fast, and extremely bright. She was pleased to note that the results indicated that these changes were not artificial but augmentations of her native abilities. Since there were no "controlling chips" involved the scanners had not changed her physicality. She remained as she had been planned, fast, strong, and smart.

There were some troubling changes to her endocrine system. The hormones that regulated her reproductive system had been artificially enhanced. Dianna looked up into the Captain's understanding eyes. "I appreciate the fact that you have not tried to artificially control me through my systems. It appears that this overwhelming desire to reproduce has been graphed into me. Would it be possible to suppress these urges without eliminating my ability to have children at some future date?"

"Certainly, Dianna! Such procedures are simple and non-invasive. Many human females put off having children until they feel that they are ready to take on such responsibilities. The scans do indicate that your planet origin is that of Earth and that you are indeed a human being from that planet so it should be a simple matter to give you control of your own body."

"Very well, I accept your offer, but that leads me to another and much more troubling question." She looked the Captain in the eyes and spoke slowly so that her meaning could not be misunderstood, "Obviously, I was on that base for a reason. If I am truly of Earth, I must have been "harvested" from there and brought to Deimos for the purposes of enhancement. The question begs, why?"

That question hung in the air between the two women. Finally, Captain Tillet answered her. "I do not know Dianna. It is plain that the Brethren have some plans for Earth. We have only begun to understand some of the facts concerning that race. It is felt that they are few in number and that they have lost the ability to reproduce. It is true that when a Brethren is killed that is not the end of that individual, but in some warped manner they appear again, sometimes almost immediately and sometimes generations down the timeline. To outward appearances they are the same and have the same memories, but they appear uniformly at an age that we judge to be thirty life cycles."

Captain Tillet looked at her gently, "It could be that they meant for you to be part of a resurgence of their race that you, Dianna would be as you said, the mother of a new race."

Dianna thought about that for a moment, and she could not fault the Captain's logic. It fit her circumstances except for one important point. "I am not a hermaphrodite. I cannot breed with myself I must have a mate!"

Captain Tillet nodded her head slowly, "I think that you are correct. Somewhere there must be a male, a Brethren, who has been manipulated as you have been. That is the purpose for which you were created. The question now remains, will you meekly submit to the dictates of the Brethren Triune or will you determine your own fate?

Dianna sat very still and ran the words of the Captain through her mind. The conclusions were logical and the question a valid one. She would not deny her purpose, the genetic programming was too strong for that, but she would not weakly submit to the control of the Brethren Triune.

"I accept the help of your medical staff to control the hormones that I have coursing through my system. I will dictate when and if I will breed. Still, I cannot help but think that the logical outcome will be one of mating and replication. I will have to think long and hard on the topic. In the meantime, may I request that you allow me to assume a position with your command, Captain? I know that from your point of view that it is a lot to ask, but I think that I need to get to know you and what you stand for better. Then when the time comes perhaps, I can make my own decisions as to the direction of my fate."

Chapter Twenty-Five

Captain Tillet sat back in her command chair. The large transport which had come in with her small fleet was now safely installed on the Martian surface. The process of developing a base from which they could unobtrusively defend the Terran solar system was well begun.

The Freshden asteroid ships had been placed in the asteroid belt between Mars and Jupiter and the seeding of the belt with magnetic mines had been accomplished. The Orion had found a secure place on one of the moons hidden inside the frozen rings of Saturn and was developing a defensive base there.

Dale Lambert the fleet Admiral was due out to visit the Earth and attend the weddings of David Peterson and Mary Rodriquez as well as that of Scott Green and Nancy Peterson. The event would be well attended, or so she had heard.

Several representatives from the Ikornian system, including Theresa the Outer Warder as well as several of the Kilorian peoples would be in attendance. Liza Tillet found herself checking schedules and dealing with logistics. "Here I thought that I would be out in old Federation space dealing confusion and defeat to the enemy fleet! Ah well I guess we all have our place."

A quiet voice spoke up by her elbow. "Captain, I wonder if you would allow me to attend that wedding on Earth? I would like to understand more of this thing you people call love." Liza Tillet was a bit startled by the request, but she had come to know Dianna somewhat over the past few weeks. There was an odd combination of innocence and sophistication rolled up into the woman that they had rescued from Deimos.

Dianna had been eager to learn and after a little while the crews of the various vessels that the Starfire came into contact with had accepted her as another crewman. While she had not assigned the woman a specific duty station aboard her ship,

Captain Tillet had attached Dianna as her personal aid. She used her as a valuable link between her and her command.

"I will pass your request along, Dianna. It is up to those being married who attends their wedding, but I could certainly see the value of the experience for you, I will ask. In the meantime, we need to prepare the system for the arrival of the guests."

The new Empire Embassy in New Mexico was busy with preparations as well. Nancy Peterson and Mary Rodriquez spent hours with their mothers discussing the fine points of the celebration. The two, who had been fast friends since their days together on the farm in New York, found it easy to compromise and create a synthesis of activities. They polished their vows and held on to each other as the realization of their futures drew near.

Scott spent a great deal of his time aboard his ship. The freighter had been delivered by a crew from Brightholme and now rested in an underground hanger bay adjacent to the Embassy proper. The activity tended to calm his nerves. The future was open to him, but a problem was niggling in the back of his mind. He had privately decided that he should establish a base on which he could build a home. A place, he thought where it would be safe to raise children. As he worked installing an auxiliary panel on the command deck a calm voice came into his mind. It was more of a remembered conversation or the whisper of a memory. "You and yours will always have a home here."

David stayed out of Mary's way and spent a great deal of his time meditating. He was applying the training that Griden had given him, developing that inner core which was his base of strength and the center of his convictions. He prayed a lot during that time, not so much appealing to God for strength but more to allow him to understand what it was that he had to do.

He of course was excited by the coming wedding, and he loved Mary with all of his heart, but sadly he knew that until his task was accomplished or he was dead, his time with his bride would be stolen moments to be treasured and held dear.

The chime of his chamber entranceway rang softly, its low melodic sound insistent. David raised himself up through his consciousness and uncurled his legs to stand briefly. He shook himself as a dog would coming up out of the water and walked the few feet to his chamber door. "Strange he thought to himself, I can't "feel" anyone there. "Enter," he invited the visitor to come in, and then stepped back as a wave of invisible force swept through the door.

The force that engulfed him was not violent and did him no harm, but it held him in its grip, unable to move. A handful of bells went off in his mind, gently chiming a strange melody. A soft laugh accompanied that melody. "Come now my brave Weapons Master, surely Griden has taught you more caution than that." The force died away and there Theresa the Outer Warder of Ikorn stood. Her shoulders adorned by the venerable Frthessig.

She looked at David who after the first moments of alarm had stood still and passive in the force that had held him. "Have I come at a bad time?" Theresa asked, a smile on her face. "It is time that you attended to your training David Peterson. I have come to begin your instructions in the use of Dark Energy."

David straightened his shoulders and returned the Ikorian's smile. "As it happens, Madam Warder I am free of responsibilities for the moment. My bride to be is busy driving everyone crazy with the preparations for our wedding and I have been told in no uncertain terms to stay out from under foot."

"Good", was all she said and then added. "I think that we had better do this on Ikorn." David started to protest but Theresa had already made a sweeping motion with her hands and his room melted away in a blaze of purple light. When his eyes cleared enough for him to see again, they stood in the middle of a large clearing surrounded on all sides by high intricately carved walls. From the bottom of the walls rank upon rank of stadium seating bleachers rose up. David felt the dark sand of arena floor under his feet, automatically adjusting his balance on its loose surface.

"This is the training stadium of the Ikorns. Here you are suspended outside of your normal time and space. At the end of each of your sessions you will be transported back to your room in the Embassy on Earth, mere seconds after you had left."

David shook his head to clear the cobwebs from his mind, still Griden had trained him well and he adjusted his thinking very quickly. "Will I be able to transfer myself as you have apparently done, at my will?"

Theresa laughed once more, "You will have this and many other powers, but I warn you that the training is very difficult, and you may fail, in which case, well that would not be very pleasant." She looked into David's eyes and asked, "Are you ready?"

Thoughts of Mary crossed his mind. He knew that she served only life, but he knew that somewhere in his future he would have to face Hymical. He understood beyond doubt that the fate of the galaxy would rest on his shoulders and that included Mary. David looked into Thresea's eyes and nodded his head, "I am ready."

Krylon sat lost in thought. His ship was on its way to the Terran system, his assignment was a strange one. He had lived within the system of the Brethren for thousands of years and had been regenerated many times during that long span of lives. Never had he felt as threatened as he did now. The Triune had given him this one last chance to serve the Brethren. Succeed or die!

He was keenly aware of the truth of this edict having been present and forced to watch as the long line of clones that should have protected his immortality were destroyed before his very eyes. His link to the future had been lost. Now the only way that he could feasibly perpetuate himself was by the ancient and to his mind crass, way of impregnating a female whose genetic makeup would be compatible enough to match his and produce viable children.

On top of that he would be required, again of necessity, to guard and rear those children so that they might survive to reach an age where they too could continue the genetic strain that was Krylon and that of his mate. He would have to be a mate that provided for his family. How archaic was this?

In the darkness of his private dome, with the security panels slid closed and the dampening fields active, he knew that no one or nothing could reach him. He was free to think. Into his thoughts that spanned many life times he dug and apart from the brief joy of discovering that he still existed as he came alive once more in the regeneration chambers, that he Krylon, was empty of everything. He no longer felt joy, he no longer treasured conquest, he was completely turned off by the thoughts of the excesses of his past lives, he was a desert, dead of all emotions. Yet still in the darkest corner of his mind he felt a stirring. A chink of light dimly illuminated the dark landscape of his life.

A voice, one that had no business being there reached him in his sanctuary. "Such a life is not so bad, my friend. To place someone else above you, to protect them and to hold them in high esteem need not demean you. Such a love and such a way of life will make your spirit grow. In that growth, there is a chance of life eternal that has been denied you through the false belief that by perpetuating the body and in some ways the mind you could achieve such immortality."

"You know what I mean. I sense the desolate landscape of your past lives. Not one has brought you any great joy. Not one has given your life meaning. You my friend, are in a position to become the father of your race. You can join the world of the living at last. Such is the gift that you have been given, although your old masters do not realize what they have started. In you the galaxy can find a new life and in you, your race can finally achieve the greatness that its past perversions have denied it."

He felt the knee jerk reaction of his kind, a swelling of self importance, of egotistical self righteousness. "You have no place in my mind, I am a Brethren Councilman. My Triune has given me life after life, and I am obligated to do as they ask. To forget all that I am, all that I have done would be impossible. Even if I found merit in your argument how could I put aside the sins of my life? I am, as are all of my race, damned for our lives of excess and self indulgence."

The voice filled his mind with a richness and compassion. "I know what you are Krylon. I know what you have done, but there is forgiveness for those that seek it. It would not be easy and the demands on you would be difficult but there is the possibility of redemption. I will show you the path, but you must walk it."

"I do not think that you understand me at all. I am satisfied with my life. I don't know any other. All bow before me, I am as a god to those that must serve me. How do you expect me to give up all that I am? For what? Now get out of my mind!"

The voice was quiet within him, but as Krylon began to think that he had experienced a psychotic episode, he heard the voice one last time. "I think that you will find it impossible to continue on. The universe will reach out to you, and you will be swept into a new pattern."

The voice was gone, and all was still, but Krylon was completely desponded. A light began to flash in the corner of his dome. It was insistent. Krylon waved his hand and the dome lifted from above him.

"Lord Krylon, we have entered the Terran system, but we are not receiving a response from our moon bases around the fourth planet out from the system's star." Krylon looked up from his seat in surprise. He knew his lowly station in the scheme of things within the Brethren ruling strata, but to have an underling verbally admit failure in his presence demonstrated how low he had sunk. "Remember," came the voice. "You do not have to be like your brothers, you are unique!"

Krylon held his breath and released it slowly, the flash of red anger drained from him leaving him calm and objective. "Very good commander, open all channels and broadcast a great and meet. We are not alone in this system."

The commander who was expecting a reprimand at the very least and instantaneous death at the worst just stood there dumb founded. Krylon turned and raised an eyebrow at his subordinate. This released the man from his stunned inactivity and with a heartier voice he commanded the communications officer to commence the broadcast. "Very good, came the voice. "You have taken the first steps to true leadership."

Dale Lambert sat back into the command chair a satisfied smile playing on his lips. When he had met Krylon during the Orion rescue mission, he had dealt with the immediate circumstances that allowed him to control the peaceful outcome of that meeting. He had scanned the Brethren commander's mind and, in that process, had implanted a few suggestions.

Dale of course had not realized where the patterns that he suggested to the subconscious mind of Krylon would go. Again, he smiled to himself, the future was in the hands of God and certainly was not the providence of mere mortals, no matter how powerful they were. He had "felt" the mind of Krylon as he was once more regenerated, and Dale was surprised to find that his suggestions had survived that awesome rebirth. Apparently, the Brethren leadership had not combed the man's mind as carefully as they may have thought.

Since then, Dale had been able to ease into Krylon's mind making other suggestions while mentoring the Brethren toward a better path. Now Krylon was entering the Terran system just as Dale himself was arriving aboard his personal transport. He would be a fool indeed if he thought that this was mere coincidence.

"Notify the Orion, I am going to make contact with Krylon's ship and more than likely board it. I want to meet him face to face." The duty commander just acknowledged the order and contacted the Orion. Dale once more sat back into his chair, closed his eyes, and concentrated on the Brethren leader. "Krylon, do you hear me?"

He wasn't very surprised to hear the voice once more in his mind. Krylon cocked his head in an attentive manner and formed his mental reply. "Yes, I hear you. I assume that this is Dale Lambert the Admiral of the Federation Fleet. You have been very busy, haven't you? I assume that the voice that has been gently guiding me has been yours?"

"Yes, indeed, but I hope that you have noted that I have only made suggestions and in no way, have I tried to force your actions or demanded your compliance. You have made all your own decisions. I am not the Brethren masters that have controlled you through all of your many lives."

Krylon smiled bitterly. "So, noted Admiral Lambert. Now to what do I owe this pleasure? You would not have exposed yourself in this manner if there wasn't something that you wanted, from me."

The next words startled Krylon to his core. "I would like to meet with you Krylon. I would like permission to board your ship and if you don't mind, I would like to sit down with you to discuss the matter of your future, say over a cup of Terran Coffee, my treat?"

The trials that Theresa had put him through may have had only an elapsed time frame of minutes in the reality of David's world, but the hours of grueling mental, emotional and physical labors demanded of him in the reality of Ikorn drained him as nothing had ever done before. He leaned heavily on the training given to him by Grieden but even with that support he was exhausted when he was transported back to his sleeping compartment.

He threw himself down on his sleeping platform and closed his eyes. Exhausted has he was sleep would not come. His mind whirled with the memory of the power that the dark energy had given him. He did not have a previous inkling of such power. His master had not warned him of it, had made no mention of it in fact. Theresa had drilled him in the safeguards necessary to wield that energy and he was grateful. No mortal man should have had access to such raw power. Without the safeguards, he would have been consumed by it.

A hand full of silvery notes rung through his head and immediately the thoughts of his trials were replaced by comfortable ones drawn from his own memory. He was asleep in seconds.

Mary had been so involved in the preparations for the upcoming weddings that she hadn't realized that so much time had elapsed. She suddenly felt very lonely, and, in that solitude, she missed David. He was a man who she had come to know as a gentle soul, who fate had selected to a higher and much deadlier calling. She knew that he did not pursue that calling of his own choosing. She decided to take a few minutes and went to find her husband to be. She paused outside of his door to listen. She knew that he spent a lot of time in meditation. She respected his need to develop his talents. He had hinted to her that there were some dire times ahead and she knew that he needed all the inner armament that the fates would give him.

Not hearing anything she palmed the door entranceway panel. Her DNA was scanned allowing her admittance. The room was dark and quiet. She was about to leave when a wash of purple light filled the room briefly blinding her. In its afterglow, she could just see David as he collapsed on his sleeping pallet. Mary was stunned for just a moment as a soft voice entered her mind. "Do not be afraid, Mary your husband to be, has been very busy putting his time to good use while you have been preparing for the upcoming wedding."

Mary turned as Theresa appeared by her side. Her voice trembled as she tried to articulate what she was feeling, "I don't know what to think. I have struggled these past months to come to an accommodation with David's, err talent. I love the man dearly, that I know, but how can we have any sort of life together, when he must go off and do, God knows what. I worry all the time for him. I worry about his safety, and I worry about his humanity." She couldn't go on and started to quietly weep.

Theresa reached out and cupped Mary's face in her hand. Gently but insistently, she forced Mary to look her in the eyes. "Your love is all that keeps David safe. He truly loves you and he is aware of your conflict over his abilities. It saddens him greatly because it causes you distress. He would give it all up in a heartbeat, but that is not his decision to make. The fate of billions upon billions of lives and many hundreds of worlds rides on his shoulders."

"The only way that he could even think of taking on that load is the knowledge that you, Mary, are there waiting for him." Theresa looked at the young woman in her care and a smile played upon her face. "One day, when this is all over you will have David completely to yourself. He will be able to be the man that you would want him to be, but now, well now he must prepare for a battle the likes of which have not been seen in this galaxy before. On his shoulders the hammer stroke will fall. Please, Mary, just love him. There will be a time when that love will be all that can save him, and us!"

David stirred in his sleep. In his dreams, he could feel the tug of the universe on him. The segmentation of powers that keep the balance was moving rapidly in two directions. When he had first felt that pull, he knew that the majority of that energy was focused on Hymical. Now he could feel it coming back to him and he could sense the scales coming into balance. Somewhere in his dreams he called out Mary's name and, in that instant, Theresa was gone, and Mary stood over his sweating and restless form. A decision was made and without further fear, Mary bent down to kiss his lips.

Stephen Goodale   282

David's eyes flashed open, and the soul of the man resided in those eyes. He reached out and swept Mary into his arms kissing her deeply with all the passion of his heart. He then released her and stood up holding her in his arms a peaceful smile plying his lips. It would be alright. He need not fear the future, he held the present in his arms.

As Dale's ship came out of its stealth mode next to the Brethren Dreadnaught, it was enveloped in a tractor beam. The beam caught and held the much smaller ship and pulled it into the waiting maw of an open hanger bay. On Dale's ship, there was an ordered calm. Dale let his mind roam through the circuits that controlled that power beam and he delved into the minds of the Dreadnaught's crew. He could find no sense of duplicity, no hint of a trap. He did notice that unlike the previous contacts that he had with Brethren crews that this crew had remarkably few of those controlled by the Brethren's chip devices. Yes, there were a few and they were well marked for latter application by Doctor Scott's devices.

Dale was content. There was a sense of change within this meeting. Something was moving in the shadows that neither he nor the Brethren had suspected. He was content to watch and to wait. When the ship was safely docked, Dale gave orders to his crew. "Under no circumstances are you to engage in any provocative action. If hostilities should occur, summon Theresa the Outer Warder and she will remove the ship from harm. Do not, I repeat do not, attempt to reach me or rescue me. I will be fine."

With that he walked the short distance to the outer hatchway and spun the controls that opened the airlock. Stepping through, he sealed the airlock behind him and waited as the ships air balanced with that of the Dreadnaught. He pressed the buttons that allowed the ramp to extend down to the hanger deck and then clicked the controls that would withdraw it the moment that he stepped off its surface.

Dale Lambert looked around with some curiosity. This was the first visit that he knew of to a Brethren ship of the line by a member of the Federation. At least, he thought to himself, voluntarily. As he stood admiring the vast space of the Hanger Bay, he was being subtly scanned. Dale felt the waves of invisible energy as they gently washed over him. He smiled again. He approved of the cautious nature of the probe, a precaution that he himself would have taken if the shoe was on the other foot.

The scanning ceased as through a portal in a far wall a small contingent of officers and guardsmen dressed in their parade best approached him. They drew to a halt in front of him and separated into two parallel lines. Waiting at the opposite end of those lines was Krylon himself. Dale recognized the Brethren's features immediately and knew the familiar flavor of the man's mind.

With an assured stride, Dale marched between the lines of the officers and guardsmen approaching his protégée. He raised his arm to chest level and extended his hand in an offering of friendship. Krylon eyed Dale and with some hesitation extended his own hand. The shock of Dale's fingers as they closed around the Brethren's hand sent a brief but not unpleasant pulse of energy through the man's system.

Krylon, clearing his throat said, "Welcome aboard the Vengeance, Admiral Lambert. If you follow me, we can convene in my office." He turned and together they walked to the waiting portal. Dale was amused that the honor guard remained and took defensive positions around his ship. "I want you to know, Leader Krylon that I have ordered my command not to take any provocative actions while we are guests aboard your vessel. There really is no need to have a guard on the ship."

Krylon barked a short laugh, "They are there not because I feel that you and yours are a threat, Admiral, but as a pretense to standard procedures. They are there to allow my people to feel safe from the alien horrors that they imagine lies within your vessel."

They fell into a companionable silence as they proceeded through the vast bulk of the Dreadnaught. "This is an amazing vessel, Leader Krylon. It must take the energies of thousands of workers and many sophisticated robotics systems years to construct."

Again, Krylon gave a short bark of laughter. "As well you should know considering you have mentally toured such ships before and are in part responsible for the destruction of many of them."

They came at last to the command deck. The activities that surrounded them ran smoothly. There was an air of quiet efficiency in the ordered way that commands were given and carried out. Dale approved. This was a far cry from the stilted responsiveness that he had felt from some of his previous encounters aboard Brethren craft. He extended his mind and was pleased to note that most, if not all the command crew were free from the Brethren control chips.

"I must commend you Leader Krylon on the efficiency of your command. The fear and stilted behavior that I have met from many of the Brethren's, ah shall we say, workers seem to be missing from most of them."

Krylon looked at Dale, a cold smile on his face. "The fear is still there but of late I have found it better to blunt my more demanding command style in favor of one tempered with patience. It is uncertain if this methodology will work or if I must revert to my old style. It is a work in progress both on my part and that of my command." Krylon cautiously led him into his "office" a rather well-appointed suite that was a combination of office, research library and living quarters.

"As for your other observation, the Triune has declared my mission of relatively low importance. They tend to feel skeptical about the need for biologically reproducing as a method of keeping our species alive. As a result, they have placed slaves in my command who have not undergone the expensive and time-consuming methods of control that are commonly found in ships of the line."

Indicating a chair in front of his work desk Krylon ask Dale to be comfortable. Dale reached out with his mind and traced the circuitry embedded in the chair. It was a passive scanning mechanism that would allow the chair to register the impulses from his brain and nervous system. With a flick of his mind, he disabled the electronics, causing them to create a feedback loop which would report absolutely nothing to the recording devices. Dale sat down enjoying the comfort that the chair provided. He did not feel that this was an attempt on the part of Krylon to subversively study him. Rather he took it as a standard piece of equipment that was used through normal shipboard activity. Either way it would not affect him.

Krylon looked briefly at the monitor on his desk and smiled. Dale Lambert had submitted himself to capture and worse by boarding his ship, but the man certainly was not defenseless. "You have asked to meet with me Admiral. You are here and I can guess at some of the purpose behind your visit. As for the rest I await my enlightenment."

Dale Lambert straightened up and looked at the man across the desk from him. Apart from the distinctive eyes which glistened like silver mirrors and the flowing blond-white hair this man could be the same as any that he had met through his life on Laurel and then in the greater galaxy as he had traveled it these past few years. Still Dale knew that this man represented the culmination of thousands of years of barbarous, vicious, and depraved living that was the root signature of the Brethren people.

"I have come to offer you an alternate possibility. You are not the same as your fellow Brethren. Yes, yes, I know that you are a relatively unimportant part of the hierarchy that is the Brethren Council and that in their eyes you represent nothing more than a minor experiment hardly worth their attention, yet you have become a nexus of change. The Brethren's policies have become unacceptable to the civilizations of the galaxy."

Stephen Goodale   286

"No longer can your tactics of friendly infiltration work among the galaxy's surviving civilizations and the rising forces that will be arrayed against the Brethren. No longer will your methods of controlling various key members of leadership work. We have analyzed your controlling chips and have devised methods which not only will negate their effect but will supply false information back to your listening posts."

"I give you fair warning that the Brethren will be opposed and defeated. In that defeat, they may face annihilation. However, I would like to offer you a chance to take your place among the free peoples of the galaxy." He paused and looked steadily at the Brethren commander before him. "Your society will surely crumble. I read more into the fact that you have been genetically altered to allow for the reproduction and establishment of a new Brethren people's than you perhaps have entertained."

"The clones that form the backbone of your current reproductive cycle are beginning to fail. The tissues have been replicated far too many times and inherent weaknesses are becoming more prominent. It is only a matter of time before they fail completely. Your Triune has foreseen this. In you they have started a program by which new tissues can be created. They envision a time several generations from now where they will once again be able to establish new lines of clones and by doing this maintain their supremacy in the galaxy."

"We will not allow this to happen. The current Brethren system will be systematically disabled and the sins against the peoples of the galaxy perpetrated by your race will cease, by force if necessary but they will stop. It is this choice that I offer you, it is the one chance that you will be given to accept an equal place in the galaxy or perish. The choice is yours Krylon and yours alone."

Krylon sneered at his guest. "I don't think that even you are powerful enough to affect the changes that you are proposing. Besides, you have underestimated the efficiency by which any

Brethren tactic is considered, formulated, and carried out. Even now my ship is headed to our bases within this system. The prospective mates that have been assigned me wait there. Once our race is well established there is nothing that you will be able to do about it."

Dale shook his head slowly. He has anticipated Krylon's stance on his position. It was only natural given the millennia in which the Brethren had remained supreme. Still, it saddened him to think that this man, this Brethren humanoid would have to be lessened before he would begin to see reason.

"If you would allow me to display a record disc on your computer terminal, I think that you will find that things are not quite how they appear." When Dale noticed the startled look, he immediately reassured the Brethren commander that the disc was untainted by any virus or hidden code. "I suggest that you pull a terminal off-line and use it as a standalone. If you discover a problem that one unit could be easily destroyed without affecting your command structure."

With a quick order, Krylon had a unit assembled and placed on his conference room table. "I know that you have mentally snooped around enough of our ships to understand the basic operating system of this unit. I would hazard a guess that you came prepared for such a contingency."

Dale smiled thinly, "Yes indeed although again I point out that we have not tried to interfere with your systems." He then settled down in the chair in front of the large viewing screen. "I must warn you, Krylon that what you are about to see is very upsetting. It is a direct result of the Brethren's rather callous way that they treat any other race but their own." He paused and looked thoughtfully at Krylon. "They even treat their own with contempt as well. You are a case in point. A fact that I hope will not be lost upon you as you view this record. Nothing that you see has been altered in any way."

Krylon settled into a chair next to Dale and sat passively looking at the screen. The images that formed replayed the events as the expedition fleet entered the Terran system, the robotic attack on those vessels and the easy defeat of the attacking force. Krylon stirred restlessly he had a suspicion of what was to come next. He watched as the Federation ships located the moon bases and sent a landing party down to Demos. He watched as they scouted the outer perimeter of that base. He saw the dead forms of the Brethren workers and the technical staff. He watched as the form of a Juancy was taken through the defensive shields. The view switched to the personal com unit of that Juancy as he was led into the main revitalization chamber. He watched as the base AI removed one of the suspended creatures, a female, from a stasis tube and had her placed on the regeneration dais. He listened in as the AI discovered too late that the Juancy was actually a part of the attack force. He watched in mounting horror as the internal defensive lasers were used to destroy all the remaining stasis tubes.

He watched as the AI directed the base's mighty defensive arrays at the oncoming vessels. He watched with some satisfaction as the original landing craft was destroyed in its attempt to rejoin that force. Then to his horror he watched as the beams of destructive energy not only failed to destroy or disable that fleet, but those deadly beams were turned back onto the base itself. The Juancy had gathered up the now reviving female from the dais and had negotiated the hidden escape tunnels. There the Juancy was rendered unconscious and was placed into one of those escape ships and a course was laid in that would bring that traitor to the Brethren sphere of influence. The female guided another of the escape ships up to the waiting fleet, the sole survivor of what was supposed to be a glorious union between himself and a harem of nubile young women.

Despite himself, Krylon admired the form and efficiency of the female human. Her strength in dealing with the much stronger and heavier Juancy was impressive. Then his mind soured. In his guts, he knew that his mission was a failure from the beginning. The words of the Triune came back to him. He had failed and the resultant was his death. Not only the death of his current corporal body but that of his genetic line. There would be no more resurrections for him.

Dale was watching him carefully and he saw the shadow of realization cross his face. "It does not have to end this way, you know. You are still very much alive and perhaps there is still a possibility of immortality out there for you." The picture of the red-haired woman reappeared on the screen. "But", and here Dale's voice grew stern, "You will not be able to order things to your liking. I think that you will find Dianna much more difficult to order around than you might think. You might have to learn how to be "human" and treat her as someone to love and cherish rather than as a chattel. This is the doom that is laid upon you."

Krylon sat heavily back into his chair and closed his eyes. He had been a faithful servant of the Brethren all through the many incarnations of his long genetic life. He had been accorded a hero's triumph and a traitor's death. Like his earlier self-examination, he looked back through the long years and found little in the way to redeem himself.

Now he was faced with a decision that he had been pushed into by the callousness of the Brethren's actions and the self delusion of his own lives. He could end it now. There was a hidden switch that this Dale Lambert could not have discovered it was so shielded. Once activated the dreadnaught would self destruct killing all aboard. It would be a great coup to kill this self-styled Admiral of the Federation. It was tempting, but his eye caught and was held by the image of the redheaded woman on the screen, perhaps Dale Lambert was right, perhaps there was more to living than satisfying the Brethren greed.

He came to a decision and with a flick of his hand disabled the self destruct switch. He turned to look Dale Lambert in the eyes and asked simply, "What's next?"

Dale smiled broadly and released the mental control that would have prevented that switch from activating, laughing he said,

"Well my brave leader I think that it is time we attended a wedding!

Chapter Twenty-Six

The Governor of New Mexico had a problem, in fact several. She had toured the new Embassy of the Empire and had been overwhelmed by the advanced technologies that she saw in use as common place tools to those that occupied that space. She had not felt threatened in any way, in fact the open way that the various representatives treated her and each other had been most satisfying. She had been even further mollified by the inclusion amongst those gathered there of humans, no that was not quite right, of citizens of the earth. She had been introduced to the Peterson clan, and the Greens and the Rodriquez family. She shook her head in amazement. The fact that all were treated as respected members of this new galactic union had gratified her most of all.

She was not that far removed from her political roots to recognize the inclusiveness of a family that had their beginnings in Mexico and had overcome the trials and frustrations of becoming citizens of the United States. Now, the Governor mused, they were citizens of the galaxy. They represented the Empire on Earth and stood as equals to any statesman or woman that this world had to offer. There was a valuable lesson to be had from this she mused.

The problem that she currently faced was the reaction of the Federal Government to the alien presence at the Spaceport. They were upset to say the least by the sudden appearance of galactic neighbors. Neighbors who have had space flight for many hundreds of years and could travel between the stars. The military, of course was leading the parade of naysayers and they had some serious weaponry behind them. There were some in the political arena who had worked up their support base and the shadow of xenophobia had reared its ugly head. "Earth for Earthers" was a political rally cry that was blaring from the television screens of many national broadcasting stations.

She had been called to the Whitehouse and had been subpoenaed by Congress to testify. While those that called the

Embassy home, a well understood political safe zone, had refused to wander away from the protection of their neutral territory. The representatives of the Empire had contented themselves with extending invitations to those that wished to meet with them. Most of those invitations were not accepted but a few had resisted the fear that seem to be building around the little corner of New Mexico and had come for state visits. Those that had come left with a sense of wonder and the satisfaction that they at least had been on the ground floor of the greatest discovery in the history of mankind. The answer to the question, "Are we alone?" had been answered once and for all!

It was the fact that these visitors had been above reproach and had impeccable reputations that had even allowed the fragile balance of peace to exist at all. Now the Governor knew that some of those that opposed the Embassy and the establishment of friendly relations with the earth's nearby neighbors had been affected by a device so insidious that the current medical expertise of Earth could not detect its presence. Lucky for us, she thought to herself, that our friends had come to Earth with mechanisms and devices that could detect these controlling chips and modify them so that they no longer did their job. They also prevented those that pulled the strings from even knowing that their devices had failed.

She had seen this demonstrated to her satisfaction. One of the Generals from the United States Army had begun to draw up forces to surround the Spaceport. In his confidence and swagger he had demanded that those Earth people representing the Empire be allowed to talk with him so that he could give them the terms of surrender of all who occupied the Embassy and the Embassy itself. To do that the General along with members of his staff had to pass through a rather innocuous metal portal. Looking for all the world like a metal detection unit and it did perform that function, but it also examined each individual for the Brethren controlling devices and nullified them as the person passed through. They individually felt nothing and were otherwise unaffected.

The resultant was that after a brief period of disorientation the General and his staff were willing to sit down and talk with the Petersons and the Rodriquez families. The Greens were busy preparing for their daughter's wedding and were unavailable for such mundane meetings. When they had been shown the obvious advantages of working with their neighbors in matters of system defense and intergalactic trade the General and his staff left with very thoughtful looks on their faces. The buildup of armed units was called off and a small detachment of soldiers was placed around the perimeter of the Spaceport as a security detail.

The General reported back to the Joint Chiefs of Staff, who immediately sent one of their number, the member most vehemently opposed to having the Embassy in place, to verify the general's findings. This person, an Admiral in the United States Navy, was passed through the arch and immediately collapsed on the other side. The aides that had accompanied him rushed to his side. The Petersons who had come to meet the man escorted the small group to a small first aid station set up outside and in plain view of all the visitors. The doctor who had been part of the delegation examined the Admiral and determined that he had just allowed himself to become too worked up. He administered the Admiral's high blood pressure medication and after a short period of quiet rest the man came around.

"Where am I?" He demanded of his hovering staff. When they had told him the man's eyes lit with curiosity. "Really? You are telling me that I am in Embassy grounds of an alien empire and that I had come here with the express purpose of destroying any chance that we, the people of Earth, could develop a peaceful dialog with such a group?" He looked at his attending staff who all nodded their heads in agreement with the Admiral's verbal assessment of their visit. The Admiral just burst out laughing, "What utter nonsense is this?" He said when he could gain control of his mirth. "I have waited my entire life for an opportunity to communicate with peoples from another world. The very last thing that I would do is to destroy such an opportunity." He looked at his astonished staff and then in his old gruff command tone added, "Well what are you all standing around here for? Get me out of this bed and let's go talk to these visitors from another world!"

The attending physician just shrugged his shoulders and after a brief but thorough examination of his cantankerous patient declared him fit enough to continue his visit. Doctor Scott who had hovered at the edge of the conversation stepped forward and introduced himself. The Admiral took in the appearance of the older man and settled his gaze on the opaque silver-colored eyes. "Forgive me for asking, but do all of your race have such eyes? They do take some getting used to."

Doctor Scott smiled, "No Admiral, these are the gift of a genetic mutation that I received on what had been my home world, Laurel. They allow me to look into the finite systems of any biologic and to determine the cause of any problems in their health. A very useful tool to my profession, don't you think?"

The admiral looked the doctor up and down and then leaned into him and whispered, "Would you be willing to examine me and see why my blood pressure keeps giving me fits? It is somewhat embarrassing to wake up in a hospital and ask the question, where am I?" The Admiral chuckled and waved his own doctor over. "This is my personal physician Doctor Folmer. He has a complete medical work up on me and carries it around with him like a treasured toy. Doctor would you object if this man, Doctor Scott examines me using his, err ah, gift?"

Doctor Folmer looked directly into the eyes of his colleague and a slow smile spread across his face. "No indeed Admiral, as long as I can monitor the examination and stand ready to assist. Does that suit you Doctor Scott?"

Doctor Scott bowed and smiled as he agreed to the man's terms. "Let's go on into the Embassy, I have a fully appointed medical facility and I think that you will find some of our diagnostic tools very interesting."

Stephen Goodale   295

The delegation moved on through the gaping entrance way of the Embassy itself. They walked slowly taking in the site of a busy and engaged staff as they went about their business. The Admiral was like a kid in a candy store turning his head this way and that trying not to miss any of the ongoing activity. He pulled up short as the bulk of Kadolic and Gloridic came into view. The two Dragons were lying next to each other their necks raised and their heads pointed to a viewing screen. Two humanoid, heck humans, thought the Admiral to himself were standing next to the Dragons talking earnestly with them.

"Excuse me, Doctor Scott." He waved vaguely at the Dragons. "Are those what I think they are?"

Doctor Scott chuckled. "Well, that depends on what you think they are, Admiral."

The Admiral shook his head as if coming out of a dream, "They look for all the world like the Dragons that we here on Earth fabricated out of ancient legend." He paused and looked at the great beasts again and added, "They are magnificent creatures!"

A soft deep voice entered his mind and said, "Thank you Admiral Willis. It is a pleasure to meet you. I am Kadolic and Vantu is my Rider. My mate is Gloridic and Darcel is her Rider. We welcome you to the Embassy and we both hope that your visit here will begin the process of bringing our peoples closer together in the spirit of friendship and mutual respect."

The Admiral stood dumbfounded and slowly gather himself erect to his full height and bowed deeply. "Thank you", he said aloud. "It is a very great honor to meet you. I look forward to a more in-depth conversation with you both, but if you excuse me, I can see that these Doctors want to get their hands on me, so I must go with them."

The two Dragons bowed their great heads briefly and went back to attending the conversation that was ongoing with their

Riders. The Admiral just walked on in a daze. Intelligent Dragons, and such nice manners. He had the feeling that he had just met with a race that had great dignity and grace. He truly did look forward to a more detailed conversation with them. Dragons of legend indeed. He would have to watch his preconceived notions if he was to get the full value from this amazing experience.

They entered the well-appointed medical facility. Doctor Scott sat the Admiral and his attending physician down around a small conference table. The rest of the entourage waited outside in the spacious waiting room. "Now Doctor Folmer, from what I am given to understand your current medical technology includes, blood screening, x-rays, Cat Scans, radioactive imagery and ultrasound." At a nod from Doctor Folmer, he continued. "What I propose will be a full body scan done in three-dimensional imagery. The separate sections of the body can then be called out for study in greater detail. In other words, you will have a complete mapping of every system in the Admiral's body. In addition, the computer algorithms will be able to detect anything within his body that falls outside of the expected norms for the Terran race. These then can be studied as needed."

"The entire procedure is non-invasive and casts no harmful radiation into the system." Doctor Scott looked at the two men in front of him and then asked, "Do you have any questions before we begin?"

Doctor Folmer cleared his throat and asked, "Will I be able to view the scan in real time." He flushed briefly, "It's not that I don't trust you Doctor Scott, but it would help alleviate any questions that might be raised later by critics of your, hem, presence here."

Doctor Scott smiled, not the least bit insulted. "Excellent thought Doctor Folmer, and yes the scan can be viewed in real time and any anomalies noted as they appear." He stood up and waved a hand toward the conference room door, "Shall we?"

Stephen Goodale   297

The three men marched out of the conference room and past the receptionist's desk. Doctor Folmer shook his head in amusement as he thought to himself that somethings never change. He was immediately disabused of that thought as it became apparent that receptionist, a very pretty brunette, was in fact a humanoid robot. He had a lot of re-thinking to do he thought grimly to himself as they walked by.

That thought was augmented and compounded as they entered the diagnostic arena. This featured several banks of complex looking machinery flanked by workstations that were manned by various types of humanoid attendants. Only a few would have been called human by the Admiral just hours before, now he perceived that they all worked together as a seamless unit and the communications that were passing between them were all done in English. At the center of the room was a raised dais on which rested a very comfortable looking bed.

"Excuse me Doctor Scott, how is it that all of these folk are speaking in flawless English? I can understand what they are saying although some of the terms are foreign to me."

Doctor Scott pointed to a rather inconspicuous device that was located on the collar of his tunic. "This is a universal translator. It allows us to "hear" what we do even though the words spoken by those around us are in a foreign language. A very useful tool, don't you agree?" Now Doctor Folmer if you will place the patient onto the dais, we can begin.

"Don't you want to have our patient change into a hospital gown? Doctor Folmer asked with amusement in his voice.

Doctor Scott just laughed. "No, we have done away with most of the customs and devices that we physicians had used to make our terrified patients uncomfortable. The scanning unit is strictly interested in the patient not his accoutrements."

Doctor Folmer laughed at the observation and helped the Admiral onto the waiting bed. Once he was comfortable, he stepped away and stood with Doctor Scott by a rather large data screen. "Admiral this will only take a few minutes. Are you comfortable?"

From the dais, the Admiral commented, "I would like to know where I can buy one of these beds. This is much more comfortable than anything that I have ever slept on."

Doctor Scott smiled and pressed the button to begin the scanning sequence. "We will begin from the feet on up," he stated as the screen before them dissolved and the space that it occupied became a three-dimensional image of the Admirals body. The systems were noted, and various "tags" were placed along areas of concern. Doctor Scott would pause the scan as these areas came into view and would bring up the analysis on an adjacent screen so that he and Doctor Folmer could discuss the findings.

As the scan continued a brief warning beep went off and the two doctors huddled over and area of concern in the region of the heart. The image clearly showed a blockage of seventy-five percent in one of the major arteries leading from the heart. Doctor Scott turned and asked his fellow physician, "Were you aware of this issue? Did your own diagnostics reveal the problem?" When Doctor Folmer shook his head, he asked, "Would you like us to eliminate the issue while we are here?"

Doctor Folmer just stared at his fellow physician. "Can you do that?"

"Yes indeed. Most of what is now considered common aliments can be treated without invasive surgery or harmful medications. If you would like we can eliminate that blockage now."

With a decisive nod of his head Doctor Folmer gave his permission and paid close attention as a bath of blue light covered the area of the Admirals body in question. That gentle illumination penetrated the Admiral and within seconds the blockage disappeared from the viewing image.

"Amazing," was all that he could say. The readings on the Admiral's vital signs immediately improved as fresh blood flowed freely to and from the man's heart. The scan then continued upwards through the Admiral's body pausing once again as a red indicator appeared in the upper lungs. The diagnostic screen indicated that there was a partial tear in the lining of the left lung very near the brachial artery. Once again Doctor Scott asked if the issue should be repaired and once again Doctor Folmer agreed. He watched in utter fascination as the tissues were cleaned and new growth appeared. The tissues then knitted themselves and the damaged area was completely healed."

"I don't know about you Doctor Scott but when the Admiral is done, I would like to be your next patient. This is utterly astounding."

Doctor Scott refrained from comment, but his smile broadened considerably. "This is just a small example of the benefits of inter system trade. Knowledge can be dangerous, but in the right hands and handled correctly it is an invaluable aid to life."

The scan continued and was quickly approaching the area where the Brethren control device had been implanted. Doctor Scott paused the scan and turned to face his fellow doctor. "I must be completely truthful with you now Doctor Folmer. You deserve the truth."

"When your group passed through our metal detection arch each member of your party was also scanned for a specific device. This device is so insidious that it would be impossible for your current technology to discover. This device has been implanted not only in your Admiral but in many of your governmental officials. The device is controlled by a race of barbarous people known throughout the galaxy as the Brethren. It is the Brethren's standard operating procedure to infiltrate and then, by use of these control devices, dominate societies that they wish to either enslave or to conquer with an eye to the natural resources of the world on which they have set their sights."

Stephen Goodale   300

"As you passed through the arch, the device was neutralized and the communications link that maintains contact with its Brethren controller placed into a feedback loop which fools the controller into thinking that the device is active and functioning correctly. This is a temporary solution because eventually the controlling master will discover that its puppet is not doing things that he or she has been ordered to do. We are now coming to the part of the Admiral's brain in which the device has been implanted. It can be safely removed, if that is your wish or it can be left in place. The only problem with leaving it is that there is a self-destruct mechanism that can be triggered if the controller can figure out a way to circumvent our inferences."

Doctor Scott shrugged his shoulders. "It would be a shame to have all of the good work that we have done come to naught because of the Brethren's heartless designs. It is entirely up to you. Ah here is the location that I am talking about."

Sure enough, the scan paused once more as the warning beep rang out. There as Doctor Folmer carefully watch was a vague intermittent image that came in and out of focus on the three-dimensional image. The read out clearly defined the object and its connections to the neural pathways of the brain and the spinal cord.

Doctor Folmer tore his eyes away from the diagnostics screen and looked thoughtfully at Doctor Scott. "You know. I have been the personal physician attached to the Admiral for the past ten years. We have been as close as any doctor patient association can be, in fact we had become good friends. Over the past two years I have noticed a subtle change in the Admirals opinions and attitudes towards topics that he and I had mulled over and agreed to for many years. He became much more aggressive and his opinions divisive. He had in fact become something of a problem as a ranking member of the Joint Chiefs of Staff. Now, if what you say is true, he has become a controlled agent of a race that we had known nothing about, with purposes of deadly intent to our world."

He shook his head to clear his thoughts. "This is way above my skill sets to understand and to grasp. I do know that if this device has a chance of killing this man, my friend, then I would like to see it removed and to have him set free."

Doctor Scott nodded his head in understanding. "If that is your wish we will proceed." Once again, the Admiral was bathed in a bluish light which deepened into purple before it began to pulse. As he watched the scan image of that device became encased in that light. At first it seemed to glance off and had no effect but as he continued to watch the light began to cling to the surface of the chip and its form stopped fading in and out as it became encapsulated in the light.

The operating theatre became deathly quiet as all those present focused their attention on the activity on the dais. A robotic attendant wheeled up next to the Admiral. It pushed a large metal cylinder on a specially reinforced carrier. The light was joined now by a green beam which grabbed the object and began to pull it though the tissues and structures of the Admirals brain and skull. Once freed from its host the beam placed the device into the container and the container was sealed.

As the robot wheeled away the carrier a dull thrump, was heard and the solid metal container became distorted. The robotic attendant beeped once and then hustled the ruined carrier out of the operating area. "Wheww," said Doctor Scott. "That was close. Someone or something must have been monitoring the Admiral very closely for that to have been detonated."

He turned his attention back to the scan and watched as the tissue that had been controlled by the device healed up and once more began its normal function. "It seems my good Doctor Folmer, that our procedure has been successful. Shall we see how the patient is doing?"

The Admiral who had been under a mild sedation was awake and aware. He had listened in with some consternation as the two doctors had dispassionately discussed his case. Now as he sat up with the help of Doctor Folmer he ran a quick mental check of his body. He felt extremely good. His heart felt strong, and he was able to breathe without that annoying stitch of pain that had plagued him for the last couple of months. His mind was clear and memories that had been clouded became focused.

He gripped his friends arm tightly as a frightening memory came flooding back. He had been in a briefing with the president and his principal advisors concerning a security issue in the Middle East. He had excused himself to go to the men's room and as he had turned to leave, he was pinned by strong arms and placed on the floor. He never saw who attacked him but as he lay there face down on the cold tile, he felt a stinging sensation on the back of his neck and a burning pain move from his neck into his brain.

He had blacked out briefly and when he recovered, he was sitting on the bathroom toilet in one of the stalls. He hadn't given his ridiculous position a thought as he rose, straightened himself up and went back to the meeting. There he suggested a position on the conflict that seemed reasonable at the time although looking back at it now, he realized that it was completely inappropriate to the resultant that was needed. He had suggested something that was not only counterproductive in the long run but counter to his personal belief system. He had been manipulated. Tears began to flow down his cheeks as other memories surfaced of activities directly influenced by him but whose nature, he would never have condoned.

Doctor Folmer reached out and hugged his friend. "It will be alright Chip. The things that you have done over the past two years were not your fault. Thanks to Doctor Scott and his technology, we have removed the causal agent of those decisions and we have brought you back. You are you, once more!"

The Admiral looked to where Doctor Scott stood patiently waiting for the emotional outpouring to slow to a trickle. "Yes, Admiral you have come back, but there are others, many others that are still under the control of those chips, and the Brethren. Now if you are up to it, I would like you to meet our Admiral, the man who was able to rescue me and many of the others that you will meet today." He waited as Admiral Willis got to his feet and then politely led the two friends from the operating theatre.

Susana Martinez reflected on her next pending problem. She had received a rather startling visitation from a certain Dale Lambert. This man identified himself as the Admiral of the Federation fleet, but she could sense beyond any doubt that he was much more than that. He did not arrive in his physical form but as an astral projection. The impact of his personality was not diminished by the lack of his physical presence. His aura was a bit overpowering, but still he was polite and included her in his plans, asking for her opinions and implementing some of her suggestions.

It seemed, like it or not, that the area around the Spaceport was about to become the nexus of great celebration and momentous occasion. Several large space craft were scheduled to land in the vicinity of the port and the Governor was thankful that certain military types had relented in their efforts to drive in force on the spaceport. In fact, she had verbal assurances from several high-ranking officials that the incoming visitors would all be treated with respect and honor. So now her problem had become one of political appeasement and public assurance.

She reached out and called in her private secretary. Together they developed a list of "guests" that would be invited to the official opening of the Empire's Embassy. Many on the list were those whose minds were open to the startling revelation that they were not alone in the universe. Others had been serious antagonists to the fact that her state had become the home to such an honor. It was these the doubters and distractors and those downright opposed to the coming events that she personally got on the phone to invite.

The press was another issue. Dale Lambert had talked about the Brethren and their methods. She had been very aware of the shift in public attitude against the "visitors" and she held some suspicions that reporters and their network bosses had changed in their reporting patterns in recent years. Their work now sought to incite and enflame rather than report. These were gathered in a special "news conference" that she had arranged to announce the coming events at the port. If Dale Lambert was correct in his assessment of the true nature of those that gathered than she would soon see a shift in attitude towards the Embassy and those that it represented.

As the time for the meeting grew near the metal detector which funneled people into the state capital building was replaced with a newer more efficient model. As the crowd entered through the device, more than a few stumbled and needed to be helped into a room off the main corridor. Once there the devices that had been implanted by the Brethren were removed. Shortly the great meeting hall began to fill with happy and excited members of the press. She mounted the podium and with the help of visual aids she was able to outline the history of the Empire and the Federation.

She did not speak of the Brethren, this was not the time for panic, but she did emphasize the importance of having the Earth become a part of a larger galaxy. She also highlighted the special relationship that Earth would play in repopulating the galaxy with Dragons and their Riders. She spoke of that long and loving tradition and of the need to allow those of the Earth who wished the chance at such a bonding the opportunity to try.

Chapter Twenty-Seven

Dale Lambert sat in a quiet office off the main floor of the cavernous hall that was the Empire's Embassy. He was not alone. Krylon had reluctantly agreed to join him on his Admiral's gig, while his Dreadnaught stayed in orbit around Mars. As Dale pointed out, while the technology of Earth was advancing it was still too primitive to detect much in its own solar system.

The Orion had taken up guardian position with the Brethren craft and what might have been a tense situation dissolved into a joyous reunion as those crewmen and officers aboard the Orion who were freed members from Krylon's original ship of the line made contact with Krylon's new crew. Many had been from the same families and some even the long-lost spouses of the crewmen and women. Those that had remained under the Brethren control, found themselves gassed and transported to the Mars base for treatment. They too quickly rejoined the two vessels once they were freed from that control.

"It would seem," Krylon stated, "That freedom is a very powerful aid in developing relationships between races in our galaxy. Not one of those who had been under control wished to return to that status once a safer choice had been made. I fear that once again you have taken my crew from me."

Dale smiled at Krylon, beginning to like the Brethren more and more. "Nonsense, the command is yours, Leader Krylon. No one has taken that away from you. A fact that you have only yourself to blame. Your milder command style and your care for others under that command has earned you the respect of your crew. I commend you sir. You are a fine Leader."

"I still don't understand you Admiral, you have compassion, a trait that I am only beginning to understand. You have great power, a fact that I do understand, but your application of that power appears to be only for the positive good of people." He smiled and then added, "All people, including me, your enemy." You have let the wolves in through the front door to borrow a phrase that I have read in a human book of fiction, yet you do not fear the result."

He paused and then looked directly at Dale Lambert. "Forgive me for saying this, but are you a god?"

A gentle voice laughingly added, "Only to his wife, and even then, he has to be careful around her." There framed in the office doorway was a very pregnant Heather Lambert. Her smile was for both men, but her eyes were for her husband only. As she moved in through the doorway both men rose to their feet.

Here in front of him was a living example of the type of immortality that he might yet experience. He watched the pair as they drew together for a brief hug and a gentle kiss. Dale placed his hand on his wife's gravid belly and whispered, and how is little Emily doing today?"

All within the room heard the female child's petulant response. "I am tired daddy. I want to nap for a bit more before I stretch my legs and kick mommy." There was a clear note of silver bells which played lightly in the air.

Dale smiled riley as he guided Heather to a comfortable chair. "Leader Krylon may I introduce my wife, Heather Lambert and of course you have already heard from my daughter, Emily."

Heather took the proffered hand of the Brethren Leader, another of the habits that Dale Lambert had grafted upon his nature. "It is a pleasure to meet such a beautiful foe," Krylon commented.

Dale arched his eyebrow at his wife and then asked, "And where is that rambunctious son of mine?" He had seen Tristen immediately after his wife had arrived, but the boy had gone missing. Despite his young age, he had developed beyond his years and had taken to going out exploring with his life mate Casric. Dale knew that Heather kept a light mental touch on her son and would respond to any emergency concerning him.

Heather closed her eyes and smiled. "He and Casric are out hunting in the hills above the spaceport. He is having a grand time," she added.

Krylon was amused by the interaction of the two Lamberts. If this meeting was a means to introduce him to a possible lifestyle that he may also share in the future, then so be it. He rather thought though that it was just the spontaneous meeting between two adult humans who loved each other and who had been parted for a time because of their respective duties and responsibilities. In any event, he found that it was a charming occurrence. Emotions of this sort were not seen among the Brethren. In fact, the daily contact between individual Brethren, male or female was mostly based on the desire for gain and the posturing of power. Alliances were only made to further yourself, Krylon mused. He was beginning to understand that there was so much more to life than greed.

A soft knock on the door alerted Dale to the presence of his next guests. "Come in Doctor Scott, I have your patient sitting next to me and she is waiting anxiously for your examination."

Heather threw her mate a dirty look and then laughed. "Yes, Doctor Scott please let me know when I can expect this next Lambert to arrive and join the fold." Quite clearly Emily made her opinion known, "Mother!"

Dale could almost see her stamping her foot. In fact, judging by the way Heather grimaced that was probably what she had just done. He sent a gentle admonition to his daughter. "Please be careful of your mother, Emily. I would like her to be around and fit for a very long time."

The doctor entered the room followed by two men. Dale immediately rose to his feet and walked over to them. "Gentlemen. I am Dale Lambert and I am very glad to meet you." Once again, he proffered his hand and shook those of Doctor Folmer and Admiral Willis. "Please won't you come in and make yourselves comfortable."

Dale turned and introduced his wife and then Leader Krylon. Then Doctor Scott helped Heather to her feet and with a gentle hand on her back led her from the room. "Gentlemen, you will have to excuse my wife and Doctor Scott, they have a prior engagement in the medical wing."

When she had physically left the room Dale Lambert continued the conversation, "We have only to await the last three members of this meeting gentlemen before we begin. In the meantime, may I offer you some refreshments?"

Scott Green was hip deep in the schematics of a rather complex design. He had received permission from the Empire to install a sophisticated navigation and tracking system that they had developed for their space fleet, and it was giving him fits. A dozen times he caught himself calling out for Nancy, his bride to be and then realized that she was busy elsewhere. He smiled grimly. The fool I am, he thought to himself, she is working on a much more complex set of designs! He looked forward to the wedding. In just two more days he would have Nancy as his bride and the life that they had envisioned for each other would truly begin.

"It's about time to. We have been grounded long enough. I feel the need to get these bones back into space and to smell the staleness of recycled air."

Scott laughed at his Dragon. He was beginning to feel the same way. "You know, our first order of business is to head back to Trillion and set up a home base from which to work. If the feelings I have for Nancy and our wedding night are any indication I must be sure that we have a proper home in which to raise the resultant child and those that will follow.

Tremolic's only reply was a snort. Then in a quiet voice his Dragon said, "We are called to a meeting Scott. We have to leave now." In a puff of purple smoke Tremolic appeared and Scott reached his hand out to touch his friend. Tremolic then transported the two directly into the conference room where Dale Lambert and his guests waited.

Stephen Goodale   309

Home World

As the brief smoke cleared the room, the startled gasps of the two Earthmen and Leader Krylon abated. This is really getting interesting thought Krylon to himself as he settled back down into his chair. If he wasn't mistaken, he was looking at a representative of those ancient foes, the Dragons although he imagined them much bigger.

"I am what I am Leader Krylon," came Tremolic's mental voice, "but outward appearances are deceiving. You of the Brethren should know all about that!"

Dale Lambert held up his hand as his mind followed the thoughts of Tremolic and Krylon. "Gentlemen, I suggest that you leave any demonstration of past differences aside during this meeting. If we are expected to make any progress at all we must use discernment in our discussions. Is that understood?"

Then he turned to his guests and introduced the newcomers. "Gentlemen I would like you to meet Scott Green, whose origins are of Earth, but who is now a free trader and a member of the galaxy. The Dragon that you see with him is his bond mate Tremolic. Tremolic comes from a very ancient and quite intelligent race whose members have plied the galaxy for thousands of years."

Turning to the two newcomers he then introduced Admiral Willis of the United States Navy, Doctor Folmer and finally Leader Krylon of the Brethren. "We who are gathered here are met with a purpose. The Earth has become a nexus of great importance to the galaxy as a whole. One whose viability many races throughout our spheres of influence need to assure. Because all of us here have a stake in this conference I have called upon Theresa the Outer Warder of Ikorn to officiate. She is quite neutral and has no vested interest in this world. She will moderate our discussion."

With that Dale Lambert bowed deeply and the room grew dark as a deep purple light enveloped them all. When it cleared the tall dark haired Ikornian stood before them and returned Dale's bow with a brief nod. "Gentlemen if you would be seated, we will begin."

"There are several purposes and very many reasons that you find yourselves assembled here. Although you, yourselves may not realize what those reasons may be. I will attempt to clarify these and, in the process, demonstrate to you that your purposes are not so very different from each other." She smiled and as she did Frthessig uncurled himself from his perch on her shoulders. He climbed down to sit on the conference table, his tail curled around him, his bright green eyes moving from face to face.

"I first would like to reveal some of the history of this world that is pertinent to our conversation. Earth is extremely unique in many ways. While it did indeed develop its own native population it also has had a significant graft placed upon that population. The Federation, albeit unknown to its leaders, supplied a significant boost to the numbers of its people. These "colonists" while not intentionally placed here, were able to intermarry and produce viable progeny with the native population of Earth. The blood of every human here has at least part of the Federation flowing through his or her veins."

Admiral Willis and Doctor Folmer looked startled. Scott Green looked thoughtful. "To validate this", Theresa continued, "I would like to invite several witnesses to contribute their testimony." With that Frthessig leaped from the table and went to the closed conference room door. He scratched at the closed panel which immediately opened to admit a small group of people.

Theresa turned and smiled a welcome and waved the group to the front of the room. "Gentlemen I would like to introduce you to Drew and Nancy Duncan and their son Christopher." With a bow, she said, "And this is the AI from that selfsame colony ship the Andromeda. He prefers to be called Cain."

"Our part in this story began when Nancy and I stumbled upon a hidden, illegal government weapons storage area buried underneath our high school in Oregon. When we had become trapped in that facility by the government, we discovered a hidden cavern which contained the entombed Federation colony ship the Andromeda. As part of our agreement with Cain, we were signed on as the Command Crew and we have been in constant contact with Cain ever since. In fact, Admiral Lambert and his wife Heather along with their life mates, Shadow Grey and Moon Glow met with us in the conference room aboard the Andromeda. Although they were in their astral forms while we were in our corporal bodies. A very interesting experience."

Admiral Willis, cleared his throat and asked, "Would that have been the East Mountain High School?" When Drew nodded his head, the Admiral spoke up. "I can validate this story. It was and still is one of the more shameful events that fell under the realm of national security."

Cain nodded his head. "I will save those present the tedium of thousands of years of waiting by playing the disc of my recorded history on Earth." He produced the disc which he placed in the projection device which sat unobtrusively on the surface of the conference room table. "I assure you that while this is an edited version the full version is available for study." With that he flipped the switch on the projector and the history of the great ship's landing and that of its crew was displayed in detail. It noted the crew's agreement to abandon the technical life that they had lived to "blend in" with the native population. The disc demonstrated quite clearly the weddings and births of the combined crew and native populations. This history finally ran out around two thousand years ago, Earth time. The final scenes reflected a momentous occasion, the images were scratchy but clearly depicted was the form a man nailed to a cross of wood. The scenes of darkening storms and the cries of frightened people did not drown out the man's last words, "Into your hands I commend my soul."

The viewer went quiet as Cain's calm voice filled the room. "Jesus Christ of Galilee as he passed into the Father's hands."

"Thank you for your testimony." Theresa once more waved her hand and the Duncans and Cain left the room. She turned back to the waiting men and Tremolic. I will now call upon another witness to describe the relationship between the Tresolins and the race of Dragons." Once more Frthessig went to the door panel and at his insistent pawing two people entered the conference room.

"Tremolic immediately straightened up from his accustomed slouch. "Hail, Vantu. Hail Darcel, and well met." His mental broadcast reached them all. Krylon also sat up in his chair and keenly watched as Vantu stood at the front of the room to address those present. "Thank you indeed Tremolic for your greeting." He then turned and looked directly at Krylon. Those present were struck by that long slow gaze. The two men looked very much alike. The silver hair and the silver eyes were identical. Finally, Vantu broke the silence. "Long has it been since one of my race sat in the same room with one of the Brethren without drawing swords. I can only hope that this meeting results in better consequences then those previous gatherings."

He turned his gaze away from the Brethren Leader and spoke to those in the room. "I am Vantu and I am a Dragon Rider. My Dragon Kadolic stands watch in the great bay outside of this conference room. Darcel is my mate and she is also a Dragon Rider. Her Beast is Gloridic and she stands with my friend. I have been asked to describe as lucidly as possible the relationship between the Tresolins and our winged brothers, the Dragons. My story would not be complete however without describing the role that the Brethren have played in our long history."

"Our story begins on Firanth 7 a planet far from here. Our race was one that loved to explore, and we pushed further and further into the space around our native system. Our technology had evolved to the point that we could travel the space between the stars. We arrived on Firanth 7 and began the peaceful exploration of the biosphere of the planet. We did this as we had always done by capturing samples of wildlife

Stephen Goodale   313

sedating them with a stasis field, studying them and then releasing them back into their native environment without harming them.

We had been on the planet's surface for a few weeks, planet time when a creature walked calmly through our force fields and into the center of our encampment. We shortly learned that this Dragon was a young emissary of his kind. The Dragons had been observing us, unbeknown to us. They had decided that our humane treatment of the life around us had demonstrated our peaceful, non-aggressive purposes on the planet. Once we had become aware that there was a sentient race already dwelling on Firanth 7 we offered to withdraw from the system. But the Dragons had other ideas. They offered us the opportunity to develop an embassy and the chance to learn each other's cultures."

"By mutual agreement we developed the embassy and after many years, our two races, being very long lived, drew even closer. At one point my ancestor bonded with a member of the Dragon race and then his mate bonded with a golden Dragon during a hatching. These four were the beginnings of a wonderful and fulfilling association between our species. Together Dragons and Riders traveled the star lanes and colonized many worlds, always in peace and in harmony with those that they touched. Never did we conquer. Never did we destroy. We worked well with the sentient races with which we met, and peace ruled through our section of the galaxy. We became the Empire, and it was good."

Vantu paused again and looked sternly at Leader Krylon. "Then came the days of conflict. It started with the arrival of tall gleaming ships on one of our colony worlds. Our peoples watched as they settled in on the planet's surface. From those ships marched a tall, proud people, their long silver hair streaming in the dawning wind. Their eyes matched those of our own people, the hair was the same as ours and we rejoiced. Here were a people who as they told their story had travelled from the far-off rim of the galaxy, a lost colony seeking the source of their origin."

Vantu smiled grimly, as he added bitterly, "You wouldn't want to tell us the exact location of your Home World, would you Leader Krylon? No? To bad, I am sure that there is enough left of the Empire that would love a chance to visit that world and repay your kindness."

"You see gentlemen that while we welcomed these newcomers, our Brethren, we invited our own deaths. Soon after their arrival an insidious transformation overcame our fellowship, lies and rumors weaved through our society. Where these came from no one at that time knew. The values of our fellowship were questioned, and to be frank some of what came up were long buried problems that any two desparative species might have experienced. These lies and rumors worked on these differences to the point that conflict broke out and old allegiances were forgotten in the heat of hate and violence."

Vantu shook his head slowly, "When the conflict had burned through the Empire and most of the Dragon and Rider pairings had been destroyed or newfound friends the Brethren, who had kept very carefully neutral, stepped in with their Dreadnaughts and Planet Killers destroying where they willed and raping resources where they wished. When they had taken everything that they wished they piled back into their ships and left for parts unknown. Those of us that remained faithful and thus survived in backwaters that held no interest to the Brethren thought that we had seen the last of their kind." He waved demonstrably in Krylon's direction, "But we were wrong."

"Now we are scattered with many of the Dragon kind born to a life without the sharing that we Riders have experienced through the centuries with our friends. There simply are not enough of us left to carry on the tradition. I was sent here to Earth some four hundred Earth years ago, to watch and to wait. I have seen many changes to the society here on this planet. I have watched as the Brethren influence has again begun to raise its ugly head twisting and misleading the peoples of Earth to suit their own purposes. Finally, my wait came to an end as two of the Dragon kind sent their son through the gate that was maintained in my home, the Embassy if you will of the Empire here on Earth. This was a very different form of Dragon, with all of the genetic coding of his parents but in a form that would allow his growth on Earth to match that of his Rider."

Vantu smiled and said, my neighbors, the Petersons had a young son whose mental makeup allowed the bond to form. Together Sam Peterson and Nemoric, "grew up" together demonstrating the bond. Latter Scott Green and Tremolic formed the bond while on Scalar." He bowed to them. "Tremolic was again of a different genetic sequence than his parents and is the first of the Dragon kind suited for life in interstellar space as well as that on planetary surfaces and in alien air."

"Unfortunately, my home, as well as the Peterson home was destroyed by the enslaved minions of the Brethren. This," and here Vantu waved his hands to indicate the immense complex, "is the new Embassy of the Empire."

"The human race, those people who developed from the melding of the Terrans and the members of the Federation seeded here have become a root source for the bonding for our Dragon brothers and sisters. Earth has become the hope of our race and that of Dragon kind. This Embassy will provide a place where those of Earth who wish to attempt the bond may come and once the process is explained thoroughly, travel on to Scalar or the few surviving worlds of the Empire where the Dragon kind live to allow the opportunity for the bond to form."

Vantu gave a brief bow and Theresa motioned to Darcel to rise and speak. She stood tall and straight, her eyes drilling into those of leader Krylon. "My story is far from unique, but I will tell it here so that it becomes a cautionary tale. For the record, I and the people that were fortunate enough to be transported to Scalar, am representative of the ruthless and callous methodology that the Brethren have used for thousands of years to conquer worlds and to destroy civilizations across the galaxy."

"Ours was a peaceful world. We had overcome the trials of any young civilization by putting wars and aggression behind us. We had achieved a stable world democracy and were just beginning to reach out into the larger region of space which was our solar system. We had placed a small colony on our moon and had developed a reasonable platform to reach out into space. We, like many civilizations had wondered if we were alone in the vastness of the universe and we were curious."

Darcel sighed, "It was this curiosity that was our undoing. The Brethren arrived in near space, and our rather primitive detection devices caught their approach. We used the communications available to us and the Brethren responded, translating our communications back to us in messages of peace and friendship. Our leaders were joyful, and invitations were sent allowing the Brethren to "send down' a delegation to our world's surface.

"The scientific leaders of our lunar colony took a quite different approach. As soon as contact was made all communication and power outputs were cut off and only passive monitoring was allowed. We received the signals from our world but did not venture to send any out." Once more she paused and raised an eyebrow in query to Leader Krylon. "That was standard procedure for your kind was it not, Leader Krylon? To offer friendship to a world that had drawn your attention, a world that held something that your Triune deemed of value to your race?"

"Our scientific leaders on the moon monitored your delegations closely and watched through the news broadcasts of our world, their travels to and fro. They were quite thorough in their investigations, which led us to believe that they had not suspected our world to be inhabited. Not that it mattered, did it leader Krylon? The delegates withdrew asking for "time" in which they could confer with their own leaders. Our world thought nothing of it granting them whatever time that they needed."

"Once they had all returned to their vessel our monitoring posts on the moon detected a change in the configuration of their ship. It began to spread and morph into what appeared to be a giant net, with power nodes in the junction of each of those strands of braided steel. The change was not lost on those below. Our world's government asked politely and finally demanded an explanation of such an aggressive behavior. They got their answer soon enough as hellish energies were unleashed form those innocuous junctions. There was a brief and hysterical plea for mercy and aid and then silence."

"Our scientific leaders immediately suspended all energy out puts in our lunar bases, including life support." Darcel's eyes now glinted with tears of remember grief and frustration. "We were forced to watch the destruction and rape of our world as your "planet killer" transported all of the natural mineral wealth of our world into its hungry maws. We were also forced to watch as we lost a full third of our base's population to oxygen starvation and the depredations of cold. I suppose that we should have counted ourselves lucky that our moon held no great mineral resources of its own, for when they had finished destroying our world the Brethren ship simply reconfigured into its original form and sedately moved out of our system. Leaving us perhaps the more horrifying death than those who died so quickly on the planet below."

Leader Krylon returned the gaze of this impassioned woman steadily. The description of the action above her home world was one that had been repeated many times in the past history of the Brethren. They had assumed the position of power in the galaxy, and none had dared to have opposed them and survive. Still, most of the conquests of others had been left to the Brethren's slaves and robotic minions. Very few Brethren actually stirred beyond the luxurious appointments of their private estates. They were the rulers of the galaxy but had no real contact with others of their domain. In the back of his mind, Krylon began to feel the stirrings of something akin to a conscious.

"A short time after the Brethren left our system, we detected another vessel of similar size as it entered our system and approach our world. We feared the worst, having just buried our dead we waited for our turn to be slaughter. Yet as the ship pulled over the still smoldering ruins of our world our passive radio detection devices picked up a call being broadcast from that ship. We managed to rig a translation algorithm and soon learned that this vessel was from a group of worlds known as the Empire. The ship was named the Vooglean and it soon sent down rescue teams to determine if any had survived the onslaught below."

"We had no choice but to attempt to communicate with these strangers and trust that these at least had good intentions at heart. A small scout was sent and landed precisely where we asked it to land. I and a small number of our survivors were there ready to meet the craft. It was a lucky thing that their technology allowed them a certain amount of shielding because as the first member cleared our airlock and stepped out into the corridor illumination, he took off his protective helmet. Silver blond hair and silvered eyes were turned to me. I fired without a thought, all the hatred in my soul behind that volley of projectiles. They met that shield, paused and then dropped to the corridor floor, like so many harmless insects."

"It was then, leader Krylon, that we learned of the amazing similarities and the daunting differences between your Brethren kind and the people of Tresolin. We were rescued and brought to a small out of the way planet within what remained of the Empire territory. Scalar suited us well and we built a life on the deserted remains of a small town under the shadow of Scalar's great mountains."

Theresa stood once more and bowed gently to Vantu and Darcel, "Thank you for your testimony." She waited as Frthessig escorted the two from the room. "I would like to call on Dale Lambert and Heather Lambert to add their testimony and perhaps shed some light on just how the Brethren have maintained their control over the galaxy."

Dale stood. His tall frame lit by more than the light in the room. Krylon and Theresa both noticed the illumination but said nothing keeping their own council on the matter. "Thank you Thresea and thank you distinguished guests. I am very grateful to see that while this meeting was not called it certainly has proved providential. For the record our world Laurel was not destroyed directly by the Brethren although as you will see they used their infiltration methods to twist and distort our society. They did not order the final attack on us, the people of the Southern Experimental station but the leaders that they left in control certainly did."

Dale looked at Leader Krylon, "You see my friend, the Brethren used our world as a test bed for the development, design and implementation of one of your most powerful weapons. The controlling chip that had been deployed to keep your chosen captive slaves loyal to your every whim. While the designer, may his name be forever damned died before his secrets could be revealed, he left prototypes which were used on certain individuals in our society. Those individuals included my father."

Leader Krylon looked at Dale with wonder. He had been privileged to know of the experimentation on Laurel. He knew that the prototypes developed there had been taken to other labs in the Brethren sphere of influence and developed far beyond the crude workings of the scientist who first conceived of the idea. He knew of laurel's destruction, and he knew of the displeasure that destruction brought to the plans of the Triune.

"I see that you know of what I speak, but all was not bad concerning the death of our world. Through our efforts we made contact with a sentient race of canines who had survived the contamination of our world. These creatures used a form of mental communication that was far beyond that of mere telepathy. Their whole social norm revolved around its use. The area that they called home was within our study range and we contacted them bringing ten individuals back to the station."

He looked at the gathered group. I will only speak now of our developing relationship with the troupe and our narrow escape through gathering storms and attack to reach the area in which they lived. It was there that we learned of their greatest secret. Lodged in the tall pinnacle of rock and stone that stood at the center of their range was an ancient starship. The Star Dancer had waited and had communed with members of the troupe for many generations, but it needed something more. Through our contact with the troupe, we learned that it had recognized our presence and had schemed to bring us to it. Once there we were examined and found suitable for service."

Dale paused and looked at his audience. "Just like the folks here on Earth we had a common link to the Federation. The Star Dancer was a Federation starship that ran afoul of an interstellar accident while exploring the section of the galaxy that Laurel had existed in. The ship had come out of hyperspace and was immediately enveloped in a cosmic storm emitted by Laurel's sun. At the same moment, it was hit by and asteroid shower. All hope of deflection and protection of the crew was wiped away by that dual attack. The crew received dangerous levels of radiation and their genetic code had become damaged. The structure of the ship had also received major damage."

"Fortunately, there was a planet with the correct atmospheric make up and gravitational requirements that could safely harbor the crew as they and the ship repaired themselves. Once landed the crew decided to leave the confines of the ship and to strike out into their new world. You see they had received such a dosage of damaging radiation that they could no longer perform the needed duties as crew. Star Dancer knew that it would take many hundreds of generations to repair that damage. So, while the crew started life once again as simple farmers and workers on the land Star Dancer encased itself year after year in a solid shielding of rock and stone. When at last it had felt the presence of our scientific community nearby on the southern continent of Laurel it reached out to us through its canine friends."

"We were taken aboard as crew and I as Captain with Heather as alter-day Captain. We watched as the leaders of our world surrounded the pinnacle of rock trying to reach us and, in their paranoia, and desperation launched a nuclear attack on the pinnacle. Star Dancer along with the aid of certain members of its new crew absorbed the energy of that attack and launched us into space. Once free from the gravity of Laurel, we watched in horror as the stresses placed upon the planet's surface caused the planet to fracture."

"Our world was destroyed and for a brief while I was overcome by grief and guilt. I assumed the responsibility of that destruction although after a time I was dissuaded from that guilt by my soon to be wife Heather. Now I have stayed over long in this conversation, I will let Heather describe our encounter with the Orion and its crew."

Heather had been admitted to the meeting while Dale was talking, sat down carefully in a comfortable chair that flexed with her gravid bulk. "I will not keep you long my fellow guests. It was a rescue response to a weak interstellar radio signal that brought us to the site of the Orion disaster. The Orion was a Federation starship similar to Star Dancer but much newer. It lay in orbit above a world that had been torn asunder. Our readings indicated some life force was left on board and some deep within the planet's surface below. These turned out to be the remaining members of the crew that survived their encounter with the Brethren and were in cryostasis."

"Once on board we discovered that the vessel had been attacked from the inside out. In the command deck area, we found an encoded message which Star Dancer aided us to decode. It was a video and audio record of the ship's mission which was to gather much needed minerals for the Federation. That was why by the way there were members of the crew down inside the planet. The away team had set up mining operations and living areas inside the planet, but I digress. A Brethren vessel entered the system and was immediately contacted by the Captain of the Orion. The Orion you

Stephen Goodale   322

understand was a top ship of the line for the Federation and as such was a fearsome opponent of any that wished it harm. However, the Brethren vessel did not vector in for an attack but instead broadcast messages of friendship and peace. The command of that vessel did everything that it was asked to do by the Captain of the Orion, which perhaps explains the ease in which it won its victory."

"The Orion had sent an away team to the Brethren ship and with that team went some of the more sensitive members of the crew. These had some psionic abilities and gently probed the Brethren ship. What they found there puzzled them. Very few of the ship's compliment were Brethren. There were many other races found there acting as crew. When that visit was over the Brethren vessel sent a gig of their own with just three representatives of the Brethren race. These toured the Orion and as they came into the command deck opened fire on the ship's crew. The automatic weapons systems of the Orion responded but the Brethren had concealed about them shielding devices that deflected all efforts to attack them. The betrayal was quick and thorough. The command deck was destroyed for the most part and as the Brethren made their way back to their gig, they selectively destroyed key components of the Orion leaving it basically helpless."

"From their vessel, the Brethren proceeded to rape the world below of its mineral wealth not caring for the fact that there were people inside the planet. Only those that made it back to the base tunnels were spared. These had been driven in areas of the planet that contained no mineral wealth. When they had taken all that the planet had to give the Brethren ship simply moved away and reaching the outer edge of the system went into hyperspace."

"Those in the tunnels and the remaining crew aboard the Orion had no hope of immediate survival. They placed those that they could into stasis tubes and sent a rescue request on the Federations frequencies, which despite the many years difference in our ships apparent age allowed the Star Dancer to respond."

"Thank you, Heather Lambert, I think that we have stressed you in your condition enough for one day, others will complete your story." Theresa walked over and gave a gentle supporting hand to Heather as she made her way to the conference room door.

As she left Doctor Scott and Life Giver paused to talk with her briefly. Doctor Scott gave the pregnant woman as gentle squeeze of her arm and then allowed her to pass. The two medical men came into the room. Theresa introduced them to the waiting audience. "These fine physicians will testify to the revival of the Orion's crew but more importantly they will talk about the methods by which the Brethren to this point have controlled their slaves."

"Ah yes thank you Theresa for your kind introduction. Life giver and I are from Laurel. You have heard of the destruction of that planet and while Dale Lambert made mention of his father, skimming over what I am sure are still painful memories of that situation, Life Giver and I will need to give you a more in-depth analysis of the controlling chips that are now currently being used by the Brethren."

Life Giver's rich melodic voice entered all the minds present. "You see honored guests, that while the victims of the chips remain cognizant of what they are doing, they have absolutely no control over their actions. They become controlled puppets of the Brethren. We have found no species, except perhaps those of Ikorn, who are immune to this method of control. The device is extremely difficult to find. It phases from this plain of existence into another depended upon the demands being placed on the subjects by their controllers. A truly insidious device. Doctor Scott and I thought that our most recent example, which was filmed in this facility not that very long ago of Admiral Willis might shed some understanding on the matter. I direct your attention to the front view screen." "Note that the device forces the victim to do the Brethren's bidding. Actions and points of view that would have been aberrant to the victim change and become acceptable norms.

This is one way in which a candidate for scanning can be selected. This was true of the Admiral. The changes began over two years ago and have become more prominent as he became more of a central player to the Brethren's purposes here on Earth."

"Please watch as the Admiral passes through what to all appearances to be a metal scanner. A station that all visitors must go through to enter the Embassy. This is standard procedure on your world Admiral Willis so that you and those that controlled you did not think that it represented anything out of the ordinary. I will pass this conversation over to Doctor Scott, for it is he who invented the scanner and to him should go the honor of describing its working processes."

"Yes, thank you Life Giver. As you see Admiral you passed through the scanner at what is a normal walking pace. The nano electronics buried in the scanner react almost at the speed of light so the process is very quick. It needs this speed because the chip that was controlling you is not always on the same plane as our normal space and time. Its actions are quick and fleeting but it still must cycle through at very rapid intervals. It is this cycling which aids us in our detection. There is a minute power burst every time it does this and every time it leaves this plane. It creates what we call a specific signature of energy."

"This allows us to narrow down the location of the chip. When its presence is detected, the subject is injected with a micro bead of narcotic designed for its own species and is completely harmless. The subject displays a brief fainting spell or moment of unconsciousness. This allows us to transfer the patient into another room and to apply a secondary scan which surrounds the chip with a unique energy barrier. This barrier forces the chip into a feedback loop which temporarily makes the controlling agent unaware that he has lost control of his puppet. During this period of uncertainty, we can either remove the chip, which was the decision that Doctor Folmer made in your case Admiral, or we can substitute a series of false responses which makes the controlling agent "think" that the commands are being followed."

"Now we come to the crux of the problem. The Brethren have become much cleverer since we first learned of the controlling chip. They have added a self-destruct switch which comes into play the moment the controlling agent feels that he has lost control of his victim. If the chip is left in place the patient can quite literally lose his or her mind." Here Doctor Scott made a motion of cutting his throat.

The video and audio playback quite graphically demonstrated this fact. There was silence in the room as all watched the heavy metal canister become distorted by the force of the blast as the chip that had been inside of Admiral Willis' mind just moments before exploded with devastating force.

Into the quiet that ensued Doctor Scott changed the topic of his lecture. "When we arrived on the scene of the Orion disaster, we discovered that the remaining medical staff had placed as many of the survivors as possible into cryostasis. Now it is something of a gamble reviving subjects from their frozen state. A deft mind and a gentle soul are needed for the task. Dale Lambert has both of those qualities. He was present as we revived the first series of subjects, and he had his hands full reassuring them that they had been asleep for almost two-hundred years."

"The just of it was that we revived enough crew both on board the Orion and from the tunnels to fashion a skeleton crew for the Orion. The Star Dancer was already shorthanded but both crews worked together to begin the reconstruction phase of the Orion, well at least enough to make her space worthy again."

"It was Dale Lambert who suggested that we keep our ears open for any approaching vessels, as distant as that possibility was now after two hundred years. He felt that the way the damage had been done form the inside out in the Orion indicated that the methodology was a considered one. He felt that the Brethren might be interested in coming back and claiming the Orion as a prize."

Dale Lambert picked up the tale again. "It was a feeling. I get them now and again which led me to suggest that we watch for incoming vessels. As an added precaution, I had the Star Dancer take an orbit adjacent to the Orion so that any ship coming at the planet from the elliptical would only see the one vessel. All of this became important a few days into the reconstruction. There was a warning on the Star Dancer's board as three vessels worked their way leisurely into the system approaching the Star Dancer on an elliptical orbit."

"Two of my crew had gone onto the fifth planet of the system to look for metals to aid in the rebuild and were in constant communication with me. These then brought their shielded craft up behind the intruders and disabled their ships. How they did this I will not speak of here. Once they were dead in space, I made a visit to the ship bearing the Rever Commander."

"The Revers, it turned out act as the Brethren's clean up squad, sophisticated space janitors if you will. Their job, I found out was to come in after the Brethren fleets did their dirty work and check for any valuable technologies that might be applied to the Brethren's ships." Dale looked at Leader Krylon and added, "This is standard procedure for the Brethren is it not?"

"Well, the Orion had caught the attention of the Dreadnaught commander who had disabled it and he had passed along the order for the reclamation crew to check out what he felt was a dead hulk circling the fourth planet in a slowly decaying orbit."

"Apparently the Orion was not a top priority or perhaps the Brethren look at things differently than we do? Who is to know? Still, it was the Orion that the Rever crews had come to reclaim two hundred years later."

"My mind was able to penetrate their shields easily enough and I soon found myself in conversation with the Rever leader. I will not mention the man's name here. Suffice it to say that he was quite surprised to find a fully functional starship facing him."

"There came a point in our conversation when it became apparent that the Juancy, who manned the ships were a member of one of the many races that the Brethren had subjugated over the millennia. These were and are a very good people forced by their masters to do a very nasty job. As the commander told me you did what you were told, you did it well or you died. It was that simple. It was this reasoning that led him to question the validity of what was apparent. He thought, as did many of his command crew that this was a test by their masters."

"Failure to carry out orders is death in the Brethren oligarchy. So, he ordered that his ships continue on toward the Orion. I disabused him of that notion and then I offered him another possibility. I offered that he and any of his folk that wish to, could join with us."

"Surprisingly enough after consideration of a power that could stop his vessel in mid-space and hold it helpless, all without firing a shot or using any apparent means whatsoever, he agreed."

"Now I need to fill you folks in on who and what the Juancy people are. They had become a spacefaring race on their own, having overcome political dispute on their own world. They traveled the nearby star lanes, colonizing where they found no other intelligent life and leaving those worlds alone that demonstrated civilization of any type. A contrast, I might point out to their current masters. In fact, the Brethren made no attempt at all to eliminate the Juancy's history from their education allowing or perhaps not caring would be a better term, that the historians of the Juancy people to relate their history from generation to generation."

"A mistake if you ask me, but more than likely simple arrogance on the Brethren's part."

"Not all of his people agreed with him, the fear of the Brethren was too well ingrained in them, I suppose. Several of his own command staff tried to kill him after he made the announcement of my offer over the ship-to-ship communications system. I stopped those projectiles from ever hitting him. Then I, and several of my staff mentally scanned all the Juancy in the three ships and divided those that had a true desire for freedom up from those that would rather stay in the Brethren service. A full one-third stayed and were placed under a light mental sedation aboard one of the Juancy vessels. The rest went with their leader and were soon aiding us in the reconstruction of the Orion, which I am happy to report went amazingly well. The Juancy have a definite mechanical and electrical knack about them."

"We brought the Juancy commander in on our strategy meetings, and it was through conversation that we learned that while the Brethren didn't much care for their slaves as individuals, they did track their equipment. So, we prepared a welcome for any Brethren vessels that might follow. The one Juancy ship we let sit in a distant orbit with its crew in cyrostasis. The ship's log reflected that it had broken out into normal space and experienced a malfunction that caused it to go dead. The crew had entered cryostasis as a precaution while waiting for a rescue mission."

Dale looked at Krylon, "A good enough ruse, for a race that brooked no failures. When your craft did come out of hyperspace it expected no trouble. The Juancy ship was recognized, and the Orion was sheltered behind the Star Dancer along with the other Juancy craft."

Theresa rose once more and thanked Dale and the two doctors. She smiled then at Leader Krylon. "I think that it is time that you took up the story Leader Krylon. You have a very unique perspective on what happened next, do you not?"

Krylon looked askance at Dale Lambert who simply shrugged. Thresesa reminded him that this was his chance to tell his story from his prospective. "An opportunity that I am sure the Triune would never afford you!"

Slowly the Brethren rose from his chair and just as slowly walked to the head of the conference table. He took a deep breath and said, "I will not try to defend or debase any of the policies or procedures of the Brethren Empire. An Empire far older than any civilization that now exists in this galaxy. I will instead stick to my part of the story. A very small part at that."

Krylon looked once more at Dale Lambert. "It is true that I was in command of the Dreadnaught that was assigned to track and punish three Rever ships that had been sent on assignment and that had failed to report in as required. It was a dull assignment suitable I suppose for one that had lost favor in the Triune's eyes. I was a very low-level member of the Brethren Council and had been sent to the particular section of space in question because of some perceived insult to a higher-ranking member of that elite body."

Krylon smirked again. "I was being punished, but little did I know at that time just how severe that punishment would be. But I am getting ahead of myself, I was sent to discover the reason for the break in protocol and I was board. I find looking back that boredom was a state that I had found myself in frequently. There just was nothing new under the many suns of the galaxy to excite me or even surprise me. As our ship broke out of hyperspace my command second informed me that one of the Rever ships was on screen and that after reporting the vessel's ident number the vessel had been scanned as procedures demanded. The result showed that the ship had come out of hyper drive and had experienced some type of malfunction. The crew, the report stated, was in cryosleep."

"The target vessel in orbit around the fourth planet was clearly visible but the reports coming back from the scans indicated a fully functional ship, not the derelict that had been reported. It did not matter to me. I had been sent to punish the Revers and destroy any that were found. I ordered my second in command to take the vector to the Rever ship and destroy it."

"What happened next is the reason that I am here. The mental power that overwhelmed the command deck on my Dreadnaught was similar but different than the only other minds that could produce such, shall we say respect from any of the Brethren ruling class. Dale Lambert's mind came to me and forbade any attempt of an attack on the Rever vessel. The power was great, and I knew that I could not resist it. As I have said the power is similar but different from the Triune that rules the Brethren Council. I was still alive!"

The Admiral of the Federation, a grouping of worlds that we had destroyed more than a century before, Dale Lambert spent time talking with me, before alleviating me of my enslaved crew, destroying my attack capabilities and freezing my navigation systems. I asked him if he would like me to deliver a message to the Triune, for that was where I was going to go. It would not do to fail to report a mind of such power. He gave me the message and I promised to deliver it unchanged in any way."

"I then set course using my restored navigation computers for the nearest Brethren out post." He looked at Dale and smiled bitterly, "I know that it is the desire of every galactic civilization to discover the location of the Brethren Home World, but I cannot help you with that. Only the Triune and a few select others have that knowledge and they would all die first before revealing it to anyone."

Dale just nodded his head gravely in agreement. "I have searched enough of the true Brethren's minds to know that you speak the truth. But each engagement, each mind that I visit, adds more evidence to its location. One day soon we will find your Home World and when we do there will be a reckoning."

"So, you have said Admiral Lambert, and I take you at your word. You have been a completely honorable man in your dealings with me, so I must believe you. Now however I must relay my tale to its completion or as complete as it has come to this point."

"Failure has never been tolerated by the Brethren and by failing to punish the Rever ships and their crews and by losing my own crew to an outside force I was in disgrace." He looked at those present and laughed. "Death is the punishment for such a lapse and death I received once they were done torturing me for a cycle or two. I was brought up to the "Examination Room", a sort of pleasure house for the Triune and on occasion members of the Council at large. I knew of course that I was about to die, but then I have died so many times before, you get kind of used to the idea. Still, it wasn't a very easy death. When the chief of the Triune entered my mind with all the force of a raging sun I was torn away and cast out. That parting was very painful. The triune took all of the data that my mind had stored and shifted it for relevant content."

"I had told the truth during the inquisition. It would never do to lie. They would torture you anyway, just for entertainment value. So that sifting only confirmed what I had told them. They learned about you Admiral Lambert of the Federation and then to they learned of the possibility that the rumors of Ikorn and their witches were true. They had forces gathering that they would need to oppose in the near future."

"You see the Brethren have a problem. I may now relate this information to you without the fear of being disloyal, as you at least Admiral, have already discovered the issue. Through the many centuries that we have existed, we have become a very selfish race. This of course is no surprise to those who have lost their worlds and the lives of millions of their people to our greed. What you may not know is that most of us, if not all of us, have lost the ability to "feel", we have no souls and we care nothing for each other. The only unifying things that we all share is the desire for more power., attack us at your own peril or leave us alone to live out our very separate, very lonely lives it really is all the same to us."

"We stopped procreating many centuries ago. We have instead instilled a system of cloning. Each member of the Brethren has a line of clones just waiting at reanimation stations throughout our sphere of influence. When one of us dies whether through political intrigue or accident, the persona of the individual is preserved. If the Triune deems you worthy or if enough time has passed, they might allow your next clone in line to become reanimated. Once that happens the complete persona and memory of the Brethren is restored. There is a brief reorientation session held by one of the Council and you are then set about completing whatever task that you are assigned."

"Dale Lambert knows that I have been restored, but what he may not know is the price. I am the last clone of my line. If I were to die right now the line of Krylon would cease and be lost forever. You see when I was reanimated it was to complete a task started by my predecessor here on Earth. The Triune has determined that while not in immediate threat of failure the continuous regeneration of clones has weakened our bodies and minds to the point where we would fail, physically and mentally to "live" up to the standards expected of us."

"The Triune has read the writing on the wall. The experiment here on Earth has been developing for hundreds of years, almost as long as Vantu has been involved here. You see we have developed several bases of our own within your solar system. One in particular on Demos was designed to take captive, young Earth girls and women and manipulate their DNA so that they might become compatible mates and produce offspring through procreation."

Admiral Willis shot to his feet his face suffused with anger. "You mean to tell me that you have had the audacity to steal our women for your breeding program? Perhaps it is time that we visited your bases and deliver some special propagation of our own!"

Dale stood up and with a calm voice said, "Admiral, you are out of line. Threats will not be tolerated here. Also, you have not heard the entire story please, sit back down." The Admiral stared at his counterpart and nodded his head in reluctant agreement.

"Very good," he made a small bow to Leader Krylon and asked in the same calm voice for him to continue. Krylon looked at the Earth Admiral and said, "Let me assure you Admiral Willis that up until a few of your weeks ago, I had no knowledge of this particular program or for that matter of Earth, which is, or I should say was a rather insignificant world in a back water part of the galaxy."

The Triune determines when a clone will be released for reanimation. Usually after a failure the clone line of the offender is suspended for a period of time, which is usually decided by the severity of the offense. When they terminated me, I knew that I would be reanimated but I thought that it would be many of our life cycles. The fact that the Brethren that was in charge of the project here on Earth was killed in battle with Vantu, and his failure to stop the transport of the Dragon Nemoric and his Rider to an unknown destination off planet caused the Triune to declare a fifty-cycle suspension of that man's clone line. It is for this reason that I was reanimated to "finish" the project here on Earth."

"Now I should explain that we, of the Brethren, lead what to you would be a hedonistic lifestyle. We have profited from our conquests of various civilizations to the point where each of us possess a kingdom of our own. A place where our rule is absolute. Our amassed wealth is truly amazing but should a Brethren operative fail in his or her duty than those lands and estates are taken from him. When he comes back to life and has had his memories returned to him, he must start life once again from the lowest level of our society."

"It is because of our virtual immortality that very few of my Brethren co-patriarchs have any fear of death. It is in essence removed from the equation. It is only the fear of the loss of their wealth that motivates them. Remove that promise of immortality and the Brethren culture will collapse into a day to day worry over the amount of life that is left to each of us. We become mortal."

"Dale Lambert has referred to the rest of the story, Admiral. Perhaps you will find it satisfying to your need of vengeance and perhaps you will understand the terrible fear that we Brethren must now face. You see while I was reanimated to complete this mission on Earth, the Triune executed a terrible sentence upon me. They held me at the reanimation satellite on which my particular clone line was based. These other selves were kept in reserve and as the whim of the Triune dictated were brought back to life to continue my immortality. On their command and in my presence, they terminated my clone line. All of my futures destroyed in front of my very eyes!"

The expression on Krylon's face was one of devastation. No one in the conference room could possibly know the loss that he had experienced but they could certainly see how it affected him. "There was nothing left for me, I longed for the final night to fall, but in the corner of my mind where all was bleak and dark a light appeared urging me to look beyond my ingrained racial memory and to consider a different type of immortality. I held on to that voice as it whispered through my mind."

"A different voice, the voice of the Chief member of the Triune was addressing me and his words came out of the dark waters. They would send me on this assignment to Earth, where if I succeeded I and the female who would bear my children would become the corner stone of a new Brethren race. Failure of course meant instant and permanent death."

"I considered the matter for only a moment before accepting the mission. I really had no choice in the matter anyway, no choice if I wanted to continue to live. I began my travels here, but the voice that had offered me hope had become a constant companion, mentoring me, guiding me and I soon found that what it had to say was true and correct. I, for the first time in my long existence, began to consider others. I began to lead and not just command. The crew on my ship were not all puppets as many of the crews are on ships-of-the-line within the Brethren fleet. These were mostly ordinary beings with backgrounds, feelings, and families. I began to treat them with respect, never of course letting up on what I expected from a smoothly functioning crew. Surprisingly as the days have gone by, I have received much better results from the crew's performance than I had ever received by meeting out death and torture."

Krylon looked around the room. "There has been much made of the way that the Brethren have treated the galaxy. There has been many stories of deceit, destruction, and devastation, all of which are true. To any other Brethren, inured in their private paradise this would all seem like the natural order of things. Certainly, a case of "might makes right," allowing whatever small conscious twinge that may occur to be rationalized away. I on the other hand, who have no hope to live on, now see things differently. I suppose I could still use our massive technology to try and dominate as I have done to often in the past, but it has been clearly demonstrated to me that there are others out there who have the means to simply "think" at my technology to neutralize it. The resultant would be true death for me, true death for my crew."

"I am now unique to my species, and as such I need to explore new patterns of thought. The voice in my mind," and here he looked directly at Dale Lambert. "Has often reminded me that I was not under his control. That I have free will to make choices and that whatever my fate will be it will not be the dictate of others, but of my own."

While Krylon had been speaking the door to the conference room had opened and Dianna, slipped in to stand quietly in the corner by the door. As Leader Krylon sat once more a quiet filled the room. It had the effect of placing all present in a cloud of their own thoughts. Finally, Theresa stood once more and into that silence spoke, "Leader Krylon, I have gazed into the eyes of many enemies over the life span that has been given me. Never in all those thousands of years has any of those moved me as you have. You are guilty of crimes far greater than most, but you have demonstrated the beginning of wisdom and a sense of regret. We who are gathered here are not judge or jury. You, I think will be judged by God, but it is hoped that as you move forward from here that you keep your heart open and your mind clear, and who knows even those that have suffered greatly at your hands may find room in their hearts to forgive."

Dale Lambert stood once more, "I have one final display of evidence, one finally demonstration of the cruelty and the blatant use of careless power used by the Brethren." From a hidden projector in the desktop of the conference room table a three-dimensional image of the events on the moon Demos played to the waiting audience. Leader Krylon who had seen the scenes displayed there before just hung his head, a tear welling in his eyes.

Admiral Willis stood in shock but apart from gasps of horror said nothing. When the images faded. "This is the doom of Earth and its great hope. The Earth has become a nexus for all of the galaxy. This small blue pearl hanging in the blackness of space holds the key to the survival of the galaxy." Theresa paused and added "As such it has fallen to all people who would like to see it take its place in the universe of free and loving beings to protect and nourish it. The people of Ikorn offer their protection Admiral Willis as do the Federation and the Empire. From this point forward no enemy, Brethren or otherwise will be allowed to cause harm to your world."

The Admiral sat back down, a morose look on his face. As he sat, he muttered, "And who is going to save us from ourselves?"

Dale Lambert smiled grimly, "Like Leader Krylon has observed the choice of your salvation is entirely up to you. But if I could start by making the suggestion, that the Brethren strangle hold on your world be removed. Those that are controlled by the chips that have been implanted in their brains be, "convinced" into having them removed. I would also suggest that any other true Brethren sequestered here on Earth be found and neutralized. I think that once these two steps have been accomplished, the rest of the Earth's population will form their own opinions concerning their changed position in the galaxy."

"As for the Brethren, I suggest that we continue to lure them out into old Federation space. We can do this by constantly harassing their fleets and preventing them from gaining any additional slaves or materials. This will force them into a desperate defense of their way of life, exposing them to mistakes in strategy."

Dale Lambert turned and looked directly at Leader Krylon, "I must propose that as we discover the cloning facilities that are spread throughout the Brethren sphere of influence that those facilities and the clones that are contained within be destroyed."

Krylon looked up shocked to his core yet thoughtful. "Dale Lambert you do not need my permission to conduct your fleet's operations, yet if you want an opinion then I will say that that you are correct. As long as our cloning system remains in place our people will remain smugly confident in their immortality. Once that is removed the remaining "mortal" Brethren might begin to form a different world view."

Theresa stood once more. "It is agreed then. Admiral Willis we will sit down and develop a strategy for removing the enslavement from your people. I would suggest that Doctor Scott, Life Giver and Doctor Folmer be a part of that process. You might look to your own medical community and offer them a free upgrade to their medical scanners. In the meantime, we will gather data on the behavior of your leaders and correlate that to see if we can find patterns. Like the webs of your Terran spiders, I think that we will discover any remaining Brethren operatives at the center of those webs."

Dale Lambert looked at Leader Krylon. "I have already taken the liberty of having those few remaining "slaves" aboard your vessel neutralized. They are all recovering and are very happy indeed for the change in their lives. I have removed the tracking devices implanted on your ship. The Brethren can only surmise that they have lost another vessel and either discontinue their plans or come to investigate. I have also taken the liberty of broadcasting a slightly edited version of the tape that was played earlier so that it will be picked up in Brethren space. It is hoped that it will find its way to the Triune and perhaps dissuade them from continuing their attempts to develop a breeding campaign from Earth's female stock."

"I would like to offer you the opportunity to join with us in the defense of this world. You can command your vessel and be part of what we have started here. The choice is yours."

Slowly Leader Krylon stood. "I thank you Dale Lambert for all that you have done on my behalf. I don't think for a moment that I would have survived long enough to have even reached the Earth much less be invited to such a conference of leaders as this without that intervention. I can see no other option than to agree to your proposal. I offer my services, such as they are to you Admiral Lambert, use me and my ship as you see fit. Then he hung his head and when he raised it once more tears welled from his eyes and trailed down his cheeks. "I am alone now, and I am frightened by that loneliness, but I am a now just a man. I will find a way to move forward for as long as the fates allow. May I make the most of that time in the service of those who once called me enemy."

There was a gasp from the shadowy figure by the door and Dianna ran from the room. Krylon, his head down neither heard nor saw her as Theresa rose one last time. "Gentlemen, I commend you for your passion and your reason. The planet Ikorn will be moved to the Terran solar system in a position that will neither be disruptive nor discoverable by Terran technology. The system will no longer be vulnerable to the Brethren. In the meantime, I call this meeting adjourned and I suggest that you all get ready for the wedding. I think that we have kept our young people waiting long enough."

Chapter Twenty-Eight

David Peterson and Scott Green stood facing the full-length mirrors that were the chief feature of the annex chamber. The fact that they had come through so many twists and turns these past two years to wind up here on Earth inside the domain of an alien Embassy amazed them. A period of time that seemed to both, a lifetime ago. While they stood having inspected their appearance for the tenth time, they were not really seeing the reflection in the glass. Both were gazing ahead into the future.

Scott had already made contact through Theresa with the planet Trillon. That sentient world had readily agreed to the arrival of the newlyweds and their acquisition of an area in which they could build a home, and a repair and readiness facility for RJ. Everything was in readiness, still Scott could not help but feel a little unsettled. This was a big step for him. He was chronologically only a seventeen-year-old youth, but his enhanced appearance and his experience made him look and feel much older.

"Relax, my friend," came his Dragon's thoughts, "You are ready. We will spend the time necessary to establish our new home and then we will be off again. The stars await us, but for now they can wait a little longer."

David's mind was very far away from the Embassy and the coming nuptials. He felt the forces of the universe flow around him once more and by concentrating as he had been taught, unveiled that other force. The dark energy played and coiled like a living thing, which as he had learned, it was in part. It danced in front of him and pulled him with it as it sped the unimaginable distances of the galaxy. It pulled him to the very outer fringes of the spiral which stood completely opposite of his current position. There it showed him a world, circling a dying star, its light so faint that it only cast a dim red glow on the planet's surface. On down into that world the energy took him. He passed through the layers of rock as if he were moving through the tissue of a living being. He came to a stop in a dimly lit vaulted chamber and faced a figure that sat encased by a lurid crimson glow. Hymical! He recognized the seated figure at once.

David studied the figure carefully. The being that sat in front of him now had changed from the previous images that David had received of him. His physical stature was much greater, but it was the pulsing energy that flowed from him that caught David's attention. This man, this thing was alive with alien energy, and it was growing even as he watched. Hymical's eyes were closed but as David watched they sprung open and looked directly at him. His mind was immediately thrown from the planet and back across the distance of the galaxy to his waking body. He knew that Hymical was aware of him and in that awareness, David had started a string of events that would bring him back into contact with this being. The final conflict was inevitable.

David sighed and released the energy which he had unconsciously drawn to himself. That was the future and there would be many more years and events that would occur before that confrontation. He shook himself, releasing the last of that vision and turned to smile at Scott. "It is time my friend. Are you ready?"

Scott merely nodded and together they walked to the portal and out into the vast expanse of the Embassy's main hall. The crowd of people human and alien stunned both young men as they stepped out into that expanse. Tremolic flew down from a perch that he had been using to observe the activities and took his place on Scott's shoulder. "Where did all these people come from, Scott whispered under his breath?'

"Aren't you just a little bit too old to be asking that question", Tremolic chimed back. "Your weddings it would seem have become the social event of the season here on Earth, and beyond! Representatives of the Freshden, with Griden and Perfeshda are here to honor David and Mary. The Ikorns have sent a small delegation, they are now Earth's near neighbors don't you know? Besides Theresa has become an Ambassador of her people and will stay here at the Embassy until the Ikorns can build one of their own. Darcel's people have sent a delegation, Scalar is about to become a very popular spot and oh yes, the Dragons of Scalar have added four more members here to honor you. You might recognize them."

Over the noise of the crowd Scott and David heard the bugling of welcoming Dragons and shortly after the bass voice of Sam as he shouted out his recognition of the pair. With Kathrine in tow, they moved through the crowd like a ship through water. He stopped just in front of his friend and his brother. He then gathered both in with a robust hug of greetings. When at last his victims pleaded for air he relented. "Scott," he said and all his feelings for his friend were evident in that single word. Then he turned and shook hands with his brother who now stood slightly less in height than his own stature.

Kathrine, stepped around her husband and hugged both men. "It is so good to see you both my friends and felicitations, and might I add it is about time!" She smiled to take the sting from her words.

Just then a loud trumpet blast was heard and quiet began to fall over the crowd. In his mind Scott could hear his Dragon urging him up towards the waiting group standing on a slightly raised dais in the rear of the huge hall. "I think that you had better get going, my friend or you will miss your own wedding!"

The four Dragons present stood slightly to the one side of the dais so that they would not block the view of their fellow guests. Their Riders stood near them on the far side of the dais. Slowly the remaining guests took their seats leaving a wide isle from the front of the Embassy to the dais at the rear. The space was filled. David smiled in amusement as he recognized the fact that sophisticated video recording devices were broadcasting this event. He wondered in some amusement how far out into the galaxy the broadcast went.

Krylon sat in one of the comfortable chairs near the front of the dais, the chair next to him remained open although there was a placard placed there reserving it for a guest who had yet to make their appearance. Once more Krylon was feeling just a little low. He was having a difficult time adjusting to these emotions, but he accepted them as part of his maturation process. Imagine a man, many thousands of years old in chronological time having to put up with what every teen-aged human experienced, emotions indeed!

He was lost in thought when he heard a voice asking him to excuse her. He looked up and quickly stood aside as a beautiful, young redheaded woman sat down in the reserved chair next to his. She turned briefly in his direction and smiled and then just as quickly looked away. He felt the breath in his chest stop and his muscles tighten. His heart skipped a momentary beat and he looked at her in wonder.

Just then the audience fell completely quiet, and the sound of beautiful music began. The music Krylon noted, when he could breathe again, came not from a recording but from a group of musicians who played their instruments in real time. The music was haunting, and the sounds provoked the emotions of the audience.

The group on the dais, David and the Petersons, Scott and the Greens and The Rodriquez family including Juan, who had come in on the Vooglean stood facing the rear of the chamber. There were three officials present. The minister from the church that the Petersons had attended on and off during David's youth and whose sermons he had found so appealing. A priest representing the Catholic Church, of which Mary and her family had faithfully attended during their time in New York. The third member of the group was the Governor of New Mexico, Susana Martinez.

There was a brief pause in the music and then a stately march began. Nancy and Mary stepped through the doorway of the annex room opposite from that which David and Scott had shared. They turned together and faced the long isle leading to the waiting party. Before them went several of Nancy's friends from her high school days and several young members of the medical staff of the Vooglean. These young women scattered flower petals in the isle as the brides walked in measured steps side by side to the dais. As they mounted the two steps their respective husbands to be extended their arms and as a group they turned and faced the officials in front of them.

The music halted and the hidden microphones picked up the ancient words of the wedding ceremony. The Minister and the Priest blest them individually and together in the appropriate forms of their own church. The unity and the rhythm of both wove a beautiful pattern of scared words. As they exchanged vows the pair were blest and in a unified voice were told, "We now pronounce you men and wives you may each kiss your bride. "

A great cheer went up from the gathered crowd and the Dragons added their own massive roar of approval. The Governor then stepped forward. As the crowd grew quiet once more, she said, "On behalf of the people of the Earth and those of the United States and the State of New Mexico, I Susana Martinez, Governor of the state of New Mexico validate the marriage of David Peterson and Mary Rodriquez, as well as that of Scott Green and Nancy Peterson under the laws of the State of New Mexico and those of the United States of America." She paused and then in a loud voice declared, "Ladies and Gentlemen and friends of all races, I am proud to present Mr. and Mrs. David Peterson and Mr. and Mrs. Scott Green, may they live together in happiness for the rest of their days!"

Epilogue

Nemoric soared into the bright New Mexico sky as below a group of parents and children watched in open mouthed awe. He and Sam did a series of intricate aerial maneuvers and then glided back to land in front of the assembled audience. A great cheer rang out as the humans pressed forward. Firenthic had curled her neck and had lowered her head to look at the small group of young girls who stood in rapt attention in front of her. She projected her mind and described what kind of life a Dragon and her Rider would have not only on Scalar but throughout the worlds in which they explored.

As Nemoric landed and Sam Peterson jumped down to stand before the excited boys he noted one that stood tall and proud. Sam walked over to him and asked him his name. "I am Allen Thresher, and these are my folk. We are from Texas, and I have come to be a Dragon's Rider.

If you have enjoyed reading this book you might be interested in reading the first three books in this series. These are:

"Adventures at the End of Childhood" First Book in the Brethren Saga
Amazon.com

"Star Dancer's Children" Second Book in the Brethren Saga
Amazon.com

"Sam and His Dragon" Third Book in the Brethren Saga
Amazon.com

"Missionary to The Stars" Fifth Book in the Brethren Saga
Amazon.com

Look for the sixth and final book in the Brethren Saga due to be released in early 2022: "The Rising"

Made in the USA
Middletown, DE
16 November 2022

15062539R00195